03839783

, 12. FEB. 1994

-5. MAR. 1994   27. MAY 199

14.

...sband and ...ourite hobby is ...TED TO DIE is her third ...owing A DRINK OF DEADLY WINE and THE SNARES OF DEATH.

F*

Charles, K.   839783

Appointed to die

Also by Kate Charles

A Drink of Deadly Wine
The Snares of Death

Appointed to Die

Kate Charles

HEADLINE

839783

Copyright © 1993 Kate Charles

The right of Kate Charles to be identified as the Author of
the Work has been asserted by her in accordance with the
Copyright, Designs and Patents Act 1988.

First published in 1993
by HEADLINE BOOK PUBLISHING PLC

First published in paperback in 1993
by HEADLINE BOOK PUBLISHING PLC

10 9 8 7 6 5 4 3 2 1

All rights reserved. No part of this publication may be
reproduced, stored in a retrieval system, or transmitted,
in any form or by any means without the prior written
permission of the publisher, nor be otherwise circulated
in any form of binding or cover other than that in which
it is published and without a similar condition being
imposed on the subsequent purchaser.

All characters in this publication are fictitious
and any resemblance to real persons, living or dead,
is purely coincidental.

ISBN 0 7472 4199 6

Printed and bound in Great Britain by
HarperCollins Manufacturing, Glasgow

HEADLINE BOOK PUBLISHING PLC
Headline House
79 Great Titchfield Street
London W1P 7FN

For my parents

Author's Note

The diocese, the city and the cathedral of Malbury are all as imaginary as their various inhabitants and denizens. Any resemblance to real cathedrals, living or dead, is purely coincidental.

Prologue

*For the foundations will be cast down: and what hath the
righteous done?*

Psalm 11.3

One night in November . . .

The piercing klaxon of the sirens shattered the customary
nocturnal tranquillity of the Cathedral Close. Canon John
Kingsley, who had not been long in bed and had been too
troubled to sleep, rose quickly and crossed to the window. The
police cars' pulsating blue lights reflected eerily on the grey
stone of the cathedral, as unnatural an intrusion into this place
as the harsh wailing of the ambulance sirens.

But there was a kind of inevitability about it, thought John
Kingsley as the drama unfolded, a few houses away around the
bend of the Close. Like the last act of a Shakespearean tragedy
– except that it wasn't the last act, but the last act but one: in
the real world, if not in Shakespeare, justice must be done, and
the guilty brought to judgement.

But who are the guilty? John Kingsley reflected painfully.
Surely we must all bear the guilt: we've all thought of
ourselves as somehow charmed, here in the Close, as though it
were a second Eden, sealed off from the wickedness of the
outside world. But we all should have realised that living in the
shadow of a holy place is no proof against human evil, against
sins of ambition, spiritual pride . . . and even murder.

As the cold blue lights flashed, casting distorted shadows,
grotesquely huge, on the east end of the cathedral, it was all too
clear what had happened. Two men had been at the Deanery
tonight, Canon Kingsley knew – two men who had good reason
to hate and fear each other – and now one of them was coming
out on a stretcher, ministered to by hovering paramedics, and
the other would soon follow, flanked by police.

1

How had it come to this? How had their little world been brought to destruction? For as the two men, the one living and the one dying, left the Deanery that night, John Kingsley knew beyond any doubt that no matter what followed, their sheltered world would never be the same again.

But let us begin the story a few months earlier, in July . . .

Act I

Chapter 1

Thou shalt prepare a table before me against them that trouble me: thou hast anointed my head with oil, and my cup shall be full.

Psalm 23.5

No one at the dinner party mentioned the empty place at table. There was certainly awareness of it; Lucy Kingsley sensed it in the occasional speculative glances cast from around the table in the direction of the empty chair. Their hostess had said merely that Canon Brydges-ffrench was indisposed and would not be joining them that evening as planned.

Lucy was surprised. She'd spent some time that afternoon with Canon Brydges-ffrench and had not noticed any signs of indisposition. But the Canon's absence was for Lucy, as for most of the dinner guests, merely a matter of curiosity, a cause for mild speculation. For the hostess, it was an unmitigated disaster.

Rowena Hunt looked at the empty chair at the head of the table with despair; there was nothing else to do, she reflected bitterly. It wasn't just that Canon Brydges-ffrench was theoretically the honoured guest, as Subdean, and thus senior member of the Chapter, and the probable next Dean of Malbury Cathedral. It wasn't even that her plan for sumptuously entertaining the entire Chapter and thereby subtly convincing them of the excellence of her culinary skills had been marred, that the opening move in her carefully planned campaign was thus a failure in spite of all her preparations. No, she thought: the main difficulty was that the numbers had been upset. They were one man short at table, and that wrecked everything. He hadn't even had the courtesy to ring until just before dinner, leaving Rowena insufficient time to remove the extra place setting and the chair, let alone to find a last-minute substitution.

The real problem, of course, was that Kingsley woman. When Rowena had planned this dinner party, weeks ago, it had looked as though there would be an extra man, and that was, although perhaps not ideal, no bad thing. Then just a few days ago Canon Kingsley had rung her, apologetic, to beg off from the dinner party. He'd just learned, he said, that his daughter Lucy was coming for the weekend. He'd happened to mention to Canon Brydges-ffrench, he'd explained, that his daughter was an artist, and the Subdean had immediately insisted that Canon Kingsley contact her and ask her to come this weekend. Planning for his music festival had fallen perilously behind, and the artistic talents of Lucy Kingsley were exactly what they needed at this point.

Rowena, of course, had insisted that Canon Kingsley must bring his daughter to the dinner party. He had protested that she was a vegetarian, and thus difficult to cater for, but Rowena had explained that she was already committed to providing vegetarian fare for Canon Thetford and his wife – vegetarianism was just one of the many 'isms' embraced by that couple.

She'd had no way of knowing that in addition to being a talented artist, Lucy Kingsley was also an undeniably attractive – some would even say beautiful – woman, with a graceful presence and a stunning nimbus of shoulder-length red-gold curls. The colour and the curl even looked natural, thought Rowena sourly, her hand going to her own glossy black hair, its stylish waves as well as its rich colour purchased and maintained at great expense. And the Kingsley woman couldn't be a day under thirty-five – it just wasn't fair that she should have hair like that.

Seated at Rowena's right, Jeremy Bartlett couldn't keep his eyes off Lucy Kingsley. It had been a mistake, Rowena now saw belatedly, to seat Lucy on Jeremy's other side. She had of course expected that Lucy, as a stranger in their little community, would talk to her father. But Canon Kingsley was deep in conversation with Evelyn Marsden, who had been left stranded by Arthur Brydges-ffrench's defection. Hemmed between John Kingsley and the empty chair, it was only natural that Miss Marsden should address herself to the former, and that he should see it as his duty to attend to the lone woman, leaving his daughter to fend for herself.

She was fending very well, ruminated Rowena with a savage poke at her tarragon chicken. With Jeremy's back firmly turned towards her, she had little better to do than to observe her dinner guests and attempt to eavesdrop on their conversations. It was true that Canon Greenwood, seated on her left, was carrying on a monologue which was vaguely addressed to her, but as she had no interest in what he was saying, an occasional nod was all that was required of her.

Rowena derived some perverse satisfaction from the fact that Evelyn Marsden must be nearly as discomfited over Canon Brydges-ffrench's non-appearance as she was herself. It had been especially galling to her, Rowena had observed, that she'd had no hint of his 'indisposition' until it had been publicly announced. Miss Marsden, proprietary as she was about the Subdean, would have expected him to have phoned her first, and to have given her all the details of whatever had befallen him, so that she could subsequently divulge the facts, or not, as she felt necessary. But she was clearly as much in the dark as everyone else about what was keeping Arthur Brydges-ffrench from this evening's festivities, and her displeasure was evident.

If she hadn't been so upset herself, Rowena could almost have felt sorry for Evelyn Marsden. It must be terrible to be so old, so poor, and so unattractive, she thought – dependent upon the virtual charity of the Dean and Chapter for the roof over your head, and with no prospects of a man ever wanting you. It was no secret in the Close that Miss Marsden would like to become Mrs Brydges-ffrench; the possibility of this actually happening seemed highly unlikely to Rowena. It was true that Arthur Brydges-ffrench was not exactly a prize catch, but at least he had a good position – especially if he became Dean – and Evelyn could certainly never hope to do better. Retired now, and in her early sixties, Miss Marsden looked exactly what she was, or at least had been: the headmistress of the local infants' school. She always dressed smartly, if dowdily, and wore her auburn-tinted hair in an old-fashioned French roll. The dress that she was wearing tonight almost concealed the unfortunate tendency towards

5

plumpness that she'd fought unsuccessfully all her life, and as she inclined her head to Canon Kingsley, Rowena observed her slightly stilted manner of speech, caused by the self-conscious way that she pulled her upper lip down in an effort to conceal her slightly protruding front teeth. She was definitely someone to be pitied, as was the poor Canon who so unexpectedly had to share her company this evening.

Canon Kingsley, though, betrayed no discomfort. He showed every evidence of interest in her conversation, nodding away as he tucked into his meal. He was definitely enjoying his food, Rowena noted, and that endeared him to her – she hoped he'd remember, when the time came, what a good cook she was. As the most recent addition to the Cathedral Chapter, who had in fact been in his position of Residentiary Canon only a few months, John Kingsley was not well known to her. But from what she'd seen of him thus far, there was nothing to dislike – apart from his daughter, of course. His manner was always gentlemanly, in a somewhat abstracted way, and there was something serenely spiritual about his long, pale face, topped as it was with a soft sheaf of silvery hair. Tallish and willowy, he was as ethereal as an attenuated saint in an El Greco painting.

His daughter took after him in build, observed Rowena, as well as in her pale complexion, and she'd made the most of it by dressing in a pastel Laura Ashley print dress. Rowena could see her animated face clearly as she turned towards Jeremy Bartlett, the blue-green eyes fixed on him and a smile curving her mouth. A shameless flirt, Rowena told herself acidly. Jeremy should see through her in a minute.

Jeremy showed no signs, though, of tiring of Lucy Kingsley's company; his back remained turned relentlessly to Rowena. She felt like crying: for weeks she'd worked planning this evening, not only to impress the members of the Chapter with her culinary skills, but also to let Jeremy know, in a subtle way, what a good wife she would make for him. She would grace his home and his table with her elegance and her good taste. She would entertain for him, help him to make a real name for himself in the cathedral world. He was a relative newcomer to the Cathedral Close, having sold up his London architectural practice and moved to Malbury as Cathedral Architect less than a year before. In

that time Rowena had made little headway with him –
hardly surprising, really, as he was such a recent widower,
and presumably still in mourning – but she entertained
great hopes of a breakthrough soon. Recently there had been
tantalising hints, in his manner towards her, that he was not
unaware of her charms, and until this evening that had been
almost enough. He was such a fascinating man, with so
many interests, and she thought that underneath his re-
strained and urbane exterior she could sense a passionate
nature that matched her own. He was certainly attractive, as
well, for a man who must be nearly fifty, with his ashy blond
hair shading naturally into silver and his neatly trimmed
beard covering a well-shaped jaw. Straining her ears, she
caught snatches of their conversation. They were talking
about music. Stifling a sigh, Rowena turned towards Canon
Greenwood: she may as well be listening to him.

If Jeremy Bartlett, the only non-cleric, was the most interesting man present, Rupert Greenwood was undeniably the
most decorative, and Rowena felt herself distracted for just a
moment, appreciating his beauty. Although he was over
thirty, he had the sort of boyish good looks that are usually
thought of as being typically English: a long-jawed, even-
featured face with guileless blue eyes and fine hair like
spun gold. Unhappily, though, the Precentor of Malbury
Cathedral had but one interest in life: music. He could talk
about it for hours, completely unaware that he was boring
his listeners nearly to tears. Now he was telling her, with
enthusiasm, about the various pieces he had selected for
Malbury's new music festival – things that had never before
been heard in England.

Probably for good reason, thought Rowena, who was not in
the least musical. Fixing a smile on her face, once again she
stopped listening, and directed her attention farther down
the table, to the three-sided conversation that seemed to be
taking place beyond Canon Greenwood.

Perhaps conversation was not really the proper word,
she discovered after eavesdropping for a moment. Canon
Thetford was lecturing, with appropriate and timely interjec-
tions from his wife. The subject seemed to be the problem of
overpopulation in the Third World, and what the Church's
response should be.

Everyone agreed, thought Rowena, that Philip Thetford

was a tiresome man – as tiresome in his own way as the one-dimensional Rupert Greenwood. It was a great shame that he was not even now where he longed to be: somewhere in Africa, ministering to the needs of the unfortunate natives. But a bad chest had kept him from the mission field, and everyone who knew him was well aware that as far as he was concerned, his position as Canon Missioner at Malbury Cathedral was at best a poor second and a waste of his talents. Physically he was unprepossessing in the extreme, with thin gingery hair – his hairline in retreat as aggressively as his chin – and pale eyes; his nearly invisible eyebrows and lashes gave him an expression of perpetual surprise, and while he was not actually a small man, he somehow gave the impression of weediness. His voice, which had a sonorous carrying quality, nevertheless had an underlying whineyness that Rowena found most unpleasant.

On Canon Thetford's left was his wife, Claire Fairbrother, nodding vehemently and occasionally adding commentary to his arguments. Feminism was, needless to say, among the 'isms' espoused by Ms Fairbrother, who had not taken her husband's name at the time of their marriage. Although she lived in the Close with her husband, and participated in the life of that insular community, she had never been a typical clergy wife; her own career as head of the Malbury family planning clinic was more important to her than cathedral politics, and she was far too uncompromising by nature to play power games. At forty, a few years younger than her husband, she was a handsome woman, tall and well built. She had a round, somewhat flat face with high cheekbones and widely-spaced tawny-coloured eyes, the kind of ageless face that looks much the same at fifty as at twenty, even without the make-up that she eschewed for political reasons. Her light brown hair was cut short, but its natural wave made it curve attractively around her head, just as she wore her Oxfam-bought clothes with a natural elegance. Tonight, Rowena noted, her dress was a dark Indian cotton, spangled all over with tiny mirrors, and even her bare unshaven legs and sandalled feet could not counteract the impression of elegance.

The same could not be said of poor Judith Greenwood, who was even now picking at her food, her eyes on her plate, as she endured Canon Thetford's lecture on overpopulation.

8

Describing Rupert Greenwood's wife as a frump would be unkind, thought Rowena, but it would not be far off the mark. She was certainly insipid, with her lank mouse-coloured hair and her shapeless home-made frock. The sad thing was that she'd evidently made an effort this evening; usually she wore no make-up – not from conviction but because she couldn't be bothered – but tonight her cheeks were unnaturally pink and her eyelids unnaturally blue. The colours, perceived Rowena, were completely outdated: it was probably the same make-up she'd experimented with as a schoolgirl, then put in the back of a drawer unused until tonight. What had the beautiful Rupert ever seen in this drab woman, Rowena wondered, not for the first time – apart from the fact that she so obviously adored him? That was a powerful aphrodisiac for many men, as she well knew.

Philip Thetford's voice penetrated her consciousness. 'And it's not just in the Third World that overpopulation is a problem,' he insisted. 'Right here in Malbury . . . well, Claire could tell you stories that would make your hair stand on end. Girls who are no more than children themselves. By the time she sees them it's too late, of course.'

Claire Fairbrother leaned across her husband. 'If you don't mind me saying so, Judith, I don't see how any sane, thinking person could bring a child into the world these days. It's totally indefensible, as far as I'm concerned. The world's resources will only stretch so far, you know. When Philip and I were married, we decided from the first not to have any children, and we've certainly never regretted that decision.'

Judith Greenwood, whose chief sorrow in life was her failure thus far to conceive a child, looked down at her plate and refrained from saying that if everyone thought that way, there would soon be no population at all.

During the dessert, Lucy Kingsley became aware of her hostess's eyes on her. It was not, she realised, a particularly friendly gaze. 'This is delicious,' she commented brightly, leaning across Jeremy Bartlett. 'What sort of chocolate did you use?'

Rowena's smile was chilly. 'I always use Swiss chocolate.'

'Would you consider giving me your recipe?'

'I never share my recipes,' Rowena replied sharply.

Lucy felt it wise to change the subject; she took her cue

from the ongoing discussion across the table, and the photograph she'd noticed on the mantelpiece of a young girl with dark curly hair. 'You have children, Mrs Hunt?'

'Yes, a daughter. She's away . . .' Lucy noticed a fractional hesitation, 'at school . . . right now.' There was a slight emphasis on the word 'school'.

'How long have you been running the Friends of the Cathedral? My father tells me that you do a splendid job of it.' Lucy smiled in what she hoped was a friendly and encouraging way; Rowena unbent slightly.

'Over six years now. Since just after my husband died. It enabled me to stay in the Close, and to keep the house,' she explained.

'Oh, I see. Your husband was a clergyman, then?'

'He was the Precentor for a number of years. Canon Greenwood's predecessor. He died very suddenly while singing Evensong – a massive heart attack.' Rowena looked down at her beautifully manicured nails and added quickly, 'He was much older than me, of course.'

'Yes, of course. You must have been a child bride,' Lucy said solemnly, and was rewarded with a gratified smile at last.

After the cheese and biscuits, the time finally arrived to leave the men with their port. Rowena had brought a very good bottle up from the cellar, mostly for the benefit of Jeremy, who would appreciate such things, and for the absent Canon Brydges-ffrench, a known connoisseur of fine wines. The other men, she thought scornfully, judging from the way they'd treated the sherry and the wines with dinner, probably wouldn't know the difference between vintage port and a £3.99 bottle from Tesco. Rowena was not averse to a glass of port herself, taken in privacy; perhaps there would be some left over.

'Well, ladies,' she said deliberately, watching Claire Fairbrother bridle at the perceived insult, 'it's time for us to retire to the drawing room. Jeremy, would you like to do the honours with the port?' She set the decanter down in front of the architect.

'Oh, I think I'll skip the port tonight,' he said easily, rising from the table and stretching. 'I've had enough to drink already.'

10

'But you don't have to drive,' Rowena protested.

'No, but I'd like to keep a clear head.' He took her hand and raised an eyebrow at her with a faintly ironic smile. 'Rowena, it's been a lovely evening, and I've enjoyed myself very much, but if you'll kindly excuse us, I've promised Miss Kingsley a tour of the cathedral by moonlight. And I think the moon will be setting rather soon, so we'd better be on our way.'

Rowena Hunt was speechless.

Chapter 2

Walk about Sion, and go round about her: and tell the towers thereof.

Mark well her bulwarks, set up her houses: that ye may tell them that come after.

Psalm 48.11–12

It was a warm Saturday evening early in July, one of the exquisitely long evenings of mid-summer; the sun had barely set as Lucy Kingsley and Jeremy Bartlett came out of Rowena Hunt's Georgian town house into the Cathedral Close. The moon was high in the sky, a pale silver disc, scarcely visible yet in the darkening sky as the shadows gathered around the ancient stone building which dominated the centre of the Close.

Lucy looked up. 'I thought you said that the moon would be setting soon.'

Her companion grinned conspiratorially. 'I lied.'

'But why?'

'Let's just say that I find Mrs Hunt a bit overwhelming sometimes. I get the strangest feeling that she has designs on me. And I'd much rather be with you,' he added.

She let that pass. 'So, what are you going to tell me about Malbury Cathedral?'

'How much do you know already?' Jeremy led her through Rowena's gate and out into the Close; they were nearly opposite the east end of the cathedral.

'Not much,' she admitted. 'I've been here before, of course. I grew up in the diocese – my father's parish was about twenty miles from here. But Ludlow was nearer for shopping, so we didn't come to Malbury all that often.'

'A little history, then, to begin?' he suggested, indicating a convenient bench which faced the cathedral.

'All right,' Lucy sat down gracefully.

13

'Stop me if I'm telling you things you already know. I tend to get carried away when I start talking about the cathedral.' He settled down beside her. 'It was founded as an abbey in 1088. Benedictine, dedicated to St Malo. The monks claimed that they had the saint's body, or at least a substantial portion of it, although Bath Abbey claimed the same thing.' Jeremy grinned. 'There was a lot of that sort of thing going on at the time. Anyway, in the original Norman east end, there was a large shrine to St Malo.'

'Remind me about St Malo,' Lucy interrupted reluctantly, ashamed of her ignorance.

'Oh, he was the apostle of Brittany. A bishop in the sixth century. But he was a Welshman, so he's always been popular around these parts. An odd man, by all reports – he liked to sing psalms, loudly, as he travelled about on horseback on his missionary journeys.'

'Sounds like a fun chap.'

'He had a few enemies, reportedly. But, as I said, the monks here built a huge Norman church and abbey, which they dedicated to him.' Jeremy gestured at the massive square central tower. 'The tower's the best bit that's left, of course. Though the Victorians did mess about with it, as they were wont to do.' The Victorian crenellations looked, in the deep blue twilight, like great discoloured teeth. 'A century or so later, after his martyrdom, Thomas à Becket became an extremely popular saint, and the monks decided to honour him as well, so they changed the dedication to St Malo and St Thomas à Becket. That's when they put in the great window in the south transept, the Becket window.'

'It's still there, isn't it?'

'Yes – it's the cathedral's greatest treasure.' Jeremy pointed to the left, at the south transept. 'But I'm afraid it's a bit difficult to see from the outside. See that wall that runs right up to the transept? That's my garden wall. It was put up in the last century, when they built the choir school – which is now my house. So you can only see the window properly from my front garden. Or,' he added with a wry smile, 'from my bedroom window. That's the best view of all of the Becket window. Perhaps I could interest you in looking at it sometime.'

Again Lucy let it pass, refusing to be drawn. 'Perhaps.' She looked at the cathedral, pushing her hair back from her forehead, and changed the subject. 'What about the east end?

14

It's very perpendicular, isn't it?' The east window, which faced them, was a soaring pointed traceried arch, and the flying buttresses stood out against the night sky.

'Oh, yes, quite late perp. During the Wars of the Roses, after the battle of Ludlow in 1459, the Lancastrians were rampaging about a bit, as Lancastrians were often inclined to do. Some of them came here, and for whatever reason they took a dislike to old St Malo. They tore down his shrine, and made rather a mess of the whole east end. So after that the east end was rebuilt in high gothic style. It's really quite splendid, with the fan vaulting in the retro-choir. The monks never rebuilt the shrine. They recovered St Malo's head, though, and put it in a gold reliquary at the High Altar. It was a marvellous thing, apparently, shaped like a head and encrusted with jewels.'

'That didn't survive the Reformation, did it?'

'No, and that's part of the legend of Malbury. When the Abbey was dissolved in 1538, the reliquary was the main thing the commissioners were after. But one of the monks, a Brother Thomas, hid it from them. They threatened him with death, but he said that he was willing to give his head to save St Malo's head – he was ready for martyrdom, it seems, like his namesake Becket. They took him at his word, and executed him on the spot. Chopped his head off.'

Lucy shivered slightly. 'They found the reliquary anyway?'

'Yes, of course. His sacrifice was in vain. Another monk lost no time in turning it over to them. It was duly destroyed, melted down, and the jewels went into Henry VIII's coffers.' Jeremy paused for a moment, looking thoughtful. 'The building didn't fare too well, either. Before Brother Thomas's defiance, there had been some indication that the church itself might be spared, that it might be one of the abbey churches that Henry named as cathedrals in 1540. But there wasn't a chance of that after Brother Thomas's wasted martyrdom. They let the townspeople have it as a parish church – for a price, of course – but not till after they'd knocked down the last three bays at the West End. That's why it's such an odd truncated shape now – there are only two bays of the nave left.

'So when did it actually become a cathedral?'

'In 1868, when the Malbury diocese was formed out of parts of Worcester, Hereford and Lichfield. And that,' he said with a smile, standing, 'is the end of your history lesson, Miss Kingsley. Now would you like a tour of the Close?'

The road curved around the east end of the cathedral, so from where they stood they could see much of the Close. 'As I said,' Jeremy began, 'over there, behind that wall, is my house. You can just about see the roof from here. The wall goes straight across the road, so that's as far as you can go in that direction. You can't actually get to it from the Close – you have to go around the west end.'

'How inconvenient for you!'

'It is a bit, but I don't often need to come into the Close, and I can go through the cathedral, when it's open.'

'You don't have a key?'

Jeremy laughed. 'I'm only the humble architect. They don't trust me with a key.'

'That building next to your wall looks very old. Or is it pseudo-gothic?' She pointed at a long stone building, two storeys high, with a number of windows but no visible doorway.

'No, that's actually the only bit of the Abbey buildings that survived. It was the monks' infirmary. I'm not sure why they didn't tear it down – I think it was used for storage for years. Around 1870 they converted it to a schoolhouse. Then in the 1920s, when they made the old Deanery into offices, the infirmary-cum-schoolhouse became the Deanery. The entrance is around on the side.'

'It's vacant now, I presume?'

'At the moment, though an announcement is expected any day now. We could have a new Dean installed by the early autumn.' Jeremy shook his head, bemused. 'I don't know how much you know about the cathedral politics, Lucy, but most people are banking on Canon Brydges-ffrench being appointed – Malbury Cathedral isn't exactly forward-looking, and that would be the best way of preserving the status quo. And I must say that Canon Brydges-ffrench himself is rather counting on it.'

'I'd gathered that much. Miss Marsden seems to think there's no question that it could be anyone else. That's what she told me before dinner.'

'Miss Marsden . . . well. She's rather counting on it, too,' he laughed. 'She rather fancies being Mrs Dean.'

'Oh. I see.'

'Not that it's necessarily going to happen, whether he gets the appointment or not,' Jeremy added, smiling cynically. 'He's

16

been putting her off for years, from what I hear.' He pointed to the house on the curve of the Close to the left of the Deanery, an eighteenth-century red brick house with stone dressings. 'Evelyn Marsden lives there, next to the Deanery. She's been there for yonks.'

'And here?' Directly opposite the east end of the cathedral was a range of three houses, built of red brick in the 1920s in neo-Georgian style. The centre house was small, one-storeyed with dormers; the two flanking houses were larger, and two-storeyed, though in proportion they were slightly pinched looking.

'Canon Brydges-ffrench lives in the one on the right, next to Miss Marsden. The one in the centre belongs to the organist, Ivor Jones. And the Precentor's house is on the left,' explained Jeremy. Next came the row of Georgian town houses that they had so recently left, set back from the Close and angled to the south-west. Each of the three houses had its own handsome black iron gate, but subtle differences in their exteriors, reflecting the respective personalities of their inhabitants, saved them from uniformity. Lucy's father's house was the first, on the right; in the few months that he had been there he had done little to differentiate his dwelling, apart from the rather half-hearted terracotta pot of wilting petunias and alyssum outside the door. Next door, though, a wooden statue, clearly African in origin and depicting a Negroid mother and her suckling child stood vigil over the entrance, betraying that this was the home of the Canon Missioner, as did the hectically-coloured native blinds at the windows. Rowena Hunt's front door, in contrast, was flanked by two tastefully sculptured bay trees in elegant containers, and there were Holland blinds in all the windows.

Jeremy pointed to an old stone barn, set back a small distance from the Close and largely concealed by the town houses. 'That's the cathedral refectory,' he explained. 'A converted barn. They serve meals there during the day. It's a bit out of the mainstream, but it serves the purpose.' They strolled along slowly. 'And the next buildings here are shops. They were built as almshouses in the seventeenth century, and converted not too long ago.' Six tall chimneys towered above the single-storey building, which now sported display windows and three smart doors. 'One is a book shop – quite a good one, actually – and one is a dress shop, as you can see. The one in the centre is the Cathedral Gift Shop.' They paused for a moment and peered in the window at the array of Malbury Cathedral mugs, tea towels, and postcards.

The next building was of an entirely different sort: an eighteenth-century gothic folly of pink stucco, massive and double-fronted. 'This was the old Deanery,' said the architect. 'It now houses the diocesan offices – the diocesan solicitor, the registrar, and so on.'

An equally large building, constructed of stone in the seventeenth century, stood to its left at the end of the Close. 'This used to be a school,' explained Jeremy. 'It's now been converted into offices, which the cathedral leases out. It all helps to pay the bills,' he added.

The Close ended at that point, opposite the west front of the cathedral. They began to cross the wide green space in front of the cathedral, an empty space that had once held the original extended west end of Malbury Abbey.

'The Bishop's House is on the other side,' said Jeremy, 'next to my house. Would you like to come round that way, and perhaps come in for a nightcap?'

Lucy nodded her assent. 'But I mustn't be too long. My father will be waiting up for me – I don't have a key.'

'The west front is pretty undistinguished,' Jeremy said dismissively as they passed in front of it. 'Victorian. They added on those side porches, to give it the extra width, so in fact the west front looks deceptively wide.' The Bishop's house, in front of them, was fairly impressive, a large neo-classical structure of grey stucco graced with huge Ionic columns. 'It was built for a rich banker in the nineteenth century. Conveniently close to the cathedral for the Bishop. He's actually got his own entrance, through the east range of the cloister. All that's left of the monastic cloister, but it's fairly intact.'

'I've been to the Bishop's house before,' remarked Lucy. 'He and my father are old friends.'

Jeremy led Lucy around the side of the Bishop's house, towards the corner where it met the cloister. 'I've actually got a little idea about the cloister,' he confided. 'I think that it would make a marvellous tearoom if it were glassed in and tarted up a bit. Much more accessible than the refectory, and it would be quite a nice project for me. Keep me out of mischief, you know.' He raised his eyebrows at her.

'That sounds like a good idea,' she responded ambiguously.

'But what do other people say? Wouldn't they think it was spoiling the cathedral?'

'Oh, I haven't mentioned it to anyone yet,' Jeremy grinned. 'Just to you. But you're right – they won't like it. Change is not very high on the agenda at Malbury. I'll have to take my time and approach it in the right way.' He paused at the mouth of the cloister. 'You can only get to my house through this cloister entrance.' By now night had fallen in earnest and it was truly dark; they paused at the sight of the medieval cloister, arched and vaulted, shimmering greyly in the moonlight. 'Actually, they say that the cloister is haunted. I've never seen him myself, but I've talked to people who swear they've seen Brother Thomas, gliding along with his head in his hands. Literally, I mean. Looking for St Malo's head.'

Lucy shivered. 'I can just about believe it, seeing it like this. The poor man – what a waste.'

Taking her arm, Jeremy guided her out of the cloister and around to his door. 'Come on in. I think we could do with a brandy.'

The sitting room was well furnished and cosy, Lucy noted approvingly. There were books everywhere, and a great number of records as well, ranged on shelves along two walls. Through a half-open set of double doors Lucy could see another room, dominated by a grand piano. 'Do you play, then?' she asked as he fetched the glasses and decanter.

'Actually, I play the cello.'

'Shades of Barchester,' she smiled. 'Mr Harding and his cello. How lovely.'

'Do you play the piano?' He handed her a brandy snifter, returning her smile.

'I used to. I haven't played for years – my house in London is too small for a piano.'

'Ah, well. We must try some duets some time.'

'I'm sure I wouldn't be good enough.'

'I'll be the judge of that.' Jeremy's smile faded suddenly, replaced by a thoughtful look, not without pain. 'My wife and I . . . we used to play together often. That's one thing I really miss.'

'How . . . how long has it been?' Lucy wasn't sure whether it was something Jeremy would want to talk about, but he was the one who had brought it up.

19

'Over a year now.' Looking down into his brandy, Jeremy went on after a moment. 'Cancer, it was. Rather protracted, and very painful. After she died, I . . . well, I didn't want to live in London any longer. There just didn't seem to be any point in all the rat race. So I sold up and came here. It was a good move. I like it here. The cathedral fascinates me – all that history. It's a bit of a dog's breakfast, architecturally, I know, but I love the building anyway. And by and large, I like the people.' With an effort, he shook himself out of his reflective mood and turned to her with a smile. 'Speaking of the people, what do you think of us all? After the dinner party?'

Lucy laughed. 'Well, that's certainly putting me on the spot!' She took a sip of her brandy. 'Collectively or individually?'

'Either. Both.'

He waited, so she tried to formulate her thoughts. 'It's an amazingly insular community, isn't it? Sheltered, almost self-contained.'

'Very. You might even say incestuous.'

'It was odd about Canon Brydges-ffrench. He seemed very well this afternoon.'

'Canon Brydges-ffrench *is* a bit odd,' Jeremy grinned. 'He has an utterly perverse antiquarian mind. You know the sort I mean – adores crossword puzzles and obscure theological riddles. He was a chorister here himself, back in the thirties. And if he had his way, we'd all do things exactly the way they were done then.'

'Sounds a bit regressive. This music festival . . .'

'All his idea, of course. He's never been able to stand being excluded from the Three Choirs Festival.'

'Really?'

Jeremy quirked his eyebrows. 'Hereford, Worcester, and Gloucester – why not Malbury as well? Why not the Four Choirs Festival? He's been going on about it for years, but no one's paid a blind bit of notice. So he's decided to show them all – he'll put on his own festival that will be better than the Three Choirs. And of course,' he added, 'it will look good on his c.v. when they get around to choosing the next Dean. Shows a bit of initiative, puts Malbury on the map. That sort of thing.'

Lucy looked dubious. 'But will it? After the meeting today, I'm not sure . . .'

'No, of course it won't. One of the difficulties, of course, is that none of them has a very realistic grasp of the finances of the whole thing. It's all being done very extravagantly, and I can't imagine that it will make any money. But the main problem is . . .' Jeremy paused and regarded her over the rim of his glass. 'The problem is that they're not good enough. Not only are they disorganised and shambolic in planning this thing, the musicians just aren't up to it. You met Ivor Jones, the organist?'

'He was at the meeting,' she nodded.

'Well, he's mediocre at the best. As an organist and as a choir trainer. And of course the choir isn't professional, in the sense that most cathedral choirs are. They closed the choir school years ago, so the boys are drawn from the local grammar school. No girls, at least – Canon Brydges-ffrench would never permit that. And the men in the choir – the lay vicars – aren't even paid. They're just a few blokes who like singing enough to give up their time to do it. Some of them are pretty dire, but we've got to take what we can get.'

'It sounds like they've chosen some fairly ambitious music for the festival,' she commented.

'That's part of the problem. It's difficult stuff, and it's so specialised in its appeal. If they could do it well, it would be one thing.' Jeremy shrugged. 'But Rupert Greenwood is so blinkered. You can't tell him a thing.'

'What about Canon Greenwood? Is he any good as a musician?'

'Oh, he's a real pro. Lives and breathes music. But he's very narrowly focused. He's chosen all the music, and it's all pretty esoteric.'

Lucy thought back to the meeting: to the impact of Rupert Greenwood's boyish good looks, and her subsequent surprise on meeting his plain, shy wife. The conversation took a diversion. 'Rupert Greenwood's wife . . . wasn't quite what I expected.'

Jeremy laughed. 'Rupert's definitely the peacock of the family. But our Judith . . . well, don't underestimate her, Lucy. I wouldn't be surprised if our Judith had hidden depths.'

Jeremy escorted Lucy back to her father's door some time later. 'It's been a lovely evening, Jeremy. I really enjoyed the tour of the Close and the potted history of the cathedral,' she said with sincerity. 'I'll look forward to seeing you again when I come back next month for the music festival.'

He hesitated for a moment. 'I'd like to see you before that, Lucy.'

'What do you mean?'

'It's not impossible for me to get to London,' he grinned. 'The trains run quite regularly, you know. If I were to come up to London one day, could I take you out for a meal?'

Her reply was a long time coming. 'No,' she said at last. 'No, I don't think that would be a good idea.'

Jeremy frowned. 'You're not married.' It was a statement rather than a question.

'No, I'm not married.' She paused. 'But I'm . . . attached.'

'Engaged?'

'No . . .'

'Good.' He nodded, reassured. 'Then I'm not taking "no" as a final answer. And if you think I'm giving up without a fight, Lucy Kingsley, then you've got a lot to learn about me.'

Chapter 3

*Thou art about my path, and about my bed: and spiest out
all my ways.*

Psalm 139.2

Canon Kingsley had left the door unlatched for his daughter;
he was on the phone in his study as she came into the house.
Lucy looked at her watch: nearly midnight. It was a bit late for
phone calls, she thought. And her father was not known for
retiring late. Choosing a comfortable chair in the sitting room,
she settled down to wait for him.

In a few minutes he emerged, a worried frown creasing his
normally placid brow. 'Oh, hello, my dear. You're back.'

'Yes, I haven't been back long. Is something wrong?'

He nodded his head abstractedly. 'I'm afraid so. A cathedral
matter. Would you like some hot chocolate?'

'Yes please, Daddy. I can make it,' she offered.

'That's very kind, my dear.'

Lucy busied herself in the unfamiliar kitchen, searching for
the tin of drinking chocolate while the milk warmed on the hob.
Knowing her absent-minded father, she realised that it could
be anywhere; eventually it turned up, improbably, under the
sink. When she carried the tray into the sitting room, her
father was in his favourite armchair, staring off into space with
the same worried look. But he smiled at Lucy as he took the
beaker. 'Thank you, my love.'

„ She sat down across from him. 'What's the matter, Daddy?
Anything you can tell me about?'

Smoothing his silver hair with his hand, he considered for a
moment. 'I suppose so. As long as you don't tell anyone . . .'

'Of course I won't.' Lucy blew on her chocolate to cool it, then
took a sip.

'Arthur Brydges-ffrench . . .' he began, then stopped and
began again. 'George rang me tonight, after I got home. He was

23

worried about Arthur.' Dr George Willoughby, the Bishop of Malbury, was perhaps John Kingsley's closest friend.

'Why? What's the matter with Canon Brydges-ffrench? He seemed fine this afternoon.'

'That's just it. He *was* fine this afternoon, until George talked to him, just before the dinner party.' Lucy looked puzzled and her father went on. 'George wanted to tell him the bad news himself. Before he heard it through other channels, that is. They've chosen a new Dean. And it's not Arthur.'

'Oh, dear. I understood that he was really counting on the appointment.'

John Kingsley shook his head sadly. 'Indeed he was, my dear. It was to be the culmination of his career at Malbury. An affirmation of everything he'd stood for, everything he'd tried to do here. He's devoted his life to this cathedral, and he was sure that he would get his reward. And he *should* have had the appointment,' the Canon added with some spirit. 'He earned it. Over the last ten years, he's been the acting Dean in all but name. It was before my time, of course, but George tells me that the last Dean was hopeless. Really past it. Left everything to Arthur to do. It was only right that Arthur should have it now, for at least a few years before he retires.'

'So whom did they choose?' asked Lucy.

'Oh, a man from London. His name is Stuart Latimer. He's currently the incumbent at a posh London church – Fulham, I think George said.'

'You don't know him?'

'I met him recently, when he visited the cathedral. The Chapter doesn't have any real say in the appointment, of course, nor does the Bishop – it's all up to the Prime Minister. But he made a point of coming round and meeting everyone. A nice enough chap, I thought. Young and dynamic. But we all thought that Arthur would get the nod, after all that he's done.'

Lucy turned the news over in her mind, twisting a curl around her finger. 'Why did the Bishop ring you?'

'As I said, he was worried about Arthur. He didn't take it at all well. George thought that perhaps I could talk to him. I've known Arthur a good many years, you know.'

'And did you talk to him?'

'Yes, I rang him just now. I know it's late, but George said he'd still be up. He was, of course. In a real state, he was. Poor Arthur.' John Kingsley sighed feelingly, took off his spectacles, and rubbed the bridge of his nose. 'There wasn't really much that I could say. All I could do was listen to him, and share his pain.'

'I'm sure that was worth a great deal to him,' Lucy said with a rush of love for her gentle, empathetic father.

'I wish I could believe that. It's been a terrible year for him, you know – his mother died last winter.'

Lucy stared. 'His mother? But she must have been ancient!'

'Oh, she was – well over ninety, I think. But she'd kept house for him ever since he came to Malbury. Very healthy right up to the last, apparently – she'd never been sick a day in her life, Arthur claimed, then she caught the flu and was dead within a week. A dreadful shock it was for him. They were devoted to one another. And this on top of it. I just don't know how he's going to cope.'

'You don't think he'd do anything . . . foolish?'

'Oh, no,' said Canon Kingsley. 'No, I don't think so.' But he looked even more troubled.

With an effort, they turned their conversation to a less distressing topic over a second round of hot chocolate. But, in discussing the forthcoming music festival, they couldn't get away entirely from the subject of Arthur Brydges-ffrench.

'What exactly did they want you to do for them?' the Canon asked his daughter. 'Arthur seemed very keen to have you come down for this planning meeting. What did he have in mind?'

'Oh, he wants me to do a painting for the cover of the festival programme. Something that they can use on posters and other things as well,' Lucy explained.

'But the festival is at the end of August – next month. Isn't that leaving it a bit late?'

'Absolutely.' Lucy laughed, pushing her hair back. 'Fortunately, though, things are a bit slow for me at the moment, and I'll be able to do it rather quickly. Probably within the next week or so.'

'They *will* pay you, won't they?' he asked anxiously. 'I told Arthur that you were a professional artist, and that he couldn't expect you to do it for free.'

She smiled. 'Oh, I'll send them a bill. But, of course, I won't charge the going rate. And I won't hold my breath until I'm paid!'

The lateness of the hour, as well as the emotions of the evening, fostered a rare intimacy between father and daughter as they sat together in the cosy room. The room itself was unfamiliar to Lucy, but the furniture was all well remembered from the rambling country vicarage of her childhood. There they lingered over their chocolate, saying little, both unwilling to break the mood.

Lucy loved her father deeply, but they had never had the kind of relationship that involved sharing confidences. Canon Kingsley was a diffident man who had never pried into his children's lives, and Lucy had always been a very private person, finding it difficult – and unnecessary – to discuss her personal life with anyone, especially her quiet, saintly father.

So when he broached the subject later that night, emboldened perhaps by their closeness, Lucy realised the depth of his concern for her.

'You seemed to be getting on well with Jeremy Bartlett tonight,' he ventured obliquely.

Lucy's reply was noncommittal. 'Yes. He seems a very nice man.'

'He's been quite lonely since his wife died.' John Kingsley paused, pressing together the tips of his long white fingers, then went on gently, 'I worry about you being lonely, my dear. London is such a big place, and you're . . .'

'Not as young as I used to be, Daddy?' Lucy laughed. 'Don't worry about me.' For a long time she'd felt that she needed to tell her father about David; now seemed like the time. 'As a matter of fact, there is a man I'm . . . very fond of.' Her father nodded encouragingly, but said nothing, and after a moment Lucy went on. 'His name is David. David Middleton-Brown. He's a solicitor. I've known him for about a year.'

'He lives in London, then?'

'Actually, he's been living in Norfolk. But he's moving to London quite soon. He's got a new position, at a firm in Lincoln's Inn. Quite a prestigious old firm,' she added, unable to keep a note of pride from her voice. 'They do a lot of work for charities, including the Church of England.'

'That's very nice, my dear.' Canon Kingsley smiled with relief, then fell silent again. Lucy was silent too, thinking about David. She'd meant to be in Norfolk with him this weekend, helping him to get his house ready to put on the market. That plan had had to be abandoned when she'd had the call from her father, urgently requesting her help with the preparations for the music festival. She couldn't very well have refused to come – her father asked so little of her. But poor David, she thought. She could understand why he'd been upset and disappointed at the last-minute change of plans. The house itself wasn't too bad: he'd done a great deal of redecoration after his mother's death the previous year, and he was by inclination a tidy man, who in addition had been well trained by his mother to keep the house in reasonable condition. But the garden was another matter; David's weekends were invariably spent with Lucy in London, and his garden had been sadly neglected as a consequence. She'd been looking forward to a satisfying if undemanding weekend of pulling weeds and pruning shrubs in the hot July sunshine. Instead, it seemed, she'd plunged headfirst into the disappointed ambitions and frustrated passions of the Cathedral Close.

When they parted at last for the night, at the door of the spare room that Lucy was using, Canon Kingsley kissed his daughter on the forehead. 'Thank you for coming,' he said. 'Good night, Lucy dear, and God bless you.'

His tender benediction, remembered from so many nights of her childhood, put Lucy into a reflective mood as she got ready for bed in the unfamiliar room. It had been a long day, beginning with a lengthy and less-than-straightforward train journey from London to Malbury, and ending here in this bed. In between so much had happened: so many new faces to assimilate.

There was, of course, the unfortunate Canon Brydges-ffrench, his appearance as eccentric as his reputation. She had been struck by his very tall figure, his frame cadaverously thin and stooped, and by his expansive domed forehead above bushy, expressive brows. The forehead would have been remarkably high even if it had been met by hair at its upper reaches. As it was, the hair – longish, greasy, and a yellowish grey – was restricted to the sides and back of his head, and the forehead merged uninterrupted into a shiny bald dome. A remarkable man.

Then there were the others at the meeting – handsome Rupert Greenwood and the small, dark organist Ivor Jones, quiet almost to the point of sullenness. And of course the dinner party. Jeremy.

Had she been fair to Jeremy? Had she led him on? She hadn't thought at the time that she was leading him on – she'd found him a pleasant dinner companion, and had sincerely enjoyed their evening together, discussing shared interests and partaking of his extensive knowledge of the cathedral and its environs. It hadn't occurred to her that he might want to take it further. Her unavailability – the strength of her commitment to David – was taken so much for granted by her that she hadn't even thought to mention it until it was too late. And had she really made it clear, even then? Jeremy certainly didn't seem prepared to accept it as final.

He probably thought, Lucy realised now, that the reason that she and David were not married, or even engaged, was that he hadn't asked her. This, of course, was far from the truth: David had asked her repeatedly and insistently to marry him. It was the lasting legacy of a short-lived early marriage to a man completely unsuitable that Lucy quailed at making this final commitment to the man she loved. She knew that her refusals made David unhappy: he was a deeply conventional man, and craved the security of marriage. But her efforts to overcome her own deep-seated antipathy to the institution had not been successful. Their current arrangement of spending weekends together was less than satisfactory, she knew; it would be an improvement when David moved to London within the next few months. The house he had inherited would not be available for occupancy for some time, so he would be moving in with her for the time being. It was almost the same as being married, Lucy told herself – at least she hoped that David would think so.

And Jeremy? He was a nice man, and undeniably attractive. She'd better edit her account of the weekend, when she shared it with David, to leave out Jeremy Bartlett. He was still so insecure about their relationship that he would find it difficult to cope with the idea of Jeremy, a self-professed rival for her affections. Lucy knew that Jeremy was no threat, but David would be profoundly threatened nonetheless – at least she could spare him that worry.

As she drifted off to sleep at last, Lucy thought about David, alone and lonely in his bed. Suddenly she missed him dreadfully. When would she see him again? Next weekend wasn't soon enough. She determined that after the morning service at the cathedral, and after Sunday lunch – they'd been invited to lunch with the Bishop – she would go to him: she would take the train back to London, and from there on to Norwich. She probably wouldn't arrive till very late, but she would stay with him for a few days. Canon Brydges-ffrench and his programme cover could wait – she needed David.

Jeremy Bartlett stood outside the house in the quiet Cathedral Close for a very long time. He had drawn into the shadows, where he would not be observed, and from whence he could watch the windows of the house. John Kingsley had not bothered to close the curtains of the sitting room, so Jeremy had a good view of the conversation between father and daughter. As he was not a lip-reader, its subject matter escaped him, but that was not important; he had much to think about.

Lucy Kingsley. From the moment he'd met her, Jeremy had found her fascinating. It wasn't that she'd been flirtatious, or even conscious of her charms; indeed, her naturalness was perhaps a large component of her attraction for him. Since the loss of his wife, and even before, he was used to women – women like Rowena Hunt – who signalled their availability to him in ways subtle and not so subtle. Occasionally, through the years, he'd succumbed to this direct approach – he was after all only human – though on the whole he found it a turn-off. But Lucy Kingsley hadn't been like that. During their evening together he'd tested her, had given her a number of openings to flirt with him, but she'd never taken the bait.

And now she'd told him that she was in fact unavailable. In some perverse way that excited him, and challenged him. She was the most interesting woman he'd met in years, and he wasn't about to give up just because of some other man's prior claim. He would pursue her, he told himself, and he would have her. It might last for a few months, or perhaps for just one night, but that didn't matter. The chase was all.

Jeremy held his breath as, at long last, the lights went out in the sitting room; a moment later the window above his head on the first floor was illuminated and Lucy came into the room. He stepped back from the house to get a better view of her, but to his disappointment she immediately crossed to the window and drew the curtains.

With a philosophic shrug, Jeremy turned and headed back

towards home. Passing Rowena Hunt's house, he automatically looked up at her front bedroom. Rowena was not so discreet: the Holland blinds were only partially lowered, and the light from the bedside lamp framed Rowena, seated at her dressing table, drawing a silver-backed brush through her glossy black hair with sensuous strokes. At this distance, with her beautiful skin and her firm body clearly visible in a lacy black night-gown, she looked no more than a girl. Under other circumstances Jeremy might have lingered. But not tonight. Rowena interested him not in the slightest.

And yet by the time he'd reached his house Jeremy had decided to ring Rowena, his curiosity piqued by the remembrance of Canon Brydges-ffrench's non-appearance. Perhaps she'd tell him more on the phone than she'd been at liberty to reveal in the gathered company.

She answered quickly from the extension in her bedroom. 'Rowena Hunt speaking.'

'Rowena? Jeremy here. I'm sorry to be ringing so late,' he began.

Rowena smiled into the phone. 'No problem. I was still up.'

'I wanted to thank you for a delightful dinner party,' he said smoothly. 'The food was delicious.'

'I'm glad you liked it.'

'Arthur Brydges-ffrench missed a superb meal. I hope he had a good excuse.'

'As a matter of fact . . .' Rowena hesitated for a fraction of a second, then went on, 'Jeremy, you must promise that you won't pass this on, but I found out later why Arthur cancelled.'

Jeremy kept his voice neutral. 'My lips are sealed.'

'I was a bit worried, so I rang him up after everyone left,' she explained. 'It's not really like Arthur to be rude, and the sudden illness didn't really sound very convincing.'

'And?'

'You won't believe it, Jeremy! He's been passed over for the appointment!'

'My God! Then who . . .?'

'A chap called Stuart Latimer, from London. Arthur just found out this evening, and it won't be announced for a few days yet.'

'Ah.' There was a long, thoughtful pause as Jeremy worked out the implications. Then he laughed softly. 'Well, well, well.

This changes everything, doesn't it? All bets are off. Just as a matter of interest, Rowena, how do you see it? Will it make it easier or harder to get what you want?'

'I'm sure I don't know what you mean,' she replied in a chilly voice.

'I'm sure you do. That dinner party tonight – it wasn't just a friendly social occasion, was it? I'm not that naïve. No, Rowena – you want something, and you want the Chapter on your side. Why don't you tell me what it is, and perhaps I might help you? After all, it might be to our mutual benefit to work together. Since we both have the best interests of the cathedral as our top priority . . .'

'I can guess what *you* want,' Rowena interrupted him.

'And what might that be?'

'What every architect wants. Immortality. Although how you intend to achieve it . . .'

Jeremy laughed. 'Clever girl, Rowena. Keep guessing.'

'And if you're so clever, you should know that I'll get what I want in the end, no matter who becomes Dean of Malbury.' She put the phone down and said aloud, almost purring with satisfaction, 'And that includes *you*, Jeremy Bartlett. I'll get you yet.'

Chapter 4

Whoso leadeth a godly life: he shall be my servant.

Psalm 101.9

Several weeks later, John Kingsley was at work in the cathedral library when he received a message from the Bishop's secretary that Bishop Willoughby would like him to call at his convenience. One of Canon Kingsley's responsibilities as Residentiary Canon at Malbury Cathedral was the care and supervision of the library, which was housed in a long, narrow chamber over the surviving east range of the cloister. Although the library was not large, it possessed a few rare and valuable volumes and a number of other books of some historic interest, and the Canon quite enjoyed the time he spent there.

Bishop George Willoughby and John Kingsley had been close friends since their days together at theological college. It had taken a number of years for the Bishop to convince his friend to accept a canonry at the cathedral; he'd always been content in his rural parish, with no ambition for higher office, but as he neared retirement age the Bishop had prevailed upon him to finish his career at Malbury. In the end he'd even had to use subterfuge: he'd had to make out that John Kingsley would be doing him a favour by sorting out the library. The Bishop knew Canon Kingsley as a modest man, spiritual and unworldly, and felt that he would be a great asset to the ego-ridden Cathedral Chapter. It was his modesty, lack of presumption and his discretion that had prompted the Bishop to send for him on this occasion.

Bishop Willoughby opened his front door himself with a grin of delight. 'John! How splendid to see you! Do come in!'

'It's not an inconvenient time, is it, George?'

'No, of course not.' He laughed heartily. 'I sent for you, didn't I? I'm glad of the interruption, in fact. I've been working all day

33

on my book, and to tell you the truth, I'm getting a bit fed up with the Albigensian Heresy. But don't quote me on that!' He laughed again, a deep belly laugh. Dr George Willoughby, short and rotund, and with a full white beard and twinkling blue eyes, looked like a cross between Father Christmas and a rather jolly Old Testament Jehovah. He was, in spite of his appearance, a scholar of some note, and an acknowledged expert on the heresies of the Early Church. In addition, his pastoral skills were considerable, and his tenure in the see of Malbury had been a long and popular one. He led his friend through the house, explaining over his shoulder, 'Pat is in the garden. Why don't we join her out there? I'll put the kettle on – I imagine we could all use a cup of tea.'

The Honourable Mrs Patricia Willoughby, better known throughout the diocese as Pat, had her back to the two men as they came out into the garden. She was expertly and ruthlessly wielding a rather wicked pair of secateurs, divesting one of her prize rose bushes of its dead blooms.

'Pat!' announced the Bishop in his rich, booming voice. 'John has come for tea! I've put the kettle on.'

Pat Willoughby turned with a smile. 'John! It's been ages since you've been to see us! I think we saw more of you before you moved to Malbury, you naughty man.' A tall, big-boned woman, she was wearing a large-brimmed straw hat to shade her fair skin from the sun, but her arms were bare and freckled.

'I'm sorry,' Canon Kingsley apologised. 'But I know how busy you are. I don't like to bother you.'

'Nonsense!' was her robust reply. She, like her husband, was extremely fond of John Kingsley. Although he was about the same age as the Bishop, the man gave the impression of being totally incapable of looking after himself, and that brought out all of Pat Willoughby's considerable maternal instincts. She had been a close friend of Elizabeth Kingsley before her early death, over twenty years before. At the time of that death Pat had been a tower of strength, looking after the newborn baby who had cost his mother her life, as well as offering immeasurable support to a stunned John and the three older children: Lucy and her two elder brothers, all in their teens. John Kingsley had never forgotten her strength and her kindness at that unbearable time, and he was constantly aware of how much he owed her.

If the Bishop was popular in the diocese of Malbury, his wife was even more so. To her great sorrow, she had been unable to have children, but rather than becoming bitter, she had rechannelled her nurturing instincts; for years now they had been directed towards the clergy of the diocese and their wives. They repaid her with loyalty and affection, and she had not a few godchildren throughout the diocese who regarded her as something of a surrogate mother. The rest of her abundant energies and her love were lavished upon her garden, her dogs, and of course the Bishop.

The dogs, on this hot, sunny August afternoon, were reclining in the shade of an ancient tree in the corner of the garden, panting shallowly. There were two of them, both Labradors: the black one was called Cain, and the golden one was of course Abel. As their beloved mistress approached with her guest, they raised their heads and wagged their tails desultorily, their great pink tongues lolling out of their mouths like thick slices of ham. John Kingsley stooped over to scratch their ears; the tail-wagging became more enthusiastic. 'Good boys,' he murmured.

In the shade were four garden chairs with faded floral cushions and a rather dilapidated wooden table. 'We'll have our tea here,' Pat announced; the Bishop obediently went off to fetch it. Pat flopped into one of the chairs and removed her hat, fanning her face with it. 'Hot work, gardening,' she remarked. 'Especially in this weather.' Her grey hair was bundled into an untidy knot at the back of her neck; escaping wisps fluttered about her face as she fanned it.

The tea appeared in short order, the tray carried by a beaming Bishop. While it steeped, Pat asked the Canon about his family.

'Oh, they're all very well.'

'Lucy has a new man in her life?'

'So she tells me, though I haven't met him yet. A solicitor. She sounds very happy with him. I'm glad,' the Canon confessed. 'I do worry about Lucy. She ought to be thinking about settling down.'

'Will he be coming down with her to the music festival?' Pat wanted to know.

'I'm not sure.'

'Did you have to bring up that blasted music festival?' interrupted the Bishop with a groan. 'I'm sick to the teeth of hearing about the music festival.'

35

His wife laughed. 'Sorry, dear.' Pouring the tea, she turned to John Kingsley and explained. 'George keeps getting these phone calls. From Arthur, mostly, but also from Rupert Greenwood and Ivor Jones. They keep second guessing each other, and are all looking for his support.'

'I keep telling them that it has nothing to do with me,' the Bishop muttered, taking his tea and helping himself to a biscuit.

'Arthur seems to be . . . coping all right,' ventured the Canon, hoping to steer the subject away from the contentious music festival. 'Don't you think so, George?'

The Bishop shook his head. 'About the Deanship, you mean? I'm not sure, John. Arthur is a deep one – it's hard to tell what he's thinking.'

'It will be worse . . . later, I suppose.'

'When the new man comes? Well, John, time will tell. That's really what I wanted to see you about.'

'About Stuart Latimer? But I've only met him once.'

'Not about him, exactly,' the Bishop replied. 'About the Chapter, really. I'm rather worried about what will happen to the Chapter when there's a new Dean in place.'

'What do you mean?'

'Well, it's a bit delicate, John.' Dr Willoughby drummed on the arms of his chair with his fingers. 'It's none of my affair, really, as you know. After all, I have to knock on the door to be admitted to my own cathedral! My business is running the diocese, not the cathedral, and I've always stayed out of Chapter affairs as a matter of policy. But I anticipate that there may be some major problems.'

'George is afraid that the balance of power will change, that the new Dean may be out of step with Malbury, with the rest of the Chapter,' Pat amplified bluntly; she had always been considered an equal partner in her husband's ministry and didn't hesitate to speak her mind. 'Arthur has had a free hand for so many years now.'

'The balance of power in a cathedral Chapter is always a delicate thing,' the Bishop added. 'Things haven't really changed for quite a few years. As Pat says, Arthur has had a free hand – the old Dean was quite useless, and did whatever Arthur told him to do, so his death didn't make any practical difference. And you fit in quite well, so your coming didn't rock the boat. But a new man, presumably with modern ideas – well,

I just don't know what might happen. Perhaps I'm over-reacting, but . . .'

Pat interrupted forcefully. 'You're not overreacting, George. I'm convinced that there *will* be conflict. But you can't allow yourself to be drawn into it! You have no authority, and no power, and if you try to get involved it will be an absolute recipe for disaster!'

'That's why I've asked John to come here,' the Bishop reminded her.

Canon Kingsley looked from the Bishop to his wife, puzzled. 'But what can *I* do? You know that I'm always willing to do anything I can for you, George, but as you say, I'm the newest member of the Chapter. No one pays much attention to me, and as far as I'm concerned that's fine. I don't aspire to any power within the Chapter.'

Dr Willoughby laughed. 'Modest as ever, John. I'm not asking you to stage a palace coup. All I ask is that you keep an eye on the situation for me, and let me know if you see any trouble coming. I'd feel a lot easier about things if I knew that I had a reliable set of eyes and ears in the Chapter.'

'Yes, of course, if that's what you want,' John Kingsley assented. 'Though I don't know how much help I'll be.'

Pat lifted the lid of the teapot and inspected its by now depleted contents. 'It looks like this might just stretch to one more cup. How about it, John?'

Chapter 5

*I will pay my vows now in the presence of all his people:
right dear in the sight of the Lord is the death of his
saints.*

Psalm 116.13

The first event of the Malbury Music Festival, on a Friday
evening near the end of August, was a performance of T. S.
Eliot's 'Murder in the Cathedral', put on by the Malbury
Amateur Dramatics Society. Appropriately, it was staged in
the south transept of the cathedral, beneath the Becket
window.

The attendance was disappointing; the hoped-for last-
minute rush of ticket buyers on the door had not materialised
to augment the poor advance ticket sales, and the crowd in the
south transept that evening was sparse.

'It's a bit embarrassing, actually,' Jeremy Bartlett said to
Lucy and her father during the interval. A large striped
marquee had been erected on the grass to the north of the
cathedral, but inside there was no long queue for drinks; a
handful of people circulated in a somewhat dispirited manner,
sipping cheap white wine or watered-down Pimms.

'Let's go outside with our drinks,' Lucy suggested. 'It's such a
lovely evening – too nice to stay inside this stuffy tent.'

A few other people had the same idea, and half a dozen tables
had been set up outside. Jeremy led them to an empty one; he
didn't want to share Lucy with anyone tonight, though he was
willing if necessary to put up with her father. 'Cheers,' he said,
raising his glass.

Lucy smiled at him. 'Cheers, Jeremy. Thanks for the drink.'

'Yes, thank you very much indeed,' Canon Kingsley echoed.
'Very kind.'

Jeremy asked the question that was uppermost in his mind.
'So, he didn't come with you this weekend? Your boyfriend?'

39

'David? No, he didn't,' she replied shortly. He looked at her inquiringly, hoping for further information, but she disappointed him.

Canon Kingsley sensed the awkwardness of the pause and volunteered, 'Lucy says that he's moving house soon, and couldn't get away.'

'What a pity,' Jeremy said with exaggerated regret, quirking one eyebrow ironically. Lucy shot him an unreadable look.

'Oh, there's Arthur Brydges-ffrench,' said John Kingsley. 'I do hope he's not terribly upset by the poor turnout tonight.'

'Perhaps you should go and have a word with him,' Jeremy suggested.

'Yes, I shall do that, if you don't mind.'

'Not at all, Canon.'

Lucy watched her father moving towards the tall Subdean. 'What did you do that for?'

'So I could have a few minutes alone with you. I wanted to ask you something.'

She was wary as she turned to him. 'What's that?'

'Who is he, this David? This chap who has a prior claim on you?'

Lucy frowned in irritation at the invasion of her privacy, twisting a curl around her finger, and took her time in answering. 'His name is David Middleton-Brown. He's a solicitor. He and I . . .' She hesitated. 'Well, that's all I'm prepared to say about him. It's really . . .'

'A solicitor? Sounds fairly boring, Lucy. You're so artistic . . .'

'. . . nothing to do with you,' she finished with some asperity. 'And now, if you don't mind, I'm going to pay my respects to Canon Brydges-ffrench.' As she walked away, Lucy realised that her anger was directed more against herself than against Jeremy, because of her failure to be completely honest with him from the very beginning, and because she had so mistakenly interpreted his initial interest in her as being of a very general and friendly sort. It increasingly seemed that she had been wrong about that, but the damage had already been done.

Arthur Brydges-ffrench was deep in conversation with her father as Lucy came up, but his gaunt face broke into a smile at her approach. It was not a pleasant sight; his teeth were

40

uneven, discoloured and heavily decayed. 'How nice to see you, Miss Kingsley. I must congratulate you on your artwork – I've had nothing but compliments on it. Don't you think that the programme looks stunning?' He held up his copy of the Malbury Festival programme book, with Lucy's painting on the cover: it was the Becket window, but done in so abstract a style that its subject was not immediately evident.

'It's a beautiful printing job,' she replied modestly. 'It must have cost a packet to have it done like that with full four-colour treatment.'

Canon Brydges-ffrench frowned suddenly. 'Yes.' He hesitated a moment, then added in a low voice, 'Much more than we expected, actually. You see, it was done by the local firm, the one that we've always used for cathedral business. They've always given us a preferential rate. They'd even given me some indication that, in this case, they'd consider a sponsorship – print the programmes at virtually no charge, as long as we'd let them run a full-page advert on the back. But as you can see, there's no advert, and they've sent me a bill for the full amount. No discount at all.'

'But what happened?' Lucy asked.

The Canon leaned towards her. 'The new Dean,' he hissed. 'His installation – it's just over a month away now. Naturally enough, the local printing firm expected the order for the invitations and the orders of service, after all they've done for us over the years.' He frowned again, creating deep furrows in his great domed forehead, and his voice was tinged with bitterness as he went on. 'But they weren't good enough for the new Dean. He had to use some London firm. Bond Street. Great stiff things the invitations are – we haven't had the bill yet, but they're sure to cost the earth.'

'I'm sure he must have had good reasons,' John Kingsley said soothingly, if naïvely.

His friend's look was scathing. 'Good reasons!' He turned earnestly to Lucy again 'And that's not all, Miss Kingsley. We've lost two other sponsors for the festival as well! The local caterers, who were prepared to take out an advert in the programme, and give us a good price on the catering for the festival, found out that he's bringing in a firm of posh London caterers for the garden party after the installation ceremony! I for one don't blame them for being upset!'

'And the other?'

'Watkins Brewery – they're the big local industry. They have historic ties to this cathedral that stretch back many years. You may not realise it, Miss Kingsley, but they provided the money that founded your father's canonry.'

'No, I didn't know that.'

'And they're always more than willing to support the things we do here in a . . . tangible way. Money, of course, but also . . . beer.'

'Beer?'

Canon Brydges-ffrench nodded in vigorous indignation. 'They would have given us free beer to sell in the marquee. Barrels of it, all we wanted. Just as they've always provided beer for cathedral events. But . . .'

'Let me guess. London beer?'

He shook his head lugubriously. 'No. No beer at all, Miss Kingsley. Our new Dean does not feel that beer is a proper drink for his garden party. Only wine will be served, he says. And Watkins . . . well, can you blame them for feeling it's a slap in the face? For withdrawing the beer from the festival, and their financial sponsorship as well?' Again he leaned towards her. 'That man,' he said with sad dignity, 'has a great deal to answer for.' He sighed heavily. 'It almost seems as if he's done it deliberately – to sabotage *my* festival!'

Before the interval was over, they were joined by a pair of young people – unlikely candidates to seek out the company of Arthur Brydges-ffrench, Lucy thought as they came up. The girl, who looked about twenty, was extremely pretty in an animated way, with masses of loose dark curls, very blue eyes, and expressive hands that wouldn't stay still as she talked. The young man at her side was tall, well-built and broad-shouldered; he had a pleasingly open face, and when he smiled, his beautiful and plentiful white teeth couldn't have been a greater contrast to those of Canon Brydges-ffrench. They were both casually dressed: she in white trousers and a brightly flowered, oversized cotton shirt, and he in a T-shirt emblazoning 'Ohio State University' across his chest above the inevitable jeans.

The girl smiled at Lucy, nodded in recognition and acknowledgement to John Kingsley, and to Lucy's astonishment, gave Canon Brydges-ffrench a hug that nearly spilled both their drinks. 'Oh, Uncle Arthur!' she burbled. 'Isn't it absolutely fabulous? I've never seen "Murder in the Cathedral" before, and I think it's the most marvellous thing!'

The Subdean regained his composure and smiled fondly at the young woman. 'You're enjoying it, then?'

'Oh, yes. That bit about the Archbishop actually *wanting* martyrdom – what an incredible way to look at it! I can't see how anyone with so much to live for could be tempted by death like that. Do *you* think he was?'

'It wasn't death he was tempted by, my dear. It was martyrdom. Two different things.' The Subdean seemed prepared to launch into a lecture, but suddenly recalled his manners. 'Miss Kingsley, I don't believe you've met Kirsty Hunt. Or Todd Randall. Todd is an American theological student, spending a year with us here at Malbury. He's been helping me to catalogue my papers.'

Lucy acknowledged the introductions, then said, 'I didn't realise that you had a niece in Malbury, Canon. Or is she just visiting?'

He looked perplexed and the girl Kirsty laughed, a charming bubbly laugh. 'Oh, he's not my real uncle, Miss Kingsley. But I've known him nearly all my life, and I've always called him Uncle Arthur. Haven't I?' She tucked her arm through his affectionately, adding, 'My mother runs the Friends of the Cathedral.'

Lucy stared at her for a second as the penny dropped. 'Oh, you're Rowena Hunt's daughter! I'm sorry, I didn't realise. I thought for some reason that her daughter was ... much younger than you are.'

Kirsty laughed again, unabashed. 'I'm not surprised. Mummy likes to give that impression.' Speaking in a humorously affectionate tone, she went on, 'She doesn't like people to think that she's old enough to have a daughter at university, you see. If she could, she'd still have me in plaits and a gymslip when I'm in Malbury.'

Feeling embarrassed for the girl as well as for her mother, Lucy shifted the subject and asked, 'So you're at university, then?'

'Yes, at Cambridge. I've just finished my first year, reading law. But that's another story ...'

Canon Brydges-ffrench interposed quickly. 'Miss Kingsley is an artist. She did the painting for the cover of the programme.'

'Wow!' The American spoke for the first time. 'I'm really

impressed!' His broad vowels had all the redolence of the mid-west; Lucy altered her mental picture of him, removing the imaginary surfboard and substituting a placid pet cow. 'You sure are talented,' he added.

Lucy gave the only possible response to such ingenuous effusion: a gracious smile and a slight inclination of her head. 'Tell me, Mr Randall,' she said, 'are you enjoying the play?'

He looked horrified. 'Please call me Todd,' he insisted. 'Mr Randall is my *father*!' He grinned at her, then continued. 'I'm enjoying it a lot. It's just too bad that . . . well, that there aren't more people here. You must be awfully disappointed, Canon,' he added.

Canon Brydges-ffrench shook his head. 'To tell you the truth, I wasn't really expecting a huge crowd tonight. After all, it *is* the last night of the Three Choirs Festival.' He gave a self-deprecating titter. 'And we're not quite as well known as they are . . . yet. No, I expect to do much better tomorrow, when people leave Hereford. Probably a good many of them will come straight on here. With the Friends of the Cathedral flower festival in the afternoon, the Festival Evensong, and the big concert tomorrow night . . . well, things are bound to pick up.'

Lucy admired his optimism while doubting its foundation in reality. Just then the bell went to signal the end of the interval. Canon Kingsley, who had remained very quiet up till then, looked at his watch. 'That means we'd better be making a move, Lucy my dear.'

'It was nice meeting you, Lucy,' said Todd immediately, having learned her Christian name. 'I guess we'll be seeing you around this weekend.'

'Yes, I'm sure.'

As they all turned and moved back in the direction of the cathedral, Lucy looked towards the table where they'd sat with Jeremy. He was still there, all alone and looking unhappy; she was overcome with guilt at the way she'd treated him. 'I won't be a minute, Daddy,' she said impulsively, 'but I must go and apologise to Jeremy for . . . something I said.'

Chapter 6

*Such as are planted in the house of the Lord: shall flourish
in the courts of the house of our God.*

Psalm 92.12

On Saturday morning, Malbury Cathedral – or to give it its
proper title, the Cathedral and Abbey Church of St Malo and St
Thomas à Becket at Malbury – was the scene of an almost
unprecedented frenzy of activity as the Friends of the
Cathedral, in the form of various flower-arrangers, sprang into
action. Ordinarily everything would have been completed the
evening before the flower festival, but the performance in the
south transept on Friday night had precluded that, and had
necessitated a very early start on the Saturday. The flower
festival would open at noon, and all must be in readiness by
then.

Rowena Hunt, as head of the Friends, had been there first,
preparing the battle-stations. The arrangers arrived to find
their spots clearly labelled by name and provided with all that
was needful (save the flowers themselves): appropriate containers and lumps of pre-soaked Oasis.

Things were already well under way when John Kingsley
arrived to take the eight o'clock service. The service would be
held in the Lady Chapel, in the centre of the retro-choir at the
far east end of the cathedral, so the majority of the arrangers
would be unhampered by it; only Evelyn Marsden, who was
doing the Lady Chapel flowers, was affected.

Lucy had accompanied her father to the cathedral that
morning. It was a gesture that pleased and somewhat
surprised Canon Kingsley; he'd protested mildly that it wasn't
at all necessary and suggested that she have a lie-in instead,
but she had insisted that she wanted to come.

She was a bit surprised herself. Although she had, obviously,
grown up in the Church, she had reacted against her

45

upbringing in a drastic way: at eighteen she had married, and almost immediately divorced, a very worldly and unsuitable man. Thereafter, during her years of living on her own in London, her connection with the Church had been tenuous, and her attendance sporadic. But in the year that she'd known David, and especially in the five months since they'd become lovers, both her attitudes and her habits had been changing gradually. The Church was very important to David, and David was supremely important to Lucy. So she'd begun to go with him to church during their weekends together, and his appreciation for the beauty of worship – and the buildings where worship took place – had communicated itself to her. She thought about it now, as she sat in the Lady Chapel waiting for the service to begin. A year ago, she reflected, she wouldn't have come with her father. A year ago she wouldn't have recognised the gilded English altar and the other chapel furnishings as being the work of Sir John Ninian Comper, and absolutely typical of the work that great church architect and furnisher did during the 1920s. Now she did recognise it, with a small shock of pleasure. She would have to remember to tell David about it, Lucy thought.

David had really wanted to come with her this weekend. He shared Lucy's love of music, and while he agreed with her that the music which had been chosen for the Malbury Music Festival was frightfully obscure and even somewhat eccentric, he had hoped to be able to attend. They both agreed, as well, that it was past time for him to meet Lucy's father, thus making even more concrete his role in her life. But David's imminent move was overshadowing everything else at the moment: his house in Wymondham had been sold, and there was much to do in preparing to leave it. He would be putting all of the furniture into storage until the future became more definite, but the accumulated detritus of three lifetimes – David's, his mother's, and his father's – had to be dealt with somehow; there certainly wouldn't be room for much more than his clothes in Lucy's small London house. And in addition to the personal side of the move, he had much to occupy him at work, clearing away paperwork and tidying up loose ends before his final departure in just over a month. So, to the regret of both David and Lucy, she was on her own in Malbury yet again.

John Kingsley entered the chapel, the silvery green colour of his chasuble emphasising the silver of his hair. As he turned to the tiny congregation, gracefully raising his hands in greeting, he looked more than ever like a medieval saint. 'The Lord be with you,' he said, solemnly yet sweetly. The Mass had begun.

Evelyn Marsden, temporarily displaced from her flower arranging in the chapel, was at the service, along with a few stray tourists. Near Lucy was another woman whose assured manner suggested that she belonged at the cathedral. After the blessing, the dismissal and a moment of private prayer, the woman turned to Lucy. 'Hello,' she said, in a clipped, upper-class voice. 'You must be Canon Kingsley's daughter.' Lucy nodded in acknowledgement. 'I'm Olivia Ashleigh. The Bishop's secretary,' she added.

Lucy tried not to betray her surprise. 'How nice to meet you, Miss Ashleigh. I've heard Bishop George speak of you.' Indeed she had: the Bishop always talked of his secretary with something approaching awe. Lucy had had a mental picture of her as a formidable old battle-axe, middle-aged or older, with gimlet eyes and grey hair in a bun. But this was a young woman – not even thirty – and an extremely attractive one; she was statuesquely tall and her face had a rare classical beauty, with a profile that looked as though it had been carved from marble. Miss Ashleigh was nonetheless formidable: she exuded an aura of no-nonsense efficiency, and she seemed to have done everything possible to disguise her physical charms, almost as if she were deliberately trying to look unattractive. Her blond hair was cropped quite short, she wore large disfiguring spectacles with heavy dark rims, and her figure-concealing clothing would have better suited a woman twice her age. 'Are you arranging flowers today?' Lucy asked.

Behind her spectacles, Miss Ashleigh's blue eyes were intelligent. 'Not a chance,' she replied with a short laugh. 'I wish that I could. Or rather, I wish that I had the time.'

'The Music Festival's keeping you busy, then?'

'Not the Music Festival.' She laughed again, but without humour. 'It's the new Dean's installation. At the end of September. The invitations have to go out this week, you see. The whole thing's a nightmare.'

'How is that?'

Miss Ashleigh rolled her eyes expressively. 'Everyone and his grandfather are being invited. The full works. Lord

47

Lieutenant, High Sheriff, Mayor, all the County. And all the new Dean's political friends – his father-in-law is an MP, you know. The guest list looks like the membership roster of the Conservative Party. I just don't know where we're going to put everyone. This cathedral isn't that big. And then there's the garden party after . . .' She shuddered.

It was Lucy's turn to laugh. 'Sounds like quite a do. It almost makes me wish I were coming.'

'Oh, you are. Or at least you're being invited.' Miss Ashleigh paused, consulting her prodigious memory. 'You and . . . Mr Middleton-something, isn't it? At the Bishop's request.'

'Oh, well. I shall look forward to it.'

John Kingsley, divested now of his chasuble, came up beside Lucy. 'I see that you've met Miss Ashleigh, my dear. She's the one who keeps everything ticking over around here. The cathedral would come to a grinding halt without her.'

The young woman made a dismissive noise, but she smiled. 'Enough chit-chat. I must get back to my invitations. The new Dean insists that they must all be addressed by hand, of course.' She regarded her fingers ruefully, and moved away with a purposeful stride.

'Breakfast?' suggested Lucy to her father.

'Not yet, my dear. I'd like to spend a bit of time chatting with the flower arrangers. To let them know their work is appreciated, you see.'

Evelyn Marsden was already back at work, in front of the Comper statue of the Virgin and Child which stood to the side of the altar, near the Mothers' Union banner. Her arrangement of spiky blue irises and rosemary seemed to be nearly completed; she was too absorbed to take much notice of her audience. 'Lovely, Miss Marsden,' Canon Kingsley murmured. She nodded abstractedly.

The perpendicular retro-choir, at the far east end of the cathedral, was by far the most attractive part of the building, with its elaborate fan vaulting and its black and white marble floor. It contained three chapels, all re-furnished by Comper in the 1920s; to the north of the Lady Chapel was a small Reserved Sacrament chapel, and to the south was a regimental chapel. John Kingsley stopped there next, where, under the frayed and faded standards of the county regiment, an elderly colonel's widow worked on a handsome pedestal arrangement in the regimental colours. Then, through the south choir aisle, Lucy followed her father into the Quire – as Canon Brydges-ffrench had always insisted on spelling it.

The Quire as it now stood was an entirely Victorian refurnishing job, with elaborately carved wooden choir stalls. As befitted the Precentor's wife, Judith Greenwood was in the Quire, half-heartedly draping posy chains along the stalls. Dressed in a faded sundress that was too snug on the top and too baggy on the bottom, in an unbecoming shade of green, and her mouse-coloured hair clearly unwashed in recent days, she was instantly recognisable.

She looked up. 'Oh, hello.'

'This is looking very nice,' said Canon Kingsley.

'No, it's not.' She shook her head and frowned. 'I know that it's not right. But it's the best I can do, I'm afraid. I'm just not cut out to be a flower arranger. I can't get out of it, though – Rupert says that I must do my bit . . .'

Lucy studied the problem with her artist's eye. 'Perhaps if you just attached the ends like this instead . . .' she suggested tactfully, demonstrating what she meant. 'It would give it a bit more shape, I think.'

'Oh, yes.' Judith Greenwood raised her head and smiled at her saviour; her plain, sallow face was transformed to something approaching beauty by the warmth of her smile. And, Lucy realised for the first time, the woman had the most astonishingly beautiful eyes, pure deep violet in colour with velvety black pupils. But they were not happy eyes; they seemed to Lucy to be brimming with deep, hidden pain. Perhaps Jeremy was right about there being more to Judith Greenwood than was immediately evident, she thought. 'Aren't you clever? That makes all the difference, doesn't it? Thank you so much.'

The Bishop's wife, up near the high altar in the area beyond the altar rails, heard the voices and looked up from her labours. 'Well, hello there!' she hailed them. 'You're out and about early. Have you come for an advance peek?'

'I took the eight o'clock service,' Canon Kingsley explained. 'And Lucy wanted to come along.'

'Then you're even more virtuous than the rest of us,' Pat Willoughby laughed. 'It's a real pain, having to do everything this morning. It's much too nice a day to be indoors – I'd far rather be in my garden.' She had nearly finished with the first of two large pedestals, one on either side of the sanctuary, composed entirely of white flowers.

'It looks stunning,' Lucy said truthfully. 'Are the flowers from your garden?'

Pat stopped for a minute and tucked a stray wisp of grey hair back into its knot, giving her arrangement a critical look. 'That's right. The garden has been good this year, and I've been able to keep the white roses going until now. Luckily.'

'Are everyone's flowers home-grown, then?' John Kingsley wanted to know.

'Hardly,' Pat said, raising her eyebrows dryly. 'Far be it from me to judge, but ... well, everyone's taste is different, I suppose. I would suggest,' she added, 'that if you want to see something completely unique *and* home-grown, you have a look at what Claire Fairbrother is doing in the south transept.'

They took her advice. The south transept, scene of the previous evening's performance, could have been part of a completely different building, so dissimilar was it architecturally to other parts of the cathedral. After a fire in the twelfth century, it had been rebuilt in Early English style, with shafted columns and exaggerated stiff-leaf capitals. Its tall lancet south window was exquisite: the famous Becket window. Somehow, miraculously, this window had survived the depredations of the Reformation and the Civil War completely intact; all the other original glass had been destroyed, to be replaced in the nineteenth century at the time of the church's elevation to cathedral status. The mediocrity of the rest of the cathedral's glass, muddy in colour and indifferent in design – Jeremy had dismissively described it to Lucy as 'bought in by the yard' – only served to emphasise the unique beauty of the Becket window, with its rich jewel-like colours and its minutely detailed scenes from the life of St Thomas of Canterbury.

Now, beneath the Becket window, Claire Fairbrother was indeed engaged in creating something unlike any of the other arrangements the Kingsleys had seen that morning. It seemed to be made up entirely of weeds, bits of sticks, and other assorted desiccated vegetable matter, without a flower in sight. She straightened up, revealing more fully her voluminous gauze harem pants and ethnic-printed cotton top, and gestured at her handiwork proudly as they approached. 'Rather splendid, wouldn't you say?'

50

John Kingsley, ever tactful, nodded. 'A most original creation.'

'Not like all the rest.' Her voice was scornful. 'It's such a waste, growing flowers just so you can cut them! I mean, really! How can they possibly justify it? And the money that some people spend on florists' flowers – it's absolutely obscene. You could feed a whole village in Africa for a year with the money that's been wasted on flowers in this place today. Those two out in front of the screen . . .' she added cryptically, then shuddered.

'I suppose you're right,' Canon Kingsley conceded. 'But surely this flower festival will raise enough money to cover . . .'

'That's not the point,' she interrupted. 'The point is the waste. All that money for flowers, and tomorrow or the next day they'll be dead. Like it says in the Scriptures, "The grass withereth, the flower fadeth".'

'Yes . . .'

A man carrying a pail of water had approached them unnoticed. 'It looks like your grass has already done all the withering it's going to do,' he laughed. 'I don't think you'll need any of this water.'

Claire glared at him and turned back to her task, determined to ignore him.

'Oh, hello, Inspector Drewitt,' John Kingsley greeted the newcomer. 'Have you met my daughter Lucy?'

'No, I haven't had the pleasure.' He gave her a discreetly appraising look, and, liking what he saw, put down his pail of water. 'Mike Drewitt,' he said, extending his hand.

Lucy returned his smile. The man was in his late forties, she judged. His open-necked shirt revealed a powerful chest; he was stocky – almost burly – yet muscular, with a physique that was obviously maintained very carefully through regular work-outs. His somewhat grizzled dark hair was worn short, and he had a trim greying moustache. It was a physical type that had never appealed to Lucy at all, yet there was something attractive in Mike Drewitt's smile.

'Inspector Drewitt is one of the bell-ringers here at the cathedral,' her father explained. 'And a member of our local police force.'

'Why the water?' Lucy asked. 'Are you filling in as a fireman in your spare time?'

Drewitt grinned appreciatively. 'Just helping out, that's all.

51

I asked Mrs Hunt if there was anything I could do, and she said that I could make sure that everyone had enough water for their flowers. Just a humble water-boy, that's me.'

'Very noble.'

Retrieving his pail, Drewitt bowed to Lucy with a droll twinkle, and nodded at her father. 'I'll see you again,' he said.

The Victorians, in their enthusiasm, had built a solid stone screen behind the crossing, completely blocking off the Quire from the nave of the cathedral. It had been an ill-judged move, according to Mr Pevsner's 'Buildings of England: Shropshire', for though the glass in the east window was as murky and undistinguished as the rest, it was a well-proportioned perpendicular window, rich with stone tracery, and it would have let a bit more light into the nave. As it was, even on the brightest summer day, the nave of Malbury Cathedral was as dark as the ship interior which gave that part of the building its name.

The two men who were arranging the flowers in front of the stone screen, however, seemed oblivious to the chill emanating from the ancient stones in the gloom of the nave. They were both dressed in shorts of the briefest kind, shorts which cruelly exposed two pairs of hairy legs and barely covered the essentials. The younger of the men, the one with the blond hairy legs, had matching wavy blond hair on his head and a rather apologetic moustache of the same hue; his plump torso was encased in a T-shirt that did nothing to flatter his figure. His companion, a few years older, was smaller, sharp-featured, dark and wiry, and wore a shirt unbuttoned to such an extent that his multiple gold chains, nestling in his stiff dark chest-hairs, were clearly evident. Their flowers were undeniably beautiful, showy, and arranged with great cleverness, but they encompassed a whole range of colours never seen in nature.

Lucy's father introduced them to her as Victor and Bert, who ran the cathedral gift shop. 'Utterly charmed, my dear,' said Victor, the blond one.

'And how nice for your dear papa to have you here to brighten his lonely life,' Bert added. 'If only for a brief time.'

'And lovely for the rest of us to have such a celebrity in our midst, as well. You did the painting of the Becket window for the festival programme, I understand?' probed Victor. Lucy nodded in assent. 'It's absolutely stunning, my dear. Just too much. We've had sweatshirts printed with your design – a thousand of them. For the Cathedral shop, you know. I do hope that you're not going to charge us royalties or anything?' Victor laughed, a gurgling laugh like a drain. 'We're expecting to do great business this weekend.'

Lucy looked at her watch. 'What time do you open? Will you be finished here in time?'

'Oh, not to worry, dear. We have heaps of time,' Bert assured her. 'And we've laid on extra help today, to cope with the rush.'

'Have we?' Victor asked sharply.

'Yes, I'm *sure* that I told you, Vic. I've asked that Hunt girl, Kirsty her name is, to give a hand. She seems reliable.'

'Oh, well.' Victor sighed in relief. 'As long as you haven't asked that American boy.'

'What's the matter with him?' Lucy couldn't help asking.

Smirking, Victor told her. 'Not a thing. That's the problem. He's just too gorgeous for words, my dear. Far too distracting.'

'Utterly wasted on the Hunt girl, if you ask me.' Bert shook his head sadly.

Suddenly Victor grinned. 'Speaking of Rowena . . .'

'Were we?' interposed Bert.

'You mentioned her daughter. Same difference, dear. Speaking of Rowena, have you seen her this morning, Canon?'

'No, not yet. Why?'

'She's absolutely spitting nails!' Victor announced with relish.

The Canon looked stricken. 'Because I haven't been to see her?'

'No, of course not, my dear man.' Victor lowered his voice to achieve some semblance of discretion. 'It's the new Dean.'

'What has he done now?' Lucy wanted to know.

'Well!' Victor made a great show of looking around to ensure they weren't overheard, and went on in a loud, carrying whisper. 'She's just found out that he's bringing in a posh London florist to do the cathedral for his installation. At least all the flowers that matter – he's allowing the Friends to do a few things for the nave and the choir aisles. And of course they won't get a look-in at the garden party afterwards. The London lot will have that all sewn up. Our Rowena really threw a wobbly when she found out. Tried to hide it, of course, but . . .' He gurgled, interrupting himself.

'Well, it's no wonder, is it, when she's got Dorothy to deal with? The Dean can't be having Dorothy doing his flowers,' Bert put in.

'She's handled Dorothy very well today, you must admit! Put her back behind the font, where she can't do much damage. Very clever, our Rowena.'

'Who's Dorothy?' asked Lucy, enjoying the exchange.

'Dorothy Unworth,' said Victor.

'She runs the refectory,' Bert added.

'And her idea of arranging flowers . . . well, my dear!' Victor rolled his eyes expressively. 'Three red gladioli, done strictly by the book.'

'Have a look,' Bert urged. 'Behind the font. You'll see what we mean.'

'And if you think her flowers are appalling . . .' Victor went on, 'you should try her food! Her sausage rolls should be registered as lethal weapons!'

'And those nauseating Bakewell tarts with the little cherries on top . . .' shuddered Bert.

'But we're not trying to influence you, my dear,' Victor finished triumphantly. 'You must see for yourself, and make up your own mind.'

As they moved off towards the back of the cathedral, John Kingsley whispered to Lucy, 'They're really not that bad, you know.'

'Oh, I thought they were quite sweet.'

He looked baffled for a moment, then said, 'Oh, no, I didn't mean them. Not Victor and Bert.' He paused. 'I meant the sausage rolls.'

They reached the font some time later, after Canon Kingsley had duly cheered on the ladies who manned the stations around the nave pillars. These six spots had been allocated to the six largest parish churches in the diocese; the parishes' prize flower arrangers were fiercely competitive and jealous of their own skills, and each display was larger and showier than the one before it. But the Canon somehow managed to make each woman feel that her arrangement was superior to all the others.

Lurking in the dark south-west corner of the cathedral, the neo-Norman font resembled a large round bath-tub, exuberantly zigzagged and dogtoothed. With its large, heavy wooden cover, it quite effectively blocked from view the triumvirate of red gladioli. Lucy and her father peered around the bulk of the font to discover that Dorothy Unworth was even at that moment adding a judiciously chosen supporting cast to show off her three stars to better effect. She was concentrating raptly, a small frown puckering her forehead, and they hesitated to disturb her. Had she not already been informed to the contrary, Lucy might have mistaken Dorothy Unworth for the Bishop's secretary: she looked the sort of woman who would suffer no nonsense from anyone, not even a Bishop. She appeared to be in her mid- to late-fifties, and could have been described as well-upholstered rather than plump; Lucy imagined that any recalcitrant bulges of fat were marshalled into a strong corset, just as her iron-grey hair was permed into regimented waves. Her mouth was small and pursed, now, in a scowl of concentration, but it was hard to imagine that mouth ever smiling in anything but the most perfunctory way. She had sturdy legs with thick ankles, encased in heavy support stockings; her only adornment, if it merited that description, was the blue- and white-enamelled Mothers' Union badge on the collar of her polyester dress. In fact, Lucy realised with a quickly suppressed giggle, Dorothy Unworth rather resembled the font in shape, and the zig-zag pattern of her dress was not unlike that which encircled the massive round bowl.

Miss Dorothy Unworth was not, and had never been, the sort of woman to entertain foolish fancies about anyone. But for some reason, perhaps because he appreciated her sausage rolls, she had a real soft spot for Canon Kingsley. As she realised that he was standing by, she looked up from the scarlet gladioli with the baring of teeth that was her version of a smile.

'Good morning, Miss Unworth,' he said. 'You have a nice quiet corner back here, don't you?'

It was the wrong thing to say. Her semblance of a smile faded immediately, to be replaced by a thunderous look. 'That Woman!' she barked – she never gave Rowena the courtesy of a name. 'Who does she think she is? She's shunted me off into this poky corner . . .'

Alarmed, he tried to repair the damage. 'But the font is a very important spot, Miss Unworth. The place where we first receive our membership in the family of God. It's a great honour to be stationed by the font . . .'

'Hardly!' She withered him with her scorn. 'That's what *she* said. That Woman. That's what she'd like me to believe. But she can't fool me that easily. *In* the font, certainly. Or in front of the font. But *behind* the font? I ask you! Is this the way I'm repaid for a lifetime of service to this cathedral?'

'I'm sure it wasn't meant . . .'

'I'm sure it was! But *he's* seen through her!' A look of satisfaction crossed her face. 'The new Dean. Have you heard? About the flowers for the installation? A real slap in the face for That Woman!' Like many people who are hard of hearing, she spoke far more loudly than she realised.

The woman in question had just finished her own arrangements, two six-foot high towers, all in green, on either side of the west door. She was therefore near enough to have overheard Dorothy Unworth's scathing comments, had she been listening. But Rowena wasn't listening. She was thanking Inspector Michael Drewitt for his labours on behalf of the Friends of the Cathedral.

'Inspector, it's been most kind of you to give up your morning like this.'

'It's been my pleasure, ma'am.' He clicked his heels together and grinned ironically. 'And please call me Mike. All of my friends do.'

'Your wife didn't mind sparing you this morning?' She raised her finely-shaped eyebrows in inquiry. 'Mike?'

'My wife,' he said, giving the word just a slight emphasis, 'has her own life to lead. And she's used to me leading my own life. Ma'am.' His eyes lingered on her just an instant too long.

'Perhaps . . .' She hesitated fractionally. 'Perhaps you might like to come round for a cup of tea one day next week. So that I can thank you properly for your hard work. When you're off duty, that is . . .'

Mike Drewitt smiled. 'Yes, ma'am. I'd like that very much.'

Chapter 7

O how sweet are thy words unto my throat: yea, sweeter than
honey unto my mouth.

Psalm 119.103

During the late breakfast shared by Lucy and her father, a
delivery was made by the local florist shop: the choicest of the
flowers that they had remaining after the cathedral's on-
slaught, a peace offering from Jeremy to Lucy. She'd been
feeling quite guilty enough about her defensive outburst
without this added burden, and so when Jeremy turned up on
the doorstep that afternoon, inviting her to accompany him to
have a look at the flower festival, she felt that she could hardly
say no.

'Daddy, wouldn't you like to come, too?' she urged quickly.

A disappointed Jeremy managed to conceal his feelings well.
'Yes, Canon, you'd be very welcome to join us,' he said with a
smile.

'Oh, no. I think I've seen enough of the flower festival,' he
demurred.

'Then perhaps I should stay with you . .' suggested
Lucy.

'Not at all, my dear. You go along. I've got a sermon to write.'
He hesitated a moment. 'Would you mind running a little
errand for me while you're out?'

'Anything, Daddy.'

'It won't take you out of your way. If you wouldn't mind
calling in at the Cathedral Shop and picking up a box of crème
de menthe Turkish Delight . . .'

'What?' She looked at him in amazement.

'Crème de menthe Turkish Delight,' Canon Kingsley
repeated. 'For Arthur Brydges-ffrench. Just a little gift to
cheer him up. It's his weakness,' he added in explanation. 'He
can't resist the stuff.'

57

Lucy shook her head. 'If you say so. But I must say it sounds rather disgusting to me.'

It had turned out to be a blazing hot day in Malbury: the sun beat down upon the Close, and in its centre the cathedral shimmered in the heat. For once, the chill of the cathedral interior was a welcome relief if something of a shock. Lucy nearly gasped involuntarily as they entered; it was almost like plunging into a cold, dark pool of water. For a moment they paused at the end of the foreshortened nave, with its massive round Norman pillars and heavy rounded arches, and waited for their eyes to adjust to the gloom.

It soon became evident that others had preceded them in the quest for a cool spot to spend the afternoon: the cathedral was full of people. 'Well!' Jeremy said with some surprise. 'It looks like old Arthur Brydges-ffrench was right! Things are definitely picking up.'

'Yes,' a voice said from beside them. It was Rowena, looking very self-satisfied – and very lovely, in a flame-coloured sundress that complemented her black hair and showed off her perfectly tanned shoulders. Had Lucy been an envious person she would have envied that tan: hers was the sort of creamy fair skin that so often goes with her hair colour, skin that turns painfully red at the first hint of sun. On days like this one she had to be especially careful, keeping her shoulders and her arms well covered; she would never dare to wear a sundress.

Rowena had an armload of programmes. 'It's going very well,' she said. 'The weather certainly hasn't done us any harm – it seems that quite a few people have come in to get out of the heat. And there have been a lot of people who've said that they'd been to the Three Choirs Festival, so it looks like Canon Brydges-ffrench was right about catching people on their way home from Hereford.'

'I must admit that I had my doubts about that reasoning,' Jeremy said. 'But I'm glad if I was wrong.'

Proffering a programme at him, Rowena smiled. 'Were you wanting to look around?'

'You're not going to make us pay, are you?' Jeremy raised his eyebrows in mock horror.

'I'm afraid so. One pound – each – for admission, and another pound for the programme.'

'No discounts?'

'No discounts.'

'You drive a hard bargain, Mrs Hunt.' Jeremy's tone was flippant but cordial as he reached into his pocket. 'But I suppose it's all in a good cause.'

'If we pop into the Cathedral Shop now,' Jeremy suggested some time later, after a detailed perusal of the flower festival, 'we should still have time for a cup of tea in the refectory before the Festival Evensong.'

'Is the refectory all right?' asked Lucy. 'I've been warned about it. By those two blokes who run the shop. Victor and Bert.'

'Oh, you mean Victoria and Albert?' He quirked his eyebrows humorously.

Lucy laughed with real amusement. 'Don't tell me. It's perfect. Do they know you call them that?'

'I doubt it.' He grinned. 'Though I think everyone else in the Close does. Anyway, they're right about the refectory. I wouldn't recommend eating a meal there – the food's pretty grim. But it's just about acceptable for a cup of tea.'

'Well, lead on then.'

The Cathedral Shop did not seem to be overrun with business when they arrived. Bert was engaged with a tourist who appeared to be an American, judging by the quantity of cameras which were slung around his neck and which bounced against his ample paunch as he leaned eagerly over the counter. 'So you're telling me,' he said in a voice which confirmed his transatlantic origins, 'that Brother Thomas isn't the same as Thomas à Becket.'

'That's right,' Bert said patiently.

'Well, that explains it.' The man nodded in satisfaction. 'We're staying at the Monk's Head Inn, here in town, and I was sure that the manager told me that Brother Thomas got his head chopped off by Henry VIII. But I got confused last night by that play.'

'Two different Thomases,' reiterated Bert with a sage nod. 'Two different martyrdoms.'

'I'm sure glad to get that cleared up. Did you hear that, honey?' he called across the shop to his wife, who was looking at T-shirts with Victor. Without waiting for a reply, he went on,

'I'll have some postcards of that Becket window. It's pretty old, isn't it?'

'Early thirteenth century,' Bert confirmed.

The man whistled, impressed. 'Now *that's* old! Where I come from, we don't have windows that old. Or anything else, for that matter. That window must be worth a lot of money! Do they have to do anything special to take care of it?'

'Oh, it's well maintained. Isn't it, Mr Bartlett?' asked Bert, deferring to Jeremy's specialist knowledge.

'Absolutely,' Jeremy assured the American with a smile. 'After all, it's Malbury Cathedral's greatest treasure. We look after it very well. It was completely re-leaded not more than ten years ago, and all the stonework was renewed.'

Bert interposed, 'Mr Bartlett is the Cathedral Architect.'

The American looked impressed. 'Well, then, maybe you can answer a question for me about those big fat pillars. If you took those away, would the cathedral fall down?'

'Most assuredly,' Jeremy said solemnly, with only a twitch of his eyebrow to betray his amusement to Lucy.

Lucy, with sort of a vested interest in the sale of the Malbury Festival sweatshirts – although she was not profiting financially, it would give her a certain artistic satisfaction to see her painting widely displayed on various chests – was eavesdropping discreetly on Victor's conversation with the American woman. The woman, whose deeply tanned bare legs were at least more attractive than Victor's blond hairy ones, seemed dissatisfied with the choice of garments available. 'But I don't *want* a sweatshirt,' she said to Victor petulantly. 'It's too hot for a sweatshirt. I want a T-shirt.'

Victor gurgled. 'I'm afraid this weather has taken us all a bit by surprise. I mean, who would actually expect it to be *hot* in England in August?'

'And I was hoping,' the woman went on in her aggressively nasal voice, 'that you'd have some T-shirts for my grand-children. You know. One that says, "GRANDMA AND GRANDPA WENT TO THE MALBURY MUSIC FESTIVAL, AND ALL I GOT WAS THIS LOUSY T-SHIRT". With a Union Jack. You know.'

'Well, no. Nothing like that, actually.'

Frowning, the woman turned and appealed to Lucy. 'Wouldn't you think that the official Cathedral Gift Shop would have something like that? Well, wouldn't you?'

Lucy merely smiled noncommittally, and escaped to the corner of the shop where Kirsty Hunt stood behind the till. Kirsty beamed in pleased recognition. 'Hello again.'

'Hello. I heard that you were helping out today – to cope with the rush.'

'Well, it hasn't exactly been a rush,' the girl laughed, with an expressive gesture. 'More like a trickle.'

'Oh, well. Maybe before Evensong.'

'Maybe.' Kirsty shrugged. 'Were you looking for anything in particular?'

'Crème de menthe Turkish Delight,' said Lucy, grimacing. 'My father said that I could get it here.'

'For Uncle Arthur, I suppose. He absolutely adores it.' The girl ran her fingers through her dark curls. 'But I'm not sure where the boys keep it. I don't think it's out on display anywhere. Not really something there's much demand for, I shouldn't think, apart from Uncle Arthur.'

'Well, I can wait until one of them is finished. No hurry,' Lucy assured her.

The American pair concluded their respective conversations and moved over to Kirsty at the till; Lucy stood aside as the man began laboriously counting out his coins. In a moment they left the shop; Lucy caught the husband's words, whispered furtively, as they went through the door. 'Honey, you don't think those two men were . . . you know?' He flapped his wrist limply. His wife's reply was lost in the slam of the door.

Suppressing a laugh, Lucy turned to Victor, who hovered nearby, his attention now fixed on her. 'My father asked me to get a box of crème de menthe Turkish Delight,' she explained. 'Kirsty wasn't sure where you kept it.'

'For Canon Brydges-ffrench, no doubt,' said Victor, kneeling down and reaching under the counter. 'There's no point giving it shelf-space – he's the only one in Malbury who eats the stuff.'

'Why do you even stock it?' she asked.

'As a special favour for the Canon. There's nowhere else in town that he can get it.'

Bert joined them and added, 'He used to buy it at a posh confectioner's shop in the High Street. But they closed down a year or two ago, and he asked us if we could keep it in stock for him.'

'He buys that much of it, then?'

61

Victor rolled his eyes. 'My dear, have you *seen* his teeth? I mean, really!'

'Arthur's not so bad,' protested Bert.

'He's an absolute poppet, darling,' Victor countered. 'Dear old Arthur. But let's be honest, my dear – he's not exactly the type to set one's heart a-flutter, is he?'

Bert's reply was forestalled by another customer, whose presence was announced by a thick cloud of cheap scent mingled with cigarette smoke. 'I need a birthday card,' said the woman; her voice, Cockney overlaid with broad Shropshire, was additionally coarsened by years of heavy smoking. 'For me old mum,' she added. 'Not that she'd appreciate being called old, mind.'

Bert looked with distaste at the cigarette. 'No smoking in the shop, if you don't mind.'

'Sorry, luv.' The woman grinned cheerfully, winking at Jeremy, then dropped the cigarette on the floor, and ground it out with the toe of her spike-heeled shoe.

The woman's dress, which was fractionally too short and too tight for her ripe figure, would have been better suited to a night at a disco than an afternoon in the Cathedral Close. It would also have been more suitable for a woman half her age. She was in her forties, though she might have been older; constant smoking had etched her face with a network of premature wrinkles, especially around her mouth. Her attempts to disguise the aging lines with make-up were largely unsuccessful, though her make-up was heavy and as overdone as her dress: she wore eyeshadow as blue, and as unnatural, as the tinted carnations in Victor and Bert's cathedral flower arrangement, and a thick application of eyeliner which ended well beyond the corners of her eyes. Her hair was platinum-coloured, and brittle from repeated bleaching and teasing.

She moved to the rack of greeting cards and began flicking through them with a chipped mauve fingernail. 'I've been over to the cathedral to see them flowers,' she said conversationally. 'Can't really see what all the fuss is about, myself.' Her remarks were addressed exclusively to Jeremy, who, as the only eligible man present, was the only one worthy of her notice. 'And that stuck-up bitch Mrs Hunt lording it over everyone – she made me pay a pound to get in! Can you beat that? After all my husband's done for that bloomin' cathedral! She even wanted money for the programme – I told her where she could put her programme!' She paused in her flicking and smiled in satisfaction at the recollection. 'She didn't know what to say! Mrs Bloody Hunt – I don't know who she thinks she is. She doesn't half fancy herself, that one.' She plucked a card, festooned with garish flowers and a cute striped kitten, from the rack. 'Here. This'll do. How much?'

'One pound,' said Victor.

'A bit dear,' she frowned. 'I could do better on the market, you know. But I guess me mum is worth it. And it's only once a year.' She fished in her handbag for the money, then slapped the pound coin on the counter.

'Thank you, Mrs Drewitt,' Victor said. 'See you again soon.'

'With prices like those, don't expect my custom very often,' she stated grandly, smiling at Jeremy over her shoulder and reaching for her cigarettes as she made her exit.

'Mrs Drewitt?' Lucy asked incredulously. 'She's not married to . . .'

'Inspector Michael Drewitt,' Bert confirmed.

'Dead common, my dear,' Victor pronounced in a melodramatic whisper.

'Tarty,' added Bert with a moue of distaste.

'And *he's* so dishy. As policemen go, that is. If you like the strong, silent type.' Victor gurgled. 'Which I do, don't I, Bert dear?' He sighed. 'Such a waste . . .'

The Festival Evensong was to begin at five, so there was still plenty of time for tea when Lucy and Jeremy got away from the Cathedral Shop shortly after four; the refectory was located just to the east of the shop, a minute's walk away. Familiar with the routine, Jeremy took a tray and led Lucy to the serving counter where the available offerings were arrayed.

Behind the counter, Dorothy Unworth presided over the Bakewell tarts with the same fierce intensity that she lavished on her gladioli. 'Would you like one?' she demanded, wielding a pair of plastic serving tongs over the sickly white tarts with their obscenely red candied cherries.

Lucy shook her head. 'It's not good for my figure,' she said with an attempt at tact. 'I'll just have tea, thanks.' The stout woman narrowed her eyes in a glare, and Lucy realised that she'd said the wrong thing.

'I'll have two, please,' Jeremy said quickly, with grave courtesy. Miss Unworth rewarded him with a grudging smile.

Lucy looked around the room. 'Where do we sit?'

'There's an empty table over in that corner.' On their way to the empty table, however, they passed Judith Greenwood, sitting alone; she caught Lucy's eye with a fleeting smile, then, embarrassed, looked down at her tray.

'Oh, hello.' Lucy stopped, glad for an excuse not to be alone with Jeremy. 'Mind if we join you, Judith?'

'Please do.' Judith smiled again, shyly. They had a brief glimpse of her violet eyes as they settled down across from her, but soon there was an awkward silence, and it was clear that her attention was elsewhere.

'Dorothy didn't intimidate you into buying one of her Bakewell tarts, then?' Jeremy, trying to make the best of what was obviously not an ideal situation from his point of view, addressed the Precentor's wife with a wry chuckle and a characteristic lift of one eyebrow.

'What? Oh, no.' Judith turned her head to look at him. 'Rock cakes. Aptly named, I'm afraid.'

Lucy laughed as Judith indicated the pebble-like crumbs on her plate. 'I can see that.' Another silence followed, longer this time; curiously, Lucy followed the other woman's gaze to a table on the other side of the room. It was in fact several tables pushed together, with Rupert Greenwood at one end and the small, taciturn organist Ivor Jones at the other, drinking tea. In between were a number of young boys in red cassocks, voraciously and single-mindedly devouring plates of sandwiches, sausage rolls, biscuits, and even Bakewell tarts. In their concentration the boys were remarkably quiet; Lucy hadn't even noticed them until now. 'The choir?' she asked into the silence.

Once again Judith's head turned back. 'Yes. Having a break from their rehearsal before Evensong.'

'Your husband seems to have them under control.'

'Oh, yes. Rupert manages his boys very well.' There was an unmistakable note of bitterness in her voice, but she forced a smile to cover it. 'His boys,' she repeated, almost to herself.

'Tea, Jeremy?' Lucy suggested brightly, pouring the almost viscous dark liquid from the small red plastic pot. Jeremy launched into some inconsequential chatter about the music festival, capturing Judith's attention at last, if only superficially. But as the choir finished their hurried snack and got up to leave, giggling and knocking their chairs about, her eyes followed them hungrily. Renewing his efforts, Jeremy began a wickedly accurate impersonation of Victoria and Albert, complete with hand gestures; Judith laughed with real amusement and Lucy, also laughing, admired not only his skill at mimicry but also his ability to distract.

A moment later, though, Judith appeared to have sunk back into contemplation. This time the object of her covert scrutiny was at the next table: a thin young woman with a pinched face and limp fair hair who was trying to set down her tray and at the same time control a toddling baby. The baby was in a harness and the woman held the reins, but the child was resisting all efforts to be put into a high chair and was pulling determinedly in the other direction, towards their table. 'Oh, bugger,' the woman swore softly as the red plastic pot tipped over on the tray; she dropped the reins and the baby toddled closer to them.

Judith's face lit up as though by a candle. 'Hello, there,' she said softly to the baby, who regarded her solemnly. It was an odd, gnomic-looking child, Lucy thought, with a huge round head way out of proportion to its body, small pinched features and no hair at all. It was dressed in an androgynous sunsuit, and Lucy assumed that it was a boy.

Her assumption was proved wrong. 'Oh, Caroline, look what you've done!' the child's mother fretted, mopping at the spilled tea with a serviette. She reached over and recaptured the trailing reins. 'I'm so sorry,' she apologised to Judith. 'She just wanted to come and see you, Mrs Greenwood. I hope you don't mind.'

'No, of course not.' Judith didn't take her eyes off the baby, and her face had an expression Lucy had not seen before, an expression of intent rapture.

It was clear that no introductions would be forthcoming from that quarter, so it was up to Jeremy to introduce Lucy to the baby's mother. Liz Crabtree, it transpired, was, along with her husband Barry, one of the cathedral bell-ringers.

'We're ringing for Evensong tonight,' she explained. 'With the festival and all, it's meant to be something special. I've come on ahead with Caroline, to get myself some tea.' She looked ruefully at the wreckage on her tray. 'Barry and his mate Neil said they'd rather have a pint. So I'm meeting them up the tower in a bit.'

'Here,' said Jeremy quickly. 'Have one of my Bakewell tarts. Have them both. And I'll go and get you some more tea.'

'Are you sure?' She smiled with gratitude as he made for the counter. 'Ta very much.'

Judith entered the conversation for the first time. 'You're not taking Caroline up in the tower with you, are you?'

'Well, I was going to,' Liz replied defensively. 'I know it's not very safe, but there's no one to leave her with, and she *does* have her reins. I attach them to the ladder, and then she can't get underfoot when we're ringing.'

'Oh, please!' said Judith. 'Please let me watch her.' Her face shone in its intensity. 'I promise that I'll take good care of her. Please!'

Lucy looked on in fascination, and made her mind up to ask her father what he might be able to tell her about the background of this troubled woman.

Chapter 8

*For they intended mischief against thee: and imagined such
a device as they are not able to perform.*

Psalm 21.11

It was early the next week when an agitated Arthur Brydges-
ffrench found Rupert Greenwood alone in the Quire, setting
out his music for Evensong.

'I must have a word with you,' the Subdean said tensely,
looking around to make sure that they were alone.

'Yes?' Canon Greenwood paused.

'It's about the music festival.'

'Can it wait? Evensong . . .'

'It's important,' Canon Brydges-ffrench insisted, moistening
his lips with a nervous tongue. 'Most important.'

'All right then.' Rupert Greenwood sat down in his elaborately carved stall, labelled 'Precentor' in gothic lettering.

The Subdean found it difficult to begin. 'About the music
festival,' he repeated.

'Yes. The music festival.'

Canon Brydges-ffrench licked his lips again. 'You know – you
must know – that the festival lost rather a lot of money.' Rupert
Greenwood said nothing, but nodded in encouragement to
continue, and after a moment he went on defensively. 'I don't
think that anyone can blame *me*. I did my best. Not *my* fault
that people didn't come on here after the Three Choirs Festival.
Not *my* fault about the weather. And the new man' – here he
sighed bitterly – 'did his best to sabotage all the sponsorship.
But . . . well, Rupert, it's dashed awkward. Don't you see?'

'Yes, of course. But I don't quite see what you expect me to do
about it, Arthur.' The Precentor picked up a piece of music and
began studying it, distancing himself from his colleague's
discomfort.

'Rupert!' The old man's voice was heavy with sorrow, and it

compelled Canon Greenwood to look up in spite of himself. 'I expect you to support me, Rupert. *You* helped in planning it all. *You* chose the music. You assured me that it would be a success and a triumph, and that it would put Malbury on the map. But no one came, Rupert! I should think that now . . .'

'Well, yes.' The Precentor drummed his fingers on his desk rhythmically and thoughtfully. 'What about the Friends?' he asked at last. 'They made a pile of money at their flower festival on Saturday. Perhaps Rowena . . .'

'Don't I know it!' frowned Canon Brydges-ffrench. 'Thousands! And don't think I haven't thought about that.' He paused and lowered his voice. 'But I've already spoken to Rowena. And she's made it very clear that she's not parting with one penny of the money. *Her* money, she calls it,' he added bitterly. 'As if she earned it all herself. And as if the Friends would have had *any* of it if it hadn't been for the music festival. *My* music festival. *Our* music festival,' he amended, looking slyly at Rupert Greenwood.

'But I rather thought that Rowena was being especially nice to us these days,' Canon Greenwood said with rare perceptiveness. 'To all of the Chapter, that is. I had rather formed the idea that she was up to something and wanted us all on her side.'

'Oh, yes,' confirmed the Subdean with a sour smile. 'That's exactly the way of it. And she laid her cards on the table with me. I'll give the woman that – at least she's honest. She *did* say that she'd be willing to help cover our . . . um . . . shortfall. But her terms were . . . unacceptable.'

At last Rupert Greenwood was intrigued. 'Just exactly what did she want?'

Arthur Brydges-ffrench leaned over from his considerable height and whispered, 'Our support. It was blackmail, to put not too fine a point on it.'

'Blackmail? Support for what?'

'She wants . . .' he paused impressively. 'She wants to run the refectory and the Cathedral Shop. She wants Dorothy Unworth out. She wants Victor and Bert out. She thinks that the Friends could do a much more professional job in running them. Add some much-needed class to a run-down cathedral, she said! Run down! I ask you!' he finished indignantly on a rising note.

Rupert Greenwood looked thoughtful. 'And what did you tell her?'

'I told her that it was out of the question, of course. Victor and Bert are my friends. Dorothy Unworth has served this cathedral faithfully for many years. It just wouldn't be ... proper! I told her that her price was too high, and she should be ashamed of herself for even suggesting such a thing.'

'And what did she say?'

'She said,' replied Canon Brydges-ffrench, looking pained, 'that she always gets what she wants. In the long run. She implied that ... that the new man might be much more favourably disposed to her plans than I.' He took out a handkerchief and mopped at his shining dome of a forehead. 'And the worst thing is, Rupert, she may well be right!'

The Precentor gave him a warning look as the volume of his voice increased and someone else entered the Quire from the south aisle.

It was Jeremy Bartlett, appearing from behind a pillar like the serpent coming from behind the forbidden tree in the Garden of Eden. He hesitated for a moment, then approached the two men with a wide smile. 'Forgive me, gentlemen. I was in the south transept just now, and I couldn't help overhearing some of your conversation.'

Appalled, Arthur Brydges-ffrench clapped a hand over his mouth. 'Oh!'

'But don't worry,' Jeremy quickly added. 'I'm in total sympathy with your problem. I'm sure that I can help you ...' He paused. 'And I believe that you might find *my* terms ... acceptable.'

In a moment he outlined an ingenious solution to their financial dilemma; all he required from them in return was their promise to support his plans to develop the cloister, and the Subdean's agreement that a major fabric restoration appeal would be launched within the year. Arthur Brydges-ffrench and Rupert Greenwood agreed with relief and alacrity. The cloister development was not the sort of thing that Canon Brydges-ffrench would, in the ordinary course of things, have approved of, but it seemed to him that he had little choice, and it was certainly preferable to Rowena Hunt's blackmail. At any rate, he told himself, anything might happen to prevent it.

For his part, Jeremy was delighted with the bargain he'd made. He smiled to himself as he left the Quire – not only the cloister, but a major restoration appeal as well! A bonus, skilfully negotiated. And he thought to himself with great satisfaction of what he'd overheard just before he made himself known to the two conspirators: he now knew what Rowena Hunt wanted. That knowledge might prove to be extremely useful one day in the near future.

Chapter 9

*Thou hast given him his heart's desire: and hast not denied
  him the request of his lips.*

                                        Psalm 21.2

David Middleton-Brown, looking for a hanger for his suit
jacket, peered into Lucy's rather full wardrobe. He was a man
in his early forties, pleasant looking and reasonably trim if not
particularly handsome, with hazel eyes that crinkled attractively at the corners when he smiled, as he was doing now. 'Are
you sure there's going to be room in here for my clothes?' he
asked wryly. 'Or are we going to have to call the whole thing
off?'

It was still technically the afternoon, and Lucy and David
had been home for only a few minutes, but she was already in
bed waiting for him. Now she sighed with exaggerated
impatience. 'Isn't it a bit late for that? And it's a fairly weak
excuse – I thought you *wanted* to move in with me,' she
laughed. 'And whatever's happened to the old passionate
David? You never used to hang up your clothes before we went
to bed. It hasn't even been six months – don't tell me you're
bored with me already!'

'Bored?' The jacket fell to the floor, forgotten, as he made
an exuberant dive for the bed. 'We'll see about that, woman.'

Later, while Lucy drowsed, contented, in his arms, David
lay awake thinking. There was much to think about, and
it was after all only early evening, though the day had
been an eventful one. It had been only that morning, a
morning late in September, that he had overseen putting
the last of his furniture into storage, loaded up his car,
signed the final papers, and turned over the keys of his house
– the house where he'd lived most of his life – to its new
owner.

71

Moving to London, to a new, interesting and prestigious job, and to be with the woman he loved – even if she wouldn't marry him – was certainly what David wanted for himself at this time in his life. But it was not without regret that he had left Wymondham, a place that encompassed so much of his personal history. Even though many of the memories were unhappy ones – his mother had been a tyrant, demanding and difficult to live with, and his personal life had been characterised by much loneliness – they were *his* memories, and his life. And he had loved his church, Wymondham Abbey, the place that had inspired his interest in the Church in all its many facets.

He had taken little with him as he left Wymondham; his law books and his files had been boxed and shipped to his new firm to await his arrival there in about a fortnight's time. And the move to Lucy's tiny mews house in South Kensington was only meant to be a temporary one: as soon as a complicated estate was settled, he would inherit, and be able to take possession of, a large Georgian mansion near Kensington Gardens. So that morning he had loaded into the boot of his car only his clothes and personal things, a few boxes of books that he couldn't bear to be without, and a small number of favourite compact discs – ones that were not duplicated in Lucy's collection.

Lucy had had to make a trip to Bond Street earlier in the day, to talk to a gallery owner who was interested in exhibiting a few of her paintings, so they'd arranged to meet for tea at Fortnum's as he arrived from Norfolk. Tea had been a festive event, celebrating his move to London. It was also one reason why he was not particularly hungry now: they'd eaten sandwiches and scones and cream cakes, and drunk pots of tea, before coming back here. David remembered, now, an odd incident during their tea. She'd been telling him about her experience at the gallery, when she'd stopped in mid-sentence. 'Oh!' she'd said softly. 'Don't turn around, David. There are some people that I'm *sure* I recognise, sitting in that corner behind you. I don't think they've seen us.'

'Who are they?' he'd asked, reasonably. 'I'm not ashamed of being seen with you . . .'

'No, but I don't think they'd want us to see *them*.' She'd shaken her head and smiled. 'I'll tell you all about it later,' she'd promised.

He thought about it now; he'd managed to catch a glimpse of them as he and Lucy had left: a strikingly attractive raven-haired woman and a powerfully built man with a moustache, neither of them young. Who were they, and why didn't they want to be seen? And why would they not expect to be seen, having tea at a public place like Fortnum's?

'Lucy?' he murmured tentatively.

'Mm?'

'Are you awake?'

She opened one eye and squinted at him, smiling. 'More or less.'

'Who were those people in Fortnum's?'

'Oh, them.' She laughed, stretched, and turned to rummage on the floor for her dressing gown. 'The woman was Rowena Hunt, the head of the Friends of Malbury Cathedral. And the man . . .' Breaking off, she turned back to him. 'I'm absolutely starving, David darling. Let's get up and make something to eat – some eggs or something. I'll tell you about them in the kitchen.'

'I'm not really that hungry,' he protested, reaching for her. 'Why don't we just stay here? We might as well – it's night now.'

She managed to evade him. 'Oh, David! We can't spend *all* our time in bed!'

'I don't see why we can't try,' he grinned, unrepentant.

They continued the conversation as they prepared their makeshift supper. 'Who was the man?' David asked. 'In Fortnum's?'

'His back was turned to us, so I couldn't really see him that well, but I'm almost positive that it was Inspector Michael Drewitt of the Malbury police. Rowena Hunt I'm sure about – she was facing us, and I'd know her anywhere.'

'But why wouldn't they want to be seen? After all, Fortnum's is a rather public place.'

Lucy looked thoughtful. 'Perhaps there's nothing in it after all. But he's a married man – even if his wife is rather frightful.' She hesitated. 'And he's not really Rowena's *class*, if you'll forgive the categorisation. Not someone she'd spend time with, in the normal course of things. If you knew Rowena, you'd understand what I mean. She's an extremely proper lady.'

'So you think . . .'

'I'm not sure what I think,' she said quickly. 'It just seems odd, that's all. And as for Fortnum's being a public place, it's not so public if you live in Malbury. They could reasonably expect to have tea there without being seen by anyone they know. It was just a coincidence that we were there.'

'They didn't see you, did they?'

'I'm sure they didn't.' Lucy smiled. 'The way it looked to me, they only had eyes for each other. But I could be wrong . . . Anyway,' she added, 'next weekend you'll have a chance to meet them. Then perhaps you can see what you think.'

For a moment he looked blank, then comprehension dawned. 'That's right – the big do for the new Dean is coming up, isn't it? With the move and everything I'd completely forgotten that we were going to Malbury next weekend.'

'You *do* want to go, don't you?' she asked.

'Of course I want to go. I want to meet your father.' David's smile was a bit self-conscious. 'I think it's past time for the two main men in your life to meet, don't you? And I want to meet all these interesting people you've been talking about for the past few months.'

'It's supposed to be quite an affair, from what I hear. Have you taken a proper look at the invitation? It's in the sitting room, on the mantelpiece.'

While Lucy laid the table, David wandered into the sitting room and returned with the invitation. 'Good Lord,' he said. 'This must have cost a bomb – look how thick the card is.'

'From a posh Bond Street firm, I was told. One of the many complaints against the new Dean.'

'His extravagance?'

'That, and his insistence on using London firms for everything – for the catering, the flowers, and the printing. He's offended all the local Malbury firms, and seemingly most of the Chapter as well.'

'This sounds intriguing.' Still fingering the invitation, David sat down to eat. 'The man's not even installed yet, and he's already made enemies – it doesn't sound as though he can expect the customary honeymoon period, does it?'

'No, not really. Do you know anything about him?' Lucy asked.

David looked at the invitation again. 'Stuart Latimer. I've heard of him, of course. He's made a bit of a name for himself in the London diocese. But I don't think he's known as a scholar, particularly, or for his spirituality either. More as just a man on his way up, if you know what I mean. His father-in-law's an MP,' he added cynically. 'It was obviously a political appointment. Father-in-law calling in a few IOUs, you know.' He reached for the pepper mill. 'Now tell me about Malbury – what the cathedral is like, and the people. You haven't really adequately prepared me for this weekend.'

Lucy considered, twisting a lock of hair; she knew that he was talking about the actual cathedral building, but she deliberately misunderstood him. 'The Cathedral Close is like . . . well, it's like it has an existence all its own. It's a self-enclosed community. Claustrophobic, I find it – like living in a goldfish bowl. Everyone seems to know each other's business. It's interesting as an outsider but I don't think I could bear to live there.'

'Start from the beginning,' he encouraged her. 'The Chapter – tell me about them.'

'Well, there's my father, of course.' She smiled. 'But I'm not exactly an unbiased source when it comes to him, so I'll leave you to make up your own mind when you've met him. And then there's Arthur Brydges-ffrench, the Subdean and Treasurer. Malbury Cathedral has been his whole life – he started out there as a chorister back in the thirties. He'd convinced himself that he was going to be appointed Dean, and was absolutely shattered when it didn't happen that way. And he's a very eccentric man.' She went on to describe the Canon's appearance and habits, then continued in the same vein with the Precentor, the Canon Missioner, and various other inhabitants of the Close.

They had finished eating and were in the midst of washing up, Lucy continuing her discourse with questions and promptings from David, when the phone rang.

'Can you get it, darling?' Lucy requested. 'I'm up to my elbows.'

His mobile mouth twisted in a self-deprecating grimace. 'You know how I hate to answer the phone – and anyway, it's not even *my* phone.'

'You're living here too, now,' she pointed out. 'It could even be for you.'

'Not very likely.' But he went into the hall to answer it; he picked up the receiver and stated the number.

There was a fractional hesitation. 'Oh, hello,' said a pleasant male voice. 'You must be David.'

'Yes . . .'

'Is Lucy available?'

'I'm afraid it's not very convenient for her to come to the phone right now. Could I take a message? Perhaps have her ring you back later?'

'Just tell her that Jeremy rang. It's not important – I just wanted to have a chat. Tell her that I'll ring back in a day or two. Before the weekend, anyway.'

'Yes, I'll tell her.'

A minute later, Lucy turned to see him come back with the beginning of a puzzled scowl. 'Double glazing salesman?'

'No.' He picked up his tea towel. 'But who,' he asked, 'is Jeremy? And how does he know who I am?'

Chapter 10

*Who shall ascend into the hill of the Lord: or who shall rise
up in his holy place?*

Psalm 24.3

'Daddy,' said Lucy brightly, with a touch of nervousness, 'this
is David. David Middleton-Brown.'

John Kingsley took the younger man's proffered hand and
smiled, liking what he saw. Solid, he thought approvingly.
Solid and dependable; nothing flashy. Just what Lucy needs.
'How very nice to meet you, David. Welcome to Malbury.'

'Thank you, Canon. I've been looking forward to this meeting
for a long time.'

'Would you like a cup of tea?' the Canon offered. 'I've just put
the kettle on. You must be tired after your long drive.'

'Oh, yes please, Daddy. Shall I make it?' Lucy suggested.

'No thank you, my dear,' he assured her. 'I have everything
ready. Perhaps you'd like to show David upstairs while I bring
the tea through to the sitting room. I've had the daily make up
the room next to yours for him – I hope that's all right.'

'Yes, of course,' she said quickly, not daring to look at
David.

David followed her up the stairs, stunned into silence.
'Separate rooms?' he said at last, outside the door that she indicated with a sheepish wave. 'Didn't you tell your father . . . ?'

'No, of course not,' she whispered, following him into the
room. 'He wouldn't understand.'

'Wouldn't understand? But surely . . .'

Lucy shook her head. 'My father is a very naïve man in many
ways. It would never occur to him, I'm sure, that two people
who weren't married would want to sleep together.'

'All the more reason why you should marry me,' David
declared with self-conscious melodrama, clapping his hand to
his heart. 'I quite agree with him that it's high time you made

77

an honest man of me. This living in sin is all very well as far as it goes, but . . .'

She rolled her eyes. 'Please, let's not get into that right now. And besides,' she added, smiling, 'you don't know my father very well. I don't think he would even understand why two people who *were* married would want to sleep together!'

'But, Lucy! He has four children! Clearly somewhere along the line . . .'

'A source of constant amazement to me,' she laughed. 'And no doubt to him as well. Come on, David darling. Let's go downstairs and have some tea. It's only for one weekend,' she added conciliatorily, giving him a brief but reassuring kiss and taking his hand; he returned her smile at last.

'The flowers are incredible, aren't they?' Lucy whispered to David as they took their reserved seats in the Quire of the cathedral a short while before the Service of Installation was to begin.

'A London florist, didn't you say?'

'I don't suppose flowers like these have ever been seen before in Malbury,' she nodded. 'White and lime green – they must have cost the earth.'

'The bills haven't come in yet, but I suspect you're right,' was the wry confirmation of Olivia Ashleigh, seated next to David. Although she was dressed suitably for the occasion, her dress was severely tailored and with her heavy black-rimmed spectacles she still managed to look twenty years older than her age.

Lucy introduced David to the Bishop's secretary. 'Miss Ashleigh has been landed with making most of the arrangements, from what I hear,' she explained to him. 'You must be glad that the great day has finally arrived, Miss Ashleigh?'

'Please, call me Olivia,' the serious young woman insisted. 'And yes, I'm delighted that we've finally got this far. But I'm afraid it's not over yet.' She looked around with an apprehensive smile. 'The potential for disaster today is almost unlimited.'

'What do you mean?' David asked, intrigued. 'It all looks very well organised, and well under control.'

'Oh, nothing *technical* will go wrong – it's all been planned like clockwork, and rehearsed to death. But ruffled feathers, hurt feelings, injured pride, trampled dignity – call it what you will. *That* is going to be the problem today.' Olivia lowered her voice. 'See all those people on the other side of the chancel? In the best seats in the house, so to speak? They're all the new Dean's political contacts. Or more precisely, his father-in-law's political contacts. Fellow MPs, some of them, even a couple of Cabinet ministers, and the bigwigs of the local Tory party. Plus the County, of course. The empty seats are for the Lord Lieutenant, the High Sheriff and the Mayor's party.'

'What's wrong with that?' Lucy wanted to know. 'Isn't that customary?'

'Certainly not on that scale. And this side is reserved for the cathedral people and the Chapter families – the Bishop insisted on that, of course – so everyone else has to squeeze into the nave. That includes the whole of the local Conservative party, as well as the Reverend Mr Latimer's London parishioners, friends, relations, and well-wishers. Which rather leaves the rest of the diocese out in the cold. To be more specific, shoe-horned into the transepts, where the visibility is absolutely nil. Or in some cases left out entirely. Do you see that empty seat?' she whispered, gesturing. In the front row on the cathedral side, next to Judith Greenwood and Claire Fairbrother, was a prominently vacant stall. 'The Bishop's wife's reserved seat.'

'But where *is* Pat?' asked Lucy, looking around. 'Surely she wouldn't miss this . . .'

'Somewhere in the south transept, with the diocesan clergy wives. She was absolutely livid that they were being stuck back there where they couldn't see, and said in no uncertain terms that she wasn't going to accept preferential treatment when her clergy wives were being treated like that.' Olivia smiled ruefully. 'It's put me in a very awkward position, I can tell you. The Bishop is my boss, but as far as this whole affair goes, I've had to take my orders from the new Dean. It's his show, and he knows exactly what he wants. He wouldn't listen to a word I – or Bishop George – said. Or anyone else, for that matter.'

'Who is that?' inquired Lucy in a whisper as an elegant woman and a distinguished-looking older man ostentatiously took their seats in the front row of the opposite side.

'That's Mrs Latimer and her father. Things must be about ready to get under way.' Olivia consulted her watch. 'Yes, just on time.'

Conversation was curtailed as the congregation stood and

the official parties began to process in; Lucy took the opportunity to observe Mrs Latimer surreptitiously. It was difficult to determine the woman's age: hers was a highly polished and well-preserved elegance, speaking unmistakably of wealth and privilege. She was very fair, with blond hair skimming her shoulders in a page-boy, timelessly fashionable. Her lids were lowered demurely over pale blue eyes; her nose was long and patrician, and her lips thin and pale pink. Gloved hands were clasped in the front of her Tory blue suit, and on her lapel sparkled a diamond bow brooch. Her father, beside her, was sleek and prosperous-looking, with wiry grey hair combed straight back from a fleshy pink face, and diagonal eyebrows angling sharply above slightly bulbous eyes.

After the Mayor, the High Sheriff and the Lord Lieutenant had taken their seats, the clergy procession moved into the chancel. Scores of diocesan clergy were followed by the Cathedral Chapter; Lucy caught her father's eye and smiled. The Precentor's golden-haired charms aside, John Kingsley was the most distinguished-looking cleric in the procession, his daughter decided, with his graceful carriage and his silver hair. He was wearing one of the cathedral's original Victorian copes, threadbare but beautiful. The Bishop, portly and smiling under his mitre, was no match for him, in spite of the impressive beard.

And then at last came the Reverend Stuart Latimer, Dean-elect, to the sound of bells and a trumpet fanfare. Lucy wasn't sure quite what she'd expected, but she would never have pictured Stuart Latimer as he now appeared before the assembled company. In contrast to Arthur Brydges-ffrench's towering height, he was positively insignificant, small of stature and slightly built. He was wearing a new cope, commissioned by him especially for the occasion; it was heavily appliquéd and embroidered in a contemporary design, but its bulk was not sufficient to disguise his smallness. And he was young, much younger than Lucy had anticipated – scarcely forty, by the look of him. It was with complete self-assurance, however, that he moved into the chancel of Malbury Cathedral, to lay claim to his new kingdom.

A closer look at Stuart Latimer, in the receiving line at the garden party, proved even more unsettling. As John Kingsley formally introduced his daughter to the new Dean, the words popped unbidden into her head, 'Esau was a hairy man.' Hairy he was: thick dark hair grew down low on his brow, and his jaw was already covered in shadow by mid-afternoon. The backs of his hands and even his fingers were densely matted with dark hairs. But if his appearance was Esau-like, his manner, in contrast, was all Jacob: oily and smooth, concealing a deep self-serving cunning. It was instantly clear to Lucy that he was a man who would get what he wanted, in one way or another. All of the things that she'd heard about him suddenly coalesced into a picture that was consistent, and deeply worrying.

'And this is my wife Anne, Miss Kingsley, Mr Middleton-Brown,' he was saying. Anne Latimer towered over her husband by nearly a head; she acknowledged Lucy and David with a cool, reserved smile.

The garden party was being held in the spacious gardens of the Deanery. Although neglected shamefully during the late Dean's tenure and in the interregnum, the gardens were in reasonable shape after several weeks of intensive attention from a – needless to say – London landscape gardening firm. A large blue- and white-striped marquee had been erected, for although the weather had been warm for late September, it was an unreliable time of year for which to plan outdoor entertaining. The marquee added an additional note of festivity to what was undoubtedly the social event of the year in Malbury. Clearly, no expense had been or was being spared. As many flowers bloomed inside the marquee as outside, and artifice outstripped nature in the elaborateness of the arrangements. The food, at whatever cost, was superb, with platters of smoked salmon and all manner of dainty things to nibble, and the wine was far removed from mere plonk. A crew of men circulated with video cameras, recording the event for posterity.

After the guests passed through the receiving line, though, they drifted into two distinct groups: the London people and the Tory faithful kept to themselves, tacitly refusing to mingle with the cathedral and diocesan crowd. So on one side of the marquee there was a distinct preponderance of cassocks and dog-collars, and on the other expensive silk dresses and Savile Row suits.

David, after his briefing by Lucy, was finding it all fascinating. In the cathedral he had surreptitiously studied his fellow guests in the south Quire, trying to put faces to names.

Rowena Hunt he had recognised instantly from his brief glimpse of her at Fortnum's, but the man with her was not the same one – this one was taller, more slenderly built, and bearded.

He'd just taken a glass of wine, and was about to ask Lucy who the bearded man was, when the man caught Lucy's eye and came up to them, Rowena following behind. Rowena, who had been looking distinctly like the cat who'd found the cream, frowned as the man kissed Lucy's cheek. 'Lucy, my dear, how nice to see you again,' the man greeted her with easy familiarity. 'Isn't Lucy looking stunning today, Rowena?' he added, grinning at Rowena's discomfiture. 'And this must be the famous David.'

'Yes. David, this is Jeremy Bartlett, the Cathedral Architect,' she put in quickly, taking a step away from Jeremy. 'Rowena, this is David Middleton-Brown, a friend of mine from London.'

Rowena appraised David swiftly and expertly, with one vertical flick of her eyes. From the way he looked at Lucy, she apprehended instantly the way things were between them and, with an inward sigh of relief, mentally crossed Lucy off her list of rivals for Jeremy's affection, at least provisionally.

'How did you like the service, then?' Jeremy addressed David.

'Oh, it was . . . most interesting.' He remained guarded; in his professional life, David frequently had to make snap judgements about people – instant assessments that more often than not turned out to be accurate – and there was something about Jeremy Bartlett that didn't quite ring true. 'It appears that the new Dean has made quite an impact already.'

Jeremy raised an amused eyebrow. 'Yes, you might say that. Ruffled quite a few feathers, even. Isn't that right, Rowena?' He looked at her expectantly; everyone in Malbury knew that Rowena considered the London florists a personal insult after the triumph of the flower festival.

But Rowena refused to be drawn. Her smile was bland and her voice as smooth as cream. 'I don't know what you mean. Mr Latimer seems to have all of the qualities necessary to make a great success of his new position.'

Jeremy's eyebrow inched still higher. 'Well, yes, I suppose you have to say that. No doubt the Friends will be working very closely with him – at least if you get what you want,' he stated provocatively, but though Rowena shot him a quick look her gracious smile never faltered. He seemed about to make a further comment, but changed his mind and turned towards Lucy. 'I thought that your father looked splendid in the old cope,' he said.

'Yes, didn't he?' she smiled.

David was not inclined to join in Lucy's conversation with Jeremy, so he turned to Rowena. 'Lucy tells me that you run the Friends of the Cathedral, Mrs Hunt.'

Looking gratified, she inclined her head. 'Yes, that's right. And what do you do, Mr Middleton-Brown?'

'I'm a solicitor.' He was surprised at her reaction to this less than earth-shattering piece of information. Rowena raised her head suddenly, smiled, and reached for his arm.

'Are you, indeed? Then you're just the man I've been looking for, Mr Middleton-Brown!'

'You need legal advice?' he guessed, puzzled. 'I'm afraid this isn't really the time or place . . .'

'Oh, no, it's not that at all. It's my daughter, Kirsty.' Rowena looked around and lowered her voice as she indicated the young woman who was slowly wending her way through the crowd towards them. 'There's Kirsty now, coming this way. You see, Mr Middleton-Brown, Kirsty is at Cambridge, reading law. For years she's wanted to be a solicitor – as long as I can remember. She's finished her first year, and now . . . well, now it seems that she's changed her mind.' Rowena frowned. 'She's come up with an absolutely crazy idea – she's decided that she wants to go into the Church! To be ordained, for God's sake!'

'Well, yes, that's usually whose sake it's for,' David joked, but Rowena looked blank, then went on.

'I've told her that the Church is no career for a woman. It's insane even to think of such a thing! I mean, if she wants a dog collar that badly, she should *marry* one, like I did!'

'But I don't understand how I can help you,' David demurred.

'You can talk to her! Tell her what a good career the law is. Give her the benefit of your experience, and your advice. She hasn't had anyone to talk sense to her, that's the trouble. She fell in with the wrong crowd at Cambridge, and they've encouraged her in this ordination nonsense. And here at Malbury this summer, she went to see Arthur Brydges-ffrench, and he told her that she must follow her . . . oh, I don't know. Her feeling of vocation, that's what she calls it. I call it nonsense!' she added with vehemence. 'A waste of a talented young life!'

David nodded neutrally as the vivacious girl with the dark curls joined them. He could scarcely say to the girl's mother that his sympathies were all with Kirsty. When he'd been her age, his own mother had treated with scorn and ridicule any suggestion that he might find a career somewhere within the Church. Not necessarily as a priest – though he'd dabbled with the idea, he'd never had a very strong sense of vocation for that calling. A church architect, that's what he would have liked to be, he thought ruefully, glancing at Jeremy. But instead he'd given in to his mother's demands, had taken the line of least resistance . . .

'Very interesting,' said David when they'd finally managed to take their leave of Rowena and Jeremy.

'What was?'

'Oh, quite a few things. He's a rather nasty piece of work, isn't he?'

Lucy nodded. 'The Dean? I'd say so.'

'Actually, I was talking about your friend Jeremy.'

She turned to him in amazement. 'Jeremy? What on earth do you mean?'

'Just what I said. He's not very nice. Didn't you see the way he kept baiting Rowena? It was quite deliberate, you know.'

Laughing, Lucy shook her head. 'Oh, I'm sure you misunderstood. It was just a bit of friendly banter.' This was exactly what she'd been afraid of, she told herself: David was obviously jealous of Jeremy. But if she accused him of jealousy, it would only make him more defensive.

'What, exactly, is their relationship?'

Lucy considered the question carefully. 'They're by no means an item. It's the first time I've ever seen them together,' she said at last. 'I've never had the feeling that Jeremy really liked Rowena, to be honest,' she added.

David had hoped not to betray his own feelings of insecurity and jealousy – feelings which, as he fully recognised, inevitably coloured his negative reaction to Jeremy – so he kept his voice as neutral as possible. 'It looked to me like *you* were the one he was interested in, Lucy. He never took his eyes off you.'

She didn't try to deny it; he wouldn't believe her anyway. 'Well, what difference does it make? I'm not interested in *him*,' Lucy declared firmly, touching his hand in reassurance. 'Not in the way you mean, anyway. He's a friend, that's all – he can be quite amusing, you know.'

'Rowena didn't seem to like it much – the fact that he was making such a big fuss over *you*.'

'I *have* always thought that she fancied Jeremy,' she admitted. 'Nothing I could put my finger on – just a feeling.'

'So perhaps you were wrong about her and that policeman,' David concluded. 'Did you see him walk by? She didn't even acknowledge him. Surely, if they were . . .'

'Oh, David,' she laughed. 'You really *are* naïve! As far as I'm concerned, that confirms my suspicions! A *tête à tête* in Fortnum's, miles away from Malbury, and when she's here she doesn't speak to him. Don't you see? She doesn't want anyone here to know!'

'*What* does someone not want anyone to know?' asked a breathy voice in her ear as she was enveloped in an enthusiastic embrace. 'Come on, Lucy dear – do tell! You know how Bert and I love a spot of juicy gossip. Like mother's milk to us, my dear!' Victor, clad amazingly in a primrose yellow dinner jacket, appeared on her left, while Bert, more conventionally attired, closed in on her right. 'And not to change the subject, Lucy darling,' he added with a gurgle, '*who* is your absolutely divine friend? You mustn't keep him all to yourself – that would be just too selfish, wouldn't it, Bert?'

Chapter 11

*An unwise man doth not well consider this: and a fool doth
not understand it.*

Psalm 92.6

Escaping from Victor and Bert was even more difficult for Lucy
and David than taking leave of Rowena and Jeremy had been.
The pair were full of bitchy comments about their fellow
guests, even as they applauded the style that was in evidence
throughout the day's events, and they certainly found much to
admire amongst the handsome young men in the Conservative
Party entourage. But eventually Olivia Ashleigh came to
rescue them. 'Wouldn't you like to get something to eat?'
she urged. 'Your father and the Willoughbys are over there –
I'm sure they'd like you to join them.' She ignored Victor's
fulsome protests, escorting Lucy and David firmly to the buffet
table.

'Thanks,' said Lucy. 'I was beginning to think we'd have to
spend the rest of the afternoon with those two.'

'Not at all. Victor and Bert are amusing in small doses, but I
could see that you were beginning to have enough.'

Olivia handed them each a plate, but their progress was
blocked by the ginger-haired Canon Thetford and his wife, who
stood with empty plates in hand, staring at the array of food
and muttering to each other. David recognised them instantly
from Lucy's descriptions, especially as the Canon was wearing
a colourful African tribal *dashiki* over his clerical garb.

Claire Fairbrother, in the dark Indian cotton dress with the
tiny mirrors that she'd worn at their first meeting, turned to
Lucy with a furious scowl. 'You're a vegetarian, aren't you?'
she demanded. 'Just look at this! All this food, and hardly
anything that we can eat! Meat! Platters and platters of it – it's
obscene!'

'Oh, I'm sure there are plenty of things for us here,' Lucy

attempted in a conciliatory tone. 'How about this mushroom paté? And all of this cheese . . .'

'This entire affair is obscene, from beginning to end,' stated Philip Thetford, a fanatic light in his pale eyes. 'An obscene waste of money and resources. It's absolutely indefensible, when you think of famine in the Sudan, children dying in Romania . . .'

'And the trees!' his wife added, reaching in her pocket for the stiff invitation to the day's festivities. 'Look at this invitation! How many trees had to give up their lives for this?'

'Doesn't the cathedral have better things to do with its money?' challenged the Canon Missioner. 'I'm surprised that Bishop George would allow such a shameful spectacle of conspicuous consumption.'

Olivia bit her lip to refrain from replying that if they found it so distasteful they might have stayed away, and said merely, 'If it's the cathedral's money you're concerned about, then you needn't worry. This is all being paid for privately.'

'Privately? By whom?' His voice was hectoring and unpleasant. 'I can't believe that the Dean is coughing up his own money for this.'

'If you must know, it's being funded by the Conservative Party. They consider it a hospitality event for the local party. And, at the Dean's insistence, they're making a very generous contribution to cathedral funds as well. So, Canon, you might even say that we're making money out of this!' With an acid smile at him, Olivia led Lucy and David away.

'Well!' fulminated Canon Thetford to their retreating backs. 'I don't understand why the Chapter hasn't heard anything about this!'

Their progress towards the Bishop's table was blocked when they were accosted by Dorothy Unworth, encased in rusty black crimplene. 'Miss Ashleigh!' she said imperiously and with great volume. 'I wish that you would tell the Bishop how very inappropriate I find the new Dean's behaviour!'

Olivia eyed her cautiously. 'What exactly do you mean, Miss Unworth?'

'The way that he has ignored faithful servants of the cathedral by bringing in all these London outsiders – I think it's disgraceful!' The stout woman seemed to swell with indignation like an angry frog. 'I've been doing flowers in this cathedral for forty years, and as for the food—!' She snorted.

'My sausage rolls are better than that fancy muck any day!' Lowering her voice to something approaching a roar, she went on, 'He may have everyone else here fooled, but I tell you, he doesn't fool me. The man is a fraud! Any true churchman – any true Christian – would never treat people the way he has. He has a great deal to answer for, Miss Ashleigh.'

Speechless in the face of this outburst, Olivia struggled for something both soothing and diplomatic to say. But she was forestalled by Evelyn Marsden, who had overheard the tirade. Joining them, the former headmistress took Dorothy Unworth's arm firmly, as though the other woman were a misbehaving pupil. 'I don't think you're being fair, Dorothy,' she stated. 'You haven't given the man a chance. He's only just got here, after all. He's young yet, and has a bit of learning to do, about diplomacy and so forth. But I'm sure that he has many excellent qualities, or he wouldn't have been appointed.'

Miss Unworth glared at her, refusing to be placated. 'Why don't you ask Canon Brydges-ffrench about the Dean's excellent qualities?' she said with a malicious, teeth-baring smile. 'I'm sure he must have some feelings on the subject.' Looking around, she added deliberately, 'By the way, where is the Canon? I don't see him.'

Dropping her arm, Evelyn Marsden turned a shade redder and looked uncomfortable. 'Well, no, as a matter of fact he's not here. He . . . didn't feel well. One of his headaches, I believe – the service did go on a bit, after all. He asked me to give his apologies to everyone.'

'Humph.' Miss Unworth was clearly unconvinced, as well as unrepentant. Fingering her enamelled Mothers' Union badge, she went on defiantly. 'I still say the man's a fraud. And that wife of his – not even a member of the Mothers' Union! I asked her, and she said she had no interest in joining! What sort of example is she going to set for the women of the diocese?'

'Oh, here you are, my dears. Do join us, please,' John Kingsley urged. 'Pat, George, this is Lucy's friend David Middleton-Brown, come to Malbury at last.'

Plates were put down, hands shaken, and appropriate greetings exchanged.

Fond as she was of Lucy, Pat had worried that this man might turn out to be as unsuitable as the one Lucy had married so many years ago. So it was with considerable relief that she observed David: he had a nice face, rendered rather distinguished by the threads of silver mingling with the brown at his temples and transformed into something even more attractive by a kind smile, and it was clear that he adored Lucy. Pat decided on the spot that she liked David very much. There was an empty seat next to her, and she beckoned him into it.

'Could I get you something to drink, Mrs Willoughby?' David asked. 'A glass of wine?'

'Oh, no, I'm fine – and you've just got here. And please do call me Pat – everyone does.'

They all settled down for a companionable chat; David fitted in so well that within a few minutes they had all forgotten that he was a stranger to Malbury and the cathedral. The conversation, inevitably, centred on the day's events.

'I thought that your sermon was splendid, Bishop,' remarked Lucy. 'Forbearance and charity are just what are needed in Malbury at the moment – though I suspect that the guests from London wondered what you were going on about!'

The Bishop smiled wryly. 'I dare say Colossians 3.12–14 isn't the sort of text one usually preaches on at an installation ceremony: "Put on therefore, as the elect of God, holy and beloved, bowels of mercies, kindness, humbleness of mind, meekness, long-suffering; Forbearing one another, and forgiving one another, if any man have a quarrel against any; even as Christ forgave you, so also do you. And above all these things put on charity, which is the bond of perfectness". But somehow it seemed as though it fitted the situation.'

'Forbearance is all very well, my dear, but in these particular circumstances—' Pat began tartly, but she was interrupted by a tactful Olivia.

'What, exactly, are "bowels of mercies"? A peculiar turn of phrase, if you don't mind my saying so.'

The Bishop's deep laugh was genuine and prolonged. 'An odd quirk of the Authorised Version. The Revised Standard Version says "compassion", which perhaps sums it all up very well.'

'It was a lovely sermon,' John Kingsley echoed. 'Just the thing, George.'

But Pat would not be silenced. 'Don't you see, though, that charity and forbearance have to work both ways? We must of course be more than willing to give him the benefit of the doubt, but it's not easy when he begins like this.'

'What do you mean?' asked David.

'Well, naturally one feels badly about the way that Arthur Brydges-ffrench has been treated. But that completely aside, there's this . . . this party, for one thing. It would be all right to do something like this in London, but Malbury isn't London, and it's not appropriate here. It gives completely the wrong impression, you understand.' She hesitated, frowning. 'And there's the issue of my clergy wives, of course. You know that they were relegated to the south transept, where they couldn't see a thing, underneath all that scaffolding. It was a disgrace.'

David saw an opportunity to change the subject. 'I haven't had the chance to have a proper look at the cathedral yet, but I noticed the scaffolding,' he said. 'What is it for?'

'Yes,' added Lucy. 'It wasn't there the last time I was here.'

'Emergency repairs to the Becket window,' the Bishop explained. 'A few problems came to light several weeks ago, according to Jeremy Bartlett – faults in the stonework. And since that window is our greatest treasure, we couldn't afford to waste any time in seeing to the repairs. The Friends of the Cathedral are helping to fund it, I understand.'

'It's a shame that I can't see the Becket window on my first visit to Malbury,' David said. 'I've read so much about it.'

'But it won't be your last visit, will it?' Pat smiled at him, mollified slightly.

'No, of course not.'

'In fact,' Pat added, 'perhaps I could talk you into coming back very soon – as soon as next weekend, in fact. I was thinking of giving a small dinner party, and we would very much like it if you and Lucy could join us.'

David hesitated a moment, thinking with regret of the separate rooms with their narrow beds. 'Yes, of course,' he said at last. 'That sounds lovely. And it will give me a chance to get to know Lucy's father better. That is,' he added, 'if it's all right with Lucy?' He looked at her and she nodded in confirmation, reaching for his hand.

As the afternoon progressed, the groupings became even more distinct, the crowd more fragmented, as people gravitated like to like. Kirsty Hunt, told by her mother – who wanted Jeremy to herself – to run along and find some young people, had encountered the American Todd Randall, and together they had found their way to the corner table occupied by the cathedral bell-ringers. The bell-ringers were primarily a young crowd, high-spirited and increasingly cheerful as they quaffed Watkins Ploughman's Bitter out of cans.

They tended to keep themselves to themselves anyway, never quite integrating with the rest of the cathedral community, but today they stood out even more than usual, their casual jeans in vivid contrast to the dressy garb of the other guests. But they were not an unfriendly lot, the bell-ringers, and so when the new Dean came to their table, late in the afternoon, they greeted him cheerily.

In the absence of Inspector Michael Drewitt – after putting in a brief appearance, he had gone home to his wife, who had been given to understand that the invitation did not include her – the natural leader of the group was Barry Crabtree, the ringing master. He was a young man, tall and thin, with shoulder-length toffee-coloured hair; at his side was his wife Liz, holding their baby Caroline, who was dressed for the occasion in a frilly pink frock with a matching bonnet on her round bald head. On Barry's other side was his best mate and constant companion Neil Beddoes, who worked with him at Watkins Brewery. Neil, with a gap-toothed grin and an oversized nose, was outgoing and talkative, while Barry tended to be the quiet one, but when he spoke people took notice of him.

It was Barry who spoke first when Stuart Latimer approached the table. 'Hello,' he said. 'Nice party. Guess we have you to thank for it.'

As they all remained seated, the Dean was able to look down on them. 'Yes.' His eyes raked their casual clothes pointedly; he was not at all sure that these people had any right to be here, as none of them had bothered with the receiving line and he had no idea who they were. 'Most of the guests seem to have dressed up rather more than you have for it.' Realising too late how critical that sounded, he tacked on an unconvincing laugh, trying to make it into a joke.

'Well, you wanted bells for the service, mate,' Neil said with a grin, refusing to take offence. 'If you'd ever been up the tower you'd know better than to wear anything fancy.'

'Ah, so you're the bell-ringers.' His voice warmed slightly.

'That's right.' Barry introduced himself and the others by name. 'Have a seat, Dean,' he invited, indicating an empty chair.

'No, thank you.'

'Want a beer?' Neil asked, proferring a can.

The Dean froze. 'Beer?' he said stonily. 'No provision was made to offer beer at this party.'

'No, that's why we brought our own,' Neil explained. 'Watkins Ploughman's Bitter, the best there is. And we should know, shouldn't we, Bar? Go on, Dean – have one.'

There was a long moment of silence as the Dean stared first at the beer, then at the ingenuously friendly faces of the bell-ringers. He clasped his hands together; his knuckles were white. 'You have insulted me by bringing that beer here today,' he said at last with controlled fury. 'It's a scandal and a shame, and a disgrace to the cathedral. *You* are a disgrace to the cathedral! All of you!'

As he turned to stalk away, Barry called him back. 'Just a minute, Mr Latimer.' His voice was soft, but carried sufficient authority to stop the Dean in his tracks.

'Yes?'

Barry chose his words carefully. 'If you think we're a disgrace, Dean, I suggest that you look at what's going on down in the cathedral. If there's going to be any scandal or shame, that's where it's going to come from, not from us up in the tower.'

'What do you mean?' demanded the Dean. The young man crossed his arms across his thin chest with dignity. 'I'm not saying any more. But if you know what's good for you, you'll make it your business to find out what I'm talking about.'

Stuart Latimer stared at him, aghast.

Chapter 12

*For they intended mischief against thee: and imagined such
a device as they are not able to perform.*

Psalm 21.11

The following day, a Sunday, Dean Stuart Latimer took his
first service at Malbury Cathedral. Although the people
present at the main morning service of Holy Communion did
not begin to reach the numbers of the previous afternoon, it
was the feast day of St Michael and All Angels and the
cathedral was by no means deserted.

There were, of course, no reserved seats for this service, but
David and Lucy arrived early enough to secure seats in the
Quire, giving them an excellent view of the proceedings. The
canons were all present in their stalls for the feast day, and the
Bishop occupied his throne.

The choir, too, were out in force. In honour of the festival, and
in an attempt to impress their new master with their skills and
accomplishments, the organist had made an over-ambitious
choice of anthem: William Harris's 'Faire is the Heaven'. The
piece requires a double choir and impeccable tuning; the first
requisite they could just about manage, but the second was
beyond their capabilities. At any rate it was a noble effort,
David judged. It was a favourite piece of his, and so he listened
and watched carefully.

Ivor Jones's skills on the organ were limited, but he took his
role as choir trainer seriously, sensing himself to be a part,
albeit a small part, of the great ongoing Anglican choral
tradition. That morning the organ scholar was playing, so the
organist threw himself wholeheartedly into his conducting
duties. His small frame seemed to swell with emotion as he
coaxed from the boys the best they were capable of delivering;
he breathed heavily, he grimaced, he quivered, he shook his
fist, he mouthed the words at them, and the boys in response

produced a rough approximation of the ideal Anglican sound, pure and strangulated.

At the climax of this performance, out of the corner of his eye David caught an abrupt movement from the Dean's stall. He turned slightly and looked at the Dean: the man was leaning forward, staring fixedly at the organist, a frown drawing his heavy brows together and his lips compressed. What, David wondered, had the Dean seen to evoke such a reaction?

There was much to talk about on the drive back to London that evening. The south Shropshire hills, steeply rolling and bespattered with sheep, flew past the car's windows as the sun dipped towards the horizon and the shadows gathered mysteriously in the folds between the hills. But the miles between south Shropshire and South Kensington sped by unnoticed as Lucy and David relived the events of the weekend, analysing and speculating; it was, after all, the first chance they'd had to talk, the first time they'd actually been alone together since their arrival in Malbury on Friday.

Given his insecurities, it was not surprising that it was Jeremy who was uppermost in David's mind. He'd awoken in the middle of the previous night thinking about Jeremy: there was something about the other man that David didn't like, and he was trying to convince himself that there was some basis for his suspicion of Jeremy other than the architect's obvious attraction towards Lucy. Although he couldn't put his finger on anything specific, he was inclined to believe in his own instincts. 'I suppose he's a good architect,' he said, almost wistfully.

'Oh, yes, I think so,' Lucy confirmed. 'He certainly knows a great deal about the cathedral, anyway. He's told me all about its history, and all about the building.'

'Why would a good architect be happy in a backwater like Malbury, though?' Perhaps, thought David, there was something in his past – some shady business dealings from which he'd been trying to escape when he took the cathedral post.

Lucy thought back to her first evening with Jeremy. 'He said that after his wife died – she had cancer, and she can't have been very old – he just didn't want the hassle of the London rat race any longer.'

'Oh.' Unfortunately, that made sense. Chewing his lip and

keeping his eyes on the road, David said at last, 'Do you think he's attractive?'

She laughed. 'I suppose so. His beard is rather nice, I think – it makes him look distinguished.'

David flinched visibly. 'Do you think I should grow a beard, then?' he asked self-consciously.

Lucy turned and regarded him with an appraising squint in the pinkish glow of the setting sun. 'No, I don't think so,' was her eventual judgement. 'I don't think a beard would suit you, David.' Squeezing his arm, she added, 'I love you just the way you are.'

His grateful sigh escaped gently as he turned and smiled at her for just an instant.

'And what about Rowena?' she teased, further attempting to distract him from his self-doubts. 'You seemed to be getting on quite well with her. I think she rather fancies you.'

'Oh, I don't think so.' The suggestion seemed to horrify rather than gratify him. 'But I'm still not convinced that you're right about her and that policeman. She seemed very sincere to me, very . . .'

Lucy smiled at him; that, and the tenderness of her voice, took the sting out of words that might have been hurtful. 'Oh, David my darling. You really don't know very much about women, do you?'

Again he sighed. 'No, I suppose not.' But he was humble rather than defiant.

Inevitably, they discussed the various members of the cathedral community. 'What was your impression of Canon Brydges-ffrench?' Lucy wanted to know.

'I didn't have much chance to form an impression of him,' David reminded her. 'He wasn't at the garden party at all, and I only met him briefly after this morning's service. 'But he seemed . . . oh, I don't know. A tragic figure. Forlorn, as though the entire foundation of his life had been knocked out from under him. I feel very sorry for him.'

'And the Dean? What did you think of him?'

'He's a real shit,' was David's succinct reply. 'Complete and unmitigated. He lived up to his advance billing in every possible way.'

Lucy was silent for quite a long time, abstractedly twisting a curl around her finger. 'No good is going to come of the appointment, you know,' she said at last, quietly. 'I feel it in my bones. It was a bad appointment, and it will end in tears.'

David's reply was equally sombre. 'If not something worse. The way the Dean is making enemies, he'll be lucky not to meet a sticky end, and sooner rather than later!'

'That's not funny.' She frowned.

'No, I didn't mean it to be.' That bald statement, bleakly offered, again stopped the conversation temporarily.

'Even Pat Willoughby,' Lucy reflected after a moment. 'She's the most tolerant person I know. But even Pat has been upset by him, and thinks that the whole thing is a terrible mistake.'

Unexpectedly, David smiled, consciously lightening his voice. 'Pat is marvellous, isn't she? I really liked her. And the Bishop too, of course.'

'Bishop George is a dear, and she's great. Everyone adores Pat. I might have told you that she was absolutely brilliant when . . . when my mother died. I don't know what would have happened without her around to organise things. She and my mother were great friends, you know.'

'I didn't know that.' Lucy had rarely spoken to him of her dead mother; in fact she rarely spoke about herself or her personal history at all, but David now felt that he was beginning to build up a better picture of her early life. He loved her so consumingly that he wanted to know everything there was to know about her – as much as one human being could possibly know about another. He wanted to know whether she'd been a tomboy, roaming the rolling Shropshire hills with her two older brothers, or whether instead she'd stayed at home, curled in a corner with a book or playing with her dolls. He wanted to know if she'd had pets, and if so what their names had been. He wanted to know if she'd kept a diary, who her friends had been, if she'd had a nickname, whether she'd been considered pretty or plain. 'I'm glad we're going back next weekend,' he said impulsively. 'It will be good to spend more time with your father, and with Pat – they can tell me all about what you were like and what you got up to when you were younger.'

'Not a very exciting story, I'm sure,' she smiled. 'But I'm so glad that you don't mind going. I'd thought that after this weekend you wouldn't want to go back to Malbury for a while.'

David shook his head. 'I'm not very thrilled about the separate rooms, of course,' he admitted. Lucy held her breath, hoping that he wouldn't resurrect the marriage issue again. This time, for once, he didn't; instead he added with a self-deprecating grin, 'And I wouldn't mind, to tell you the truth, if Jeremy Bartlett were suddenly called away to some far-flung corner of the world. But there's a sort of morbid fascination about the place. I have to be honest, Lucy – I don't really like it much, but it fascinates me in spite of that.'

'Why don't you like it?' she probed. 'I would have thought that a Cathedral Close would be just your cup of tea.'

He thought for a moment. 'You said that it was like a goldfish bowl,' he said slowly. 'But it's more sinister than that – at least in a goldfish bowl you can see what's going on, and it's all pretty straightforward, even if everyone knows your business. Malbury is more like a stagnant pond, with all sorts of nasty things growing under the surface where you can't see them. It's not a nice place, Lucy, and nothing there is really what it seems. But that won't stop me from going back . . .'

Chapter 13

I will smite them, that they shall not be able to stand: but fall under my feet.
Thou hast girded me with strength unto the battle: thou shalt throw down mine enemies under me.

Psalm 18.38–9

Although Stuart Latimer had been installed in his new position on Saturday afternoon and had taken the communion service on Sunday morning, it was not until Monday morning, when he sat at the head of the table at his first Chapter meeting, that he felt as if he had truly arrived. He looked around the table at the other four men, savouring real power for perhaps the first time in his life. Everything else he'd done, up to and including the church in Fulham, had been preparing him for this moment, he knew. And of course this would not be the end of it, by any stretch of the imagination. This was only the beginning, the first major stepping-stone. By the time he was fifty, or possibly even forty-five, Stuart Latimer knew that he would wear a bishop's mitre. And not just the mitre of a minor suffragan, either – no, he would be a major diocesan bishop, with a seat in the House of Lords. After that – who could tell? The current Archbishop of Canterbury was older than he, would reach retirement age well before he did. On this Monday morning at the end of September, Stuart Latimer felt certain that the future was his for the taking.

Now it all begins, he said to himself with satisfaction and anticipation. His initial skirmishes with Malbury Cathedral – his involvement in the arrangements for the installation service and the garden party, for instance – had been mere preliminaries to the battle which was now to begin, shots fired over the bow to signal his intent. So for a moment he sat silently, enjoying the moment. He looked down at his hands, folded on the table in front of him: deceptively small hands, with neatly trimmed and well-cleaned nails, the dark hair creeping out from his cassock sleeves to cover them in thick growth. After a moment he raised his head and levelly regarded the four men who stared back at him, four men who exhibited varying degrees of consternation, apprehension, and even fear.

The Subdean, Canon Brydges-ffrench, was the worst, of course. How that man could have possibly thought that he had a chance to become Dean was beyond the power of Stuart Latimer's imagination. He had no vision, no new ideas, no initiative, only the desire to preserve what had been, to enshrine the past and thus to ensure a stillborn future. He was so very weak, practically trembling now at the horror of what had happened, what was about to happen; Stuart Latimer despised weakness, and he despised Arthur Brydges-ffrench.

Philip Thetford, the Canon Missioner, was an insignificant weed, the Dean judged, with his invisible eyebrows and his thin gingery hair. Endlessly carping on about the Third World, about deprivation and hardship elsewhere, without ever noticing what was going on around him right here at the cathedral. Stuart Latimer had taken his measure immediately on his first visit to Malbury, before the appointment had been made. It hadn't been difficult to win him over to his cause, to ensure that when the members of the Chapter were asked by the Prime Minister's Secretary for Appointments for their feelings about Stuart Latimer he could count on Canon Thetford's support. All that had been necessary were a few hints about future plans: new arrangements for the cathedral's catering might vacate the current refectory, he had suggested, and it was quite possible that the building might be suitable for conversion into low-cost housing. Canon Thetford had leapt at the suggestion, delivering a gratuitous sermon on the problems of homelessness in rural Shropshire. And the sweetener had clinched the bargain: ten percent of cathedral income to be given to foreign missions. Black babies, the Dean now said to himself contemptuously, dismissing Canon Thetford as any serious challenge to his power.

Precentor Rupert Greenwood was similarly ineffectual, he told himself. He could almost pass for a choirboy himself, with that golden boyishness, and he was so wrapped up in his music that the cathedral could burn down around his ears and he would only notice when the crackling of the flames drowned out the organ. He, too, had been easy to convert, with a vague promise of a new organ and perhaps refounding of the choir school. 'Stuart Latimer? Oh, yes, a forward-looking chap. Just what the cathedral needs,' was what Canon Greenwood must surely have told the Appointments Secretary.

It was more difficult to get the measure of John Kingsley, the newest member of the Chapter. He'd barely arrived when Stuart Latimer had made his first visit, and did not have an evident vested interest in any particular area of the cathedral's operation other than the relatively insignificant library. So he'd been able to make him no promises, apart from general ones about ensuring the cathedral's future. He'd sensed that Canon Kingsley was not impressed, but he dismissed him as powerless and unimportant in the scheme of things. A friend of the Bishop, yes, but the Bishop himself was powerless in the running of the cathedral. His business was the diocese; the Dean knew himself to be supreme within the world of the Cathedral Close. So John Kingsley was not worth considering as an opponent. Getting a bit beyond it, probably, at his age. Stuart Latimer could not be aware of the strength of mind and spirit that lay behind John Kingsley's gentleness; indeed, if he was aware of the gentleness at all he misinterpreted it as a manifestation of weakness.

Judging that the tension had built up sufficiently, the Dean smiled, a smile totally without humour. 'Gentlemen,' he said, 'it's gone ten o'clock. Time for us to begin.' Begin as you mean to continue, he added to himself. Now is the time.

'In the months since I was appointed,' Stuart Latimer said, 'I have been attempting to familiarise myself with cathedral affairs. Although many things have been made available to me, I have not had complete access to all of the files, or the books and the accounts – naturally enough.' He looked around the table; Canon Brydges-ffrench's head was averted, unwilling to meet his eyes. 'I'm going to need a great deal of help from you all in the near future, as I try to get to grips with things.' He slapped his open palm down on the table, and Canon Brydges-ffrench jumped. 'I will expect your co-operation!'

John Kingsley was the first to speak. 'Of course,' he said. 'Just let us know how we can help you, Dean. That is the job of the Chapter, to assist the Dean.'

103

If any of them were expecting the informal approach, the friendly 'Please call me Stuart – we're all in this together', they were disappointed. The Dean merely inclined his head in acknowledgement, and launched into his agenda.

'From what I have seen,' he said, 'Malbury Cathedral has, for not a few years, shamefully failed to move with the times. As far as the operation of this cathedral is concerned, we might as well still be back in the thirties, if not the nineteenth century!' This amounted to a direct attack not only upon his late predecessor, but also upon one of the men seated at the table; the rest of them knew it, and avoided looking at Arthur Brydges-ffrench as he fumbled in his cassock sleeve for his handkerchief and mopped his high forehead.

In the pause that followed the Dean's pronouncement, the sound of the Subdean's voice was unexpected. 'And what's so bad about that?' he asked defiantly. 'We've managed quite well up till now . . .'

Stuart Latimer turned to him, his brows drawn together. 'What's so bad about it?' His voice dripped scorn. 'Canon, we're living in the nineteen-nineties, not the thirties. It might reasonably be assumed that my appointment was intended to take Malbury Cathedral into the twenty-first century – instead I find resistance to leaving the nineteenth! I must say, Canon Brydges-ffrench, I find your attitude extraordinary! I expected to find you obstructive and difficult, but I did not expect such perverse stupidity!'

The Subdean's eyes filled with tears; he convulsively gripped his handkerchief but was unable to speak. Rupert Greenwood looked away and Philip Thetford stared down at the table, but John Kingsley met the Dean's eyes. 'That wasn't really necessary,' he said quietly.

The Dean ignored him; his voice became crisp, businesslike. 'Shall we move on, then? We have much ground to cover, and I'd like to be finished by lunch time. Item: the cathedral refectory.' The juxtaposition was not deliberate, or meant to be funny. 'I'm sure you will all agree with me that the quality of the food currently on offer in our refectory is appalling. Clearly not of the sort of standard one expects of a major cathedral these days. Sausage rolls and dried-up sandwiches – it just won't do.' He paused, and consulted his notes. 'I have had an informal discussion with Mrs Hunt of the Friends about this issue, and she has made a few suggestions for improvement of the service. I'm not yet prepared to discuss these with you in detail, but I want it clearly understood that major changes are going to be made as soon as it is feasible to do so. Mrs Hunt,' he added, looking up, 'has been most helpful. I look forward to working with her – she is obviously a competent and accomplished woman, and a great asset to this cathedral.'

'Does this mean . . . will the refectory be moved to another location?' asked Philip Thetford, trying to keep the eagerness from his voice. Canon Brydges-ffrench shot him a quizzical – almost hurt – look, but the Dean remained impassive.

'That will definitely happen eventually, though I'm not prepared to discuss my plans for new buildings quite yet,' he replied obscurely, then took perverse pleasure in adding, 'I will tell you, though, that it is my intention that the current refectory will be done up and let as offices when new premises are available.'

'Offices?' Canon Thetford's invisible eyebrows shot up to meet his ginger hair. 'I was given to understand . . . that is . . .' he floundered, uncharacteristically at a loss for words.

'The suggestion that I made to you about low-cost housing?' the Dean suggested smoothly, enjoying the Canon's discomfort. 'I'm afraid that's not financially viable. I've looked into it, and we – the cathedral – would have to bear the cost of the conversion, a cost we simply can't afford at the moment. If it's let for offices, the tenants can be made to pay for the conversion themselves. Altogether a more satisfactory solution, you must admit.' Canon Thetford, speechless with anger and embarrassment, made no reply, so after a moment the Dean went on. 'Item: the Cathedral Shop. Again, not a situation that can be allowed to continue.'

Arthur Brydges-ffrench opened his mouth, then shut it again; it was left for John Kingsley to ask, 'What situation is that, Dean?'

'For one thing, it's all in the most appalling taste. The . . . gentlemen . . .' he raised a sardonic eyebrow, 'who run it seem to have very little idea about the sort of merchandise that is appropriate for the image this cathedral wishes to project.'

'But surely . . .' Canon Kingsley began, but the Dean cut across his protest.

'Furthermore, from the records I've seen, the shop has consistently failed to make any money. On the contrary, it has been a drain on the cathedral's resources for the last several years! It was not my impression that a cathedral shop was a charitable enterprise!' he snapped. 'I have not yet been able to discover the terms of the lease, but it is my intention to replace the current tenants with someone who will run the shop properly.'

'But Victor and Bert . . .' began Canon Brydges-ffrench in agitation.

He was ignored. 'And while we're on the subject of leases,' the Dean continued, 'I would like a summary of all of the leased properties within the Close, the terms of the leases, and their expiration dates. No more peppercorn rents will be permitted. It's about time that these properties were made to pay for themselves. Will you see to that, Canon Brydges-ffrench?'

The Subdean nodded, reaching again for his handkerchief, as the Dean consulted his notes. 'Item: the cathedral library.' John Kingsley looked at him enquiringly as he continued. 'Canon Kingsley, I would like you to prepare for me a list of the most valuable books in the cathedral library. I am particularly interested in any book worth over five thousand pounds.'

'Might I ask why?'

'You might.' The Dean smiled humourlessly. 'There is currently quite a good market for antiquarian books. Many of our books, I'm sure, have no particular significance for this cathedral. They could be sold to provide us with valuable income.'

'That just won't do!' exploded Arthur Brydges-ffrench. 'I'm afraid I can't just sit by and let the cathedral library be flogged off!'

'Oh, I'm sure that you can, and will,' the Dean said, steel in his voice. 'And that brings me to the next item, Canon Brydges-ffrench. I would like you to prepare a list as well, of the cathedral plate and any items in the treasury. You are the Treasurer, aren't you, Canon? I'm sure that there must be some things that are surplus to our requirements, even though it's perhaps not the best time to be selling ecclesiastical silver.'

Canon Brydges-ffrench stared at him, appalled, his mouth working painfully.

The meeting went on in the same vein. Next on the agenda was the music. 'Canon Greenwood,' the Dean said, 'there are several matters regarding the music in the cathedral that I would like to speak to you about in private, at your earliest convenience. Nothing that need concern the rest of the Chapter. Yet.'

'About the new organ?' Rupert Greenwood asked. 'I've talked to an organ builder, and have some tentative specifications drawn up.'

'There will be no new organ.' The Dean's words dropped like lead; the Precentor gaped at him.

'But you said . . .'

'There will be no new organ,' repeated the Dean, even more forcefully. 'Organs don't make money, organs only cost money.'

'But the organ is nearing the end of its life!' Canon Greenwood argued. 'Already it's showing quite a few faults, and the organ builder said that repairs will cost a bomb! In the long run, it will be much more economical to have a new one.'

'There will be no repairs. There is no money to be spent on the organ.'

The Precentor was unable to comprehend what was being said. 'Then what . . . ?'

'The organ is good enough as it is for the time being,' stated the Dean. 'And if it becomes completely unplayable, it will be replaced with an electronic model. Some of them make quite a reasonable noise, I understand. Most people would never be able to tell the difference.'

'Electronic organ!?' sputtered Rupert Greenwood. 'Not be able to tell . . . !'

'And now,' said the Dean, consulting his list, 'regarding the budget for repairs and renewals. I'm afraid that next year's budgeted sum will be required for redecorating the drawing room of the Deanery. It's in a disgraceful state – I can't imagine how my predecessor could have lived with it! My wife and I will be doing a great deal of entertaining, and it's out of the question to ask my wife to put up with such sub-standard decoration. As it is, she'll have to wait until the following year's budget becomes available to deal with the hall and staircase.'

By now Arthur Brydges-ffrench had recovered sufficiently to say, 'But the cathedral fabric . . .'

'There are,' said the Dean, 'no major repairs needed in the cathedral that I can see.'

Before the meeting broke up, the Dean looked again at his list.

'One more matter,' he said. 'Just a small one. Canon Brydges-ffrench, I would like, at your earliest convenience, to see the accounts for the Malbury Music Festival.'

'The music festival accounts?' the Subdean echoed weakly. His eyes darted to Rupert Greenwood and he moistened his lips with his tongue.

'Yes. You remember the music festival? Last summer? Surely you can remember back that far.' Stuart Latimer's smile was sarcastic as he rose. 'And now I must be on my way – my wife will be expecting me for lunch. Thank you for your attention. I look forward to working with you all, for a very long time.'

As he swept from the room, the four canons remained frozen, staring at each other in disbelieving horror.

'What are we going to do?' whispered Rupert Greenwood at last.

'There's nothing we *can* do,' countered John Kingsley.

'It's monstrous!' Philip Thetford said in a slightly louder voice.

But Arthur Brydges-ffrench had the last word. 'He has betrayed us all,' he stated with forlorn dignity, mopping his domed forehead with a very damp handkerchief. He looked around at the others with sudden calculation. 'But as long as we all vote together, we've got him outnumbered. We're four against one. Don't forget that!'

'United we stand,' murmured Rupert Greenwood. 'Divided . . . doesn't bear thinking about!'

After the meeting, Arthur Brydges-ffrench walked home through the Close, unable to bear the thought of facing any of his colleagues. But there was one person that he knew he must talk to – Jeremy Bartlett – and he decided that the telephone was the best way to do it.

Before he reached his door, though, he spotted Jeremy in the Close, coming from the direction of the Deanery. They met in front of Evelyn Marsden's house, by the gate into her garden. 'Miss Marsden's flowers are lovely for this time of year, don't you think?' Jeremy remarked in a passing-the-time-of-day voice. 'I was admiring them earlier. Does she use anything special on them, do you know?'

Canon Brydges-ffrench held on to the gate for support, nervously playing with the latch. 'I don't know.'

Jeremy studied the late roses with every evidence of interest. 'I must ask her.'

'Never mind that.' The Canon's voice came out in a sort of squeak, not unlike that of the latch; Jeremy looked at him in some surprise.

'Is something the matter?'

The Canon gulped. 'Yes, something jolly well is the matter.' He leaned over from his considerable height and said softly, 'We've just had a Chapter meeting. It was . . . hell. That's the only way I can describe it.'

Jeremy raised his eyebrows. 'That bad?'

'The Dean. He's mad!' It was delivered in a melodramatic hiss; Jeremy drew back from the spray of spittle.

'Well, I'm sure we'll all survive.'

If this reassurance was meant to offer comfort, it fell far short of its intention. 'No! You don't understand!' moaned the Subdean, reaching into his sleeve for his handkerchief. 'He's asked for the music festival accounts!'

'Ah.' Suddenly Jeremy looked interested. 'And what did you tell him?'

'I didn't tell him anything. He didn't give me a chance! He just said that he wanted them!' Arthur Brydges-ffrench wiped his shining brow. 'What am I going to tell him? What should I do? If he finds out . . .'

'If he finds out, we're in a great deal of trouble,' said Jeremy quietly, thinking aloud. 'He mustn't find out.'

'Then what can I do?'

Jeremy studied the roses for a moment. 'You must stall him. Tell him that the accounts haven't been prepared yet. Maybe he'll forget about it, if we're lucky. If not . . . well, we'll think of something. But he mustn't look at those books. Not if we want to stay at Malbury Cathedral!'

Chapter 14

*Deliver me not over into the will of mine adversaries: for
there are false witnesses risen up against me, and such as
speak wrong.*

Psalm 27.14

Looking back on them later, the next few days had something
of the quality of a nightmare about them. At the time, though,
at least on the surface, life in the Cathedral Close seemed to go
on much as usual. Dorothy Unworth continued to create and
dispense sausage rolls and Bakewell tarts, Victor and Bert to
sell postcards and tea towels. Pat Willoughby still tended her
autumnal garden and walked her dogs; her husband the
Bishop wrote a few more pages of his treatise on the
Albigensian Heresy. Each day Claire Fairbrother went off to
her work at the Malbury Family Planning Clinic, walking past
the house where Judith Greenwood brooded over her barren-
ness, and each night Jeremy Bartlett sat alone in his great
hulk of a house, nursing a drink and dreaming of immortality.
With the end of the long vac at hand, Kirsty Hunt packed her
things and looked forward to returning to Cambridge, while
her mother continued to scheme and plan, sharing her
thoughts with no one. The giant pantechnicons from London
had been and gone at the Deanery, and no requests for
neighbourly help in settling in had been forthcoming; it was as
if the Latimers had always been there. And, sitting at her first
floor window above the Close, Evelyn Marsden continued to
watch it all, avidly interested yet somehow detached.

In the cathedral itself, even more than in the Close, the
rhythm of life, the daily pattern of Morning Prayer, Communion services and Evensong went on unchanged. At noon
each day Philip Thetford boomed forth from the pulpit, asking
for prayers for those less fortunate throughout the world.
Periodically the bell-ringers made their intrepid way up the

spiral staircase and across the south transept to the tower to ring for services or for their own pleasure. Daily the choir gathered for rehearsal, for Evensong, enduring or ignoring Ivor Jones's groans and grimaces. Stuart Latimer was little seen: he was too busy pursuing his own affairs to spend his time in the cathedral. Seen or unseen, though, it is safe to say that he was never very far from anyone's mind during those few days.

But on Thursday afternoon the Dean appeared in the cathedral, suddenly and unexpectedly, taking his stall for Evensong. He spoke to none of his colleagues, though all were present: Rupert Greenwood was of course singing the office, Arthur Brydges-ffrench was reading the first lesson and John Kingsley the second, and Philip Thetford was leading the intercessions. It was not necessary for them all to be at Evensong, but unconsciously they seemed to be seeking out each other's company more than usual, for solidarity, for some sort of comfort, or even for mutual protection.

It was a wet, miserable afternoon, unseasonably dark already by five. Early October was not prime tourist season in Malbury – if indeed there were a prime tourist season in Malbury – but it was a popular time of year for walkers in the Shropshire hills. A few of them were in the cathedral that afternoon, seeking shelter from the weather; they sat in sodden clumps in the Quire, water dripping from their wet anoraks. Several of the women from the Close were there as well: Evelyn Marsden, who usually attended, Olivia Ashleigh, finished with her day's work for the Bishop, and Rowena Hunt, who had spent the afternoon at the Friends of the Cathedral's information stall in the south aisle. Jeremy Bartlett, another habitual attender, was there, as was the American Todd Randall, and just before the choir procession came in, Pat Willoughby slipped into a stall seat, shaking the droplets from her headscarf.

Throughout the service the Dean sat impassively in his stall, the most elaborately carved on the *decani* side of the Quire. No one dared look at him for long, but everyone (save the alien walkers) was aware of his presence. There was an intensity about his stillness – concentrated, concentrating – as though he were waiting for something.

The service lasted no longer than usual, but to Jeremy, sitting on the *cantoris* side where his view of the Dean was unimpaired, it seemed to go on for an age. The opening psalm set for the day, number eighteen, was a long one; its 'hailstones and coals of fire' gave the organist much scope for facial contortion and manual gesticulation. The Dean, Jeremy observed, remained unnaturally still, watchful, the whiteness of his knuckles the only indication of some strong emotion.

Arthur Brydges-ffrench, on the other hand, was visibly moved. When the choir sang, 'He shall deliver me from my strongest enemy, and from them which hate me: for they are too mighty for me', he glanced in the direction of the Dean, chewing on his lower lip. And when he read the Old Testament lesson, hunching his tall frame forlornly over the lectern, the lugubrious words of Job Chapter 10 took on new pathos.

'My soul is weary of my life; I will leave my complaint upon myself; I will speak in the bitterness of my soul,' read the Subdean. His voice shook, and as he continued the occasional tear trickled down his cheek. 'I will say unto God, Do not condemn me; shew me wherefore thou contendest with me. Is it good unto thee that thou shouldest oppress, that thou shouldest despise the work of thine hands, and shine upon the counsel of the wicked?' His passion mounted as he read, but the final verses he finished almost on a sigh, very quietly. 'Are not my days few? Cease then, and let me alone, that I may take comfort a little, before I go whence I shall not return, even to the land of darkness and the shadow of death . . .'

Still the Dean did not move.

The choir's anthem was a short one: 'O Taste and See' by Vaughan Williams. The young treble who sang the opening solo made a valiant job of it, his voice quavering ever so slightly, and when it was over Ivor Jones beamed; as he moved back to his seat he went so far as to ruffle the boy's fair hair affectionately in passing.

Stuart Latimer started, controlling himself with an effort, Jeremy observed. For the rest of the service – the prayers and the final hymn – his eyes remained fixed on the organist, burning with some strong emotion. He stood as the choir procession trailed out, then remained standing, distanced somehow from the rest of the congregation, as people said their final private prayers and began collecting their things.

It was when Ivor Jones returned to the Quire to retrieve his music from its stand that the Dean finally moved. His movement was sudden, unexpected; he hurtled down to the music stand and clamped his hand over the music. 'Just a moment,' he said forcefully and loudly, his voice echoing from the vaulted ceiling.

Everyone stopped, all motion frozen, as the scene was enacted before them in the centre of the Quire.

'What is the matter?' asked Ivor Jones, as yet unalarmed.

'I saw what you did, and I know what you are.' The Dean's voice was controlled, and not particularly loud, yet it carried perfectly in the acoustic marvel of the Quire. 'I cannot allow such behaviour in my cathedral. You are dismissed, Mr Jones. Immediately. Please leave now, and do not return.'

The organist's face registered complete bafflement, nothing more. 'What are you talking about, Dean?'

'I am talking about the way you . . . fondled . . . that boy. In public, in God's holy place! I've seen the way you've looked at them all, the gestures you've used. I was warned about you, and I've been watching you. But I'm telling you, Mr Jones, I will not have paedophiles employed in this cathedral! Such things may have been overlooked in the past – might even have been encouraged, for all I know! – but I will not stand for it!'

Both men were short, practically of a height, and they stared at each other eye to eye. But suddenly Ivor Jones seemed to dwindle in stature, to shrink inside himself. His face paled; his mouth opened in a horrified, soundless 'O'. For an instant that stretched into an eternity, no one – neither the participants in the drama, nor its audience – moved. Then, with a strangled cry, the organist fled.

They all reproached themselves afterwards, of course. They should have said something, should have spoken up for the man. But everyone had been too shocked, too embarrassed; they hadn't even talked about it amongst themselves until the next day. And who could have known that Ivor Jones would take it so hard? Who could have known that he would bolt to the sanctuary of his solitary house in the Close, write an impassioned letter affirming his innocence, and then swallow the contents of an entire bottle of sleeping tablets?

Act II

Chapter 15

*For when thou art angry all our days are gone: we bring our
years to an end, as it were a tale that is told.*

Psalm 90.9

When Lucy and David arrived in the Cathedral Close the next
afternoon, they were unprepared for what awaited them. They
saw no one: the stillness was surreal and complete, as though
plague or nuclear holocaust had wiped out all of its inhabitants. John Kingsley opened his door to them with a grave
expression, and the kiss he gave his daughter was abstracted,
almost perfunctory.

'Daddy, whatever is the matter?' Lucy pulled away from him
and scanned his face anxiously.

'Lucy dear, I'm afraid that something terrible has happened.'

'The Dean,' she blurted, thinking to herself: Something has
happened to the Dean. David was right.

John Kingsley looked surprised. 'Oh, no. Not him.' He led
them into the sitting room. 'Tea?' he offered automatically.

'Yes, please. But what's happened, Daddy? Do tell us.'

Tea forgotten, the Canon sank into his chair. 'It's the
organist, Ivor Jones. He's dead. His daily found him this
morning.'

'Good Lord.' David leaned forward, speaking for the first
time. 'But . . . what? How did it happen?'

Swallowing painfully, John Kingsley turned to him. 'He . . .
killed himself. A bottle of sleeping tablets.'

'Oh.' There was a moment of silence as the news sank in.

When John Kingsley spoke again, it was so quietly that for a
moment they were not sure they'd heard him correctly. 'I blame
myself.'

'What did you say, Daddy?' Lucy frowned.

'I blame myself,' he repeated, taking off his spectacles and
rubbing the bridge of his nose. 'Oh, my dears, I should have

done something. I should have spoken up. Perhaps he'd still be alive if . . .'

'Whatever are you talking about?' In her concern, she spoke more sharply than she'd meant to; her father flinched.

Starting from the beginning, he related to them the story of the previous afternoon, sparing none of the painful details. 'So you see, my dears, we were all to blame – all of us who were there, and said nothing. We all allowed it to happen – we allowed him to be . . . hounded to death!'

'But that's monstrous!' David, agitated, would have said more, but Lucy intervened.

'Of course you mustn't blame yourself, Daddy,' she asserted. 'There's only one person to blame, and that's the Dean. How could you have known what would happen?'

Her father sighed and shook his head. 'I should have known. And that's not really the point – I should have done something in any case. I should have gone round to see him later . . .'

'But what's going to happen *now*?' David demanded. 'What is the Dean going to do about it?'

Removing his spectacles again, the Canon said quietly, 'I know it's unchristian of me to say this, but . . . Stuart Latimer is not a nice man.'

'Not a nice man?' exclaimed David. 'Good Lord! That's the understatement of the year. He's an absolute . . .'

'He is not a nice man,' John Kingsley repeated with slightly more emphasis. 'He is a bully and a tyrant.' He told them, then, about the Chapter meeting, and the way that Canon Brydges-ffrench had been reduced to tears by the Dean's deliberate cruelty. 'I'm not sure what he means to do with this cathedral,' he concluded, 'but I am fairly sure that none of us is going to like it.'

The doorbell rang; Lucy answered it to find Pat Willoughby on the front step. 'Lucy! I'm glad you're here,' Pat said. 'I've come to have a word with your father. Is there a cup of tea going, or do I need to make some?'

'We were going to have some, but we never got around to it. David and I haven't been here long.' Lucy stood back gratefully as the older woman took over with typical brisk efficiency, going straight to the kitchen and filling the kettle.

John Kingsley rose from his chair as Pat carried the tray into the sitting room. 'Pat! You should have let me do that.'

'Nonsense, John. Sit down and I'll pour you a cup.'

He obeyed, and after greeting David she dispensed tea all around. Pat was behaving much as she always did, Lucy observed, but she seemed to have acquired a few extra lines on her face in just a week, and her grey knot of hair was a bit more dishevelled than usual. Now she tucked a few stray strands in, absent-mindedly, as she came to the point of her visit. 'It's a terrible business, this.'

'I feel so guilty, Pat,' John Kingsley confessed. 'I should have done something.'

'Nonsense, John,' she repeated robustly. 'We were *all* there, we all heard it. If you're guilty, we *all* are.' But her eyes were suspiciously misty as she spoke. 'Anyway, I don't know what anyone could have done. Ivor Jones was an odd, secretive little man. None of us really knew him. He always kept himself to himself, never really mixed with the rest of the Close.'

'Maybe *that* was our fault, too. Maybe we never made him welcome,' the Canon suggested.

'You must stop blaming yourself,' insisted Pat. 'We all know who's to blame – I need not mention his name.' Her face took on a harder look at the thought of the Dean. 'That man has a great deal to answer for. None of it was true, you know,' she added.

'The . . . allegations?' asked David the solicitor. 'The things the Dean said?'

'That's right.' She hesitated a moment, then revealed, 'Inspector Drewitt has been to see George. He showed him, in confidence, the suicide note.'

John Kingsley's face creased with pain. 'Can you tell us what it said?'

'I probably shouldn't, but I will,' she decided. 'He categorically denied everything that the Dean accused him of. And I believe him,' she added. 'He also said that he didn't want his funeral at the cathedral, where "that man" would have anything to do with it. The ignominy – the stigma. He just couldn't cope with it.'

'The poor man,' Lucy whispered, near tears. 'How he must have suffered.'

'Mike Drewitt told George something else,' Pat went on briskly, perceiving that John Kingsley was about to break down. 'It seems that he knew Ivor Jones rather better than the rest of us.'

David raised his eyebrows at this intriguing statement. 'How so?'

'Apparently he'd had the odd pint of beer with him, at the Monk's Head. After Evensong, occasionally, when the Inspector had been ringing. It appears that the two men found that they had something in common – wife trouble.'

'Ivor Jones has a wife?' gaped Lucy. 'Did you know that?'

'*Had* a wife. And no, none of us knew it. No one but Mike Drewitt, that is. He was ashamed, I think. She'd left him before he came here. And he'd told the inspector that before that she'd . . . well, you can imagine. Run around with other men, that sort of thing. And apparently she had a drink problem as well. I don't know if you've met Mike Drewitt's wife Val . . .'

'Yes,' Lucy remembered. 'I met her once, or at least saw her. She wasn't . . . what I'd expected.'

'No,' Pat agreed bluntly. 'I think he must have said something to Ivor Jones about her, about Val, and after the organist had had one too many pints, he spilled out his own problems.'

'The poor man,' Lucy repeated. 'It was . . . unconscionable . . . of the Dean to say anything without checking out the facts first. Can't anything be done?'

'Ah, well. That remains to be seen.' Pat refilled David's tea cup. 'I've just taken George to the station. He's caught the 3.32 to London – he's going to Lambeth Palace.'

David leaned forward. 'He's going to see the Archbishop about it?'

'Yes, first thing in the morning – he phoned ahead for an appointment. And on Monday he's going to see the Prime Minister's Appointments Secretary, and possibly the PM as well. I don't know if they can do anything, but it's worth a try. After all, they got us into this mess.'

'George will be away all weekend?' asked Canon Kingsley. 'Won't there be things to . . . see to?'

'Actually, John, that's one reason I'm here,' Pat admitted. 'George asked me to see you. He would have come himself, of course, but he had to rush to catch the train.'

The Canon sighed. 'What does he want me to do?'

'Well, first I must tell you that George spoke to the Dean before he went. The Dean rang him, in fact. To say that he doesn't want any fuss made in the cathedral over all this.'

'What?' David was indignant. 'He has a lot of nerve.'

Pat smiled grimly. 'You can say that again. Anyway, George thought that it would be . . . appropriate . . . to do something, especially as there won't be a funeral at the cathedral.'

'Did he tell the Dean that?' John Kingsley asked.

'He told the Dean that he wanted some mention made – some sort of commemoration – at tomorrow morning's eight o'clock service. The Dean said that it must be kept completely simple. No choir, no bells, nothing to draw attention to it. And as we all know,' she said with ill-concealed bitterness, 'the Dean is in charge.'

'What does George want me to do?' Canon Kingsley repeated.

Pat observed him keenly. 'You'll be taking the service as usual, won't you? George said that you'd know what to do. He's relying on you, John – to do the right thing, he said.'

After Pat had gone, John Kingsley turned a troubled face to his daughter, sitting with David on the sofa. 'Lucy dear, I don't know what to do,' he confessed.

'What do you mean?'

'Surely you're not going to let the Dean intimidate you?' David demanded indignantly. 'He has no right!'

'Oh, no, not that.' The Canon smiled, a manifestation of his gentle strength. 'No, I don't care what the Dean says. But don't you see? The man committed suicide.' He took off his spectacles; his eyes were misted with tears. 'I just don't know what to do tomorrow, what to say. I was brought up to consider suicide a sin – an unforgivable sin.' He rubbed his eyes; impulsively Lucy reached out and put a comforting hand on his knee. 'But now, my dears . . . I just don't know. I think . . .' he hesitated. 'I think that, really, the only sin is . . . not trusting God.'

Chapter 16

*My song shall be of mercy and judgement: unto thee, O
Lord, will I sing.*

Psalm 101.1

For Lucy it was the kind of night in which it seems at
the time as if one is not sleeping at all, but in retrospect
is filled with bizarre, half-remembered dreams. She had not
known Ivor Jones well: she had only met him once or twice,
and on those occasions he had not made a great impression
on her. She remembered him only as a silent presence, a
small, dark, taciturn Welshman; the information Pat had
imparted about his wayward wife cast only a small amount
of illumination, making him scarcely less a cipher in death
than he had been in life. But the futility and the injustice of
his death had struck her as forcibly as it had the others in
the Close, and her father's anguished feelings of guilt disturbed her deeply. Again and again through the restless night
she wished that she could go to David, and find comfort in
his arms. But she was stopped by the realisation that her
father's sleep was probably as troubled as hers, and he would
surely hear.

Towards dawn, though, her door opened silently, and a
dressing-gowned David appeared beside her.

'Ssh!' she whispered as he squeezed next to her in the single
bed. 'My father will hear.'

'He's downstairs already. He's been pacing in his study for
nearly an hour. My room's above the study, and I could hear
him.'

'Oh!' Lucy sat up. 'I must go to him, then. He needs me. I
should make him some tea, or some breakfast.'

'Not so fast, Lucy love.' He sat up as well and put his arms
around her. 'Stay here with me just a minute more. *I* need you,
too.'

121

Sighing, she laid her head on his shoulder. 'We need each other,' she amended.

'As I keep saying.' He stroked her sleep-tousled curls; with her hair framing her face in a rosy halo, and dressed in a high-necked, long-sleeved nightdress of virginal white eyelet, she looked absurdly, heartbreakingly young. 'Marry me, Lucy?' It was half a demand, half a query, but said with the hopeless air of one who did not expect an affirmative reply.

He didn't receive one; neither did he receive an outright refusal. She shook her head negatively, but all she said was, 'Just hold me, David.'

A short while later, sombrely dressed, they sat in the kitchen, drinking tea. John Kingsley had gone off to the cathedral at about seven o'clock, too upset to talk to them, too upset to do anything but sit in the Quire and think about what he would say in his sermon. A rack of toast sat between them on the table, untouched. Lucy had made it, mostly just to keep busy; David always fasted before Communion, and in any case neither of them felt like eating.

'We both knew that something . . . unpleasant . . . was bound to happen,' said Lucy. 'But did you ever think that it would happen so soon? Within the week?'

'No.' He rubbed his eyes wearily and sipped his tea.

She attempted a wan smile. 'Well, at least it's over now. Maybe things will settle down.'

'I wish I believed that.' David sighed. 'No, Lucy. It's not over. This wasn't the end – it was just the beginning. The Dean's not going anywhere, and as long as he's here . . .'

'Then you don't think . . . the Archbishop of Canterbury won't be able to do anything?'

David shook his head, putting his mug down none too gently. 'He can't intervene. It's too late for that.' Rising, he added, 'Come on, Lucy. It's half past seven – let's go over to the cathedral. I can't bear sitting around here any longer.'

Perversely, it was a beautiful morning: opposite John Kingsley's house the east end of the cathedral shimmered golden rather than grey in the early morning sun, rising like a great ship from the faint autumnal mist which lingered in the grass around it and amongst the buildings of the Close. Somewhere a bird sang, full-throated and joyous, with a sound so piercingly pure that no

122

Malbury chorister could ever hope to equal it. David and Lucy walked around the Close on the north side of the cathedral in silence, entering through the great west doors.

The service would be held in the Lady Chapel in the retro-choir, so it was in that direction that they went, along the north aisle and behind the Quire. The sun streamed through the east window, dappling the stone walls with colour and catching the gilding on the Comper English altar, setting it alight and haloing its angels with golden effulgence.

But the Comper angels were not alone in the chapel: two women were there already, arranging flowers on either side of the altar. One was Pat Willoughby, who looked up and greeted them briefly as she added a fragrant sprig of rosemary to the pedestal; her arrangement was simple and dignified, fashioned from what was available in her garden.

On the other side of the altar, surprisingly, was Rowena Hunt. She smiled at David first, then at Lucy, though her smile was subdued. 'I had to come,' she explained, indicating the flowers, an arrangement of expensive cut blooms. 'I . . . I was there on Thursday, after Evensong, and when Inspector Drewitt told me what had happened, I knew that I had to do something. The flowers from my drawing room – they were all that I had to offer.'

Guilt, reflected Lucy with surprise. It was not an emotion which sat easily on Rowena, but evidently it had affected in various measure all of those who had remained silent while a man's self-esteem, reputation – and ultimately his life – were publicly destroyed.

Inspector Drewitt himself appeared then, out of the shadows. Acknowledging Lucy and David with a nod, he said to Rowena, 'I'm going to go up to the tower. Someone should ring the passing bell. Looks like it's going to be me.'

Rowena frowned and, oblivious to the onlookers, put a restraining hand on his arm. 'Do you think you should, Mike? Don't you know that the Dean has forbidden any bells?'

With a short ironic bark of a laugh, he raised his eyebrows. 'So I've heard. But I'm a big boy now, Mrs Hunt. I can take care of myself.' He turned smartly on his heel and was gone before she could make any reply; she looked after him, chewing on her lip.

Tactfully Lucy and David withdrew, preparing to take seats for the service. But a solitary figure hurrying up from the south aisle intercepted them. For a moment Lucy failed to recognise Judith Greenwood: it was not just that she was wearing a long black dress that had once been elegant, though it was some years out of fashion and uncomfortably tight-fitting. More importantly, she moved with none of her usual tentative, self-effacing diffidence but instead like a woman who knew where she was going. 'Your father is taking the service?' she asked.

'Yes, that's right.'

'I need to see him. Now, before the service.' Her violet eyes, usually downcast, met Lucy's forthrightly.

'He's probably in the sacristy,' Lucy said. 'Why don't we go there and find him? David, if you want to find us some seats, I'll be back in a few minutes.' He nodded. Lucy led Judith Greenwood around into the choir aisle to the inconspicuous door leading to the sacristy. She tapped on the door. 'Daddy?'

'Come in, my dear,' replied John Kingsley in a quiet voice. As they entered he turned from his contemplation of the small crucifix on the wall. He was vested in readiness for the service, wearing his own old-fashioned white chasuble, one which he seldom wore: it had been given to him at his ordination by his beloved parish priest and it was beginning to show its age.

'Daddy, Mrs Greenwood wanted to see you.'

He smiled at Lucy, then took Judith Greenwood's hands and looked into the violet eyes. 'Yes, Judith?'

'I understand that there's to be no choir at the service,' she said, raising her chin. 'I should like to sing at the offertory.'

'Sing?' he echoed.

'I'll take full responsibility, if the Dean doesn't approve.'

'Oh, I'm not concerned about that. But . . .'

Judith smiled gravely. 'You don't know whether I'm capable or not, do you? I suppose you think, like everyone else, that Rupert is the only musical one in the family.' She paused, and squared her shoulders in the snug black dress. 'I am . . . I *was* . . . a professional singer,' she explained. 'I may be a bit out of practice, but I won't disgrace you. The organ scholar has agreed to accompany me on the chamber organ.'

'Yes, of course,' Canon Kingsley agreed without hesitation. 'I'm so pleased that you want to do it. And I'm sure that Rupert is pleased, as well.'

She looked back over her shoulder as she left the sacristy. 'Oh, Rupert doesn't know,' Judith said, smiling. 'I haven't told him.'

Lucy lingered a moment before following her. 'Are you all right, Daddy?' She looked at him anxiously, noting the dark circles under his eyes.

'I still don't know what I'm going to say,' he replied elliptically. 'But I have faith that the Holy Spirit will lead me. God hasn't let me down yet, not even ... when your dear mother died. He'll give me the words to say.' He bowed his head for a moment; the sunlight which found its way through the small grilled window struck silver sparks from his hair.

Lucy, loving him, searched for some words of reassurance, but in the end merely kissed his cheek. Just then the tenor bell began to ring: sonorously, ponderously, tolling desolately for a life cut short. The passing bell.

The chapel, Lucy found to her amazement, was overflowing with people. In the few minutes she'd been away they'd streamed in silently, filling every available seat of the small, shallow chapel. Pat Willoughby was there, of course, in the front row, with Evelyn Marsden, Judith Greenwood, and Olivia Ashleigh. Rowena had found a place beside Jeremy; Canon Thetford and his wife were both there. Victor and Bert sat near the back, looking far more subdued than she'd ever seen them, while Todd Randall and the bell-ringers had abandoned their customary casual garb, looking almost as respectable as Dorothy Unworth. Word had clearly spread throughout the Close and the town; a few of the choristers were there with their parents, and all of the lay clerks had come. As Lucy squeezed into her seat, jealously guarded by David, she realised that the only people missing were the Subdean and the Precentor. Odd, she thought, that they should allow themselves to be intimidated by the Dean when everyone else had turned out in defiance of him.

Lucy was wrong, however: the Subdean and the Precentor were present. Unable at the last minute to face the crowd, Arthur Brydges-ffrench had sought out his stall in the Quire, where he could pray in peace and hear the service from behind the reredos. Seeing him there, alone and with tears on his cheeks, Rupert Greenwood had joined him in his own adjacent stall, just to keep an eye on the older man.

The passing bell continued its hollow, sombre tolling; all else was silence. John Kingsley took his place before the altar and lifted his hands. 'The Lord be with you.'

* * *

Canon Kingsley was conscious of the many pairs of eyes fixed upon him as he rose to deliver his sermon. In the early hours of the morning he had made copious notes, but had discarded them all; now he merely folded his hands in front of him, and with a quick silent prayer, began.

'A few minutes ago I read to you the New Testament lesson, 1 Corinthians 13. It is a chapter that we all know well, from many weddings and other joyous occasions throughout the years. You may wonder why I've chosen that lesson for such a sad occasion as this, and why I'm now taking it as my text for this short meditation.

'"Though I speak with the tongues of men and of angels, and have not charity, I am become as sounding brass, or a tinkling cymbal."

'As familiar as this opening verse is, it is the final verse on which I'd like to concentrate. "And now abideth faith, hope, charity, these three; but the greatest of these is charity."

'Faith,' he said, 'comes first, before all. Without faith, there is nothing else. And to me, faith means trusting in God, trusting in Him through all the adversities of life. Sometimes one of the most difficult areas for trust is forgiveness. We can't bring ourselves to believe in God's forgiveness on a personal level – we want to believe that what we've done is so horrendous, so sinful that God cannot possibly forgive us. This, my friends, is in itself a serious sin, perhaps the worst sin, for it shows a lack of faith, a lack of trust in His all-encompassing love.' He paused, looking around.

'Today we are remembering a life that has been lost. Some might say that the manner of that death has placed the man beyond God's forgiveness: to take one's own life shows a depth of despair that must exclude faith. But I would say to you that nothing can place us beyond God's forgiveness, not even our own feeling that we are unforgiven or unforgivable. No sin is too great for His love to wipe out, whether we are able to accept it or not.

'Some of us – many of us – may feel a measure of guilt, of complicity in what has happened to Ivor Jones. Guilt that we didn't get to know him better when he was here among us, and guilt that we were somehow involved in his death through our silence. But through this guilt, in which I share, there is hope of a closer relationship with God through forgiveness.

'That brings us to hope, the second in the trio of virtues. You may think that there is not much to inspire hope in the events that have brought us here today. But again, God is bigger than our imaginations, and is always able to bring good out of evil. Ivor Jones's death may yet result in good, if we are able to put it behind us and travel on together in hope. In hope, that is, that the clouds of suspicion and fear that have lingered over this cathedral recently can and will be dispelled by God's love.

'And so to charity, the greatest of all. Charity, also translated as love. For it is charity that we are all called upon to exercise now. Charity towards each other, towards our brother Ivor Jones, and above all towards the man whom many of us hold responsible for what has happened.' There was a collective indrawn breath and for a moment John Kingsley stood silent, meeting the eyes of the congregation one by one. When he continued his voice was quiet but firm. 'We all know that I am speaking of Stuart Latimer. An action of his triggered the events that resulted in Ivor Jones's death. I'm sure that the Dean regrets this as much as anyone – much more, perhaps, since he must surely bear it on his conscience. And so, in Christian charity, we must forgive the Dean, as God has forgiven him, and work with him to ensure that nothing of this kind will ever again happen in Malbury. We must rise above our own personal interests and put the interests of the cathedral first. Or perhaps I should say the interests of God, for He is why we are all here. If this is our aim, we cannot fail, for He will be with us in all that we do. "For now we see through a glass, darkly; but then face to face: now I know in part; but then shall I know even as also I am known. And now abideth faith, hope, charity, these three; but the greatest of these is charity."'

In the Quire, Arthur Brydges-ffrench sobbed quietly; Rupert Greenwood knelt beside him, patting his arm. The words of the sermon had come through the reredos clearly, but the Subdean had broken down in tears during the Creed. Now it was time the offertory. The chamber organ played a few bars of introduction, and 'I know that my redeemer liveth', a soprano voice sang suddenly. It was a voice both pure and rich, bursting with hope and faith, and it filled the cathedral with its glorious lambent golden sound, soaring to the fan vaulting, cascading down the walls, and echoing round the pillars. For a moment everyone in the cathedral was transfixed with the beauty of it. 'Yet in my flesh shall I see God . . .'

'Judith?' Rupert whispered in astonished recognition. 'Good Heavens – Judith . . .'

Chapter 17

*Lord, how are they increased that trouble me: many are they
that rise against me.*

Psalm 3.1

After the final blessing, John Kingsley made his way back to
the sacristy, followed shortly by his daughter. 'Daddy, it was
wonderful,' she said impulsively, hugging him. 'You said
exactly the right thing.'

'Did I? I can't really remember what I said – just that it
seemed right at the time.'

'What do you mean?'

'Well,' he said slowly, considering his words, 'the best way I
can describe it is like a gramophone record, with God at the
centre. The centre is still, but the record spins around, and the
farther you are from the centre the faster you spin. That's what
I was doing earlier, spinning around the outside of the gramophone record, trying to make sense of it all on my own terms.
But when I got up to speak I let God carry me towards the
centre, and the nearer I got the more certain I was that He
was in control. There's tremendous peace in letting go like
that.'

Canon Kingsley, with Lucy, returned to the Lady Chapel as
soon as possible to greet the retiring congregation. A number of
people had left already: the lay clerks had slipped out
immediately after the service, and the choristers and their
parents had gone. Victor and Bert had rushed back to the shop,
and Dorothy Unworth to the refectory. Pat Willoughby circulated among those who were left with an invitation: 'Do come
back to my kitchen for a bit of breakfast. It won't be anything
fancy . . .'

Most accepted with alacrity, but Evelyn Marsden hesitated.
Throughout the service she had been craning her neck

discreetly, searching for Canon Brydges-ffrench. 'I'm concerned about Arthur,' she admitted. 'I was sure that he would have come – I saw him set out from his house, but he doesn't seem to be here.'

'I think,' said Pat, 'that he might be in the Quire. I heard some noises coming from that direction.'

'Ah.' Evelyn sighed in relief. 'In that case, I'm afraid I shall have to decline your kind invitation. Arthur will need looking after – I shall take him home and feed him.'

'He's included in the invitation, of course.'

'Very kind,' Evelyn repeated, 'but I don't think he should be with other people just now. I'll see to him.'

'Perhaps that *would* be best,' agreed Pat.

Evelyn hurried off towards the Quire as Rowena paused and spoke to Pat. 'Mike . . . Inspector Drewitt . . . has been up in the tower, tolling the passing bell. I assume he's invited as well?'

'Yes, of course.' Pat's face, well-schooled as it was, betrayed nothing of her curiosity at Rowena's telling question, and the degree of intimacy exposed by her unintentional use of the Inspector's Christian name. 'Will you let him know? I'd be most grateful.'

'Yes, I'll do that.' As Rowena turned to go, Pat's eyebrows rose a fraction. Rowena and Mike Drewitt? she asked herself, filing it away for future reference.

Approaching the door to the spiral staircase in the south transept which led eventually to the tower, Rowena stopped and drew back as she saw the compact figure of the Dean moving in the same direction with a determined stride. He reached the doorway just as Mike Drewitt emerged from the staircase.

'Were you responsible for ringing the bell just now?' the Dean demanded belligerently, drawing his brows together.

Mike Drewitt's face was impassive. 'Yes, Dean.'

'Were you aware that I had forbidden the bells to be rung, Inspector?'

Calculating that it would infuriate the Dean even more, he took his time in answering. 'Well,' he said at last, deliberately, 'today *is* the feast day of St Faith. I couldn't let that go by without ringing the bells.'

'That's ridiculous! Have you ever rung the bells for St Faith before? In other years?'

'Well, no,' drawled Inspector Drewitt. 'But you can be sure that I will from now on. Every year, as a commemoration of what's gone on here today, Dean.'

The Dean went purple. From Rowena's vantage point, they were almost ludicrously mismatched: powerfully-built Drewitt, standing on the last step, towered over the Dean, emphasising his small stature. And Drewitt's amused composure made the Dean seem like nothing so much as a spoiled child, insisting on his own way. 'I've had enough of your insolent behaviour!' snapped Stuart Latimer, contriving to seem menacing but sounding only petulant and childish.

Mike Drewitt smiled, showing his teeth. 'I'm not answerable to you for my behaviour. You may be able to bully everyone else around here, but you don't frighten me with your tough talk. So if you'll excuse me . . .' He pushed past the Dean and strode off towards Rowena.

Although the sun was shining, it was a chilly morning, and the Aga in Pat's kitchen threw off a welcome warmth. It was a large room, but the heat from the stove made it cosy; the red quarry-tiled floor was covered with colourful woven throw-rugs and dotted about in the corners with a cheerful clutter of green wellies and dog dishes. The dogs themselves, Cain and Abel, joined their mistress in welcoming her guests, bestowing indiscriminate sloppy kisses as Pat collected coats and jackets and handed out mugs of steaming coffee. Trays of bacon were waiting in the Aga, and soon everyone was feasting on thick slabs of juicy bacon wedged into fresh bread rolls, served on paper napkins to save on the washing up. People who, an hour earlier, might have said that they weren't in the least in the mood for food – wouldn't be able to imagine eating that day, in fact – suddenly found themselves ravenous when faced with Pat's bacon rolls.

'I haven't forgotten that you're a vegetarian,' Pat assured Lucy, giving her instead a warm roll with melted cheese. 'And there's plenty of fruit, as well.'

'You don't know what you're missing,' stated David with relish, biting into his bacon roll. 'This is wonderful.'

Lucy eyed it. 'I must admit, it looks good – almost enough to turn me back into a carnivore. I think I need some moral support – where are the Thetfords?' She looked around for the

131

vegetarian canon and his wife. 'Or should I say the Thetford-Fairbrothers?'

'I don't think they're coming,' said Pat. She surveyed the gathered company; Judith Greenwood, pale in her black dress, sat alone at one end of the scrubbed pine table; her husband had collared John Kingsley and was hovering near the Aga, discussing the procedure for replacing the organist. 'Excuse me a moment,' Pat added. 'I want to have a word with Judith.'

Judith looked up with a smile. 'The food is lovely. It's very kind of you to do this.'

'Not at all.' Pat drew up a chair and lowered herself to Judith's level. 'I just wanted to tell you how marvellous your singing was, my dear. Quite extraordinary. Thank you so much for doing it.'

Blushing, Judith lowered her head. 'I . . . I wanted to. I *had* to, in a way.'

Pat regarded her appraisingly for a moment. 'Why,' she said gently, 'have we never heard you sing before, my dear? What a talent you've been hiding under a bushel!'

When Judith answered, there was a surprising note of bitterness in her voice. 'Why?' she replied. 'Because there are no women in the cathedral choir. Because there are no opportunities in a place like Malbury for a female singer.' She paused, looking down at her hands on the table, and started again more softly. 'When we lived in London, just after we were married, I did a lot of singing. With some of the professional early music groups, mostly – ensemble work, solo work, even one or two recordings. I . . . I loved it. It gave a real purpose to my life. But here in Malbury . . . there's nothing for me. Here I'm only . . . Rupert's wife. Less than that, even: the Precentor's wife.'

Impulsively, Pat covered the young woman's hands with her own and gave them a brief squeeze, thinking of the unspoken component to Judith's problem, her childlessness – a pain that she had also suffered, and had dealt with in her own way. It could never be mentioned, of course, but it gave her a real feeling of empathy for the young woman; her voice, when she spoke, was matter-of-fact, practical. 'I know what you mean, Judith. It's something every clergyman's wife has to come to terms with, in one way or another. It's been easier for me, of course – I've got my garden, and my dogs, and I've been happy here in Malbury. Partly it's my generation, as well – it's not so easy for you young ones. You're better educated, more qualified than we were. I'll tell you what,' she added briskly. 'You ought to have a chat with Lucy Kingsley. She's not a clergyman's wife, but she's near your age, and she's a woman who's managed to do something with her life in spite of a few . . . setbacks.'

'*And* she lives in London, not Malbury. I don't know how she could help. I don't know what *anyone* can do to help.' Judith looked up suddenly. 'But yes, I think I *will* talk to her. It can't hurt. She's nice. And it would be good to . . . just to have a friend.'

Pat's kind heart contracted with pity, and with guilt that she hadn't done more to make this lonely young woman feel more welcome in Malbury, in the Close. She'd spent years traversing the diocese from one corner to the other, cossetting various clergy wives; here was one under her very nose, desperately hurting, and she'd failed her. She hadn't even known that Judith could sing . . . Cain, the black dog, pushed a large wet nose into her hand, recalling her from her pensive mood. 'Good boy,' she said absently, scratching his ears, then, wasting no time, she got up and led Judith to where Lucy stood with David. 'I was just telling Judith what a marvellous treat it was to hear her sing,' she addressed them.

In a moment Lucy and Judith were deep in conversation, and Pat moved on to dispense more food; efficient Olivia had seamlessly taken over while she'd been with Judith, but after all it was *her* kitchen. David was disappointed: the dinner party that had been the reason for the weekend trip to Malbury had of course been cancelled, and he'd hoped to have the chance for a long chat with Pat. Feeling distinctly superfluous, he wandered over to Todd Randall, whom he'd met at the garden party with Kirsty Hunt. The tall young American, with the golden Labrador lying contentedly at his feet, looked faintly ridiculous, standing as he was under the wooden clothes-drying rack which was suspended from the ceiling. His head nearly grazed a pair of the Bishop's enormous spotted drawers, giving David a conversational opening. 'I see that he doesn't wear purple underneath it all.'

Todd looked blank, then, glancing upward, grinned in appreciation. 'Green polka-dots. Not really what you'd expect of a Bishop, is it? Where *is* the Bishop, by the way?' he added.

That recalled David to the solemn occasion that had brought them there. 'In London, I believe,' he replied circumspectly.

That led on to a discussion of the events of the last few days, a subject which most of the people present in Pat's kitchen were trying to avoid, having talked of nothing else for the past twenty-four hours.

'It's a real shame about the organist,' said the young man ingenuously. 'He was an okay guy, I thought. Not very friendly, but I guess maybe he was just shy.'

David thought aloud; there was something that had been bothering him, nagging at his legal brain, since John Kingsley had recounted the story to them the day before. 'The one thing I don't understand,' he said, 'is why the Dean thought that Ivor Jones was . . . interfering with the choirboys. From what I hear, he accused him outright. And if it wasn't true, he can't have had any evidence. What would even give him the idea?'

Todd's placid forehead wrinkled in concentration. 'I'll bet I know the answer to that,' he offered. 'Last Saturday, at the garden party, Kirsty and I were sitting with the bell-ringers, having a beer. The Dean came along, and got kind of nasty with us, mostly about the beer and stuff. He said that we were a disgrace, if you can believe it. All we were doing was having a few beers! So Barry, one of the bell-ringers, got pretty mad, and said to the Dean that the real scandal was happening down in the cathedral. I'll bet that's what gave him the idea. He was just looking for trouble after that, I guess.'

'Good Lord. I wonder what they meant?' David absorbed the story thoughtfully, then with determination attempted to lighten up the conversation. 'Kirsty's not here today?' he asked.

'No, she's gone back to Cambridge. She left yesterday morning.'

'Oh, that's right. She did say that it was her last week in Malbury before term started. Did she . . .' He hesitated delicately. 'Has she decided to go on with the Law, or is she still planning to change her course?'

'She's going to read Theology,' Todd said. 'Her mind was made up.'

'Well, I rather thought so when I talked to her. I don't know why her mother thought it would do any good for me to talk to her about it,' David added self-consciously. 'I felt a right prat doing it, too. But her mother insisted.'

'Yeah, Rowena's like that.' Todd laughed easily. 'Not the easiest mom in the world for poor old Kirsty.'

'You'll miss her, I expect.'

'Oh, yeah. We've sort of hung out together this summer, I guess you'd say. Just friends. No strings or anything like that – I've got a girlfriend back home in Springfield. But Kirsty's a nice kid.'

'What exactly are you doing here in Malbury? I'm not really clear on that.'

'Oh, I'm spending a couple of semesters on leave from my theology studies. Helping Canon Brydges-ffrench to catalogue his papers, and working with him on a couple of research projects. One of my professors knew Canon Brydges-ffrench a long time ago, and set it up for me. It's been real interesting. I've always wanted to see England.'

'You live in the Close?'

'Yeah, I lodge with Evelyn – Miss Marsden. She's a real nice lady, and a good cook.'

'And have you seen much of the country?' David asked.

'Not as much as I'd like. I spend most of my time stuck in Malbury.' The young man made a wry face. 'Some weekends I manage to get away, take a train someplace and see some sights.'

'If you're ever in London,' David heard himself saying somewhat against his better judgement – but he liked the forthright young American – 'do look us up in South Kensington. We'd be happy to show you around a bit. I know a few nice churches . . .'

Todd grinned with pleasure. 'Why, that's really nice of you, David! I might just take you up on that one of these days.'

At about the same time, Lucy was writing down her address on a spare paper napkin for Judith Greenwood. 'You must come and see me some time,' she said. 'Any time.'

'Does that invitation go for me as well?' asked Jeremy, strolling up, eyebrows raised.

Judith scuttled away shyly, leaving Lucy alone with him. 'Well, I'm not so sure about that.'

'You're a hardhearted woman, Lucy Kingsley.' His voice was lightly mocking.

'That's what they all say,' she laughed.

'All of your discarded suitors? Are they all as goodlooking as me? Or as persistent as me?'

'No,' she said. 'You're in a class of your own, Jeremy Bartlett.'

'Good.' His expression grew serious. 'Honestly, Lucy, I would like to see you some time.'

'It's just not possible,' she stated quietly.

'Because of David?'

'Because of David.' Deciding that it was perhaps the time for some painful honesty, she looked at him squarely. 'You see, Jeremy, David and I . . .'

'David and she have to be going,' the man in question interrupted, coming up from behind and taking her arm. 'Lucy,' he addressed her, 'I've just promised Pat that we'd take those daft dogs of hers for a walk, and get them out from underfoot. It was either that or washing up the coffee cups, and you know how I hate washing up.'

'Goodbye, Jeremy,' Lucy said, shamefully glad to be reprieved. 'I'll see you again soon.' And to deflect David's questions about her conversation with Jeremy, she began with a diversionary tactic. 'Do you *see* Rowena over in that corner with Mike Drewitt?' she asked as they collared the wayward dogs. 'Just like that day at Fortnum's – *now* do you believe me?'

Breakfast at the Deanery that morning was a quiet affair. As was customary on the occasions when they were both at home, Stuart Latimer and his wife breakfasted in the dining room, distanced from each other by the length of the polished mahogany dining table. The central heating had not yet been switched on, and the blinds had been pulled against the intrusive sun – which did no good to the furniture, and nothing but harm to the carpet – so there was a definite chill in the air.

They began as always with muesli, purchased expensively in London, while Anne Latimer discussed the morning post. 'One or two tradesmen's bills,' she said. 'Which reminds me – *are* we going to be able to find a decent butcher here in Malbury? We can manage with everything else, but it's a bit of a nuisance to have all the meat sent from London.'

'I'll ask the Bishop,' promised the Dean.

'Or his wife,' she suggested, glancing again at the post.

'Letters from the boys?' asked Stuart Latimer; their two sons were boarders at Marlborough and wrote dutiful weekly letters which usually arrived on Saturday.

'From Christopher. He says that Stephen's had a tummy bug. Nothing serious, I'm sure, or the school would have let us know.'

'I'm sure.' He tried to sound hearty and reassuring.

Anne Latimer plucked a crustless triangle of toast from the silver rack beside her plate; the large stone in her ring glittered down the length of the table at her husband like the eye of some great dead fish. For a moment the only sounds in the room were the ticking of the carriage clock on the mantelpiece and the dry rasp of the knife spreading a thin glaze of Flora on the toast.

The Dean cleared his throat. 'Bad business about the organist.'

His wife put down her knife. 'Since you brought the matter up,' she said coldly, 'I have something to say to you about that.'

'Yes?' He clenched his hands together, trying to hide his nervousness.

'I heard all about it yesterday, Stuart. About what *you* did to trigger his suicide. From my cleaning woman! My cleaning woman!' she repeated for emphasis, her voice maintaining its genteel chilliness. 'Do you realise how embarrassing that was? To find out from my *cleaning woman* what my husband had been up to, and to learn that the entire Close is talking about him? That they all hate him, and want him to go back where he came from? Stuart, that's just not on!'

'I'm sorry, Anne. I should have told you.'

'It's not good enough, Stuart.' She raised her chin and glared at him defiantly. 'Daddy stuck his neck out, and called in a lot of favours, to get this job for you – this bloody cathedral in the back end of beyond that you wanted so badly! – and in the space of a week you've managed to ruin it!' She tapped her manicured fingers on the polished table, waiting for a reply, but the uncharacteristic profanity had shocked him into silence. After a moment she continued, 'Daddy will not be pleased to hear about this, Stuart. He will not be at all pleased. I shall leave this afternoon for London. I must ask Daddy what can be done to salvage this appalling situation.'

Stuart Latimer bowed his head, silently acquiescent.

Chapter 18

*All thine enemies shall feel thy hand: thy right hand shall
find out them that hate thee.*

Psalm 21.8

Late one evening the following week, the day of the Bishop's
return from London, John Kingsley opened his door in
response to the bell to find his old friend on the doorstep,
his breath hanging in frosty white puffs like clouds of
incense wreathing his genial face. 'Come in, George,' the
Canon greeted him, beckoning him indoors. 'Cold, isn't
it?'

'Bitter, especially for this time of year,' he confirmed. 'It's not
too late for you, is it, John?'

'No, not at all. I was just going to have a cup of cocoa – would
you like to join me?'

'Sounds just the thing,' the Bishop agreed. He divested
himself of his tatty old sheepskin jacket and his even tattier
college scarf and hung them over the bannister, following John
Kingsley into the kitchen.

The Canon found two mismatched mugs while the milk
heated. 'What brings you out on a cold night like this, George?
Not that it isn't always a pleasure to see you.'

'I think you can guess.' The Bishop blew on his chilled
fingers. 'Pat sent me – she thought that I ought to tell you about
what happened in London. I would have come in any case, of
course, but I probably would have waited till daylight.'

'Good trip?'

'Oh, as good as could be expected. I don't really like London,
you know,' he admitted. 'Much too dirty and crowded for my
taste. Give me Malbury any day, John.' He added, 'And I hate
leaving Pat, even for a few days. I'm glad it doesn't have to
happen very often.'

'The train was all right, then?'

139

'Could have been worse.' The Bishop grinned. 'You'll never guess who travelled back on the same train.'

'Surprise me.'

'Mrs Latimer.'

John Kingsley looked bemused. 'You didn't have to sit with her, did you?'

'Good heavens, no!' The Bishop laughed his rumbling belly-laugh. 'She was travelling first class. The Latimers may be able to afford that sort of nonsense, but Pat would have my guts for garters if I tried putting on those kind of airs. No, as it happens, I didn't see her until we were getting off the train, and we shared a taxi back to the Close. I would have walked, of course, but she insisted. Not befitting my dignity as a bishop to walk, she said!' He laughed again. 'Can you imagine?'

They carried their mugs into the sitting room and made themselves comfortable. 'So,' said John Kingsley. 'How did it go at Lambeth Palace?'

Bishop George shook his head. 'Well, it was about what I expected. But the long and short of it is, we're stuck with Stuart Latimer. For as long as he chooses to stay.'

His friend sighed. 'Yes, I thought so.'

'Not that the Archbishop wasn't completely sympathetic,' the Bishop added. 'But there's nothing he can do. Just "continue to monitor the situation", whatever that means.' He pulled a wry face. 'You know and I know – and the Archbishop knows – that Stuart Latimer was directly responsible for a man's death. But unless the Dean actually commits cold-blooded murder, no one can touch him. The Archbishop told me in confidence,' he went on, 'that it was a real set-up job, the appointment. As you know, Deans are always appointed by the Crown, which means, of course, the Prime Minister. Mrs Latimer's father had been angling for a Cabinet post after the last General Election but didn't get one, and according to the Archbishop, this was his consolation prize from the PM – a Deanship for his son-in-law. So once the Reverend Mr Latimer decided he wanted to come to Malbury, it was a foregone conclusion. And the Prime Minister isn't answerable to anyone for the appointment – it can't even be raised in Parliament, either before or after the event.'

'So where does that leave us?'

The Bishop regarded him shrewdly. 'Well, John, our

positions are slightly different. I can't do anything *but* stay out of it, which in a way makes it easier for me. But you're a member of the Chapter. You have to deal with the man, to make it all work one way or another. Do you think you can do that?'

Looking into his cup, John Kingsley formulated his careful reply. 'I shall have to. I don't like the man – I don't like what he stands for, or the way he operates, let alone what he's done. And you know me, George – there aren't many people I can't get on with! But for the sake of the cathedral, I shall have to work with him.'

'What about the rest of the Chapter?'

The Canon shook his head. 'I don't know. It's not a very hopeful situation. From what I've been able to gather, he's already double-crossed both Philip and Rupert by reneging on promises he made to them before he got the appointment, and they both loathe him for that. They're not likely to come around. And poor old Arthur, of course, will never be reconciled.'

'How is Arthur doing?'

'Not well at all. He takes it all as a personal insult. I don't think he will ever come to terms with being passed over for the appointment.' John Kingsley lowered his voice. 'To be perfectly honest, George, as much as I hate to say it, the way that Arthur has been behaving recently makes me realise that perhaps it was just as well he *didn't* get the appointment. Perhaps he's a little too emotionally unstable to make a good Dean.'

'You may be right. What . . .' the Bishop hesitated delicately. 'What can be done about Arthur? As long as he's in such a state, he's not doing anyone any good, himself included.'

The Canon took his spectacles off and rubbed his eyes. 'I've been giving it a lot of prayerful thought lately. And I think that perhaps it would be best for everyone – best for Arthur himself – if he were to . . . retire. Resign. He's over sixty. He could take retirement now quite respectably, and no one would think any the worse of him for it. If he stays on here, with the way things are now – and seem likely to continue – he will only make himself ill, and possibly even have a nervous breakdown. For his own good he should go of his own free will, before he cracks up and has to go, or before the Dean finds some way of getting rid of him. Which I have no doubt he will do in time, and probably sooner rather than later,' he added.

Bishop George nodded, relieved. 'Yes, you're right, John. That would be best. Do you think that perhaps you . . . might have a word with Arthur? Try to make him see the wisdom of it? He'd take it from you – he knows that you have his best interests at heart.'

Canon Kingsley bowed his head, his eyes closed, as if in prayer. At last he said, heavily, 'It's a great deal to ask of me, but I shall try.' Forcing a smile, he made an attempt at humour. 'But you'd better watch out, George. Now that I've practically got a solicitor in the family, you may find me suing you for misrepresentation! Remember when you talked me into taking this job? You said that it would be a nice easy way to end my career.' He paused to deliver the punch line. 'Believe me, George – in spite of the occasional power-hungry church-warden, megalomaniac lay reader or temperamental organist, parish ministry was never like *this*!'

That same evening, predictably, around the bend of the Close at the Deanery, another dialogue was taking place.

Stuart Latimer, never much of a believer in the restorative powers of cocoa, had poured himself a stiff drink to help him through the evening. His wife permitted herself only a small dry sherry, to aid her digestion and to combat the chill of the Deanery drawing room.

'Your father is well?' he asked with false heartiness. Strategically, he had chosen the most massive chair in the room.

'Daddy is very well.' She decided on a full frontal attack, hoping to catch him unprepared. 'At least he *was*, until he heard about what has been going on in Malbury.'

The Dean groaned inwardly. So it was to begin already – clearly no quarter was to be given. Hoping to postpone the evil moment, he tried to turn it into a joke. 'Why – did he know Ivor Jones?'

Her scathing response was what he deserved. 'Don't be ridiculous, Stuart. That's *not* funny. It's in the worst possible taste, under the circumstances.'

'Sorry.' He wasn't, really – only sorry that it hadn't worked.

'If you're not going to take this seriously, I might just as well have stayed in London for a few more days – do you think I *like* being in this godforsaken place, or intend to spend any more time here than is absolutely necessary?' she demanded, then went on with cold dignity, 'Do you or do you not want to know what Daddy had to say about the mess you've got yourself into?'

There was nothing for it, he realised. He was going to have to take his medicine. With a quick gulp of his drink to fortify him, he said humbly, 'What did Daddy have to say?'

Anne Latimer arched her finely shaped eyebrows, looking significantly at the whisky glass. 'First of all, it must be said, he doesn't know how you've managed to make such a balls-up of it in just a week. Those are *his* words, *not* mine,' she added primly. 'He's handed you this cathedral on a silver plate, and you've—'

'We've been through this bit before,' he interrupted, his voice weary and verging on the petulant. 'Get on with it. What does he suggest that I do now?'

'He suggests,' she said, deliberately putting the knife in, 'that you pull your socks up and get on with it. That you start thinking like a politician instead of a woolly-minded cleric.'

He winced. 'And what does he mean by that?'

'You've got to *sell* yourself a bit, Stuart! You've got to think about your image.'

The Dean had a fleeting nightmare vision of powder-blue cassocks, elevator shoes, electrolysis treatments, and cosmetic surgery. 'Image? You mean I'm to market myself, like soap powder?'

'Don't be dense, Stuart. You know what I mean.' Taking another gulp of whisky, he waited to be told. 'In the first place,' she said, 'you've got to start thinking about making a few friends instead of enemies.'

'Curry favour with people, you mean?' he asked snidely. 'That's not my style.'

'Not your style – except with people like Daddy and his crowd,' she retorted, ice in her voice. 'You can be nice enough to *them* when it suits you. But I suppose that's different.' There was much truth in what she said, but it sent him back into his glass. Finding it empty already, he rose and went in search of the bottle.

When the Dean returned, his wife tried a different approach. 'Daddy suggested,' she said in a reasonable tone, 'that you try to make allies of the Chapter. Wouldn't it make sense to have them on your side, instead of battling against them?'

'You don't know the Chapter very well,' he muttered self-pityingly. 'They were prejudiced against me before I ever came, because they all wanted that revolting Brydges-ffrench to get the appointment.'

'That's not the way I heard it,' she said. 'I had it from my cleaning woman, who had it from the Greenwoods's cleaning woman, that you'd promised them things before you got here – things that you had no intention of delivering.'

'Oh, that.' He looked down into his drink, sullen.

'Yes, that.' Her voice was still quiet but it had a sharp edge to it. 'It's true, then?'

The Dean frowned. 'Only those two fools Greenwood and Thetford. If they don't have enough sense to recognise a campaign promise when they hear one . . .'

'So you *are* a politician after all.' She spoke with satisfaction, almost with congratulation, smiling suddenly. 'Daddy would approve of that.'

'But now they're never going to go along with anything I say. They won't—'

'Then you must get rid of them,' Anne Latimer stated, pragmatically brutal. Her husband was shocked.

'Get rid of them?'

'Yes. If they won't work with you, then they'll have to go. I'm sure you'll be able to manage that. These things are easily done: a little pressure, judiciously applied . . .' She nodded decisively. 'Then you can get your own people appointed, and you can do anything you like. What about the Subdean?'

'Old Brydges-ffrench is pathetic,' he told her, curling his lip. 'He's like a whingeing old woman. Completely useless.'

'And you don't think you'll be able to bring him round to support you?'

'Not in a million years. He wanted the appointment too badly – he'd oppose me on principle if I was the Second Coming of Christ.'

'Then he's got to go,' the politician's daughter said crisply. 'It should be easy to get rid of him – he's old enough to retire, isn't he?'

'I don't think he'll go without a fight.'

She gave him a Lady Macbeth-like stare. 'Surely you're more than a match for a pathetic old man?'

Mentally he reached for the dagger. 'Of course I am.'

'All right, then. What about the other one? Kingsley, is it?'

The Dean thought for a moment about John Kingsley. 'Kingsley is a different matter,' he said at last. 'He's not a man that I could *buy*, but I think he's a man who might listen to reason.' He thought a bit longer. 'He might even be useful,' he continued, 'because he knows the rest of them so well, and they respect him. If I could get John Kingsley on my side . . .'

'Kingsley stays, then,' she decreed. 'At least if he cooperates. Now, who else is there here in the Close who might be a useful ally?'

The Dean relaxed at last. This was more like it: he and Anne were working together as a team, as he'd always hoped they could; somehow, though, it had never seemed to happen. Leaning back in his chair, he swirled the whisky in his glass pensively. In his mind he ran through the list, discarding most of them.

'Rowena Hunt,' he said finally. 'She's a lady who knows what she wants, and as it happens she has a great deal to gain from working with me.'

'She's the woman who runs the Friends of the Cathedral? The attractive dark-haired one?'

'That's right. She talked to me after the installation – she didn't waste any time, either. She's interested in taking over all of the cathedral catering, having the Friends run the refectory. That fits in beautifully with my plans – I was planning on sacking that dreadful woman who runs the refectory anyway. I could even offer her the Cathedral Shop as well.'

'You're getting rid of those poofs, then.' It was a statement rather than a question.

'Without a doubt. Their lease is due to expire before the end of next year.'

'And you think Rowena Hunt would want to take it on?'

'I'm sure she would.' The Dean smiled. 'Yes, I'm sure she would. I suspect she'd love to build a little empire for the Friends – and for herself.'

'Good. I think that you ought to see her as soon as possible.'

He nodded. 'Right. I will.'

'Who else, then? One ally isn't enough.'

Stuart Latimer sipped his drink. 'Jeremy Bartlett,' he said. 'The Cathedral Architect.'

'Ah,' remembered his wife. 'The chap who was with Rowena Hunt at the garden party? Good looking, bearded?'

'That's the one. He's a widower, I understand. He's only been here a year or so.'

'So he hasn't really been around long enough to get in with the Establishment?' she reasoned.

'There's that, plus the fact that I have a rather attractive carrot to dangle in front of him – professionally speaking, that is.' He rubbed his hands together, pleased with himself. 'I've decided that the way forward at Malbury – the only way forward – is to build on the green space at the west end. A new refectory, a song school, a chapter house, and offices. What could be a bigger temptation for a cathedral architect than the promise of immortality?'

Anne Latimer smoothed her fair hair and nodded, satisfied. 'Get on with it, then,' she ordered. 'And I'll ring Daddy. I'll tell him that you – that *we* – have it in hand.'

The Dean smiled.

Chapter 19

*Nevertheless, they did but flatter him with their mouth: and
dissembled with him in their tongue.*

Psalm 78.36

One afternoon a day or two later, Stuart Latimer strode
through the Close to the cathedral, his long black clerical cloak
flapping in the raw October wind. Somewhat to his own
surprise, he found himself humming – a sign of rare good
humour. His meeting that morning with John Kingsley had
gone well, far better than he could have hoped for. He was
going to be able to do business with Kingsley, he told himself
gleefully. Not that the Canon had been obsequious or toadying;
on the contrary, his manner had been somewhat distant. But
he had listened to what the Dean had to say about Canon
Brydges-ffrench, and in the end he had been persuaded by the
unassailable logic of his arguments. Brydges-ffrench had to go.
He'd convinced Kingsley of that, he congratulated himself
now. Kingsley had even agreed to act as something of a go-
between, to make Brydges-ffrench realise how untenable
his position was at the moment, and how advisable – even
necessary – it was for him to resign. The recalcitrant Subdean,
who would never listen to *him*, would surely listen to a man
like Kingsley. Stuart Latimer rubbed his small, hairy hands
together with satisfaction as much as with cold as he entered
the cathedral. Now it was time to begin phase two of his
campaign to enlist allies: now was the time to talk to Rowena
Hunt. He hoped, on this afternoon, to find her in her usual spot
at the Friends of the Cathedral stall in the south aisle.

He was in luck. Rowena was chatting to a tourist, smiling
her winning smile as she reeled off figures on the cost of
running the cathedral and keeping it open daily, quoting
amounts on a cost-per-hour as well as a cost-per-visitor basis.
The tourist seemed impressed; he opened his wallet and

wandered off towards the donation box by the door to make a generous contribution. The Dean was impressed as well: this woman is on the ball, he thought. She will make a valuable friend.

She turned her smile on him as he approached. 'Good afternoon, Dean.'

'How are you today, Mrs Hunt?'

'Fairly well, as long as I don't stop to think about how cold it is in here.' She shivered slightly, pulling her cardigan across her chest.

'It *is* cold,' he agreed sympathetically.

Rowena smiled. 'I think that the heating system in this cathedral was due to be replaced about . . . oh, about a hundred years ago, I'd guess. But there's never enough money for little things like keeping people warm.'

The Dean was solicitous. 'Do you feel the cold, then?'

'Well, I'm the one who's most affected by it – I'm the only person who has to sit in the cathedral all day.' She shrugged. 'But I cope – I've learned to pile on a few extra layers when it's cold. In other words, about ten months of the year!'

'You're here all day, then?'

'I usually keep the stall open until it's time for Evensong.' She indicated her stall, with its neat stacks of brochures and its rack of post cards; a few books were displayed as well. 'I find that I do quite a good trade in post cards – not everyone makes it to the Cathedral Shop, and people appreciate being able to buy a card or two here. And Victor and Bert's selection of books tends towards the frivolous, so I have a few things available here. I also like to be available to answer questions and generally keep an eye on things. The vergers,' she said dismissively, 'aren't always as well informed, or as vigilant, as they might be.'

Even more impressed, the Dean asked, 'Don't you ever get a break, then?'

Rowena nodded. 'Oh, there's a rota of volunteers from the Friends who take over for an hour at noon, so I can slip home for a bit of lunch.' Or something else, she thought. Smiling, she added, 'Once in a while someone takes pity on me, and brings me a cup of tea in the afternoon. And sometimes I even get a day off.'

With a frown he looked around the near-deserted cathedral. 'Isn't there anyone here now who could take over from you for a few minutes? I was hoping you'd join me for a cup of tea in the refectory.'

'I would love to join you for a cup of tea,' she said immediately, looking at her watch. 'It's after four, and I haven't been very busy today – too cold for the tourists. I'll just close down early, if you don't mind.' The Dean nodded his permission, so she locked the cash box into a drawer, pocketed the key, and set a 'Closed' sign on the counter.

Having successfully avoided Dorothy Unworth's Bakewell tarts, though they did not escape the baleful glare of that worthy woman herself, the Dean and Rowena settled down at a secluded table with their red plastic pots of tea. The refectory was as empty of people as the cathedral, so it was not difficult for them to conduct a private conversation without fear of being overheard by other customers. The Dean had considered calling on Rowena at her home, or asking her to come to his office at the Deanery, but had decided that on the whole a very public meeting would be best: Rowena was such an attractive woman that a private meeting might engender unhelpful gossip at best, or vicious rumour at the worst, in the small world of the Cathedral Close.

'You indicated to me during our previous discussion,' the Dean said without preamble, 'that you would be willing to undertake the coordination of the cathedral catering on behalf of the Friends.'

'Yes, that's right.' Knowing that Dorothy Unworth was hard of hearing, Rowena nonetheless looked in her direction; it gave her a sort of perverse pleasure to know that the woman who watched them so avidly and whose future they were discussing so dispassionately couldn't hear a word they said. She put a hand in front of her mouth, just in case Miss Unworth was a skilled lip-reader. 'Though talking about it here, with her watching us, seems a bit like "Thou preparest a table before me in the presence of mine enemies". I doubt, somehow, that Miss Unworth will be very keen on the idea.'

He laughed with appreciation, remembering that Rowena was a clergy widow. 'No, I don't think you could say that her "cup runneth over" at the moment.'

'How will you manage it?' she asked baldly. 'She won't give it up without a fight.'

'Oh, don't you worry about that, Mrs Hunt,' the Dean assured her. 'It will be an easy matter. I'm sure you're aware that she's granted the contract to operate the refectory on the payment of an annual fee to the Chapter. It has to be renewed annually, at the beginning of each calendar year – up till now it's always been an automatic renewal. This time, though, we'll just decline to renew her contract as of 1 January. Couldn't be simpler. Then you take over. You must know how it works,' he added. 'You occupy your house in the Close under a similar arrangement, I believe.' If there was a veiled threat behind his words, it was carefully hidden in his smile.

'But . . .' Rowena hesitated, searching for a delicate way to articulate her doubts. 'Won't it have to be voted on by the Chapter as a whole?'

'Yes, of course.'

'And . . . can you be sure that they'll vote the way you want them to? I mean . . .' she floundered, uncharacteristically, 'I didn't think you were exactly on the best of terms with the rest of the Chapter at the moment.'

'Just leave the Chapter to me, Mrs Hunt,' the Dean stated with confidence. 'As of 1 January, the refectory will be yours.'

Rowena relaxed, leaning back in her chair. 'All right, then. I shall begin to make plans accordingly.'

'I think that we will work together very well, Mrs Hunt. And with that in mind, there's one other possibility that I wanted to . . . explore with you.' He looked down at the table but watched her out of the corner of his eye, and was pleased to see her unguarded reaction.

'Yes? What is that?' She leaned forward in anticipation, her interest caught.

'The lease for the Cathedral Shop will also be coming up for renewal next year,' the Dean said circumspectly.

Her eyes registered comprehension along with satisfaction, but she was determined to make him spell it out. 'I assume, though, that Victoria and Albert will wish to continue.'

It was the first time he'd heard that nomenclature, and it amused him. 'I have no doubt that they will,' he said with a smile. 'But it is not my wish that they should be granted a renewal. I find their merchandise inadequate, and their behaviour . . . inappropriate. If you understand me.'

Rowena understood him very well. 'And you wondered whether the Friends might be interested in taking it on as well?'

'The thought had crossed my mind.'

She appeared to take a moment to consider the idea, though they both knew what the answer would be. 'I think,' Rowena said at last, 'that it might be a very good thing for the Friends to take on.'

'Consider it done,' said the Dean.

They smiled at each other, knowing that a bargain had been struck, and both understanding the terms perfectly. For Rowena knew that the knife cut both ways: as long as she did things on the Dean's terms, all would be well. But if she failed to produce the goods, or withheld her loyalty from him, she would be just as expendable as Dorothy Unworth. Rowena was very fond of her house in the Close, and had no intention of losing it. If that meant casting her lot with Stuart Latimer, then that was what she would do.

His reservations about calling on Rowena Hunt at home did not extend to Jeremy Bartlett, so that evening Stuart Latimer set out for the architect's house. Although it was immediately adjacent to the Deanery, the wall which ran the entire length of its garden meant that there was no direct access, and the Dean found to his annoyance that he either had to traverse the Close completely, going around the west end of the cathedral, or alternatively use his keys to cut through the cathedral, entering through a small private door into the south choir aisle – by tradition called the Dean's door because of its proximity to the Deanery – and exiting through the south transept into the remnant of the cloister. He decided upon the latter course as being far shorter, and indeed it brought him out virtually at Jeremy's front door.

He had not informed Jeremy of his intention to call, feeling that the element of surprise might well work in his favour on this occasion. He knew that he was taking a chance on finding the architect at home, but it seemed that he was in luck: a crack of light showed between the drawn curtains of the front room, and the faint sound of music drifted out into the night. The Dean was no expert on music, but he recognised the melancholy strains of the Elgar cello concerto as he rocked back and forth on his heels, waiting for a response to the bell.

Jeremy opened the door cautiously, not expecting callers at that hour. 'Dean!' He hesitated a moment, caught by surprise. 'Would you like to come in?' he asked at last.

'Thank you, Mr Bartlett. I hope it's not an inconvenient time to call.'

'Not at all.'

They stood for an uneasy moment in the entrance hall; the Dean volunteered no information as to the reason for his visit. 'Could I offer you a drink?' Jeremy said, finally.

'Yes, please. That would be very nice.'

Leading the Dean into the sitting room, Jeremy asked over his shoulder, 'Brandy? Whisky? Something else?'

'Whisky, please.' Stuart Latimer surveyed the room quickly and chose the largest chair. When Jeremy had dispensed the drinks and had settled down on the sofa, looking at him quizzically, he repeated his opening remark. 'I hope it's not an inconvenient time to call.'

'I was just . . . listening to some music.' Jeremy indicated the stereo. 'It's what I do most evenings.'

The Dean leaned back and took an appreciative sip of the single malt whisky. 'I suppose you're wondering why I've come.' Jeremy nodded but said nothing, so after a moment he went on. 'There's something I wanted to speak to you about, in private. Before I talk to anyone else about it, and before it becomes general knowledge.'

'Yes?' The architect displayed polite interest, nothing more.

'It has become very clear to me that Malbury Cathedral is lacking in certain basic facilities – a chapter house, for one, and a song school. And there are other services, such as the refectory, that we could provide much more efficiently in new, purpose-built premises.' He went on, concisely, to outline his plans for building on the green space at the west end of the cathedral. 'I think that it's the only way ahead for us,' he finished. 'It will take Malbury Cathedral into the twenty-first century – put us streets ahead of Hereford and Worcester, for example.'

At some point during the narrative Jeremy had jumped up and begun pacing the room, trying to take it all in. Now he turned to the Dean with barely suppressed excitement. 'And you want me to be involved?'

'Of course. You're the Cathedral Architect. You're here on site. And I presume that you know the people who matter in London.'

'It's a big job . . .'

'It will be an enormous job. But of course you will have all the assistance you require.'

'It will cost a bomb. The money . . .'

'You needn't worry about that,' said the Dean dismissively. 'I'm not expecting you to be a fund-raiser as well as an architect! The money will come. My father-in-law is in a position to tap into corporate grants, and so forth. The money won't be a problem.' He tilted his head back to meet the eyes of the standing Jeremy. 'Are you with me?' he asked.

'Yes, of course I'm with you!'

'Then I'd like you, as soon as possible, to prepare some preliminary costings, based on the sort of requirements we've been talking about. If you want to sketch out some ideas at this point, I'd be happy to look at them. I'd like to have something to present to the Chapter at the next meeting, the end of this month, and I understand that the Patronal Festival is coming up in the middle of November. That might be a good time to unveil the preliminary plans.'

Jeremy frowned. 'That doesn't give very much time.'

'I'm sure that you'll be able to manage.'

Thinking aloud, he said, 'I shall have to go to London early next week.'

'I leave it to you.' Stuart Latimer rose. 'Thank you for the drink, and for your . . . cooperation. We'll talk again soon, Mr Bartlett. And . . . I'm sure I don't need to mention that at this point, it goes no farther than this room?'

'Of course.'

'And,' added the Dean, 'that in return I expect your complete loyalty? To me personally, rather than to the Chapter?'

There was no hesitation. 'That goes without saying, Dean.' Jeremy saw the Dean to the door, then returned to the sitting room and automatically poured himself another drink. The cello concerto had ended, but he didn't notice.

It was unbelievable. Major building projects like this didn't go on at cathedrals any more – none of them had the money. It was an architect's dream – the sort of thing they all thought about, and hoped for, while knowing, if they were at all realistic, that they were in fact there to keep those magnificent medieval edifices from crumbling to dust, preserving them in their anachronistic beauty for yet another generation of sightseers and God-seekers. This was, thought Jeremy, more than he could ever have hoped for, and what every architect yearned after: the perfect way to crown a career and leave a lasting monument to one's talents. Immortality.

There was only one little problem: Brydges-ffrench and the music festival accounts. If only he hadn't been so stupid and offered his help to the blundering old fool. Clearly he'd acted too quickly, and had backed the wrong horse. For the quid pro quo he'd extracted from the Subdean – the cloister development and the fabric appeal – was a mere drop in the bucket to the promises made by the Dean. If the Dean were to find out . . . Resolutely Jeremy pushed the thought from his mind. He knew that he was clever enough to manipulate the situation, to ensure that he wasn't caught out. The Dean wouldn't find out, *mustn't* find out. That would be fatal.

Into his musings another element intruded, bringing an involuntary smile to his face. London, he thought. Next week.

Lucy. He was obsessed with her, he realised. Thus far his attempts to win her had met with no success at all, which merely fuelled his obsession. Next week he would be in London. One way or another, he would manage to see Lucy Kingsley.

Chapter 20

*Lord, I have loved the habitation of thy house: and the place
where thine honour dwelleth.*

Psalm 26.8

Interlude: Sunday afternoon, Malbury Cathedral Close. The
lull between Sunday morning's service of Holy Communion
and Evensong, a quiet time for Sunday lunches and Sunday
papers and tea. A family time, often lonely and protracted for
people on their own, people like Rowena Hunt and Jeremy
Bartlett, like John Kingsley and Evelyn Marsden. But on this
day John Kingsley was not alone: he had enjoyed a bountiful
lunch with the Willoughbys, eating his fill – and more – of
roast beef, Yorkshire pudding, roast potatoes, fresh vegetables,
and Pat's renowned apple crumble with great dollops of
custard.

Neither was Evelyn Marsden alone. In the months that Todd
Randall had been lodging with her she had enjoyed cooking for
him – fattening the boy up, she called it to herself – and Sunday
lunch was an especially good time for her to show off her
cooking skills. This day, however, was even more special:
Arthur Brydges-ffrench had consented to join them for lunch.
Todd always had a good appetite, though he never seemed to
put on an ounce of weight, Evelyn thought ruefully as she
switched on the kettle for tea; it seemed that she only had to
look at food to add to her already thickening waistline. Todd
would be sure to do justice to the cake she'd baked for tea – a
layered sponge, slathered with cream and decorated with
precious raspberries from the freezer. She hoped that Arthur
would appreciate the cake. He hadn't eaten much at lunch; he'd
seemed to enjoy the pork, but he'd only picked at the
vegetables, and the extra portion of crackling that she'd served
him had been left on his plate. Poor dear Arthur was so thin –
thinner even than Todd, she fretted. It was clear that, being on

his own as he was since his mother's death, he wasn't used to eating enough to keep a bird alive.

At least he seemed to be in a better humour today, Evelyn reflected. Last week, after the service for Ivor Jones, he had been so distraught that, though she'd managed to get a few morsels of food into him, he had hardly been able to speak. Today, over lunch, he'd been undeniably less cheerful than of old, but he'd chatted with Todd about some project they were working on, and he'd even made a few feeble jokes about the Dean's size. 'I wonder if he has to buy his clothes in the children's department? Or maybe in *London* they have special shops for midget clerics,' he'd said, with his hooting laugh. It was a good sign.

'Tea?' she said brightly, carrying the heavy tray into the sitting room. Todd jumped up to take the tray from her; Arthur Brydges-ffrench remained seated, a few faint lines creasing his brow as he contemplated the half-finished *Times* crossword puzzle, saved over from the previous day to be enjoyed at leisure, in his lap.

Farther along the Close, Philip Thetford finished the washing up while his wife prepared a speech about teenage pregnancy to be presented to the WI; next door Rowena put the finishing touches on a tea tray of delicacies, expecting a visitor. And at the Precentor's house the Greenwoods were also preparing to have their tea.

Throughout lunch, and the balance of the afternoon, the Precentor had been telling his wife about the difficulties of finding and employing a new organist, and of keeping the cathedral music ticking over in the interim.

'I won't have time for more than a quick cup, you know,' Rupert warned. 'I've got to get back and get the music sorted before Evensong.' He picked up a piece of sheet music from the table in the sitting room and looked at it. 'Sumsion in G. It's on the music list for today so we've got to do it, but the boys always have trouble with the opening bit. I don't know why.'

Judith poured his tea. 'Rupert,' she said, her voice quiet but laden with emotion. 'Rupert, we've got to talk.'

'Hmm?' He looked up. 'Oh thanks.' He took the tea and resumed his study of the music. 'Trouble is, until we can get a new organist, I've got to conduct the choir so I can't sing the office. John Kingsley is all right, I suppose – he's got a fairly

156

nice voice,' he admitted begrudgingly, 'but it's not fair to expect him to do it indefinitely. Not part of his job.'

'And conducting the choir isn't part of *your* job, either,' Judith put in sharply. 'Rupert . . .'

'But can you imagine old Arthur singing the office?' Rupert laughed, amused. 'He's got a voice like a rusty gate. Philip's not much better, of course. Can't say that I've ever heard the Dean sing, but a pipsqueak like that can't have much of a voice, can he? So I guess it's got to be John until we get a new organist. At least the organ scholar is competent enough to play for the services, even if he's not brilliant. But then Ivor wasn't exactly the world's greatest organist, either.' He took a sip of tea. 'Any biscuits?'

Silently she proffered a plate of chocolate digestives.

'Thanks.' Again he flipped through Sumsion. 'Good piece of writing, even if my boys don't do it justice. Still, I'm not sure I don't prefer Sumsion in A.'

Judith tried once again. 'Rupert, there are some things we really need to talk about.'

He looked up. 'Did you say something, dear?' Over her shoulder he caught sight of the clock. 'Is that really the time? I must dash!' He jumped up, and with a last gulp of tea, he was gone.

In his haste, Rupert had knocked a cushion on to the floor. Judith Greenwood retrieved it, plumped it up, and sighed.

Chapter 21

Their throat is an open sepulchre: they flatter with their tongue.

Psalm 5.10

The long train journey to London gave Jeremy plenty of time to plan his strategy. He would have to stay over for at least two nights, so on the day he arrived he'd just check into his club and get acclimatised to being back in the city. Perhaps he'd ring up one or two of his old friends and suggest meeting for a drink that evening, or maybe there would be an unmissable concert on at St John's Smith Square or the Royal Festival Hall – he should have checked the papers before he left, he realised belatedly. The next morning he would go to his old office and do some work on the Dean's project; he no longer owned the practice, but he could brainstorm with some of his old colleagues, and perhaps begin to come up with some realistic costings.

And then . . . he would try to see Lucy. The fact that she was reluctant to spend time with him – her quality of elusiveness – made her all the more attractive to him, and made him determined to somehow break through the barriers that she had erected between them. If he rang her up and said that he was in town on business, would she agree to see him? Would she perhaps meet him for lunch, or for tea? On the whole he rather doubted it. Dinner, with or without a concert or something in the evening, was almost definitely out, he realised. Even if she were willing, David would certainly not approve of that, and Jeremy had no intention of including David in his plans.

What exactly, he wondered, was her relationship with David? He had never really inquired. They weren't married, or even engaged – he knew that much. Lucy had admitted it. She'd said she was 'attached', but if it were a serious relationship, wouldn't there be some effort to make it permanent? In his day, thought Jeremy, conscious of his age, there would have been: if you loved a woman, and were free to do so, you married her. Were they living together? There was only the one time that David had answered the phone at Lucy's, but there had been several occasions lately when Jeremy had had the definite impression that Lucy hadn't been alone when he'd rung.

Those phone calls, once or twice a week, were his link with her. He would have liked to ring her more often, but he strictly rationed himself to no more than two calls a week. She didn't seem to mind his calls – in fact she rather seemed to enjoy his gossipy chatter about their mutual acquaintances in Malbury. It was only when he saw her in person, on her occasional visits to the cathedral city, that she kept him so firmly at arm's length.

That must be the difference, Jeremy reasoned now, watching the crisply furrowed fields of the heart of England as they rushed past the window. On the phone his manner was light, humorous, non-threatening, but when he was with her he seemed, increasingly, to have a compulsion to come on too strong. That was obviously not the right approach. If he saw her in London – or rather *when* he saw her in London, for surely if he rang her and told her he was in town she would not refuse to see him – he would consciously adopt his telephone persona. He would be the amusing, clever Jeremy Bartlett rather than the heavy-handedly seductive one. Slow and steady wins the race, old boy, he told himself. I *will* have her, no matter how long it takes.

He frowned to himself, then, as he remembered the other cloud in his sky: the problem of Canon Brydges-ffrench and the music festival accounts. The Subdean had spoken to him after Evensong on the Sunday afternoon, just long enough to tell him that the Dean had once again asked for the accounts. Brydges-ffrench had managed to put him off, he'd explained to Jeremy, but he wasn't sure how long he could stall.

Jeremy grimaced. The hopeless old fool! How had he ever managed to get himself involved with such a loser? He must have been out of his mind. Now he must dissociate himself from the Subdean and his coterie of bunglers before the Dean could begin to suspect what had happened. The accounts hadn't even

160

been done yet, so surely Jeremy would be able to cover his tracks adequately. He'd told Brydges-ffrench to keep putting the Dean off – surely he'd be able to manage that.

It was all going very well, Jeremy told himself the next day as he left his old office, laden down with rough drawings and scribbled figures. This would give him a good starting point. Tomorrow he could return to Malbury and get started on preparing some things for the Dean to look at. But first, this afternoon . . . he must try to see Lucy. If she couldn't see him today, he could always postpone his departure for one more day – he just couldn't bear the thought of going home without seeing her. He'd go back to his club and get rid of all these papers, then he'd ring her and suggest . . . what? Or perhaps he should even just turn up on her doorstep, and then she wouldn't be able to refuse him. He tried to imagine what her reaction would be, the expression on her face, if she opened her door and found him standing there.

'Jeremy?' he heard. So intent was he on the Lucy of his imagination that he actually failed to see the flesh-and-blood Lucy who stood before him on the pavement, and when he finally registered her presence, it took an instant for him to realise that she wasn't an apparition.

'Jeremy?' She looked at him closely. 'It is you, isn't it? You look like you've seen a ghost!'

'Lucy! I just . . . wasn't expecting to see you, that's all.'

She laughed. 'But *I* live in London! It's me that should be surprised – *you're* not supposed to be here. You're supposed to be in Malbury. You never told me that you were coming up to town!'

'I didn't really know myself until a day or two ago,' Jeremy heard himself saying. He still couldn't believe that she was standing in front of him, laughing up at him, her hands jammed in the pockets of her trench coat. The spell was broken as an angry-faced woman, bristling with shopping bags, pushed past her on the pavement. 'We're holding up the traffic,' he said, laughing, consciously assuming his charming and witty persona. 'Where are you heading?'

'To Piccadilly Circus to catch the tube, and then home.'

'No, you're not. You're having lunch with me. At a very nice restaurant just around the corner where I used to go for long and expensive business lunches. That is if they're still in business – you never know these days, do you? A year or two can make a great deal of difference.'

'Yes, all right.' She hesitated for only an instant before allowing herself to be swept along.

'And you still haven't told me what you're doing in this part of town. Rather far from home, aren't you?'

'I've been to a gallery that's just hung a few of my paintings. I wanted to see how they looked.'

'And which gallery is that, pray tell? I used to know quite a few of them around here.' Turning to look at her as they walked along, he added, 'Never mind. After lunch you shall take me there, and I'll see for myself.' And later, he said to himself, I shall go back and buy one.

They reached the restaurant. It was still there: a small, intimate and very expensive cave, so discreet that you'd pass right by if you didn't know it was there. Gratifyingly, the *maître d'* remembered him, and showed him to his old table at the back, a table where many clients, over the years, had agreed to part with very large sums of money. He deposited his armload of papers on a chair, helped Lucy out of her coat, gave it to the hovering *maître d'*, and pulled out a chair for her. 'A bottle of champagne,' he said to the waiter who had silently materialised by the table. 'Your best. And you *do* serve vegetarian meals, don't you?'

'The finest in London, sir,' he was assured.

Jeremy turned back to Lucy, raising an eyebrow. 'There you are, Lucy. You heard what he said. Nothing but the best.'

'I'm very gratified.' Smiling, she picked up her napkin, glacially white and starched stiff as cardboard. 'I've come clean with you, Jeremy, and told you what I was doing this morning. But you *still* haven't told me why you're in London. And what are all those mysterious bits of paper? I confess that I'm quite curious.'

Be witty and amusing, he cautioned himself. 'Oh, I've been sent,' he said with a mysterious smile. 'But lest you think it was some heavenly visitation – the Archangel Gabriel, or one of his brethren – that ordered me hence, I must tell you that it was none other than our august Dean.'

'The Dean?'

'Yes, the Very Reverend Stuart Latimer. Or His Tiny Majesty, as he is affectionately known to his close friends.

Whomever they might be. You remember the Dean, don't you? From the installation ceremony? The little chap in the hideous new cope – the one with the machine embroidery and the bugle beads?'

'Oh, Jeremy!' Lucy, on the brink of giggles, raised her napkin to cover her mouth.

Grandly he uncorked the champagne bottle and poured a stream of golden bubbles into her glass. 'As to the reason he sent me here – it may surprise you to hear that our beloved Dean, who, if he can't claim the title of the Biggest Shit in Christendom, may be in the running for the Smallest, has an Edifice Complex!' And without a thought for the Dean's injunction to secrecy, through the layered vegetable terrine and the tagliatelle with wild mushrooms and the rum and chocolate roulade and even the coffee, he entertained Lucy with tales of Malbury in which the plans for the new building loomed large.

Travelling on the Piccadilly Line from Holborn to South Kensington during the rush hour that evening, David Middleton-Brown was not fortunate enough to have a seat. Or rather, he had a seat, but relinquished it at Covent Garden to a young woman, heavily pregnant, her hair in hundreds of tiny plaits each tipped with a shiny silver bead. She smiled at him with impersonal gratitude, and he rode the rest of the way quite happily hanging on to one of the dangling grey balls. In the second week of his new job, commuting by tube was still enough of a novelty that its inconveniences didn't bother him.

The job, at a venerable old firm of solicitors in Lincoln's Inn, was proving quite interesting. Naturally enough, he'd been apprehensive about making such a major change in his life: change had never come easily to David, who was very much a man for familiarity and routine. But his new colleagues had proved to be welcoming, and the work, while very different from the sort of run-of-the-mill country practice matters he'd handled in Norwich – wills, divorces, magistrates' courts – was varied, rewarding, and well within his capabilities. Not to mention well paid – fees were considerably higher than the going rate in Norfolk.

But the best thing about it, he thought, was that it enabled him to be with Lucy. As he left the South Kensington tube station, his steps quickened involuntarily. He was going home.

It was almost as good as being married. Almost. If only she would marry him: it was the one niggling thought which blighted his happiness. Try as he might – and he *had* tried, over the six months that they'd been lovers – he couldn't understand her reluctance to legalise their union, to have it blessed in the sight of God. It would make everything so much easier; conventional as he was, he always worried about what other people might think – his new work colleagues, for instance, and not least of all Lucy's father, whom David had come to love and greatly respect in their short acquaintance. And it would give him the security and permanence that he craved. As things stood, she could change her mind tomorrow, and where would that leave him?

Always lurking in the back of his mind, as well, was the worry about what would happen when the house he would soon inherit – as soon as a complex estate was settled – was ready for him to take possession. It was a matter that he and Lucy never discussed: her invitation to move in with her had been on the understanding that it was a temporary arrangement only, and he had to assume that she still regarded it in that light. He didn't even want to think about the problems inherent in the situation, so the back of his mind was where he resolutely pushed all thoughts of that house.

David turned into the mews, smiling as he always did at the sight of Lucy's tiny, immaculate house. Putting his own key in its lock still gave him an undiminished shock of pleasure: now it was his home too.

To his surprise, Lucy was waiting by the door for him; usually she was in her studio or in the kitchen when he arrived home. She kissed him with unexpected enthusiasm. 'Mmm. I'm glad you're home, David darling,' she said. 'How was your day?'

'Oh, fine. I'll tell you about it later. How about you?'

The hesitation, if there was one, was too brief to be noticed. 'Nothing special. I went to the gallery this morning and saw how they'd hung the paintings.'

David sniffed the cooking fumes that wafted from the back of the house. 'Something smells marvellous. Were you planning on eating soon?'

'Are you awfully hungry?' Lucy fiddled with his tie and twisted one of his shirt buttons. 'The casserole is in the oven, but it can wait. I thought we might . . . Oh, David,' she said in a strangely small voice, 'Wouldn't you like to take me upstairs to bed?'

'I thought,' he replied, 'that you'd never ask.'

Chapter 22

*They hold all together, and keep themselves close: and mark
my steps, when they lay wait for my soul.*

Psalm 56.6

Just before Evensong one night the following week, Canon
Brydges-ffrench had a quick, quiet word with two of his
colleagues. To the Precentor and the Canon Missioner he said
merely, 'Would you mind coming round to my place? After
Evensong. It's important.' Rupert Greenwood nodded, incurious, but Philip Thetford looked rebellious. 'It's important,'
the Subdean repeated urgently, drawing his great tufted
eyebrows together in emphasis, so at last the man agreed.

About an hour later he ushered them into his study. It was a
high-ceilinged, old-fashioned room, dimly lit and crammed with
books: books filling the floor-to-ceiling bookshelves, spilling
over on to the threadbare Persian carpet and covering the desk
in untidy piles. There were even books on the ancient leather
sofa; the Subdean removed them to the floor before inviting the
other two men to sit down. They did so reluctantly – dark
rectangles in the dust on the sofa showed where the books had
been, and demonstrated how long they had been there. Philip
Thetford ostentatiously took out his handkerchief and flicked
the dust from one cushion before sitting down on it.

The Subdean unearthed a box of crème de menthe Turkish
Delight from his desk and offered it around; both Canons
waved it away with expressions of distaste. Shamefacedly he
popped a sticky green sweet in his own mouth before offering,
'Would you like a sherry?'

'Not on a week night.' The Canon Missioner pursed his thin
lips self-righteously.

'Perhaps I will,' said the Precentor. 'A small one, though.
Dry, please.'

The cut glass decanter was as dusty as the sofa, but the

sherry inside was excellent; Arthur Brydges-ffrench was well known for keeping a good cellar, though since his mother's death he rarely entertained. He poured one for Rupert Greenwood and one for himself, then took a seat in his shabbily comfortable leather chair. This chair was where he spent much of his time, so it, at least, was free of books.

'What is this all about, Arthur?' demanded Canon Thetford. 'Couldn't it wait till some other time? This is not convenient for me – Claire will be expecting me to have dinner ready when she gets home from the clinic tonight. And I haven't soaked the lentils yet.'

The Subdean leaned forward nervously. 'I don't think it can wait,' he said, then paused. 'The Dean has asked to see the accounts for the music festival.'

Philip Thetford gave an impatient shrug. 'Yes, I heard him say it at the Chapter meeting. So what? Give them to him, then.'

There was a soft hiss of indrawn breath from Rupert Greenwood. 'He's asked for them again, Arthur?'

'Yes. He asked me on Sunday, and then again this morning, after Communion. He said that he wants to see them right away, before next week's Chapter meeting. And if the accounts aren't available, he'll settle for the books.'

'Ah.' The Precentor leaned back thoughtfully and sipped at his sherry, avoiding the Subdean's eyes.

'So what's the problem?' The Canon Missioner's voice took on a hectoring note. 'As I said, just go ahead and give them to him. I don't see why you had to drag us all the way here to ask our permission for that! I know that you're under stress, Arthur, but surely it's within your capabilities,' he added with a sarcastic sneer.

'You don't understand, Philip.' The Subdean's brow was beaded with sweat.

'No, I don't! I'm waiting for you to explain it to me!' he exploded truculently. 'And preferably before the Last Trumpet!'

Canon Brydges-ffrench found his handkerchief and wiped his forehead. 'Philip,' he said quietly, 'I can't give him the books. There are certain . . . ahem . . . irregularities . . . in the books, and I don't think that the Dean would be particularly . . . um . . . sympathetic.'

'Irregularities? What are you talking about?'

'We lost so much money,' the older man said, almost in a whisper. 'We had to do *something* . . .'

'Let's just say,' Rupert Greenwood put in, 'that certain . . . creative accounting . . . was used that wouldn't stand up to very close scrutiny. If it was ever made public . . .'

'There would be Hell to pay,' finished the Subdean on a groan. 'Oh, what are we going to do?'

'*We?*' Canon Thetford demanded, visibly drawing away from Rupert Greenwood on the sofa. 'This has nothing to do with *me*! You two may have got yourselves in deep water, but *I* am not involved! I had nothing to do with your blasted music festival, and nothing to do with the books!' He stood up, as if to go.

Canon Greenwood laughed, a dry unamused laugh. 'That's where you're wrong, my friend. I'm afraid, Philip, that you're very much involved.'

The Canon Missioner's pale eyes bulged even more than usual, his invisible eyebrows stood out on a suddenly red face, and he sat back down with a thump. 'But that's absurd! Impossible!'

'The cheques,' the Precentor explained succinctly. 'You were a signatory on the music festival account. Three signatures required, remember? Arthur's, mine . . . and yours, Philip.' He paused for emphasis. 'You signed blank cheques, Philip. I asked you to sign them, and you didn't even ask me what they were for.' Rupert Greenwood smiled with a certain grim pleasure. 'So you see, Philip, you're in it as deep as we are. If we go down, you go down with us.'

Canon Greenwood strode back home through the Close, past the vacant organist's house, humming a phrase from the evening's Psalm, 109, as he thought appositely of the Dean: 'Let his days be few: and let another take his office.' As he put his key in the lock, his thoughts moved ahead to dinner. Tuesday, he calculated. Curry. Tuesday was the night to finish up the final remnants of Sunday's joint, so tonight it was bound to be chicken curry. Rupert liked chicken curry; his mouth began to water in anticipation.

But no spicy smell of garam masala and cumin and coriander greeted him. In fact, there was no smell of anything, and the house felt cold, as though the central heating had not been on for some time. 'Judith?' he called tentatively. There was no reply.

There was, however, a note, in Judith's fluid handwriting, placed neatly on the kitchen counter. Rupert picked it up, disbelieving: Judith was *never* away when he got home, not even when she got roped into baby-sitting that revolting Crabtree infant while its parents were off ringing bells or drinking at the pub or whatever they did to give them an excuse to get away from their progeny. No, she always insisted on bringing the child here, letting it toddle around the house and get into his things, bang on the piano and slobber on his music.

'Dear Rupert,' said the note. 'I have been trying for days to talk to you, but you just won't listen. You don't even seem to know that I am around. Perhaps if I am not here for a while you will notice.' It was signed, 'With love, Judith.'

Rupert stared at the note, stunned.

Chapter 23

The sorrows of my heart are enlarged: O bring thou me out of my troubles.

Psalm 25.16

By the time that Rupert received her note, Judith Greenwood was many miles distant from Malbury. Earlier that afternoon she had packed her bag and walked to the station, catching the 3.32 to London. So as Rupert stood, gaping at her note, she was well on her way to Paddington Station, clutching the paper napkin with Lucy's address in her hand like a talisman.

The nights were drawing in quickly now, and already it was quite dark. But Judith stared out into the blankness, watching the pinpoints of light that marked scattered houses and villages, the evenly-spaced topaz lights dotting the dual carriageways, and the eerie pinky-yellow glow which spread through the sky as they approached a major town. Swindon, Reading, and then it would be London Paddington.

It was only as the train drew nearer to London that Judith Greenwood realised, her stomach muscles contracting with excitement, how much she had missed the capital city. It had been literally years since she'd been there – all those wasted years in Malbury, she thought.

Judith paid off the taxi driver at the entrance to the mews – not knowing this part of London very well, and uneasy to be wandering around on her own after dark, she had splashed out on a taxi. She found the house and rang the bell nervously. Now that she was here standing on the doorstep, she belatedly began to have second thoughts about the wisdom of this enterprise: would Lucy be glad to see her? Would she even be there?

After a short delay the door opened, and the surprise on

Lucy's face must have rivalled that on Rupert's earlier. 'Good heavens! Judith!'

'Hello, Lucy,' she said timidly. 'You said that I could come . . .'

'Well, come in, then!' Lucy beckoned her inside, taking in the case with a quick glance. 'Rupert isn't with you?'

'No, he's not.' Judith suddenly felt terribly awkward. 'I had to get away from him – away from Malbury – for a few days. I'm really sorry – I didn't know where else to go. I remembered that you said I could come any time, and—'

'Yes, of course,' Lucy cut across her stammered explanations. 'Have you had anything to eat?' she asked practically.

Judith thought back; in her haste to get away, and her excitement at the journey, food had been the farthest thing from her mind. 'No,' she said. 'Not since breakfast.'

'Then you must be starving. Come on through to the dining room – we were just eating. Don't worry, there's plenty.'

Judith trailed behind her in an excess of embarrassment. 'Oh, you have company, then? I don't want to interrupt anything. I'm so sorry – I really should have rung. I shouldn't have come at all, really, only—' She stopped at the dining room door as David turned. 'Oh!' she said, recognising him. 'Oh, hello, Mr . . .'

'David,' he stated with a smile.

'Judith has come to stay for a few days,' Lucy explained to him.

'I'm so sorry to interrupt, Lucy. I should have realised that you might be entertaining,' she began again, looking as if she might turn and flee at any instant.

'Oh, no, it's not like that,' said Lucy matter-of-factly. 'David is living here.'

David frowned involuntarily, partly out of embarrassment and partly because of Lucy's choice of words: 'is living here' sounded so much more temporary than 'lives here' would have done. Seeing his frown, Judith grew even more embarrassed. 'I . . . I didn't know,' she floundered, blushing.

Lucy had the grace to look slightly abashed. 'Well, no, there's no reason why you should have known. I haven't exactly publicised the fact in Malbury,' she said wryly, adding, 'My father doesn't know. And I'd just as soon . . .'

'Oh, I won't tell him,' Judith assured her. 'That is, if I ever go back to Malbury.' Her voice was wistful, yet tinged with bitterness.

After Judith had eaten, ravenously, they began to discuss her situation in a roundabout way. David, who realised early on that his presence was not required, and might even be counter-productive, made diplomatic excuses: 'Would you mind awfully, Lucy, if I disappeared and left you two to do the washing up? I really must have a look at a few papers before tomorrow.' Lucy nodded, smiling, and Judith rewarded him with a grateful look.

He retreated into the sitting room with his briefcase; there really were papers that he needed to look at, but his mind kept wandering to another matter which was troubling him. His vague suspicions that Jeremy Bartlett was not precisely the genial, witty man he presented to the world – and more especially to Lucy – had continued to nag at David's awareness, and at last he had taken some action. That afternoon he had made a few discreet telephone calls to people who might be in a position to know something about Jeremy, and the evasion with which his questions had been answered was not reassuring. In one sense he felt justified: perhaps there really was some basis in fact for his distrust of the man. But it was also worrying, in that he scarcely knew what to do next. There was no concrete evidence that Jeremy had ever been involved, in his years of practice in London, in anything strictly illegal or even unethical. But the hints were there: should he follow them up further? He knew that he couldn't mention it to Lucy; anything that he said about Jeremy would be interpreted by her as a manifestation of jealousy. In a sense, of course, it was that as well, for Jeremy was clearly interested in Lucy, and David had never managed to completely overcome his own insecurities about their relationship. But the sound instincts that made him a good lawyer convinced him that, all personal feelings aside, Jeremy Bartlett was not a nice person.

As he turned these things over in his mind, reaching no conclusions, David ceased to hear the voices – and the clatter of washing up – in the kitchen. Sophie, the marmalade cat, made herself comfortable on his lap, as she often did in the evenings; with his mind occupied and the inert animal warmth, he was unaware of time passing. When the mantelpiece clock struck midnight he looked up, surprised that it was so late, and realised that Lucy and Judith were still in the kitchen, and still talking. Reluctantly, for since he'd been in this house it had never happened before, David went upstairs and went to bed alone.

After a time he slept fitfully, waking when Lucy crawled in beside him at last. 'What time is it, love?' he murmured.

'After three. I'm sorry – I tried not to wake you.'

'I don't sleep very well when you're not with me.' He turned over and reached for her. 'Come here.'

'Mm, you're nice and warm. And my feet are cold,' she warned him, snuggling close.

He flinched only slightly. 'So are your hands. Did you get Judith settled in for the night?'

'Yes, downstairs on the sofa bed. She ought to sleep well – she's exhausted, poor thing.'

'And did you get her sorted out?'

'It will take more than my advice – and more than one night – to get her sorted out.'

'Tell me about it,' David urged. 'She's left Rupert?'

'Not exactly left *him*. I think it's really more that she's left Malbury, and he happens to be there.' Lucy sighed. 'To make a long story – and it's a very long story, believe me – short, Judith is one very frustrated woman. She met Rupert at the Royal College of Music, before he had any thoughts of ordination. They married, she went on to have a very promising career as a singer, and he went ahead and got ordained. After a curacy in London, he got the post in Malbury. They've been there about six years, and she's absolutely miserable. There are no professional outlets for her in Malbury – no women in the cathedral choir, and no decent amateur choral societies. She has no friends, no peers, no one she's felt she could talk to, and Rupert seems to neglect her shamefully. He lives for his music, and for "his boys", as he calls the choir, and doesn't seem to have much energy left over to make his marriage work.'

'Why doesn't she just tell him—'

'That's just it. She's been trying to tell him how unhappy she is, but he won't listen. It doesn't help that she has no self-confidence, and has been robbed of all sense of personal esteem by the circumstances of her life. And the other thing . . .' Lucy hesitated. 'She finally broke down and told me, after hours of talking, that she's been desperate to have a child, but it just hasn't happened. Not too surprising, either – she confessed that it's been months since they've made love, and that their lovemaking has never been very frequent, even in the beginning. Rupert just doesn't seem that interested, she said.'

'Perhaps Rupert just has a low sex drive,' David suggested. There were such people, he knew: indeed, he had always considered himself to be one of them. If you'd asked him a year ago, David would have said that sex wasn't at all important to him, that he could live very well without it, and had in fact done so for quite a few years. It was only in the last six months that he'd discovered, with Lucy's help and to his considerable delight and surprise, that this was far from the case.

'It seems likely. But again, it's something she and Rupert have never discussed. She's afraid, deep down, that he doesn't care, doesn't even want a child – after all, she says, he has "his boys". It's all added to her sense of personal failure, of inadequacy. Her very worth as a woman is in question. And of course the great unspoken fear is that Rupert doesn't really love her at all, that he just keeps her around as a domestic convenience.'

'But she loves Rupert?'

'Oh yes, she loves him very much. That's what makes it so difficult – if she didn't love Rupert so much, she could just leave him and make a life for herself in London.'

'So her coming here today . . .'

'I think it was really a cry for help, a signal to Rupert that something is desperately wrong. It was the only way she could reach him, she said. She'd tried talking to him, and he wouldn't listen. So she had to do something to make him notice her, to force him to acknowledge the problem.'

Lucy, who had drunk a great deal of coffee through the long night, was still wide awake, but David was beginning to grow sleepy. After a minute he roused himself. 'Does Rupert know she's here?' he asked.

'She didn't tell him where she'd gone, only left a note to tell him she was going. But I rang my father. He said that Rupert was frantic – running all over the Close asking people if they knew where she was. So I told Daddy to let Rupert know that she was here, and safe. I thought it was only right to put his mind at rest.'

'And now what? How long is she going to stay here?'

'I think,' said Lucy, 'that I've talked her into going back, tomorrow or the next day. She realises that she can't run away from the problems forever. She knows that she has to talk to

Rupert – they've got a great deal of talking to do. And I think that now he just might be prepared to listen.'

'What is it about you,' David asked rhetorically, just before sleep claimed him, 'that makes people you scarcely know queue up to tell you their innermost secrets? And I speak from experience – it happened to me, too. Remember the first time I came here for tea, and ended up telling you my life story, things I'd never told a living soul before?' He chuckled sleepily. 'Not that you're not a brilliant artist, but I think that some of your more singular talents are wasted on art. You ought to be a shrink – or a detective, Lucy love.'

Chapter 24

The Lord hath heard my petition: the Lord will receive my prayer.

Psalm 6.9

In the end, two days later, Lucy drove Judith back to Malbury in David's car. Judith declared that she couldn't face the return train journey, and David was not able to get away, so it seemed the best compromise. David was slightly uneasy about it, particularly about Lucy's return trip on her own, but she reminded him that she was a good driver and that she would be careful.

Much of the intervening day had been spent shopping. Realising that many of Judith's problems stemmed from her low self-image, Lucy had tried to remedy the situation in one frantic day. She'd helped Judith to choose some new clothes, not necessarily fashionable but flattering to her figure, a figure which was more than acceptable when divested of the baggy, shapeless garments she usually wore. The colours, too, were carefully chosen: rich mauves and blues to emphasise her beautiful violet eyes rather than her customary drab browns and muddy greens. There were even new underclothes, silky and feminine, and an extravagantly provocative nightdress in shimmering amethyst satin. Judith had been dubious about all of this, particularly the last item, but Lucy had remained adamant. 'You won't regret it,' she'd promised.

At the end of the day they'd visited Lucy's hairdresser, again with half-hearted protests from Judith. But about the results there had been no protest at all. Judith had always worn her hair unbecomingly long and straight, trimming the ends haphazardly herself when necessary; the hairdresser had left it long, but had sparked up the mousy colour with a few subtle plummy highlights, then had layered it and shaped it around her face in such a flattering way that she had stared at herself in the mirror almost without recognition. 'Rupert won't even know me,' she'd whispered, delighted.

There was ample opportunity during the drive to Malbury to discuss her new image and its implications. But the nearer they got to Malbury, the more apprehensive Judith became. 'Whatever am I going to say to Rupert?' she fretted. 'Tell me, Lucy.'

'I can't tell you what to say to him. But you know the things that you need to talk about, Judith. Be honest with him. Tell him the truth about how you feel about Malbury, and about your situation there. And get him to make love to you,' she added frankly.

Judith coloured. 'Oh, but I couldn't.'

'Why ever not? Don't you *want* Rupert to make love to you?'

'Yes, of course. But what if . . . what if he doesn't want to?'

'Oh, for heaven's sake, Judith! He's your husband! I'm not suggesting that you seduce some man off the street, just that you get your husband to take you to bed.' Lucy glanced at her with some asperity.

Refusing to meet her eyes, Judith twisted her hands in her lap and spoke quietly. 'But I . . . I wouldn't know how.'

Lucy laughed, not unkindly. 'Oh, Judith – you *have* got a lot to learn. Put on that nightgown we bought you, for starters – that ought to get him thinking in the right direction. Tell him that you find him irresistible, and that you missed him dreadfully. Unbutton his cassock, and take off his dog collar. And if all else fails, just grab him by the hand and drag him upstairs.'

They arrived in Malbury in the early afternoon. Lucy dropped Judith off at her house, refusing her pleas to come in with her, and went on to have a pleasant lunch with her father, filling him in – in a general way – on what had happened. Later, she decided to pay a visit to Pat Willoughby and enlist her help in keeping an eye on Judith.

While respecting Judith's confidences, she was frank with Pat about the depth of the Greenwoods' problems. Pat, who still felt guilty that she had not made it her business to befriend Judith years ago, promised to do what she could.

'Marriage,' said Lucy, shaking her head with unguarded bitterness. 'It really makes you wonder, doesn't it?'

'What do you mean?' Pat regarded her questioningly.

Realising too late that Pat was not going to let her get away unchallenged, Lucy carried on. 'Well, it doesn't say very much for the institution of marriage that a talented young woman like Judith Greenwood is in such a state. I mean . . .'

'Are you talking about Judith, or are you talking about something else?' asked Pat shrewdly. When Lucy didn't answer, she seemed to change the subject, pouring her another cup of tea. 'It's a shame that your David couldn't come with you this time. I'd like to see him again.'

'Yes.' Lucy's voice was neutral.

'I like him very much, Lucy dear. Not least because he so obviously adores you.' Pat paused. 'He's just what you need. I know it's none of my business, my dear, but I do care about you, and I'd hate to see you throw away something valuable just because of . . . something that happened a long time ago. That's what it is, isn't it?'

Lucy frowned. 'You've been talking to David, haven't you? What did he say to you?'

'We did have a little chat that morning you were all here for breakfast,' the Bishop's wife admitted. 'He told me how much he loves you, and that you were . . . reluctant . . . to marry him. Forgive me if I'm interfering, my dear, but I just want to see you happy.'

Averting her face, Lucy spoke softly. 'I'm not going to throw anything away, Pat. And I appreciate your advice. But . . . I just can't forget what a disaster my marriage was, and how unhappy it made me.'

'You're older and wiser now.'

'Older, certainly. I wish I could be sure about wiser.' She pushed her hair back from her face and deliberately changed the subject, her voice bright. 'So. Tell me the latest developments with the Dean. What has he been up to this week?'

As she left the Bishop's House, Lucy involuntarily glanced at the next house. Jeremy, putting an empty milk bottle outside his front door, straightened up at the sight of her. 'Lucy! What are you doing in Malbury?'

'Have we had this conversation before?' she laughed. 'It sounds familiar.'

'Come in and have a cup of tea.'

Lucy demurred, 'I've just had my fill of tea.'

'Something else, then? Sherry?'

She hesitated. 'No, I don't think so.'

'There's something I want to ask your advice about,' he said with ingenuity born of desperation. 'I need your advice on hanging a painting.'

'It's not by any chance,' she asked, 'the one of mine that you bought from the gallery last week?'

'How did you know about that?'

Lucy smiled. 'It's customary for the gallery to let the artist know the name of the buyer when they sell a painting.'

'I should have realised that I couldn't get away with anything!' Jeremy raised an expressive eyebrow. 'So are you going to come in and see it?'

'Oh, all right.' She followed him into the house and into the sitting room with only a slight tremor of apprehension. 'Have you got any farther with the plans for the new building? I'd like to see what you've done.'

Jeremy debated how to reply; he realised that he'd made a mistake, had betrayed the Dean's confidence, by telling her about the building plans, but was unsure how best to control the damage. At last he decided on honesty. 'Lucy,' he said, 'you haven't told anyone about the new building, have you? It's still a secret.'

She thought about the question. 'No. I didn't know that it was a secret, but I haven't told anyone. There have been more important things on my mind, to tell you the truth.'

'You haven't told . . . David, then?'

'No,' she admitted, reluctantly. 'I didn't even tell David that I'd seen you. I thought that . . . well, I thought that he might be upset about it, and I wanted to spare him that.'

Jeremy hid his jubilation, turning to the sherry decanter. She had lied to David about seeing him – it was the thin end of the wedge, he told himself. 'Are you sure,' he said, 'that you won't change your mind and have a sherry?'

'Well, perhaps just a small one,' she conceded.

The following morning, Stuart Latimer sat in his Deanery office, awaiting the arrival of the Precentor. Canon Greenwood had rung earlier, asking for an appointment to see him, but had volunteered no details. What could it be about? wondered the Dean without any particular interest or feeling of anticipation. Probably something to do with the organ, he decided, or the appointment of a new organist. Something very mundane and time-wasting, no doubt. The Dean had heard that the runaway wife had turned up, so it wouldn't be about that. She'd gone to London, he'd heard. Stuart Latimer's wife went to London all the time – he didn't see that it was anything to get excited about.

It was with some surprise, therefore, that he rose to greet Rupert Greenwood on his arrival. The Precentor's manner was agitated, as agitated as it had been a few days earlier when his wife had gone missing. He looked weary, and uncharacteristically unkempt; if he had looked old enough to shave, thought the Dean with amusement, he might even have appeared unshaven.

'Sit down, Canon Greenwood.' He gestured to a chair.

The Precentor sank into the chair gratefully, but almost immediately got back up and began pacing in front of the Dean's desk. 'I just don't know where to begin.'

'Compose yourself, Canon, and start at the beginning. What is this all about? The organ?'

'Oh, no, not that.' Rupert Greenwood stopped in front of the desk. 'My wife. You know she's been . . . away?'

An interesting way to put it, thought the Dean. 'Yes, I think that everyone in the Close has been aware of that fact,' he said sardonically. 'But she's back, I understand?'

'Well, yes. And she . . . well, I just had no idea about how she felt.'

'Felt about what, Canon? You're not making yourself very clear.' The Dean was beginning to grow impatient with Rupert's unfocused ramblings. 'And please do sit down. You're making me nervous.'

Abruptly, the Precentor collapsed back into the chair. 'About Malbury. About living here.' He paused, and the Dean waited. 'She hates it. She's always hated it. She says that there's nothing for her here, no outlet for her talents – Judith used to be a singer, you know,' he added, almost proudly. 'A good one. But in Malbury there aren't any opportunities for her.'

The Dean began to see where this might be leading – or at least where it might lead, if he played his cards right – and consciously suppressed his own rising excitement, retaining his careful neutrality. 'And how,' he asked, 'can I help you with this . . . problem?'

Rupert clasped and unclasped his hands for a moment, framing his words. 'Judith wants to leave Malbury,' he blurted at last. 'She . . . insists. She wants me to get a position in

London. She said . . . she suggested . . . that you might be able to help.'

The Dean took his time in answering, allowing Rupert to suffer as long as he could. 'Well, yes,' he said, consideringly. 'That just might be possible. We should be sorry to lose you here, of course, but I certainly understand how difficult wives can be!' He laughed in a matey sort of way. 'My wife doesn't think much of Malbury either!'

'Then you think . . .' Rupert raised his head and looked at him with hope, for the first time seeing a possible escape from his thorny dilemma.

'Leave it with me, Rupert.' The Dean used his Christian name for the first time; his voice was reassuringly soothing. 'I know enough people in London – it shouldn't be difficult. That is, if you're *sure* . . .'

'Yes, I'm sure.' The Precentor sighed.

'Then I shall do my best for you, Rupert. I assume that you would want to go as soon as possible?'

'Oh, yes.'

'In that case, I shall make some phone calls this morning, and may have some news for you within a few days.' Stuart Latimer smiled, showing his teeth, and shook his head sympathetically. 'Ah, Rupert. The things we men do to please our wives.'

Chapter 25

*For he spake, and it was done: he commanded, and it stood
fast.*

Psalm 33.9

Stuart Latimer approached his second Chapter meeting, at the
end of October, with even greater anticipation than his first.
In spite of a few setbacks in his initial week, he reflected,
he had recovered brilliantly, and had made great strides
towards his eventual goal of making Malbury Cathedral a
going concern.

They were gathered once again around the table in the room
of the diocesan office building which was used as a makeshift
Chapter House. Not an ideal situation, but one which would be
remedied with a purpose-built Chapter House when the new
Cathedral Centre was built, for that was the name with which
he had decided to christen his project.

But that would come later. As he had done at the first
meeting, he looked around the table at the four men. Philip
Thetford met his gaze, bellicose. John Kingsley, too, looked
back at him steadily, though his face was unreadable in its
customary serenity. Rupert Greenwood appeared detached,
looking off into space, managing somehow to give the
impression that the proceedings had nothing to do with him.
It was only Arthur Brydges-ffrench who quailed before the
Dean's stare. His dark-spotted hands, trembling slightly,
rested on a ledger book in front of him on the table.

'Good morning, gentlemen,' began the Dean. 'Are there any
matters arising from our last meeting?'

Canon Brydges-ffrench swallowed, sending his Adam's
apple up the length of his scrawny throat. 'Here are the books
from the music festival that you asked for,' he said feebly,
pushing them across the table to the Dean. He darted
apprehensive glances at Rupert Greenwood, who continued to

look off into space, and at Philip Thetford, who took a sudden and inexplicable interest in his fingernails.

'Thank you, Canon.' The Dean scarcely looked at the volume, pushing it dismissively to one side. 'Anything else? How about the lists I asked you for?'

'Here is the list of books in the library that you wanted,' volunteered Canon Kingsley without expression.

'Thank you. And the treasury list?' He turned his attention back to Arthur Brydges-ffrench.

'Um. No. That is . . .' The old man blinked rapidly and swallowed again 'That is,' he burst out passionately, 'I won't allow you to sell the cathedral's silver! It's our heritage – our history!'

The Dean's jaw clenched. 'We will discuss this in private, Canon,' he said in a controlled, steely voice. 'Later.' He moved on quickly, before he lost control of his temper and the meeting. 'At our last meeting I mentioned the matter of leases. I believe that I shared with you a few of my thoughts about the refectory, and its current tenant. As I'm sure you all know, Miss Unworth operates the refectory under contract, renewed annually. It is my intention not to renew that contract. Likewise, the lease of the Cathedral Shop is up for renewal next year. I am convinced that the way forward for us is to turn both of these concerns over to the Friends of the Cathedral to operate. Mrs Hunt has expressed a willingness to take them on.'

'Yes, I'll bet she has,' muttered Canon Thetford snidely.

The Dean ignored him. 'It will mean a great deal of extra work for Mrs Hunt, and I for one am very grateful to her.'

'I will never agree!' Canon Brydges-ffrench burst out defiantly. 'You can't treat people like that! Victor, Bert, Dorothy Unworth – they've all served the cathedral faithfully for so many years! As faithfully as . . . as . . . I have. You can't make a decision like that on your own. Surely it will require a vote in Chapter, and I will never agree!'

In the silence following that outburst, John Kingsley spoke quietly. 'I'm sorry, Dean, but I must side with Arthur on this. Faithful servants of the cathedral are not to be cast aside on the scrapheap for a whim, like last year's Paschal candle. And Arthur's right. It will require a vote.'

The Dean did a quick calculation, and decided not to take the risk. 'Very well. We will postpone the vote until our next meeting.' Anything, he told himself, could happen between now and then to alter the vote. He must ensure that he didn't let Rowena down. 'I have discovered,' he went on smoothly, 'that there is one more lease which will be expiring within the next year: that of the house now occupied by Miss Evelyn Marsden.' There was an indrawn breath from Canon Brydges-ffrench, but the Dean continued. 'She has been paying a derisory rent for many years. That situation cannot be allowed to continue. The rent is to be raised to . . .' He consulted his notes and named a figure several times higher than the current rent. 'If Miss Marsden does not wish to renew her lease under these new terms, I have another prospective tenant in mind.' He allowed a note of jocularity to creep into his voice. 'Although many of us – not to mention our wives,' he added, glancing at Rupert Greenwood, 'may not consider Malbury the second Garden of Eden, there are many in London who yearn for the country life, at least part of the time. One of my father-in-law's colleagues, who was here for my installation ceremony and who found Malbury enchanting, has expressed an interest in renting a property in the Close for use as a weekend retreat.'

Arthur Brydges-ffrench opened his mouth as if to speak, but the Dean forestalled him. 'We will not discuss the matter further at this time,' he stated. 'There is no hurry, as Miss Marsden's lease has several months yet to run. I will put it on the agenda for next month's meeting. In the meantime, of course, I would appreciate it if none of you would mention the matter to Miss Marsden. I plan to speak to her myself in due course.' He looked hard at the Subdean, who refused to meet his eyes.

'Now,' said the Dean, pausing a moment to change gears as he reached for the roll of sketches that Jeremy had drawn. 'I have something to share with you that is possibly the most exciting development this cathedral will have seen in this century. Gentlemen . . .' He unrolled the drawings with a dramatic flourish, 'the Malbury Cathedral Centre!'

The announcement took them all completely by surprise. As the Dean unveiled his plans, detail by detail, he was met by stunned silence.

'So you see,' he concluded, 'that all our needs will be taken care of, now and for the foreseeable future.'

'No,' Arthur Brydges-ffrench whispered, drawing his hand-kerchief from his sleeve. 'You can't possibly consider building on the green. It would alter the character of the cathedral beyond all recognition! And it's consecrated ground, where the Nave used to extend . . .' He mopped his forehead and regarded the Dean with something approaching hatred. 'I shall do everything in my power to block this . . . this desecration!'

The Dean narrowed his eyes and snapped, 'You haven't a hope of stopping me.'

Canon Thetford couldn't resist mouthing the old cliché. 'While there's life, there's hope,' he said unctuously.

But the Subdean had the last word. He sat up very straight, towering over the Dean, and spoke with ominous dignity. 'Or as a wise old clergyman I once knew was fond of saying, "While there's *death* . . . there's hope."'

There was yet one more bombshell to be exploded in their midst. Just before the meeting ended, Stuart Latimer said, 'I'm sure that you will all be sorry to hear what I am about to tell you.' He watched as they all turned interested eyes in his direction – all, that is, save the Precentor, who had yet to speak or even make eye contact. 'Sorry, that is,' he amended, 'on a personal level, though it is of course good news for one of our number.' He paused for effect. 'Rupert Greenwood will be leaving us by the end of the year.' There was a generalised gasp from the other three Canons.

'Perhaps I should elaborate,' the Dean went on. 'Last week Canon Greenwood came to see me. He felt that the time had come for him to leave Malbury, and asked for my advice.' He smiled, most unconvincingly. 'Naturally, I said that we would be very sorry to lose him, but that we would not wish to hold him back. Precentors, after all, are strange birds of passage. Their unique talents mean that their stay in a cathedral is usually brief. Canon Greenwood has been at Malbury for six years, and he is now ready to move on.' It was difficult for him to disguise his feelings of triumph as he continued, 'I do have a few connections in London,' – here he chuckled modestly – 'and fortunately I was able to help Canon Greenwood to locate a new position appropriate to his talents quite quickly. He will be taking over the living of a church in London where he can continue to exercise his musical skills with limited parochial responsibilities. And might I add,' the Dean said with a noticeable lack of subtlety, his gaze moving around the table but lingering on Philip Thetford, 'that I would be happy to do likewise for anyone else who felt that . . . perhaps it was time for them to move on elsewhere. I am not without influence, especially in London. As I said,' he concluded, 'we will be very sorry to lose Canon Greenwood. But I'm sure I speak for all of you when I say that we send him forth with our very best wishes for all possible success in his new appointment.' Rupert, still not meeting anyone's eyes, inclined his head slightly in acknowledgement.

They all lingered for a few moments after the Dean had gone home to his lunch. John Kingsley pored over the plans for the Cathedral Centre which the Dean had left behind for their inspection, while Philip Thetford rounded on Rupert Greenwood.

'Oh, Rupert!' he hissed. 'How could you do it? How could you sell us out to that unspeakable man?'

The Precentor spoke at last. 'I didn't sell you out, Philip. I had to do it.'

'What sort of pressure did he use on you?' questioned Canon Brydges-ffrench in a moan.

'No, you don't understand.' Rupert's voice was calm. 'I had to do it to save my marriage. It was either leave Malbury or lose Judith. He ... the Dean ... helped me. He was very understanding. He found me the new appointment.'

'Helped you?' the Subdean echoed with scathing sarcasm. 'You can't be that naïve! He wanted to get rid of you! Divide and conquer, you know. As I've said before, united we stand, divided we fall. Whatever will become of the rest of us when you're gone? When he replaces you with his own creature?'

'That,' said Rupert remotely, 'is none of my affair.'

Philip Thetford thought aloud. 'If Rupert is going, then perhaps we should all go. As Arthur says, losing Rupert will alter the balance of power completely. Perhaps we should just cut our losses and leave. He's offered to help us find new appointments. He helped Rupert. He'd help the rest of us as well. So what if it's only because he wants to be rid of us? At least we'd be out of the mess we're in.'

Canon Brydges-ffrench turned on him as though he had suggested burning down the cathedral as a remedy for woodworm. 'Don't be absurd! We can't possibly go!'

The Canon Missioner's pale face was mottled with emotion. 'We could, and we probably should. I, for one, am going to consider the Dean's offer very carefully, and I think that you should do likewise, Arthur.'

Fat tears ran down the channels on either side of the Subdean's mouth, and his voice quavered, revealing how close he was to losing control. 'The rest of you may do as you like. Sell your souls to the devil, if that's what you want to do! But I will never abandon this cathedral. Not as long,' he pronounced, 'as there is breath in my body.'

Chapter 26

*For they have cast their heads together with one consent:
and are confederate against thee.*

Psalm 83.5

The Feast of St Malo falls on the fifteenth of November;
at Malbury Cathedral it was customary to celebrate it as the
Patronal Festival, on the weekend nearest the fifteenth.

So it was late on the following Friday afternoon that David
and Lucy began the long drive to Malbury. David had been
somewhat reluctant to go, for various reasons: it meant an
early departure from work, and there was the unsatisfactory
situation of the sleeping arrangements at Canon Kingsley's
house, but even more importantly, he had come to dread the
feeling of unease that Malbury always roused in him. But Lucy
was anxious to see Judith Greenwood. She'd had an ecstatic
letter from Judith, and had phoned her once or twice, but
wanted an opportunity to talk to her face to face and to assure
herself that things were indeed working out for the other
woman.

David was even more interested in the political ramifica-
tions of Rupert's resignation, news that they'd heard not only
from Judith but from Jeremy and from Lucy's father. 'It will
change the balance of power in the chapter,' he ruminated as
they approached Malbury. 'Assuming that the rest of them
would all vote together against the Dean, that is. Now, if the
Dean can swing one more vote, or manage to get rid of one of the
others . . . What does your father say about it?' he asked
curiously.

'Only that he thought that Arthur Brydges-ffrench was less
than pleased.'

'I can imagine.'

'But David – the important thing is Judith. She'll be so much
happier in London. And the fact that Rupert was willing to

189

make such a big change . . .' She shook her head. 'Arthur Brydges-ffrench and the rest of them will get over it,' she predicted, confidently if naïvely. 'In a few months' time they won't even remember what all the fuss was about.'

But David wasn't so sure that it would be that simple.

The dinner party at the Bishop's House which had been cancelled in the wake of Ivor Jones's death had been rescheduled for that evening, though in a different form than originally planned. Only Lucy, David and Canon Kingsley would be dining with the Willoughbys, but their intimate meal was preceded by a festive drinks party to which the entire Close had been invited.

This time the gathering was in the drawing room rather than the kitchen. It was a large and rather grand room, seldom used by the informal Willoughbys, who preferred to do their entertaining on a smaller scale.

The guests of honour arrived a few minutes early, and David endeared himself immediately to Pat by offering to help her with the dispensing of drinks and food. 'How kind!' she said. 'George is absolutely hopeless when it comes to such things. He gets sidetracked talking to someone, and forgets that he's meant to be refilling glasses. Not the ideal host, I'm afraid.'

'I don't know what you're talking about, my dear,' the Bishop grumbled, leading John Kingsley off to his study for a long discussion of cathedral business.

David and Lucy followed Pat to the kitchen to help her with her final preparations, and they had a few minutes to chat before the other guests began to arrive. 'I don't suppose that either one of you knows too much about the rather peculiar format of our Patronal Festival,' Pat said. 'Have you been before, Lucy?'

'I remember coming years and years ago with the family, when I was quite young. When my mother was still alive.'

David looked puzzled. 'What makes it different from any other Patronal Festival?'

Pat laughed. 'If you're expecting the rarefied incense-vestments-procession of some spiky London church's version of a Patronal Festival, I'm afraid you may be disappointed. We're much more homespun out here in the country.'

'You intrigue me,' confessed David, taking it upon himself to give a last-minute polish to a trayful of glasses.

'I suppose that the term "Patronal Festival" is really a misnomer when it comes to what goes on here,' she explained. 'It just happens to take place around the Feast of St Malo. But it could be better described as a diocesan country fête, a real Barbara Pymish affair. It's not the least bit smart or grand – far from it. It's primarily for the bell-ringers, the diocesan Mothers' Union, and the parochial clergy – they're all encouraged to come, from all the country parishes, and everyone mucks in together and has a good time.'

David smiled maliciously. 'Somehow it doesn't sound exactly like the Dean's cup of tea.'

'Oh, I'm quite sure it's not.' Pat laughed again. 'But it was all planned long before he came – it was too late for him to alter it. It's been going on like this since long before George and I came to Malbury. George thinks it's important to make everyone feel that they're a part of the diocese, to realise that they matter.'

'What, exactly, does it involve?' asked Lucy. 'My memories of it are pretty dim – I just remember that Andrew – my oldest brother—' she explained in an aside to David, 'wanted to come because he was a bell-ringer.'

'Yes, it's quite an event for the diocesan bell-ringers,' Pat confirmed. 'Through most of the day there's a big striking competition, with plenty of beer – Watkins always sends along a barrel of Ploughman's Bitter. Of course we have open house here at the Bishop's House all day for the diocesan clergy and their families. And in the afternoon, by long-standing tradition, the Mothers' Union, or at least the diocesan committee and the Enrolling Member of each chapter, is entertained to tea at the Deanery.' She chuckled.

'The Deanery?' David raised his eyebrows in amusement.

'Yes, the Deanery! And believe me, those Mothers' Union women can be pretty formidable *en masse*. I wouldn't want to be in Stuart Latimer's shoes if he tries to cross them!' Pat smiled at the mental picture of an army of women with permed hair, pleated skirts and sensible shoes storming the Deanery. But she grew suddenly sober as she went on, 'But I suppose we'd all better enjoy it this year, as it will probably be the last. I'm sure that the Dean will put a stop to it from now on.'

The Greenwoods arrived, and Lucy was pleased to see how

happy – and how attractive – Judith looked. She was wearing a dress that Lucy had chosen for her on their London shopping trip, and her cheeks glowed with a natural colour that was far more becoming than make-up. She greeted Lucy with delight, and together they retreated to a corner for a long chat.

'I'm not saying that things are perfect between Rupert and me,' confided Judith, 'but in the last few weeks we've talked so much more than ever before. He just never had any idea how I felt about Malbury.'

'You never told him before,' Lucy pointed out reasonably.

'No. I'm not blaming him,' Judith was quick to reply. 'I shouldn't have expected him to read my mind. But I just thought . . . well, I thought that if two people were married, and loved each other, they ought to know how each other felt without saying anything.'

Lucy's voice was wry. 'I'm afraid it doesn't work like that. No matter how much you love each other.'

Judith smiled shyly. 'Oh, Lucy. London is going to be like a new start for Rupert and me. I can hardly wait.'

'How does Rupert feel about it?'

'He's looking forward to it, too. The new church sounds ideal – it has a fine musical tradition for him to build on. Though he'll be sorry to leave Malbury, of course. He's a bit worried about what will happen when he's gone.'

Lucy frowned slightly, remembering David's concerns. 'About the balance of power in the Chapter, you mean?'

Judith's reply was puzzled. 'No, he hasn't mentioned that. He's just worried about the lack of supervision for the music until a new organist and a new Precentor are appointed.'

The balance of power in the Chapter was one of the matters that the Bishop was discussing with John Kingsley. 'Rupert's resignation has changed everything,' George Willoughby assessed cogently. 'You realise, don't you, John, that if just one more of you goes, the Dean will be in a position to get his own way on anything he wants?'

'I'm not planning on resigning,' Canon Kingsley assured him with a half smile.

The Bishop laughed heartily. 'Oh, I didn't mean you, John! But what about Arthur? Do you think he'll go?'

John Kingsley considered the question seriously for a moment before replying. 'I think he might,' he said at last. 'I think he realises how futile his resistance will be, with Rupert breaking ranks. And Philip threatening to go as well.'

The Bishop's furry white eyebrows rose. 'Oh, is he, now?'

'I don't know if it will come to anything,' his friend hastened to assure him. 'But it all makes Arthur feel rather abandoned, I'm afraid.'

'Have you talked to him about it?'

'Yes, just yesterday, in fact.'

'And what did he say?'

'You want to know honestly? I think that he's almost at the point of deciding to go. It wouldn't take much persuasion to push him over. He's a desperately unhappy man, George.'

The Bishop stroked his beard thoughtfully. 'And how do you feel about it, John? Do you think that he should go?'

Again John Kingsley considered his answer. 'I have very mixed feelings.' He sighed. 'I'm not sure that it's a good thing for the Dean to get what he wants, especially when it comes to the Cathedral Centre. In itself it's a good thing, I suppose, but the cost is too high.'

'Too high? But raising the money will be his problem, not yours.'

'I don't mean in money, George. I mean in human and emotional terms. Think about poor Dorothy Unworth, and about Victor and Bert. And Arthur too, of course.' He sighed again, deeply. 'That's why, in the end, I think it's best for Arthur to go. For his own peace of mind. If he retires now, he can do it with dignity and with a chance of rebuilding some sort of emotional equilibrium. If his going means that it's easier for the Dean to get his own way . . . well, so be it. We'll have to live with the consequences. But Arthur is the most important consideration now. And I shall continue to do my best to move him in that direction, for his own good.'

Arthur Brydges-ffrench was also being discussed in the drawing room. 'He said he didn't feel well enough to come here tonight,' Todd Randall confirmed to Olivia Ashleigh and Rupert Greenwood. 'So Evelyn said that she'd look after him – make sure he got a nice meal and everything. It was a good thing that I was coming here – Evelyn told me, in the nicest possible way, to get lost for the evening.'

Olivia laughed, proffering a bowl of crisps. 'Poor Todd. Have a crisp.'

He eyed the tiny bowl dejectedly. 'There aren't enough potato chips in that little bowl for one person, let alone a whole room full. And there's no McDonald's in Malbury – I'll starve!'

Rupert looked around the room, his eyes lingering for a moment on the corner where his wife chatted vivaciously with Lucy. 'I don't see the Dean here,' he commented. 'Isn't he coming? Or wasn't he invited?'

'Oh, he was invited, all right!' Olivia assured him. 'But I think that he had more important fish to fry, so to speak. Rumour has it that he's entertaining Canon Thetford and his wife to dinner tonight.'

'Ah.' Rupert contrived to look disinterested.

'Don't mention dinner,' Todd groaned, patting his empty stomach melodramatically.

Jeremy was also keeping a discreet eye on the corner where Lucy talked to Judith, waiting for his opportunity to pounce. At least David was fully occupied helping Pat, he thought with a smile; David had recently refilled his glass with a barely concealed glare of suspicious antipathy, following Jeremy's gaze.

Almost as if by chance, Rowena materialised beside him, raising her glass in a friendly way. She, too, was aware of where Jeremy's attention was fixed, and she bit back a waspish comment about the charms of Miss Kingsley. 'So, tomorrow is the big day,' she began conversationally.

Jeremy frowned, uncomprehending. 'What do you mean?'

'Isn't tomorrow the day the Dean unveils his grand plans for all the world – or at least for the Malbury diocese – to see?'

'Oh, that.' Jeremy was cautious, unsure how much she knew.

'The grand Cathedral Centre,' Rowena amplified. 'The Dean's bid for immortality in the cathedral world. And yours as well, I suspect,' she added shrewdly. 'It's something we have in common, you and I,' she went on. 'An interest in the Dean's plans. An interest in seeing them carried out.'

Jeremy's mind worked quickly. 'So you got what you wanted?'

Rowena's smile was deliberately bland, though tinged with triumph – and perhaps with something else. 'I've told you before – I always get what I want. And you?'

The architect gave a noncommittal nod as he tried to gauge to what extent Rowena had been taken into the Dean's confidence. 'Perhaps we should pool our information. For our mutual benefit – and protection.'

Rowena turned puzzled eyes on him. 'Protection? What do you mean?'

'Well, it never hurts . . . to be cautious.'

Studying her drink, Rowena remembered the Dean's veiled hints about her lease. 'Do you think he's a man to keep his word?' she asked quietly. 'Do you think we can trust him?'

Jeremy took a sip of wine before he replied. 'I hope so. But I'll give you a word of advice – if I were you, I'd have the lease of your house drawn up in your own name, rather than as head of the Friends. Just to be on the safe side.'

'I see.' Her voice was thoughtful.

'And then there's the problem of Canon Brydges-ffrench,' Jeremy added.

Rowena nodded. 'Come round and have a chat some time.' She kept her tone cool, lowering her eyes. 'Perhaps between us we can come up with a way to deal with Arthur. From what I understand, he's being awkward and obstructive.'

'And I'm afraid that your feminine wiles, though they may have captivated the Dean, won't get you very far with that one.' Jeremy raised an eyebrow with a malicious grin. 'I'm not so sure, in fact, what sort of a bribe you could use to get on the good side of the Subdean. An antiquarian book, perhaps?'

'Crème de menthe Turkish Delight,' Rowena countered immediately. 'He can never resist it.' She smiled. 'Perhaps that's not such a bad idea after all. At any rate, it couldn't hurt. I'll get a box tomorrow, and I suggest that you do the same!'

Jeremy laughed. 'Well, that's the Subdean taken care of! Now if we can only manage to keep the Dean sweet . . .'

Chapter 27

For thither the tribes go up, even the tribes of the Lord: to
testify unto Israel, to give thanks unto the Name of the
Lord.

Psalm 122.4

It was Saturday morning at the Deanery, and all was in
readiness for the afternoon's hospitality: ranks of cups, saucers
and plates had been lined up in the drawing room, cakes and
scones had been baked, and now it was time for Anne Latimer
to give her husband a pep talk.

This was administered, briskly, over breakfast in the dining
room. 'I know,' she said, offering him the milk for his
cornflakes, 'that you think this is a waste of time.'

'A waste of time *and* resources,' he confirmed, not bothering
to hide his scorn.

'And so it may be. But the fact remains, Stuart, that it must
be done, and it must be done well.'

'But all of those dreadful old dragons from the Mothers'
Union . . .' he began peevishly.

His wife pressed her lips together. 'It won't hurt you to be
nice to them, just for one afternoon. And I'm not just talking
about the tea, Stuart. I'm talking about the whole day. I want
you out there, around the cathedral precincts, shaking hands
and kissing babies. All the rustics will expect it, and you'll give
it to them. And I'll be right there with you, smiling like the
perfect Dean's wife.' She stood up, slim and elegant in her pale
blondness, dressed already in her well-cut woollen suit and
pearls. 'It's just a shame,' she added, 'that the boys couldn't be
here. They'd make a good impression on the old dears, handing
round cups of tea.'

The Dean's face, as he finished his cornflakes, was as sulky
as a recalcitrant child's. But he knew, and she knew, that he'd
do as she said.

Things began happening quite early in the refectory. It was there that the beer for the bell-ringers was delivered and set up, and there also that the Mothers' Union gathered for morning coffee and cakes. The morning hospitality, in contrast to the afternoon affair at the Deanery, was provided by Dorothy Unworth, who was in addition to her other responsibilities the diocesan chairman of the Mothers' Union. As the thirsty bell-ringers gathered at one end of the refectory, making an early assault on the barrel of Ploughman's Bitter, the more genteel phalanx of the Mothers' Union began to arrive, each parish representative armed with her banner. The banners would be left in the refectory, in Dorothy's safe-keeping, throughout the day's festivities, until they were required for Evensong.

The Dean, in his black cassock and with his wife smiling serenely at his side, was very much in evidence throughout the morning, as was the Bishop, in his purple; Pat Willoughby, however, was occupied entertaining the diocesan clergy at the Bishop's House. Victor and Bert hovered around the refectory as well, armed with a camera. Victor marshalled each parish ringing company, in turn, into an artistic arrangement, flanked by the purple cassock on the one side and the black on the other, while Bert recorded the moment for posterity. 'Say Brie,' ordered Bert each time, while Victor cooed approval.

'Ooh, Bert! Some of those bell-ringers don't half have nice muscles,' Victor couldn't help whispering. He was quite enjoying his side of the enterprise, which sometimes entailed – perhaps more often than was strictly necessary – grabbing those selfsame muscular arms to move the ringers into position.

'It's pulling on those heavy bell-ropes, you know,' Bert explained. 'Develops upper-body strength.'

'Maybe *I* ought to take up bell-ringing, Bert dear. What do you think?'

Mid-morning there was a lull in the photo taking, as the ringers concentrated on their beer and the Mothers' Union on their coffee and cakes. Bert and Victor pinched a few cakes, fastidiously avoiding the Bakewell tarts. The Dean sloped off to the library, housed in the medieval storey above the cloister, where Jeremy's plans for the Cathedral Centre were on display for the inspection, primarily, of the diocesan clergy. 'I must put in an appearance there,' he explained to his wife. 'I've got to sell the idea to the clergy – we may want their help in fundraising.' Anne Latimer went back to the Deanery to oversee final preparations for tea, and Dr Willoughby returned to the Bishop's House to mingle with the clergy.

In the refectory, a raucous voice suddenly cut through the concentrated sounds of drinking and munching. It would perhaps be an exaggeration to say that everyone in the refectory was instantly aware of it, for by that time many of the bell-ringers were rapidly losing awareness of where they even were. But Victor and Bert, half-hearted at best in their enjoyment of their purloined food, moved quickly in the direction of the woman who had stumbled in and was moving somewhat erratically towards the beer. 'Is that them bell-ringers?' demanded Val Drewitt, her slurred voice indicating that she'd already had more than beer to drink that morning. 'Is my husband there, that lousy no-good bastard? *He's* a bloody bell-ringer. Or at least that's what he tells me. He's probably too busy screwing that stuck-up bitch to get near a bloody bell these days.'

It was loud enough that even Dorothy Unworth heard, and she turned, quivering with indignation; such language, to her knowledge, had never before been heard in the sacred precincts of the Cathedral Close. 'Get her out of here,' she hissed at Victor and Bert.

But Mrs Drewitt arrived at the nearest of the bell-ringers' tables before they could reach her. 'Is he here?'

Barry Crabtree, as the ringing master of the cathedral ringers and thus the self-appointed host, rose politely. 'He's not here, Mrs Drewitt. I think he may be up in the tower. Would you like some beer?' he added.

She frowned bellicosely and fumbled for a cigarette. 'No, I don't want your bloody beer! Isn't there any real drink around this place? Gin?'

Victor and Bert flanked her, one on each side. 'Come with us, Mrs Drewitt,' Bert urged. Hearing the masculine voice, she turned on him with an automatic flirtatious smile, then realised that her charms were wasted.

'We've got a bottle back at the shop,' Victor added with a persuasive smile.

With a sudden mood swing, she dropped her belligerence and

her expression turned to one of calculated cunning. 'Don't mind if I do. And if you're extra nice to me, boys, I may tell you some things you don't know about one or two people around here!' She glared around at the assembled company. 'People think I don't know anything, but I keep my eyes open, and some of these holier-than-thou types aren't exactly what they seem to be. And I don't just mean that Hunt bitch!'

Dorothy Unworth bristled with angry indignation, but at the bell-ringers' table, Barry Crabtree caught his friend Neil's eye and nodded thoughtfully.

The Friends of the Cathedral's contributions to the day's events were two-fold. On behalf of the Friends, Inspector Mike Drewitt – unaware of his wife's surprise appearance – had organised and was conducting tours of the tower, primarily for the benefit of the country clergy and their families. And in the retro-choir, Rowena had arranged a small exhibition sampling the cathedral's treasures: the Victorian cope, several rare books from the cathedral library, and, with pride of place, a few pieces of plate, most notably an Elizabethan silver-gilt alms dish. The exhibition was presided over by Canon Brydges-ffrench, who insisted that he would trust no one else with the cathedral's treasures.

'Though,' as he said to Evelyn Marsden, who stopped by to bring him a sandwich at lunch-time, 'I hardly know why I'm bothering. In a few months it may all be gone.' He sighed heavily. 'The books and the plate. Probably the cope too, for all I know.'

'Surely not!'

Arthur Brydges-ffrench lifted the alms dish lovingly, squinting at his distorted face as reflected in its rich patina. 'This was presented to the cathedral – when it was Malbury Parish Church – by a grateful parishioner nearly four hundred years ago,' he said softly. 'When the Cromwellians came, looking for things they could melt down, someone hid it and kept it safe until such time as it could be brought out again. Like Brother Thomas hiding St Malo's head, generations before. Now,' he went on, his voice rising on a swell of bitterness, 'he wants to sell it. That unspeakable man, that Vandal! And this time there's no one to hide it – no one to stop him!'

'But surely,' stated Evelyn, shocked, 'he *must* be stopped!'

The Subdean merely shook his head with a shuddering sigh.

David and Lucy decided, that afternoon, to go up to the cathedral library to have a look at the plans for the Cathedral Centre. The Dean had left by that time, returning to the Deanery for the afternoon's festivities; to David's dismay it was Jeremy who stood by the display to explain it to interested parties.

With the barest of greetings to the architect, David turned to study the display with every evidence of great interest. Lucy, however, moved over to speak to Jeremy, and soon they were deep in conversation. Unsure whether or not he really wanted to know what they were talking about, David alternated spells of reluctant eavesdropping with periods of deliberately ignoring them, concentrating his mind on the drawings. It was during one of the former episodes that he overheard a disturbing exchange.

'Thanks,' said Jeremy in an almost conspiratorial whisper – David had to strain to hear him – 'for not telling anyone about the building. The Dean would not have been amused if he'd known I'd told you at that early stage.'

'Far be it from me,' Lucy smiled, 'to get you in trouble with the Dean.'

As soon as Jeremy was engaged in explaining why the Cathedral Centre was an essential step forward to a curly-haired, cherubic-faced clergyman, David beckoned Lucy out of earshot, leading her to a secluded area of the library between two rows of shelving. He turned to face her, speaking quietly but with intensity. 'What did he mean, thanking you for not telling anyone about the building?'

'David! You were eavesdropping!'

He had the grace to look abashed. 'Well, yes. I was. But what did he mean? When did he tell you?'

Lucy thought for a moment before answering, deciding at last that it was time for honesty; compounding the lies at this point would only make matters worse, she realised. Her voice was gentle, and she put a hand on his arm. 'He told me about a month ago. I ran into him in London, purely by accident – he was there in connection with the plans. We had lunch together. I didn't tell you about it because I didn't want to upset you, darling. I know how insecure you are. I was wrong not to tell you, but I honestly thought I was doing the best thing – for you, for us.'

The hurt on his face, in his voice, was palpable. 'You had lunch with Jeremy in London and didn't tell me?' David turned away and blundered towards the steep stone staircase that led down to the cloister. Lucy, realising that perhaps it was best for him to be alone, didn't follow.

Scarcely aware of where he was going, he went out of the cloister, past the Bishop's House, and around to the west front of the Cathedral. There he stood for a long time, staring at the vast green space which, he reflected, if the Dean had his way, would soon be covered with a very large and probably extremely unsightly building. That, he realised at the back of his mind, was being uncharitable, for all other considerations aside – considerations of his own personal feelings, and of Jeremy's professional integrity – Jeremy Bartlett was a skilled architect with a real feel for ancient buildings, and he could be counted on at least for a sympathetic design. Still, it was a great pity that this open space, which gave the cathedral much of its charm, would be lost. By force of will he concentrated his thoughts on the Cathedral Centre, resisting the tug back to the subject of Lucy and Jeremy. It was just too painful to think about right now. Lucy had lied to him. What else was she concealing?

'Pretty, isn't it?' spoke a voice at his side. Pat had joined him, gazing out at the green. 'In the summer, the children play there.' David could picture it in his mind: young children in brightly-coloured clothing, rolling in the warm grass on a long, twilit summer evening. Now, though, it was the province of a few large crows, strutting about self-importantly. 'I don't know if you know its history,' she went on conversationally. 'As in so many of the monastic churches, the town owned part of it. At the Reformation, when the Abbey was closed, the townspeople tore down their bit – this part, at the west end – mostly so they could re-use the building materials, the stones and the lead. But they soon realised that they'd been rather short-sighted, as they no longer had a church. So they bought the rest from the Crown for use as the parish church, which it remained until it was elevated to cathedral status in the last century.'

'How interesting.'

Pat turned to look at his troubled face appraisingly. 'I don't often see you on your own. Where is Lucy?'

'In the library. Talking to Jeremy.'

Perceptive as she was, she was able to read a great deal into those stark sentences; Jeremy's interest in Lucy over the last several months had not escaped her attention. 'Is something wrong?'

Her genuine concern was almost enough to finish David off, but he managed to maintain control, at least at first. 'No. Well, perhaps,' he admitted wretchedly. 'Jeremy . . . he fancies Lucy. I can tell.' He was tempted to go on and confide in her about his suspicions of Jeremy's trustworthiness, but decided that such a confidence would be premature as well as inappropriate to share with the Bishop's wife.

'But Lucy loves *you*, not Jeremy,' stated Pat.

'Oh, I know. Or at least I think so. And I love her more than I ever thought possible. But . . . it's so difficult when we're here in Malbury. It seems as if we never have any time alone together – we almost seem to lose touch with each other somehow.' David looked out at the green, unable to meet her eyes.

'Ah.' Reading between the lines, Pat considered the problem. 'Well,' she said practically, 'I think it's now high time for you to spend some time alone together. What are you waiting for? Go back up to the library this minute and get her. Take her to the nice little teashop in town, out of the Close.' She thought further, going on in a brisk voice, 'Or better yet, take her back to her father's house for tea, and spend some time . . . talking.'

'But her father . . .'

'Her father is at my house, chatting with some of his old friends. I will contrive to keep him there until Evensong, by force if necessary! So you won't be interrupted. You have an empty house, and nearly two hours before Evensong. Now *go*!'

He raised his head, galvanised to act. 'Yes, I will. Thanks, Pat.'

'Don't mention it.' She grinned and gave him a conspiratorial wink as he turned and strode back towards the cloister with determination.

In due time, after their tea at the Deanery, the Mothers' Union processed into Evensong with their parish banners aloft, filling the Quire and overflowing into the Nave. David and Lucy, arriving almost at the last minute, were afraid that they might have to sit in the Nave, where the visibility was almost nonexistent, but Pat had thoughtfully saved them seats. They were flanked on the other side by Todd, who greeted them with a cheerful grin. 'Doesn't the cathedral look nice?' he whispered, indicating the gold festival hangings on the altar.

David nodded. 'And I see that they've got the scaffolding down in time for the Patronal Festival.'

'Yes, and they've done a fantastic job of repairing that window. It looks exactly the same as it did before.'

The verger entered, bearing his verge in front of him solemnly; they all stood as the clergy and choir processed in to take their places.

'O Lord, open thou our lips,' intoned Rupert Greenwood's pure voice; the service had begun.

It was a beautiful service: the choir, under Rupert's tutelage, had never sung better, and the darkness of the sky outside lent a kind of hushed magic to the candlelit Quire. The climax, for John Kingsley, was the Nunc Dimittis; Noble in B minor was not the showiest or most spectacular setting of the Canticles in the repertoire, but the Canon found its old-fashioned simplicity deeply affecting. 'Lord, now lettest thou thy servant depart in peace,' the trebles sang. John Kingsley glanced at the next stall, where Arthur Brydges-ffrench sat with head bowed, then looked up towards the Bishop's chair and caught George Willougby's eye. He knew that they were both thinking the same thing: Lord, please let Arthur go in peace.

Chapter 28

Thy rebuke hath broken my heart; I am full of heaviness: I looked for some to have pity on me, but there was no man, neither found I any to comfort me.

Psalm 69.21

After the early communion service on the following Monday, John Kingsley sought out the Dean for a brief word. The Dean had taken the service, so the Canon followed him to the sacristy, where they would not be overheard.

'It's about Arthur Brydges-ffrench,' he said. 'I had a long talk with him last night, after Evensong.'

'Yes?' the Dean tried not to sound impatient, but he was anxious to get home to his breakfast.

'I believe that he has just about made up his mind to go.'

The Dean turned on him with a smile. 'Ah.'

'He has nearly made up his mind,' Canon Kingsley repeated for emphasis, 'but he will not be forced. Not by me, and not by you. You'll have to take it very carefully from here.'

This brought a frown to the Dean's face. 'Well, what do you suggest I do?'

John Kingsley chose his words carefully, aware of how much was at stake. 'I think that you need to tell him that you are as concerned about the cathedral's future as he is – that you're only doing what you feel you must do to ensure its survival. And it might be more effective if you could do it in a non-threatening situation – say, if you were to invite him over for a meal, and spend some time just chatting. Then it might come up naturally, and it wouldn't seem so calculated or deliberate. I wouldn't wait very long, though – he could change his mind again any time.'

'But Anne is away in London this week. I'm not really set up for entertaining on my own.'

'I think it would be even better this way,' urged the Canon. 'Just a simple supper – some bread and cheese, perhaps. And if you really want to please Arthur, and convince him of your sincerity, you could get a box of crème de menthe Turkish Delight.'

The Dean looked baffled. 'Crème de menthe Turkish Delight?'

Smiling, the Canon explained, 'Arthur loves it – he eats it by the boxful. It's his greatest weakness.'

'But where on earth would I find such a thing?'

'At the Cathedral Shop. Victor and Bert keep it in stock for him.'

The Dean nodded decisively, making up his mind to do what had to be done. 'Very well, then. It may as well be tonight. I shall go immediately and ask Canon Brydges-ffrench to have supper with me this evening.' By this time he had finished in the sacristy, so he hurried off, hoping to catch the Subdean before he left the cathedral.

John Kingsley remained in the sacristy for a moment, fixing his eyes on the crucifix and saying a silent prayer. At last he spoke aloud, half to God and half to himself: 'How I hope I've done the right thing.'

Arthur Brydges-ffrench had been in his stall throughout the service, kneeling almost motionlessly; he hadn't even gone forward to receive communion. His mind was in turmoil, and he prayed fervently that God would give him a sign, show him a way out of what seemed to be an impossible situation. The service ended without his noticing as he prayed on, oblivious to the ache in his knees.

'Arthur?' The Dean spoke quietly, standing in front of him; interrupted, Canon Brydges-ffrench gave a violent start. It was the first time, he realised, that the Dean had ever addressed him by his Christian name. Was this the sign he'd waited for?

'Yes, Dean?'

'I was wondering whether you might be free to join me for supper this evening. Anne is away, so it won't be anything elaborate – just a simple meal, and just the two of us.'

For a moment the older man blinked up at him uncomprehending, licking his lips nervously. He said nothing, so the Dean went on in a rush, almost as if he were trying to convince himself as well. 'I think it's about time for us to have a little talk. Get to know one another. Try to reach an understanding.'

Canon Brydges-ffrench reared back on his heels, suddenly aware of his aching knees. He stood, stretching to his full height with a little groan, and looked down at the Dean. 'Yes. All right,' he agreed. 'All right.'

'About eight, then?' He had to tilt his head back to see the Subdean's face; he felt that it put him at a real disadvantage.

'I shall be there.'

Today, Stuart Latimer resolved, would be the day in which he would sort out all the little issues that had been pushed to the bottom of the list, all the necessary evils that had to be accomplished before his plans could reach fruition. This morning he would inform Evelyn Marsden of his intention to raise her rent, and then he would tell Dorothy Unworth and Victor and Bert that their days were numbered. The bully in him rather looked forward to these encounters, for in them he would unquestionably have the upper hand.

He had prepared a letter for Evelyn Marsden, setting out the proposed rent increase, but he intended to deliver it in person, so that he could see her face when she realised that she would be losing her home.

Miss Marsden opened the door to him with well-concealed puzzlement; the Dean was not known for paying calls in the Close, either alone or with his wife. 'Would you like a coffee?' she offered. 'I've just fixed myself some.'

'Yes, that would be very pleasant,' he agreed, rubbing his hands together.

She led him to her first-floor sitting room with its unimpeded view of the cathedral, the Close, and most particularly the entrance to the Deanery. Her chair was by the window; as she assumed what was clearly her accustomed seat with an automatic glance down into the Close, it was very clear to the Dean that she spent much of her time sitting there, spying on his comings and goings. In his mind that justified, somehow, what he was about to do to her – the nosy old cow, he thought self-righteously.

She poured him a cup of coffee from a little filtered pot – no instant granules for Miss Marsden – and sat back to await some indication of the reason for his visit. The coffee, the Dean had to admit, was extremely tasty, as was the home-made biscuit that she offered him. He must not allow himself to be deflected, but perhaps a bit of small talk would be in order.

Casting his eye around for a likely topic of conversation, he spotted a bag of knitting next to her chair. 'What are you making?'

'Oh, this.' Her laugh was self-conscious as she held it up. 'It's a sleeveless pullover, for Arthur. To wear under his cassock. He's not as young as he used to be, you know, and I do believe he feels the cold more than he used to. With winter coming on . . .'

The Dean didn't really want to discuss Arthur Brydges-ffrench. 'You enjoy knitting, then?'

'Oh, yes. It relaxes me, I find – and I've been doing it for so many years that I can do it without looking.' As if to demonstrate, she picked up the black wool and within a moment the thin steel needles were clicking rhythmically, though her eyes never left the Dean's face.

'A useful talent,' he declared heartily. 'My wife could never be bothered to learn to knit.'

'Somehow I never imagined that Mrs Latimer was a knitter.' She said it in a humorous way, intending to be friendly, but it reminded the Dean once again that this woman was in the habit of spying on his family. He put his hand to his pocket and drew out the letter.

'I have a letter here for you, Miss Marsden,' he said without preliminary. 'I believe that it is self-explanatory, but I have delivered it in person in case you have any questions.'

She put down her knitting, took the letter from him, opened it without any evident apprehension and began to read; the Dean watched her as the blood drained from her face. At last she raised stricken eyes to him. 'What is the meaning of this?' she asked in a choked whisper.

'As I said, I think it's self-explanatory. The figure named will be your new rent, as from next year.'

'But . . . but I can't possibly afford that much!'

The Dean looked suitably grave. 'I'm sorry to hear that. In that case, I shall have to begin looking for a new tenant.'

Evelyn took a deep breath. 'But it's monstrous! I've lived here for over thirty years, and my rent has never gone up before!'

'My point exactly, Miss Marsden. Your rent has been artificially low – far too low – since you've been here. This property must be made profitable – the cathedral is not in the business of charity, much as we would like to be. If you tell me that you can't afford the increase . . .'

'I'm living at the limit of my income as it is!'

He shook his head sympathetically. 'Then it seems we have no choice. Much as we may regret the fact, Miss Marsden, we must all live within our means. You should, I suppose, count yourself fortunate that you've been able to stay here in the Close for so many years.'

Her voice trembled as she tried to take in the enormity of what was happening. 'But I have nowhere else to go . . .'

'This has come as quite a shock to you,' he said with unctuous composure. 'You will have a few months to make alternative arrangements, and I'm sure that when you've had a chance to calm down and think about this rationally, you will be able to find a solution to your little . . . problem.'

A short time later, Evelyn Marsden stood at the door of Canon Brydges-ffrench's house, holding herself rigid to counteract the trembling sensation in her legs. She took a deep breath before pressing the bell; the old-fashioned chime sounded faintly somewhere in the house, barely audible to her.

After a moment the Subdean appeared, blinking, as if his mind were elsewhere. 'Hello, Evelyn.' He summoned up a courteous smile and looked expectantly at her hands; she often called on him like this with some little token of friendship, a cake or a pot of marmalade or a pair of hand-knitted socks. On these occasions he never invited her in, but accepted her offerings on the doorstep.

So he was surprised that her hands were empty, and that she was looking beyond him into the dim entrance hall. 'Can I come in, Arthur? I must talk to you.' Her voice was controlled, but only just.

'Yes, of course.' He stepped aside to let her past.

She had not been inside his house in quite some time, she realised – probably not since just after his mother's funeral, nearly a year past. During the reign of the formidable Mrs Brydges-ffrench, Evelyn had occasionally been invited round to take tea with that lady and her son, but now she was the one who entertained Arthur, when any entertaining was done. The change in the house since she had last been there was marked: all traces of Mrs Brydges-ffrench's rigorously immaculate housekeeping had been eradicated, and there was a dusty, almost seedy, feel to the place. How shocked Gertrude Brydges-ffrench would have been, thought Evelyn, to have known that one could have written one's name in the dust on her hall table.

He stood irresolute in the hall, unsure where to take her, then led her into his study. Sitting behind his desk, he indicated a chair to her, but she remained standing, clasping her hands in front of her as if in unconscious supplication.

'The Dean has been to see me this morning,' Evelyn began, keeping her voice steady.

'Yes?' He now had some idea what this might be about.

'He gave me a letter to inform me that next year my rent would be raised to an absolutely ridiculous figure. Were you aware of this?'

The Subdean lowered his head and busied himself with an untidy pile of papers. 'Yes, I was. But I'm afraid there is absolutely nothing that can be done about it.'

'Can't you use your influence, Arthur?' Her voice quavered, just a little. 'Surely it will require a vote in Chapter.'

Canon Brydges-ffrench sounded weary, and he shaded his eyes with his hand. 'I've done all that I possibly can do. I've protested to the Dean, but he has failed to heed me. It *will* require a vote in Chapter, but with Rupert going and Philip set to follow him in deserting us, the Dean will win. He won't call a vote until he's sure it will go his way.'

'But, Arthur! It means I will have to leave the Close! And I have nowhere else to go!'

'I am very sorry, my dear. I wish there were some way out, but I can't see one.'

The utterance was flat, and drained of emotion, but the sentiment it expressed gave Evelyn the impetus she needed. She stood very still for a moment, screwing up her courage; the knuckles on her clasped hands were white. 'There is one way out,' she said in a very quiet voice. 'I could come here to live.'

At first he looked merely puzzled, as though she had suggested joining the circus or emigrating to Australia. 'What on earth are you talking about?'

'I could come here to live,' she repeated, suddenly shy. She went on, increasingly agonised, 'I always knew that as long as your mother was alive, it wasn't possible. But I'd always understood that when she was . . . gone, that you . . . that I . . . that we might. . . marry.'

'Marry?!' The look on his face, the tone of his voice, registered the most complete and utter incredulity. 'But how absurd!'

Evelyn wished at that moment that the floor might open up and swallow her forever. She paled, then flamed red, whispering painfully, 'I'm sorry, Arthur. I thought . . .'

He stared at her. After a moment he said, with gentle dignity, 'There seems to have been some misunderstanding. Such a thing is out of the question, naturally. But the blame must be mine – if I have done anything to mislead you, Evelyn – and I clearly must have done – I apologise most sincerely.'

Before she could react, there was an almighty crash as Todd Randall, trapped behind the sofa sorting through a pile of books since their conversation began, attempted to creep out and tripped over still another stack of books. 'I'm sorry,' he said sheepishly.

Mortified, Evelyn Marsden fled. 'I'm so sorry, Arthur. I'll let myself out,' she murmured over her shoulder.

Todd looked guiltily at the Subdean's stricken face. 'I'm really sorry about that. I should have said something sooner to let you know that I was there, but I didn't realise . . .'

'Oh, that's all right, Todd.' Canon Brydges-ffrench gave him an abstracted, forced smile. 'I don't mind. But Miss Marsden . . .'

The young man thought quickly. 'Perhaps it would be better for me to go away for a few days, don't you think? When the coast is clear, I'll sneak up to my room and grab a few things. I can go to London.'

'Yes, perhaps that would be best,' the Subdean agreed.

So Todd departed, leaving Arthur Brydges-ffrench alone at his desk. Broodingly, he opened the box of crème de menthe Turkish Delight that was always near to hand, and selected one of the last few pieces; in a few minutes the box was empty.

Chapter 29

*I will pay my vows unto the Lord: in the sight of all his
people: in the courts of the Lord's house, even in the midst
of thee, O Jerusalem. Praise the Lord.*

Psalm 116.16

Driven partly by his craving for Turkish Delight and partly by
an unformulated need to get out of his house and breathe some
fresh air, Arthur Brydges-ffrench set off for the Cathedral Shop
in the early afternoon.

As he came out of his house, he stood for a moment looking
across towards the cathedral – his cathedral, the one passion of
his life. It was a raw November day, heavy with a damp chill
fog that had never lifted, and the cathedral appeared as
nothing more than a huge formless bulk in the mist, its well-
loved details blurred into nonexistence. Yet in the Close there
was activity. He passed Judith Greenwood hurrying along; she
acknowledged him with a wave, although, walking with his
head down, he was scarcely aware of it.

A moment later, though, he encountered Jeremy Bartlett,
who was heading in the opposite direction, and Jeremy was not
about to let him pass unchallenged.

'Canon Brydges-ffrench!'

He looked up, startled, and hesitated momentarily. 'Oh.
Hello.'

Jeremy stepped in front of him to block his path. 'I've just
seen Rupert Greenwood in the cathedral,' he stated.

'Oh?'

'And he told me that you've turned the music festival books
over to the Dean.'

The Canon snapped out of his preoccupation. 'Yes . . . um.
That's correct.' He cleared his throat apologetically.

'Why the bloody hell did you do that?' Jeremy blazed. 'I told
you to stall him!'

213

'But I *did* stall him as long as I could.' In spite of the chill air, the old man felt himself going uncomfortably hot, and he fumbled for his handkerchief. 'He kept insisting.'

'The accounts weren't even prepared!'

Canon Brydges-ffrench coughed to cover his agitation, then protested feebly, 'I told him that. And he said that if I couldn't give him the accounts, he'd have the books instead. I couldn't see how I . . .'

'So you just bloody gave them to him?' demanded the architect. 'Without even telling me?'

The Canon had never seen this side of Jeremy Bartlett before, and it frightened him. 'Yes, well. I suppose I should have told you. But there didn't seem any point in alarming you . . .'

'No point? My God, Canon, you're a bloody old fool!' His volume was low but his tone was passionately intense. 'And has the Dean perchance taken a look at the books?'

'I don't know. I don't think so. At any rate he hasn't said . . .'

Jeremy took a deep breath. 'Then you can be sure he hasn't looked at them. If he had, we'd have heard by now. There are holes in those books that you could drive a lorry through. As you well know.'

'Yes. Well.' The Subdean looked over Jeremy's head, refusing to meet his eyes.

For a moment the architect stood still, thinking. 'Are the books at the Deanery?' he asked suddenly, in a more controlled voice.

'I don't know. That is, I suppose so.'

Jeremy's anger flared again. 'I just don't believe that you could have been so idiotic!' he snapped. 'And now—' He broke off as Rowena opened her front door and came towards them.

'Good afternoon, Rowena,' said the Canon with a gusty sigh of relief at his deliverance.

'Arthur,' she began, but he was already in motion.

'Later, my dear,' he piped over his shoulder as he hurried on in the direction of the shop.

Rowena looked at Jeremy quizzically. 'What was that all about? You sounded rather angry.'

He regained his composure quickly, smiling at Rowena with conscious charm. 'Oh, nothing. You know what a funny old bird he is.'

Noting the way his fists were clenched, she remained unconvinced. 'I think you're holding out on me,' she said, her tone lightly teasing. 'I thought that we had an understanding.'

'Indeed we do.' They walked along together in the direction of the Deanery. Jeremy wondered, but didn't ask, where Rowena was going; she had a carrier bag, but he couldn't tell what it contained. Pausing in front of Evelyn Marsden's house, Jeremy looked up at her first floor window. 'She's watching us, you know,' he said conversationally.

'Poor old thing,' Rowena replied with transparently false sympathy. 'You've got to feel sorry for her – nothing better to do than spy on other people.'

'And knit,' he added, quirking an eyebrow. 'Like Madame Defarge at the guillotine. So who's going under the blade first – you or me?'

'Oh, please!' She gave an extravagant shudder and Jeremy laughed at her reaction. 'Seriously, Jeremy,' she went on. 'I think we need to have a talk. There are several things . . .'

'Yes, of course,' he said. But he was not looking at Rowena as he said it; he was looking over her shoulder at the Deanery, and his expression was speculative.

When Arthur Brydges-ffrench arrived at the Cathedral Shop, he discovered that, unusually, Victor was there alone.

Victor was also uncharacteristically subdued, greeting the Canon with no more than a hint of his customary exuberance. Knowing what the cleric was likely to have come for, he ordinarily made some joke in questionable taste regarding the delights of certain Turks he had known, but today he said merely, 'Your usual, dear?'

'Yes, please.'

'You're in luck – my last box,' Victor remarked, reaching under the counter. 'There's been an absolute run on the stuff in the last few days. I would have thought you'd be well stocked, since I assumed they were all buying it for you. No one else in his right mind would eat it, Arthur dear.'

The Subdean frowned, puzzled. 'But no one's given me any. You're sure Bert hasn't just moved the supply without telling you?'

'Oh, no. I'm telling you, I've sold it all.' He ticked them off on his fingers. 'Saturday morning it was Miss Marsden. Then in the afternoon I sold a box to Rowena Hunt, and later on one to that architect bloke. Now *he's* a rather dishy number,' he added with a hint of his old twinkle.

'How odd.'

'Then this morning I sold a box to the Dean.' At this Victor looked decidedly pained, glaring accusingly at Canon Brydges-ffrench. 'He said that you were coming to supper tonight and he wanted to surprise you.'

He lifted his eyebrows. 'Yes . . .'

'I hoped that he'd got it wrong,' Victor said stiffly. 'I must say, Arthur, I never thought that you'd sell us out to that dreadful man.'

The Subdean recoiled. 'Sell you out? What makes you think I would sell you out?'

'Well, you *are* going to supper with him, aren't you? Doesn't that mean you've joined his camp?'

'He has invited me for a meal,' replied Canon Brydges-ffrench cautiously. 'I haven't joined anything.'

'There are rumours . . .' Victor hesitated. 'There are rumours that you're going to resign. It's not true, is it?'

'I should think that you would know better than to believe everything you hear in the Close,' the Canon countered. 'But why . . .'

Victor could contain himself no longer. 'He told us that our lease was not going to be renewed! When he came to buy the Turkish Delight!'

'Oh.'

'Bert – why, Bert was beside himself! He's had to go home and take some tranquillisers, the poor darling. I mean, it's outrageous! After all the years we've been here, after all we've done.'

The Subdean lowered his eyes. 'Victor, I'm sorry.'

'And Dorothy too! She came in later to tell us that he's giving her the boot as well! Can you imagine?!'

'It's a very bad business.'

'Dorothy may manage to beat him – after all, she's got the entire diocesan Mothers' Union behind her. They're more than a match for that puny, miserable sod of a Dean. But think of *us*, Arthur! Bert has a very nervous disposition, and my heart can't take this kind of strain. It could kill us both, to be thrown out in the streets with nothing to our names.' Victor fixed him with a piteous stare, like some Victorian waif selling matches in the snow. 'Can't you do something to stop him, Arthur? Something to help us, to save our lives? I implore you! After all, we've always been friends, haven't we?'

Arthur Brydges-ffrench put his money down on the counter and picked up the Turkish Delight. 'I'm so sorry, Victor. I've spoken up for you in Chapter meeting, but there's nothing more I can do.' Trusting himself to say no more, he escaped quickly into the Close.

He thought of going into the cathedral, but didn't want to run the risk of meeting anyone; he had the idea of nipping in through the Dean's door, privately, to his stall. He felt in his cassock pocket for his keys, but remembered, belatedly, that he had loaned them to Jeremy Bartlett the day before so that the architect could take down the display in the library at his leisure. He'd asked Todd to get the keys back, but the events of the morning had driven such a trivial matter from his mind – and from Todd's as well, presumably – until just now. Besides, coming such a short way, he'd come out without a coat, and now realised that he was chilled. Shivering, clutching his box of sweets to his thin chest, he turned back towards home.

Sweets. The Dean had bought him a box of sweets. 'Out of the strong came forth sweetness,' he thought. There was something apposite about Samson's riddle: the strong Dean bringing forth a box of Turkish Delight, a peace offering. The hirsute Dean, hairy like Samson. Was his strength in his hair? And would he end up in pulling the cathedral down around his ears out of selfish ambition, as Samson had done in selfless sacrifice with the house of his captors? It was in itself a riddle, and it gave Arthur Brydges-ffrench an idea.

His steps quickened; when he arrived home he went straight to his study and found a reasonably clean sheet of blank paper under a pile of books. Uncapping the heavy gold fountain pen which he used each morning to do *The Times* crossword puzzle, he sat down at his desk and began to jot some notes in his crabbed, nearly illegible hand, pausing only to remove the cellophane wrapper from the new box of Turkish Delight.

A short time later, Bert walked through the Close, passing the Cathedral Shop with hurried steps and looking circumspectly over his shoulder to make sure that he had not been observed by Victor. He was so intent on stealth that he failed to see the woman in the Close until she was practically on top of him. 'Hi there, mate,' hailed Val Drewitt. 'Where's your other half?'

Startled and guilty, Bert jumped. 'Don't do that!' he gasped. 'You nearly frightened me out of my skin!'

Val chuckled in amusement. 'Caught you, did I?' She looked at him speculatively. 'What are you up to, then? Cheating on Victor?'

He blinked. 'What do you mean?'

Nudging him in the ribs, Val gave a ribald snort. 'Who is it, then? Not the Dean – I don't think he's your type, is he?' She laughed uproariously for a moment. 'And not that cow Rowena Hunt – she's *certainly* not your type!'

Bert smiled thinly. 'I don't know what you're talking about.'

'Wait a minute. Let me think.' Val leaned close and peered at his face. 'I'll bet it's that Rupert Greenwood. I know he's married, but that don't really mean anything, does it? He's a bit too fond of those choirboys for a happily married man, wouldn't you say?' She winked broadly. 'Don't worry, I won't tell Victor.'

'But Mrs Drewitt . . .'

'Please, call me Val! After all, we're mates, aren't we?' She tucked her arm through his. 'I'll tell you what, Bert. I'd love a glass of gin. How about it?'

'You drank the whole bottle on Saturday,' he protested.

'Oh, come on,' she wheedled. 'We can go down to the off-license, and then to my place. Buy me some gin, and I'll tell you things that I'll bet you don't know about the people in the Close. You like gossip, don't you? I could tell you things . . .'

'That's what you promised on Saturday,' Bert reminded her. 'But you passed out before you told us anything.'

Val giggled. 'I did, didn't I? But this time I'll deliver the goods.' She looked up at Evelyn Marsden's first floor window with a knowing grimace. 'Believe me, mate, I see more of what goes on around here than that dried-up old crow does.'

Just before seven o'clock that evening, Arthur Brydges-ffrench rang John Kingsley's bell.

'Arthur! Do come in,' the Canon invited, surprised to see the other man.

'I'm going to supper at the Deanery,' he said abruptly. 'And I wanted to talk to you first.'

'Yes, of course.'

The Subdean was carrying a Turkish Delight box which he

put down on the hall table. 'I've brought something for you, John. Something I'd like you to have.'

'Thank you, Arthur. That's very kind. But . . .'

'If . . . if I give the Dean my resignation, I may have to leave immediately. We may not meet again.'

'Oh, surely not,' John Kingsley protested. 'The Dean wouldn't be that brutal. He'd give you all the time you needed to settle your affairs.'

'Nevertheless.'

In spite of the fact that he had used the conditional 'if' when speaking of his resignation, Canon Kingsley sensed that Arthur Brydges-ffrench was a man who had made up his mind at last. Gone were the near hysterics of recent meetings: he was sad, but calm. 'Would you like a drink before you go to the Deanery?' he offered.

'No, not that. But I'd like you to hear my confession, John.'

'Surely that's not necessary.'

The Subdean smiled gravely. 'Perhaps not, but it would make me feel better. You're not refusing, are you?'

'Of course not. Anything you like, Arthur.'

So confession was made, and absolution given. Canon Brydges-ffrench made ready to take his leave. 'I have just one more favour to ask of you, John.'

'You know I'll do anything I can to help.' Canon Kingsley put his hand on his friend and colleague's sleeve, noticing abstractedly that the cuff of the old black cassock was beginning to fray.

He sighed. 'I'm a bit worried about tonight, John. The Dean – well, I'm not sure that he'd stop at anything to get what he wants.'

'Whatever do you mean, Arthur?' He looked at the Subdean keenly.

'I'm not sure what I mean. But I have a very uneasy feeling about it. The invitation itself seems so uncharacteristic of the man – I'm afraid he's up to something.'

'I'm sure that he's making a genuine effort to sort things out,' John Kingsley reassured him. 'I think he's sincere, if a little misguided sometimes.'

'You always have given people the benefit of the doubt, haven't you, John?' Canon Brydges-ffrench gave a slightly sardonic laugh. 'I believe that it's your biggest fault. You can't really bring yourself to believe that people are capable of evil.'

'I don't like to think so,' he admitted. 'Perhaps that is unrealistic. But in this case, I'm sure . . .'

'Promise me one thing,' the Subdean interrupted. 'Promise me that you'll ring the Deanery at ten o'clock. Just to make sure that all is well.'

'It hardly seems . . .'

'Promise me,' he repeated urgently. 'Please.'

'Yes,' John Kingsley agreed with some reluctance. 'Yes, I will.'

'Thank you, John. Don't forget. Ten o'clock.' And with that Arthur Brydges-ffrench departed for the Deanery.

It was ten o'clock exactly; John Kingsley heard the cathedral clock chime as he dialled. The Dean answered after several rings. 'Stuart Latimer speaking.' His voice sounded somewhat impatient.

Canon Kingsley felt rather foolish; he scarcely knew what to say. 'Oh, hello, Dean. This is John Kingsley. I . . . just wanted to be sure that everything was all right. With Arthur, I mean.'

There was a sharply indrawn breath. 'Well, in fact, Arthur's being . . . awkward.'

'What do you mean?'

'At first he was fine. We seemed to be getting on quite well, and making real progress in our discussion. We had a nice, civilised meal, with no daggers drawn. But just a few minutes ago, he suddenly said that he was not prepared to resign under any circumstances. He said that in his opinion I was attempting to destroy the cathedral, and he would never forgive himself if he took the easy way out and stood aside to let me do it. He said that he would never willingly resign, and that I couldn't force him.'

'But I don't understand. I thought . . .'

'*You* thought! *I* thought!' The Dean's puzzlement flared into anger. 'Damn it, John! The man's impossible! There's just no way to deal rationally with him!'

'Perhaps if I were to talk to him again . . .'

'What good would that do? We could both talk to him till we're blue in the face, and he wouldn't pay a blind bit of notice.' He laughed ironically. 'No, John, I'm beginning to think that for all our efforts, we're going to be stuck with Arthur Brydges-ffrench until death us do part!'

* * *

And yet, an hour or so later, when John Kingsley was roused from his sleepless bed by the ear-splitting screech of the ambulance, he was not prepared for what had happened. His emotions were complex: shock, grief, and guilt over his own complicity in the events of the evening; he, after all, had been the one to suggest that meal at the Deanery. For it was all too clear what had happened when Arthur Brydges-ffrench was carried out on a stretcher, near death, and when, a short while later, Dean Stuart Latimer, dwarfed by the two muscular officers who flanked him, accompanied the police to the station to 'assist them with their enquiries'. How had such a thing ever happened? How had it come to this? But how could he blame himself? He couldn't possibly, thought John Kingsley, have seen it coming.

Act III

Chapter 30

O go not from me, for trouble is hard at hand: and there is none to help me.

Psalm 22.11

'Poisoned!' David stared at Lucy incredulously. 'Arthur Brydges-ffrench?'

'That's what Daddy said.' She, too, looked stunned.

Todd spoke for the first time. 'He's dead?' Todd, a grimy red nylon backpack slung round his shoulders, had arrived unannounced late the previous afternoon, and had spent the night on the sofa-bed, but had been strangely reticent about his reasons for leaving Malbury so precipitously.

Lucy nodded. 'Yes, he's dead. He died in hospital during the night.' She sat down abruptly and looked at the two men across the breakfast table, twisting a curl around her finger. In as few words as possible she related the substance of her father's telephone call. 'He went to supper at the Deanery. He'd told my father before he went that he was worried that something might happen, but Daddy didn't believe him. After supper he was taken ill, the Dean called for an ambulance, and he died later in hospital. All they know at this point was that it was poison – they're not sure what sort, or how it was administered, but they've taken the Dean in for questioning.'

'The Dean?' gasped David. 'Good Lord! But surely the police don't think the Dean of Malbury Cathedral has committed cold-blooded murder?' As soon as he said it, he realised that he could quite easily believe the Dean capable of committing murder, if he were sufficiently motivated: he was single-minded enough, and certainly ruthless and selfish. The great surprise, really, David thought, was that it wasn't the Dean himself who had been murdered – for that crime there would be a multitude of likely suspects.

'He hasn't been charged yet, as far as Daddy knows.'

'It's a bit early for that,' David said.

She nodded. 'But the Bishop has gone to see him, and Daddy will get back to me as soon as he knows any more.' Lucy hesitated, realising that she was about to tread on delicate ground. 'He asked me to get in touch with you, darling, to see if perhaps . . .'

'No,' he stated resolutely. 'Absolutely not. I'm not getting involved in this. My firm would never allow it. They don't touch criminal work.'

She decided to bide her time. 'All right. I'll tell him that when he phones again.'

Throughout this exchange, since his initial involuntary utterance, Todd Randall hadn't said a word. Now he spoke at last, shaking his head rapidly as if to clear it. 'I can't believe it,' he said. 'I was with him yesterday. He can't be dead.'

But dead he was, and in the event it was Pat Willoughby rather than John Kingsley who made the next phone call. She had a few words with Lucy, then asked, 'Is David there?'

Lucy hesitated fractionally. 'Yes.'

'I thought he might be. Could I speak to him, please?'

David had come out into the hall, but was surprised when Lucy covered the mouthpiece and held the receiver out to him. 'It's Pat. She wants to talk to you.'

'You told her I was here?'

'She seemed to expect you to be.'

He took the phone with a great show of reluctance. 'Hello, Pat.'

'Good morning, David,' came her brisk voice down the wires. 'I'd hoped I'd catch you before you left for work.'

'I was just going,' said David, who in fact had no intention of leaving the house until he'd satisfied his curiosity about the momentous developments in Malbury.

'George wants to know how quickly you can get to Malbury. It would appear that the Dean is likely to be charged, and he needs to see a solicitor as soon as possible.'

'No,' he repeated, as firmly as he had spoken to Lucy. 'I can't get involved, Pat. Tell Bishop George to get in touch with the Dean's father-in-law – I'm sure he has all sorts of tame solicitors in his pocket, the type of high-powered chap he needs.'

'But you know the setup here, and you know all the people

224

involved. George and I have agreed that you're by far the best person for the job.'

'It's out of the question, Pat. My firm would never agree. Fosdyke, Fosdyke and Galloway don't take on criminal work. Why, old Fosdyke, the senior partner, would have a coronary on the spot if I even suggested such a sordid thing.'

'Is that Crispin Fosdyke?'

'*Sir* Crispin Fosdyke,' he amplified.

'I've known him for years,' the Honourable Pat informed him with considerable satisfaction. 'He was at school with my older brother – used to come home with him for the holidays. Fossil Fosdyke actually quite fancied me at one time, if you can believe it. I'll deal with him – you needn't worry on that score.'

'But . . .' he protested weakly.

'So how soon can you and Lucy be here?'

David tried again. 'I just don't know, Pat.' Even if he *wanted* to take on the case, and he wasn't by any means sure that he did, there were other problems to contend with: he thought about the separate rooms in John Kingsley's house, and about the uncomfortable proximity of Jeremy Bartlett.

'One other thing,' she said, as if reading his mind. 'You may have to stay in Malbury for some time, and it's not really fair to expect Lucy's father to put you up. John loves having you both, I know, but he's used to being on his own, and I'm sure it's stressful for him to have to think about meals and all that palaver. We've got a nice spare room here at the Bishop's House, and you'd be most welcome to stay with us for as long as necessary.' The offer was tactful and delicately put, but its meaning was unmistakable.

'Bless you, Pat,' he said, acknowledging defeat. 'All right. We'll come. If you can really clear it with Fosdyke, that is.'

'Oh, that should be no problem,' Pat chuckled. 'Leave it to me. Though I may have to resort to blackmail. You see, I know a few things about Fossil Fosdyke that I don't think he'd like me to tell his new associate. So we'll see you soon?'

'As soon as possible,' David agreed. Lucy looked at him questioningly as he put down the phone with a bemused smile. 'Fossil Fosdyke. Well, I never!'

David went upstairs to pack while Todd helped Lucy to wash up the breakfast dishes. 'Well, you had a short visit in London!' she said. 'I hope you don't mind.'

'I'd really rather not go back to Malbury right away,' Todd demurred. 'I think it would be best if I didn't have to face Evelyn for a while.'

'But whatever has happened?' Lucy probed curiously.

The tall American looked chagrined. 'I'd really rather not tell you the details. It doesn't have anything to do with . . . what happened afterwards, I'm sure. But she and Canon Brydges-ffrench had sort of a . . . scene. And I overheard it by accident – it was really embarrassing, for me and for her. I don't think she'll want to see me just yet.' He thought for a moment. 'I don't know what to do. Maybe I'll just go to Cambridge for a few days and see Kirsty. I'm sure she could find me a bed someplace.'

'You don't have to do that,' said Lucy. 'You can stay here if you like – keep an eye on the house, and feed Sophie. That would save me having to put her in kennels while we're gone. And you could explore London at your leisure.' As if summoned by her name, the marmalade cat materialised on the kitchen table, poking her nose daintily into an empty cereal bowl.

'Yeah, that sounds like a great idea – you know I love animals.' Todd scratched Sophie's ears and was rewarded with a purr. 'As long as you and David don't mind, Lucy.' He sat down at the table abruptly, and his face creased with unsuppressible pain. 'And that way we can talk on the phone and you can tell me the details of what happened. I just can't believe that he's dead. I keep trying to tell myself, but I can't take it in. He was such a nice man, Lucy – a little odd, but harmless. He'd never hurt a fly. How could someone want to kill him? Maybe it was just an accident – maybe he took something by mistake, some pills or something. If I'd stayed in Malbury, maybe he'd still be alive . . .'

Lucy put a comforting arm around the young man's shoulders. 'You mustn't think that, Todd.'

The guest room at the Bishop's House was spacious and well proportioned, yet there was a cosy homeliness about it, from the cheery sprigged spread on the double bed to the pile of well-thumbed books on the bedside table to the vase of over-blown late roses and greenery from the garden that adorned the chest of drawers. And the view was magnificent: the large sash window overlooked the south-west corner of Malbury Cathedral, with its remaining range of medieval cloister.

'I hope this will suit,' said Pat, throwing open the door.

'Oh, Pat, it's lovely,' Lucy assured her.

'Perfect,' added David fervently, catching Pat's eye; she gave him a quick wink.

'Go ahead and unpack if you like – there are hangers in the wardrobe if you want to hang up your clothes. I'll go down and put the kettle on – join me when you like. We've got a lot to talk about.'

'Thanks, Pat,' David said. 'For everything.'

When they came down into the kitchen a few minutes later the kettle had just come to the boil. Pat deftly filled the teapot as they sat down around the table.

'Well,' remarked David, 'I must say that when we left on Sunday I wasn't quite expecting to be back in Malbury on Tuesday.'

Lucy was concerned about her father. 'Did Daddy know that we were coming?'

'Yes, and I told him that you would be staying here – I just said that we had plenty of room for both of you.' Pat smiled wryly. 'He understood the logic of it. He'll be around to join us for supper tonight.'

'So what is going on?' David demanded, unable to contain his curiosity any longer. 'And when am I to go and see the Dean? Is he still being held at the police station? Has he been charged?'

'Hold on!' Pat laughed. 'One thing at a time! No, he hasn't been charged. Yes, he's still being held. And you can see him . . . soon.' She poured a drop of tea into her cup to test its strength, finding it still rather weak.

'Has he asked to see me?'

'Well, no. Not exactly. That is, George has been to see him,' Pat explained. 'First thing this morning. And as I told you on the phone, George and I agreed that you were by far the best person to take this on. But . . .'

'Doesn't the Dean want me? I could have saved myself a long trip if I'd known that.'

'It's not that he doesn't want you,' Pat put in quickly. 'But he says he won't talk to any solicitor until he's seen his wife. And she's not back from London yet. She's not expected back until late afternoon.'

David sighed. 'Well, I suppose you may as well fill us in on what you know. Lucy and I work as a team, you understand,' he added. 'I don't have any secrets from her.'

'I approve of that.' Pat nodded. 'George and I have always been a team.'

'What I really want to know,' Lucy interposed, 'is – did he do it? Did the Dean really poison Arthur Brydges-ffrench?'

Pat raised her eyebrows expressively. 'Well, that's the question, isn't it?'

'Did he?'

'He says not.' She tested the tea again; this time it was ready, so she poured it out. 'He told George that he didn't poison him, that he doesn't have any idea how it happened. He said that they had supper – just some tinned soup, and some bread and cheese, and he'd bought some of that Turkish Delight that Arthur was so fond of, as a sort of peace offering. The Dean didn't eat any of the Turkish Delight – he had some fruit instead, but Arthur ate several pieces of it. Then a bit later Arthur became violently ill, with nausea and chest pains. The Dean called the doctor, who sent the ambulance, but by the time they arrived it was too late. He died a few hours later in hospital.'

'How terrible,' Lucy said, frowning. 'Poor Canon Brydges-ffrench.'

'And the poor Dean,' added Pat. 'Everyone wants to believe that he did it, you know. You're not going to be very popular here in the Close, trying to prove otherwise.'

'Do *you* think he did it?' David asked shrewdly.

She chose her words with care. 'I believe that he was capable of doing it – Stuart Latimer is not a nice man. But if he tells George that he didn't do it – and George is his spiritual director – then I have to believe him. The difficult thing is, though, that if the Dean *didn't* kill Arthur Brydges-ffrench, it means that someone else here in the Close did. And I hate to think where that line of thought will take us.'

'Yes,' said David. 'I see what you mean. I'm beginning to think that I should have followed my first instincts, and stayed in London!'

Just then the phone rang in the hall; Pat went off to answer it, returning after a moment. 'It was Anne Latimer,' she told David. 'She wants to see you at the Deanery. Immediately.'

Chapter 31

For thou shalt save the people that are in adversity: and
shalt bring down the high looks of the proud.

Psalm 18.27

David had only met Anne Latimer once, briefly – at her
husband's installation. His memory of her as a chilly blonde
had been reinforced by comments that others in Malbury had
made about her; Jeremy Bartlett always referred to her as 'The
Ice Queen'. The impression was not dispelled as she met him
at the entrance of the Deanery: dressed in arctic blue, she
extended a formal hand to him, and her fingers were as cold as
her blue eyes. 'Good evening, Mr Middleton-Brown. Thank you
for coming so promptly.'

She led him into the drawing room and offered him a drink.
Though her glass looked as if it contained pale sherry, David
felt that he could really do with a whisky, so that is what
he asked for, and hoped that he was imagining the dis-
approval that he thought he saw in her eyes as she gave
it to him.

'I have been to see my husband,' she began in her clipped
voice. 'It is his wish that you should represent him. He has been
advised by the Bishop on this matter.'

'And you don't agree?' he blurted out without thinking, and
immediately regretted his rashness; although he didn't really
want the case, he found to his surprise that he was
disappointed at the prospect of losing it.

She shot him a look which might have been interpreted as
congratulation on his perspicacity, or censure at his presumption. 'Not really,' she allowed. 'I told him that my father would
be able to find someone suitable. Someone from London, with a
national reputation in criminal law.' David said nothing; Anne
Latimer appraised him for a moment before going on. 'The
Bishop seems to feel that your inside knowledge of Malbury

Cathedral and the inhabitants of the Close give you a real advantage in this matter. My husband agrees with him. I have spoken to my father, and he is willing to concede the point. So I am asking you, now, if you would be willing to undertake my husband's defence.'

Did he really want it? 'Very well,' David heard himself saying.

'There is one condition.' Anne Latimer took a sip of sherry, regarding him over the rim of her glass. 'When the case comes to trial, my father would like to choose counsel. He has someone in mind already, I believe – an eminent QC.'

Though stung by her evident distrust of him, David smiled. 'Of course. Though if I do my job properly, perhaps it won't come to that.'

She looked at him with something approaching pity, and her voice dripped chill scorn. 'Don't be ridiculous. Of course it will come to trial.'

Hurt, once again he found himself opening his mouth without thinking. 'Does that mean that you think he's guilty?'

'What I think doesn't matter.' Dispassionately, Anne Latimer inspected a pale pink fingernail. 'What does matter is that I will stand by Stuart. And that you will do your best to get him off.'

Later that evening, while David was at the police station with his new client, there was an unexpected visitor at the Bishop's House. Pat ushered Inspector Mike Drewitt into the kitchen as he explained, 'I've been taken off this case because of my connection with the cathedral. But Bishop George asked me to keep him up to date, on an informal basis, about what is happening, and I thought you'd like to know what we've found so far.'

'It's very kind of you to come,' said Pat. 'Would you like a drink? Coffee? Something stronger?'

'Whatever you're having.' The Inspector greeted John Kingsley and the Bishop, and gave a special smile to Lucy. They were sitting around the kitchen table with mugs of coffee; Pat poured one for the Inspector.

'So what do you have to tell me?' Bishop Willoughby asked. 'We haven't been given any information – only that it was poison.'

Mike Drewitt pulled up a chair and joined them. 'This is

230

strictly off the record, you understand,' he began. 'But the poison was administered in that Turkish Delight. Or should I say *on* it – it was sprinkled on top like icing sugar. That's why the Dean wasn't affected – he didn't eat any of the Turkish Delight.'

They received the information in silence, too stunned to react. Lucy spoke at last. 'What sort of poison was it? Do they know where it came from?'

Drewitt nodded. 'It was a fairly common mouse poison. An empty – or nearly empty – container has been found.'

Pat was almost afraid to ask. 'Where was it found?'

He hesitated for just a moment before replying, 'In Evelyn Marsden's garden shed. She claims to know nothing about it, of course, though she admitted that it was hers. And anyone in the Close might have had access to it, including the Dean, who lives next door. Neither the gate into her garden from the Close nor the shed is kept locked, and the poison had been there for quite some time.'

'Arthur Brydges-ffrench lived next door, too – on the other side,' Pat pointed out. 'Could he have taken the poison himself, before he went to the Deanery?'

'No, it was definitely administered in the Turkish Delight,' the policeman explained. 'And he was there for several hours before he was taken ill – even if he'd taken it himself, beforehand, it would have acted more quickly than that. No, when I said that anyone might have had access to the poison, I wasn't thinking of the victim.'

'Does that mean . . . there are other suspects?' Lucy queried.

Drewitt stroked his chin thoughtfully. 'Not at the moment. Let's just say that it is considered that there is sufficient evidence to charge the Dean.'

'He's going to be charged, then?' put in the Bishop. 'With murder?'

It was the first time the word had been uttered. 'Yes. He'll be charged tonight. In the morning they'll take him to Shrewsbury magistrates' court to be remanded. And bail won't be granted. Not on a murder charge.'

John Kingsley sighed, 'How dreadful.'

'But thank you for telling us, Mike,' the Bishop said. 'We really appreciate being kept informed.'

'Yes,' his wife added. 'Feel free to drop in any time that you have some news.'

The policeman looked slightly embarrassed. 'Not at all. But if anyone asks, you didn't hear anything from me.'

'He swears he didn't do it.' It was hours later, and David and Lucy were alone at last in the guest room, but David was far too keyed up to sleep. He moved to the window, pulled the curtain aside, and looked out at the cathedral, a dark shape against the faintly moonlit night.

Lucy came to stand beside him. 'How is he?'

Abstractedly he put an arm around her shoulders. 'About what you would expect of the Dean. Peevish, ungracious, even rude. Underneath it all, frightened witless, of course. But he swears he didn't do it.'

'And you believe him?'

'I'm inclined to, in spite of everything. But the interesting thing is – I get the distinct feeling that his wife's not at all sure that he's innocent.'

'Hm.'

'But if he didn't do it,' David thought aloud, 'then who did? And why? I mean, he was such an inoffensive old man. The Dean was the only one with a very good reason for wanting him dead. Let's be realistic – the Dean was a far more likely candidate for murder than poor old Canon Brydges-ffrench.'

Lucy turned to him, struck with a new idea. 'Is it possible that it wasn't meant for him at all? That someone was trying to murder the Dean, and killed the Canon by mistake?'

He considered the possibility. 'Then why,' he said at last, 'poison the Turkish Delight? Everyone, apparently, knew that Canon Brydges-ffrench was the only person in Malbury to eat crème de menthe Turkish Delight.'

'You're right,' she admitted, deflated. 'It was the one way to be sure of killing him, and no one else. It's quite clear that he was the intended victim. But who could have done it?'

'There are a quite a few things that I'd like to know,' David stated. 'Starting with who has bought crème de menthe Turkish Delight recently.'

'The Cathedral Shop is the only place in Malbury that stocks it, so that should be quite easy to find out.'

'You're brilliant, my love!' David tightened his arm around her shoulders. 'Then that's where I'll begin tomorrow, after I get back from the magistrates' court. And after that perhaps I'll have a little chat with Evelyn Marsden. Find out what she knows about the mouse poison in her garden shed.'

'And I'll ring Todd. He knows something about Evelyn Marsden that he hasn't told me – and it might be important.' Gazing down into the cloister, Lucy shivered slightly.

'Are you cold?' he asked, concerned.

'A bit,' Lucy admitted. 'And . . . well, I just remembered something that Jeremy told me. The cloister is supposed to be haunted, by Brother Thomas's ghost.' David frowned and was about to say something; she forestalled him quickly. 'But let's not stand here all night talking about it, David darling. Come to bed.'

His frown relaxed into a smile. 'If you think you're making me an offer I can't refuse,' he murmured into her ear, drawing the curtain, 'you just may be right.'

Chapter 32

*I have watched, and am even as it were a sparrow: that
sitteth alone upon the house-top.*

Psalm 102.7

Stuart Latimer's appearance before the Shrewsbury magistrates was a formality, lasting but a few minutes. He affirmed
that he was The Very Reverend Stuart Latimer, of the
Deanery, the Cathedral Close, Malbury, Shropshire, and when
informed that he had been charged with the murder, on 19
November, of the Reverend Arthur Brydges-ffrench, he stated
his innocence in a firm voice. Nevertheless bail was denied and
he was remanded in custody, to await committal for trial.

Naturally enough, the case had garnered a great deal of
national notice; after all, Stuart Latimer was a prominent
churchman with, if not national fame, at least a position
sufficiently exalted to attract attention when associated with
such a grievous crime as murder. So David, when he came out
of the courtroom, had to run the gauntlet of bristling
microphones. He made a brief statement, which managed to
say very little but which would appear on the evening news in
any case, and made his escape back to Malbury.

Lucy and Pat were waiting for him in the kitchen of the
Bishop's House. Pat made him coffee while he told them about
the morning's events. 'I'm very much afraid that it will be in all
the papers, and on the telly. The press love this sort of thing,
and you must admit that it's fairly out of the ordinary for a
cathedral Dean to be charged with murder. There were dozens
of cameras – it was just a good thing that I'd prepared
something to say.'

Lucy's face shone with pride. 'You mean that you're going to
be a television star?'

'My few seconds of glory,' he admitted with a self-
deprecating smile.

'That's all very well, but what do you do now?' asked Pat, practical as ever. 'Lucy's been telling me about that other business that you were involved with earlier in the year – how the two of you managed to uncover enough evidence so that the case never made it to the committal stage. Is that what you have in mind doing here? A bit of independent investigation?'

'Well, I suppose I was thinking of something like that,' he admitted. 'As you said yesterday, if Stuart Latimer didn't poison Arthur Brydges-ffrench, then someone else in the Close did. Perhaps I can talk to a few people and see what I can find out. If you don't think it would be overstepping propriety?'

'I think it sounds like a very good idea,' Pat assured him. 'You've already met everyone in the Close, and you'll be able to talk to people without arousing too much suspicion. Where will you start?'

'I thought I'd start at the Cathedral Shop – find out who has bought crème de menthe Turkish Delight recently.'

'I've already done that for you,' said Lucy with a smile. 'I went this morning while you were in Shrewsbury, and had a word with Victoria and Albert.'

'And what did they say?' He turned to her eagerly.

She shook her head. 'They were very cut up about Arthur Brydges-ffrench – they had a real soft spot for him. And Victor was feeling particularly distressed because he'd parted from him on a rather bad note on Monday, before it happened.'

'What do you mean?'

'Well, apparently the Dean had just told them that morning – Victoria and Albert, I mean – that he didn't intend to renew their lease for the shop. And when Canon Brydges-ffrench came in later, Victor more or less went for him, accused him of being in league with the Dean. He said that Canon Brydges-ffrench was quite upset, and now he feels very badly about it.'

'That's very interesting,' David said. 'Especially the fact that the Dean had alienated them just that morning. But I'm not sure that it actually has any bearing. What about the Turkish Delight? Did they remember who had bought it recently?'

Lucy smiled. 'You don't know Victoria and Albert very well if you can even ask a question like that. Of course they remembered.' Echoing Victor, she ticked them off on her fingers. 'Evelyn Marsden on Saturday morning. Rowena and Jeremy each bought a box on Saturday afternoon. On Monday morning the Dean bought his box, and Canon Brydges-ffrench came in to replenish his supply a bit later. That, Victor said, was their last box. They're still waiting for a new delivery.'

'Though of course they won't need it now,' Pat put in pragmatically.

'No, of course not. Victor had tears in his eyes when I pointed that out to him.'

David drummed his fingers on the kitchen table. 'But do you realise what this means? Assuming the police are correct and the poison was administered on the Turkish Delight, it practically had to be one of those people who poisoned him!'

'I don't think that really follows.' Lucy frowned thoughtfully. 'I mean, even if someone else had some Turkish Delight which they'd poisoned with the mouse poison from Miss Marsden's garden shed, how could they have administered it? Are you suggesting that someone broke into the Deanery, or entered by some more straightforward means, and swapped their doctored box with the box the Dean had bought?'

David rubbed his forehead. 'I'm not really suggesting anything so concrete as that. It sounds far-fetched when you put it like that, though it's a possibility, I suppose. But I just have a feeling that if I could figure out how it was done, I would know who had done it. And it must have been one of them. Or,' he added, struck by a sudden thought, 'it might have been Victoria and Albert. We have only their word that they sold all the Turkish Delight – they may have kept a box for themselves, for just such a purpose.'

'Surely you couldn't think that Victoria and Albert would have poisoned Canon Brydges-ffrench!' Lucy protested.

'Well,' said David, 'they can't be discounted entirely. After all, if they thought he'd betrayed them to the Dean . . .'

'So what is your next step?' Pat asked again

'I'm going this afternoon to pay a call on Miss Marsden.'

Pat looked at him sharply. 'You suspect Evelyn?'

'I didn't say that.' David raised his eyebrows. 'But it was *her* mouse poison, after all. And she *did* buy a box of Turkish Delight. So I suppose that, to be completely honest, I'd have to put her at the top of my list.'

'But she had no motive,' protested Pat. 'She was very fond of Arthur.'

'I shall go and pay a call on her,' David repeated.

'Alone?' queried Lucy.

'Yes, alone. I think that would be best, don't you? And in the meantime perhaps you can ring Todd – didn't you say that he knew something?'

Evelyn greeted David with every evidence of welcoming his visit, producing her silver teapot and a plate of home-made biscuits. But though she was polite, she seemed somewhat abstracted. She took a few sips of her tea, put the cup down, and picked up a skein of black wool. Within a moment her fingers were flying furiously, the needles clicking, though her eyes stayed fixed on David.

His fund of small talk nearly exhausted, and not yet ready to tackle the questions he'd really come to ask, David looked out of the window. 'You have quite a nice view here.'

'Yes, a wonderful view of the cathedral,' Evelyn agreed. The fingers never faltered as she gazed down into the Close. 'I love having it just outside my window, you know. Most people think of it as just a building, but to those of us who have lived with it for years, it's so much more than that. It's more like a person in some ways, with different moods as the seasons change, in different weather, and at different times of the day. The way the light strikes the east end on a summer's morning – why, it's just magical. And on a foggy winter day, when you can scarcely see it . . .' She sighed. 'It's a marvellous place to live.' But Evelyn Marsden's eyes were not on the cathedral, David noted; she was, instead, watching the movements of a tall figure who was striding purposefully through the Close, past her house and into the entrance to the Deanery: Pat, he recognised with a small shock. But before he'd had time to assimilate Pat's unexpected presence, he was struck with a singular realisation.

'From here you can see who comes and goes at the Deanery,' he blurted.

'Yes.'

It was manifestly evident to David that she spent much of her time doing just that. There wasn't time to frame his next question carefully; he had to know the answer. 'On Monday night – you were sitting here at the window?'

'Yes.' She registered no curiosity at the question, just a small flicker of some emotion at the mention of Monday night.

'Looking out?'

'I was knitting, as I usually do in the evenings.' She paused.

238

'Yes, I suppose you might say that I was looking out. Not spying, mind you,' she added, defensively. 'I'm not nosy. I'm just interested in what goes on in the Close.'

'And did anyone go to the Deanery?'

Again there was a flicker of emotion in her eyes. 'Arthur Brydges-ffrench.' She swallowed hard.

David leaned forward, unable to suppress the urgency he felt. '*Only* Arthur Brydges-ffrench?'

'Yes, just Arthur. And the Dean, of course. He went out for a time in the late afternoon – I supposed he was going to Evensong.'

'No one else? Think carefully, Miss Marsden. It could be very important.'

But she had no need to think carefully. She remembered very well; Monday night was not something she was likely to forget. 'There was no one else,' she affirmed. 'I was at the window all afternoon and all evening, until . . . well, until the ambulance came.' Again she swallowed visibly, then went on, 'Todd . . . well, he wasn't here, so there was no need for me to fix a meal. And I . . . well, I wasn't really hungry, so I just stayed here all evening knitting. No one but Arthur went to the Deanery that evening. I would swear to that. If someone had, I would have seen.'

With difficulty, David controlled his excitement: it had suddenly become a locked-room mystery. Unless, he thought. Unless Miss Marsden had done it. 'Would you mind if I asked you one or two other questions?'

She had regained her composure. 'Not at all.' The fingers continued to fly at a remarkable speed.

'You bought a box of Turkish Delight on Saturday morning?'

Evelyn didn't seem to find the question odd; perhaps the police had already covered this ground. 'That is correct. I always try . . . tried . . . to have a box on hand, just in case Arthur were to come by. He was here for supper on Friday night, and finished the last of the box that I had, so on Saturday I bought a new one.'

That was straightforward enough, thought David, and a plausible story as well. *Had* the police asked her? To probe about that might arouse her suspicions of his motives for asking, so he contented himself with another question; this one was fairly delicate. 'The mouse poison that was in your garden shed. Had it been there a long while?'

She pressed her lips together, stretching them over her prominent teeth. 'Yes.'

'When was the last time you . . . noticed it?'

'Oh, not for some months. I'd had a few mice in my kitchen last winter, or perhaps it was the winter before.'

'Would it have been possible for someone else to get into your garden shed?'

'Quite a simple matter. It wasn't locked, nor was the gate into the garden.'

He noted that the garden gate was not visible from her window, which meant that at any time on the previous day, while Evelyn was watching the entrance to the Deanery, someone could have entered her garden shed unobserved. David decided that he had learned enough; he stretched out his teacup with a conscious smile. 'Could I trouble you for another cup?'

'Yes, of course, Mr Middleton-Brown.' She dropped the knitting into her lap and reached for the teapot. 'Would you mind if I asked *you* a question?'

'No, not at all.'

'What will happen to the Dean? If he's found guilty of murder, that is?'

David was taken slightly aback. 'Why, he'll go to prison for a very long time.'

'Good.' He caught a glint of satisfaction in her eyes before she lowered them quickly to her knitting. 'Stuart Latimer is *not* a nice man, Mr Middleton-Brown,' she added with some heat.

Chapter 33

Yea, with thine eyes shalt thou behold: and see the reward of the ungodly.

Psalm 91.8

Lucy was alone in the kitchen when David returned; he found her concocting a sweet for their evening meal. 'I thought I might as well make myself useful while Pat was out,' she explained. 'Did you discover anything interesting?'

'Oh, yes.' He kissed her as Cain and Abel padded over to greet him, swinging their tails; he leaned down and gave them each a pat. 'Can I help?'

'You could grate some lemon rind while you tell me what you've found out.'

'Well,' he began, picking up a lemon, 'what she told me about the mouse poison was pretty much the same as you learned from Inspector Drewitt – basically, that anyone could have got into her garden shed at just about any time, including yesterday.'

'And she wouldn't have seen them?'

'Well, no. That's just the point, in fact.' In his excitement, he tossed the lemon into the air and caught it again. 'You see, Miss Marsden spent all afternoon and all evening at her window, knitting and spying on the Deanery. She would quibble at the word, of course – she claims that she's not nosy, just interested – but the fact is that if she's telling the truth, no one but Arthur Brydges-ffrench went to the Deanery in all that time.'

'So your theory that someone else got into the Deanery somehow and swapped the Turkish Delight . . .'

'Seems to be a nonstarter,' he admitted.

'You said "*if* she's telling the truth",' Lucy observed. 'What did you mean by that?'

'Don't you see, love? Evelyn Marsden might have done it

241

herself! *She* might have been the one who popped into the Deanery, while the Dean was at Evensong. Don't they always say that poison is a woman's weapon?'

'Yes, but . . .'

'If only I could see a motive. I can't really think why she would want to murder Arthur Brydges-ffrench. The Dean, yes – she seems to share everyone else's hatred of the Dean. But not Arthur Brydges-ffrench.'

'There might be a motive,' Lucy said, reluctantly.

David dropped the lemon. 'What? What have you found out?'

'Well, I finally reached Todd on the phone. And he told me something . . . it's probably nothing,' she demurred. 'He didn't want to tell me – he insisted that it had nothing to do with what happened. And he's probably right. But still . . .'

'Tell me!' David demanded.

'He said that they'd had a . . . well, he called it a scene. Evelyn Marsden and Arthur Brydges-ffrench. On the Monday morning. Todd happened to overhear it, and that's why he left Malbury, and was too embarrassed to return and face Miss Marsden.'

'But what happened?'

'She came to tell him that the Dean had been to see her, to inform her that her rent was being raised to an amount that she had no hope of being able to pay. So in effect she was being thrown out of her house.'

David whistled soundlessly. 'Good Lord. No wonder she hates the Dean.'

'Well, exactly.'

'But Arthur Brydges-ffrench? What happened between them?'

'Apparently she came to him for help. She thought he might be able to do something to block the rent increase, in Chapter. He said that he'd already done everything that he could.' Lucy hesitated, frowning. 'Then she . . . well, Todd said that she more or less proposed to Canon Brydges-ffrench. Said that she'd always thought there was an understanding between them that they'd marry after his mother was gone.'

'And what happened?' he asked, afraid that he knew the answer.

'He turned her down flat – apologised for anything he'd done to mislead her, but said that it was out of the question.'

David was surprised at his instinctive feeling of empathy for the beleaguered old man. 'Well, of course it would be impossible. He wasn't really . . . the marrying kind, was he?'

Lucy, for her part, was indignant on behalf of the rejected woman. 'Oh, honestly, David! I don't see why not! They might have provided some companionship for each other, and it would have solved her housing problem. It really wouldn't have hurt him to say yes.'

He raised his eyebrows in mock amazement. 'I can't believe my ears – Lucy Kingsley actually arguing in favour of marriage? There must be some mistake.'

'I'm not talking about us.' She glared at him. 'But don't you see? The poor woman – to be rejected like that. It must have wounded her terribly.'

David clutched at his heart melodramatically, rolling his eyes. 'Just like you wound me to the quick, every time you reject my honourable proposals of marriage.'

The sight was so comical that Lucy couldn't help giggling, dissipating her irritation. 'It's hardly a comparable situation, David darling!'

He sat down at the table, suddenly serious. 'But you're right, of course. About the motive. The woman scorned – it's one of the oldest motives in the book, isn't it? Anger at being spurned, revenge for the hurt to her pride, or however you want to explain it. I'm afraid this really does make Evelyn Marsden a viable suspect.'

'Surely not,' Lucy protested.

Absent-mindedly David picked up the lemon and tossed it back and forth from one hand to the other as he thought it through. 'The woman scorned,' he repeated. 'She decides to murder the man who rejected her, and at the same time to get her revenge on the other man whom she has reason to hate, by setting him up to take the blame. It could have happened that way, Lucy! She could have planned it so that it would look as if the Dean was the only one who could have done it.'

'Do you really think she's that calculating?'

'After seeing her today . . . I don't know, Lucy. It doesn't seem that hard to believe. She seemed so . . . well, so cold. Emotionless. She just sat there knitting away – like Madame Defarge, it seemed to me at the time. And it's a short step from picturing her beside the guillotine to being able to imagine her poisoning the man who humiliated her. As I said, poison is a woman's weapon. And it was her mouse poison, remember.'

Lucy sighed. 'It's possible, I suppose, but you haven't convinced me. I'd like to talk to her myself – perhaps there's something you've missed.'

'Be my guest,' he invited. 'I'd be glad to have your opinion. And people do tend to talk to you – you might find out something she didn't tell me.'

'I'll talk to her tomorrow,' Lucy decided. There were noises from the front of the house and the dogs, who had been sleeping in the corner, lumbered to their feet, wagging their tails in anticipation. She added quickly, 'Promise me that you won't say anything about this to Pat, though. It would upset her to think that you really suspected Evelyn. Let me talk to Evelyn first.'

'All right,' he agreed as Pat, laden down with several carrier bags, pushed open the kitchen door.

'You've been to the Deanery.' David didn't mean it to sound accusing, but realised as he spoke that it had rather come out that way.

'Yes,' said Pat mildly, raising her eyebrows at his tone. 'Among other things, like shopping. I went to see Anne Latimer, to see if there was any way I could be of help.'

'Oh.'

'You see,' she explained, dropping the carrier bags on the counter and reaching down to stroke the dogs, 'I thought that she might be needing a bit of support – George told me that she'd been to the early service in the cathedral this morning, all by herself. She doesn't usually attend any of the weekday services.'

'I didn't realise that you were on friendly terms with Mrs Latimer,' said Lucy.

'Oh, I'm not. Far from it.' Pat shook her head. 'Our paths just haven't crossed that often – she spends most of her time in London, and, as I said, she doesn't regularly attend services at the cathedral. We've had the Latimers here for a meal once, naturally, though at the end of the evening I didn't feel that I knew her at all – she doesn't expose very much on the surface. And all she wanted to know about me was where I buy my meat! But it seemed just common decency to go to see her, and offer help if it were needed.'

David was curious. 'And what did she say?'

Pat laughed astringently. 'That she didn't need or want my help, that she could manage very well on her own. I said that I'd

244

be happy to attend services with her, just to offer a bit of moral support, and she replied that it wouldn't be necessary – that it looked better if she were alone!'

'Ah!' David had seen this sort of thing before in the course of his work. 'The grieving wife, bearing up bravely in the face of adversity, supporting her falsely-accused husband with her public prayers.' His smile was cynical.

'That can't be true,' Lucy objected.

'I'm afraid so, my dear,' confirmed Pat. 'All very calculated, probably after lengthy consultation with her father.'

'But she must be upset about her husband being in jail.'

'She didn't seem very upset. In fact, when I offered my sympathy, she said that Stuart was his own worst enemy and was probably better off where he was – that it was about time he learned some humility, and that being in jail might be a salutary experience for him!'

Lucy shook her head in disbelief. 'The more I hear about Mrs Latimer, the sorrier I feel for the Dean!'

That evening there was little pooling of information and opinions around the kitchen table. David felt constrained by his misgivings about Evelyn Marsden; he felt that to voice his suspicions would distress not only Pat but also Lucy's father and the Bishop. So the main topic of conversation was David's appearance on the evening news. 'Do I really look like that?' he groaned. 'Is there really that much grey in my hair?'

'You looked very distinguished,' Pat insisted stoutly.

'You were wonderful, darling,' added Lucy. 'I was so proud of you.'

After supper Jeremy dropped by, which further discouraged discussion of David's investigations. Jeremy had seen David's appearance on the news, had rung the house in London to find out from Lucy what was happening, and had discovered from Todd that Lucy was in fact in Malbury, just next door, so he had been unable to resist calling round.

But it was Jeremy, onerous as his presence was to David, who said the thing that David would later remember from that evening. 'I realise that I'm in the minority,' he said, laughing. 'I must be just about the only person in Malbury who wants to see the Dean get off. After all, without him, where will the plans for the Cathedral Centre be? And where does that leave me?'

Chapter 34

*They go up as high as the hills, and down to the valleys
beneath: even unto the place which thou hast appointed
for them.*

Psalm 104.8

Approaching Evelyn Marsden's house, Lucy could see her
clearly, sitting in her perch above the Close; it gave her an idea
for a question to ask, when the time was right. Miss Marsden
must have seen her as well, for she answered the bell quickly. If
Evelyn Marsden was surprised to have two uninvited visitors
in as many days, she was too polite to say so. 'Hello, Miss
Kingsley,' she greeted her.

'I was passing this way,' said Lucy, 'and thought I'd call
to tell you how sorry I was about Canon Brydges-ffrench. It
must have been a terrible shock for you – I know that you were
close.'

There was an indrawn breath. 'Yes. Thank you, Miss
Kingsley. How very kind of you to think of me. Would you like
to come in and join me for a cup of tea? Can you spare the time?'

'That would be very nice,' Lucy agreed.

While the tea, in the silver teapot, brewed, there were the
inevitable pleasantries about the weather (cold, but what could
you expect in November?) and the fact that the evenings were
drawing in. Lucy, sensing the emotion beneath Evelyn's
controlled and matter-of-fact exterior, was reluctant to mention the events of Monday. As Evelyn picked up the black wool
and began knitting, Lucy, like the Dean before her, seized upon
the activity as a possible neutral topic of conversation.

'You knit very quickly,' she remarked, watching Evelyn's
flying fingers.

'Yes. I'm . . . I'm trying to finish this.' Evelyn's voice sounded
strained.

'What is it? A jumper?'

'It's a pullover.' She held it up for inspection. 'For . . . for Arthur.' Seeing Lucy's shocked, uncomprehending expression, Evelyn gabbled on in a rush. 'I started it last week, before . . . Before. And now . . . well, it's to be my last gift for him. I must finish it, so that it can go in his coffin.'

Lucy didn't know what to say. 'Oh. What a lovely gesture,' she managed at last, deeply touched.

A single tear trickled down Evelyn's cheek and trembled on her chin. 'I must do it, you see. For Arthur. For all the years . . .' She gulped, stifling a sob; the knitting dropped to her lap and she covered her face with her hands. 'I'm sorry,' she gasped. 'You must forgive me, Miss Kingsley. It's just that . . .'

Impulsively, Lucy rose and went to the older woman, kneeling beside her and putting her arms around her. The unexpected gesture of sympathy was too much for Evelyn's self-control; she burst into wailing sobs, crying for the first time since Arthur Brydges-ffrench's death. After a few minutes of sobbing she struggled to speak. 'Don't worry,' Lucy assured her. 'You don't have to say anything. Just let it all out.'

So she cried on until the first storm of her grief was past. 'I loved him,' she managed to say at last. 'I loved him for so many years. I just can't believe that he's dead. And the way we parted . . . well, we'd had words. I'll never be able to forgive myself for that.'

Lucy squeezed her shoulders. 'How awful for you. But I'm sure he wouldn't have wanted you to feel that way. I know he would have wanted you to remember . . . what you've shared through the years.'

Evelyn pulled away from Lucy and looked at her searchingly; her eyes were swollen with tears and her face, never very attractive at the best of times, was mottled, ugly. 'But do you think . . . ? I'd always thought . . . hoped . . . that Arthur loved me. In his own way, that is. I loved him so, you see.' She ended feebly, on a half-sob.

'I'm sure he did,' Lucy stated firmly. 'In his own way, I'm sure that he loved you. Men don't always express things as we do, or in the way we'd like them to, but that doesn't mean the feelings aren't there. I'm sure that Arthur loved you,' she repeated.

For the first time there was hope in Evelyn's brimming eyes. 'Oh, if only I could believe that. I think then that I could just about bear the thought of going on without him.'

To create the opportunity for a private discussion, Lucy and David offered to take the dogs for a walk later that afternoon. Pat accepted, realising perhaps that they needed time alone together, so they set off out of the Close, dressed in borrowed Wellington boots and Barbour jackets and dragged along briskly by an exuberant Cain and Abel.

When they got into the countryside they turned the dogs loose and caught their breath, walking more slowly. Deep shadows were gathering in the valleys between the hills, and the slanting rays of the setting sun illuminated Wenlock Edge, some miles distant. 'Well?' asked David, when they had at last achieved a normal pace. 'Did you find out anything?'

Lucy kept her eyes on the dogs, tearing after one another up a steep hill as they shed their customary lumbering lethargy. 'Evelyn Marsden could not possibly have murdered Arthur Brydges-ffrench,' she stated at last.

'But why not? She was alone – she doesn't have an alibi. She had a motive, and it was her mouse poison that poisoned him.'

'You don't understand, David darling. She couldn't have murdered him because she loved him.'

'Loved him?' he echoed, uncomprehending.

'Yes, loved him.' She smiled. 'She'd loved him for years. I know it seems hard to believe – he wasn't a particularly attractive specimen – but she loved him very much. Everyone in the Close knew that she'd hoped to marry him one day, but I think they all just assumed that she wanted the security and the position. That may have been part of it, of course. The fact is, though, that she genuinely loved him. She wouldn't have killed him.'

David was loath to abandon his theory. 'Not even when he rejected her? When he made it clear that he could never return her feelings?'

'Never is a long time.' Lucy took his hand and squeezed it. 'As you should well know. Circumstances change. People change. And she's convinced herself that in his own way he *did* love her. Perhaps he did – I don't know. Anyway, it's important for her to believe that.'

'So she didn't kill him.'

'No.' Lucy was firm, and her certainty convinced him. 'The poor woman – David, you should have seen her. She was absolutely devastated by his death.'

'But she seemed so cold yesterday, so distant. As if she didn't care.'

'Oh, darling. You really don't understand women. She was trying to put a brave face on it, in front of you. But she broke down completely when I showed her a little sympathy. It was heartbreaking.'

They walked along in silence for a few minutes, hand in hand. 'But if she didn't do it,' said David finally, 'who did?'

Lucy shrugged. 'I wonder . . .'

'If no one else went to the Deanery . . .'

'That's something I was going to mention,' said Lucy. 'It's not impossible that someone else did go to the Deanery.'

'But what do you mean?' David raised his eyebrows, turning to look at her. 'Miss Marsden didn't leave the window.'

'Of course she left the window. You don't think that she could sit there for ten or twelve hours, without . . . answering the call of nature?'

'Of course! But why didn't she tell me . . .'

'She wouldn't have mentioned it to you, naturally. Her delicacy would prevent her from bringing it up. She might not even have remembered it. But when I asked her, she said that she'd gone to the loo a couple of times.'

'And someone . . .'

'Someone might have gone to the Deanery while she was away from the window. I noticed as I approached her house that she's very visible there in the window, even in daylight. And in the dark, with a light on behind her – she would have to have a light for her knitting – you would be able to see her very clearly. If someone had wanted to go to the Deanery unobserved, they could have waited until she left the window. Or if they were just coming along and she happened to be away from the window, they would have been able to tell that they weren't being watched. After all, I think that most people in the Close probably know that she sits there keeping an eye on things.'

'Ah.' David considered the new information. 'So we're back to where we started, then.'

'Perhaps.' Lucy hesitated. 'You know that you said, darling, that poison was a woman's weapon. Well, I've been thinking about that. And I was wondering about Rowena Hunt – if there's any woman around here who would be capable of poisoning an old man who got in her way, it would be Rowena.'

David frowned. 'I don't know what you've got against Rowena,' he protested. 'She's always seemed very nice to me.'

'Well, of course she would.' Lucy tried to suppress the scorn in her voice. 'You're a man. And Rowena is a man's woman, if you know what I mean. She reserves all her charms for men. But you have to admit, David, that she's utterly ruthless. She's the sort of woman who likes to have her own way, and will do anything to get it. Including murder, if you ask me.'

He looked stubborn. 'You've just got it in for her, Lucy. She wouldn't have any reason to kill Canon Brydges-ffrench.'

'I'm not so sure about that. Don't forget what my father told us – that she wanted to run the refectory and the Cathedral Shop, and the Subdean was opposing her, or rather opposing the Dean, in Chapter. Rowena might have reckoned that if she got rid of him, it would be smooth sailing for her. And didn't she have a grudge against him because of Kirsty? Because he advised Kirsty to go ahead and read Theology, against her mother's wishes?'

'You're overreacting,' David stated. 'I happened to see Rowena earlier this afternoon, and she seemed as upset as anyone over the Subdean's death.'

'You saw Rowena?' It was Lucy's turn to raise her eyebrows.

'In the cathedral. I went in to have a poke around while you were at Miss Marsden's, and she was at the Friends' stall. Naturally I had a word with her.'

'You didn't happen to ask her where she was on Monday night, did you?'

'As a matter of fact I did,' he replied defiantly. 'Or at least it came up, more or less accidentally. I asked her if she'd heard the sirens.'

'And what did the fair Rowena say?'

'Actually, she wasn't very forthcoming,' he admitted with reluctance. 'She said that she'd been home, but that she hadn't heard the sirens. She didn't seem to want to talk about it. She was so evasive that I thought for a minute that she might be hiding something.'

Lucy looked satisfied. 'Something like murder, for instance? Or perhaps she just didn't want you to know that she was entertaining Inspector Mike Drewitt in her bedroom on his night off, and was too . . . involved . . . to hear the sirens.'

'Lucy! You can't know that for sure!'

She smiled. 'No, but I know Rowena. Don't forget,' she added, 'that she bought a box of Turkish Delight on Saturday. Why would she do that, if not for some devious purpose? A kindly impulse doesn't exactly fit in with her character.'

David stopped and called the dogs. 'It's getting dark – I think we ought to go back.' He turned to her as a sudden thought struck him. 'If you're going to say that about Rowena,' he said agitatedly, 'then why not say the same thing about your great friend Jeremy? He bought Turkish Delight, too, you know. And he had as much reason as Rowena to want to get rid of Canon Brydges-ffrench – the Subdean wasn't exactly a strong advocate of the Cathedral Centre! No, Lucy, I won't accept what you say about Rowena. If I have to put my money on anyone, I'll put it on Jeremy Bartlett.'

That evening Inspector Drewitt paid another call at the Bishop's House. He found them much as before: Pat and George Willoughby with Lucy and John Kingsley around the kitchen table, though this time David was there as well.

Pat made him welcome and found him a seat at the scrubbed pine table. 'We're just about to have our pudding,' she told him. 'You'll join us, won't you?'

'I shouldn't, but I will.' The policeman grinned, patting his trim waistline.

The Bishop looked down at his own substantial paunch with a rueful twinkle. 'I promise I won't tell your wife.'

'Have you met David?' interposed Lucy. 'My friend, David Middleton-Brown?'

'No, I don't believe we've actually met.' Drewitt extended his hand across the table. 'Though I've seen you about the place once or twice. I understand you're representing the Dean.'

'That's right.'

Pat dished up the fruit crumble. 'Any news, Mike? Any developments in the investigation?'

The Inspector cast a dubious glance at David. 'I shouldn't really be here, you know. But as long as you all understand that this is strictly off the record . . .'

'Yes, of course,' David put in quickly. 'Any help that you can give me will be very much appreciated, of course, but I won't say a word.'

Drewitt relaxed slightly. 'Mind you,' he laughed, 'I don't know why I should do anything to help the Dean's case. The man is a total shit.'

'Don't I know it,' David agreed with feeling. 'And that's off the record, as well.'

'Think of it as helping Malbury Cathedral instead,' suggested Pat.

'Yes. I don't like seeing the cathedral receiving this kind of bad publicity,' the policeman agreed.

Pat prompted him again. 'So do you have anything to tell us?'

'Yes, one or two things, as a matter of fact.'

They all turned to him and waited expectantly; he took a bite of his crumble, nodded in approval, then went on. 'The Deanery was searched immediately after the murder, of course. We took away quite a few things to have a look at. One of them – well, it's given us something to think about in terms of motive.'

'What's that?' Pat looked at him keenly.

'We're not sure yet exactly how, or if, it fits in,' he cautioned. 'But it's something that might be significant. The books for the Malbury Music Festival, which the Dean had in his study. One of our men who knows something about accounts took a look at them, and he says that they don't make sense, though he can't put his finger on exactly what's wrong. We've sent them away to an accountant to go over them with a fine-tooth comb, so we won't know for a few days what the problem is. But it gives us something to think about, doesn't it?'

'You think someone's been cooking the books?' Pat asked with her customary bluntness.

'Well, it's possible. All I can say is that our man thinks there may well have been a hand in the till somewhere along the line. We're hoping that the accountant may be able to tell us whose hand, and that that might shed some light on what's happened. After all, the music festival was Canon Brydges-ffrench's baby, and presumably he kept the books.'

'And if the Dean found out or suspected that something was wrong . . .' David thought aloud.

'You might ask him,' Drewitt suggested.

'Did you search Canon Brydges-ffrench's house as well?' Lucy asked.

'Yes, of course.'

'Anything significant?' Pat questioned.

'I don't think so,' the Inspector admitted, 'though of course we may discover something later. On the desk in his study there was an opened box of Turkish Delight, with several pieces missing – nothing surprising in that. Whacking great piles of books everywhere for the men to trip over. Heaps of papers on and around his desk, but nothing that seemed to relate to the music festival. The paper that was on top of everything else on his desk – so presumably it was the last thing he was working on – was some sort of list of scripture references. Sermon notes, I suppose.' Drewitt sighed. 'Poor old bugger. That was one sermon he never got to preach.'

'Arthur never was a very inspiring preacher, I'm afraid,' the Bishop put in, apropos of nothing.

John Kingsley looked at him with reproach. 'George, the man is dead.'

But Pat had the last word. 'That doesn't alter the fact that his sermons were nothing to write home about.'

As Inspector Drewitt made ready to leave, David caught his eye tentatively. 'Would you mind if I asked you a question?'

'Fire away.'

'Presumably the police have checked with everyone in the Close about that night, and would have on record everyone's whereabouts. Would it be possible for me to know what they found? To put not too fine a point on it, who has an alibi and who doesn't?'

'I'll see what I can do,' the Inspector promised. 'I'll drop by tomorrow evening, if that's convenient.'

'That would be very kind,' agreed David with gratitude.

After the policeman had gone, they all nursed their coffee in silence for a few minutes, thinking about the implications of what he had told them.

Pat was the first to speak. 'I don't know what to think. Maybe the Dean *did* murder Arthur after all.'

For almost the first time that evening, John Kingsley spoke. 'Oh, no, I don't think so.' His voice was mild but definite, and everyone's head swivelled to look at him.

'Why do you say that?' queried Lucy.

'Because, my dear, of what he told me on the phone that night. He told me that Arthur was being difficult, was refusing to resign under any circumstances. And after we'd all been so hopeful that he was about to see reason.'

'But I don't see . . .' David began.

'All the more reason for him to murder him, I should have thought,' the Bishop stated.

'But don't you understand? If he'd decided to murder him –

had in fact already poisoned the Turkish Delight – he wouldn't have told me that. It gives him a motive that he wouldn't have had if Arthur had carried out his promises and gone quietly. He needn't have told me that Arthur had changed his mind – he could have let me go on thinking that Arthur was willing to resign, knowing that Arthur would be dead and couldn't contradict his account.' The Canon shook his head and took off his spectacles to rub the bridge of his nose. 'No. As convenient as it would be in many ways to believe that the Dean was guilty, in that phone call he proclaimed his own innocence.'

David exchanged glances with Lucy, recognising the truth of what had been said, and acknowledging as well an enhanced respect for her father.

Chapter 35

God shall wound the head of his enemies: and the hairy scalp of such a one as goeth on still in his wickedness.

Psalm 68.21

The next morning, Friday – the day that the story of the Malbury murder hit the front page of the weekly *Church Times* – David arranged to see his client in Shrewsbury prison, for the first time since the remand hearing. He found Stuart Latimer's temperament unimproved by two days of incarceration; the Dean drummed his hairy fingers on the table of the interview room and glowered at David as he entered. 'I see you haven't managed to get me out of here yet,' he greeted him.

'It's only been two days.' David took a seat opposite his client, noting that he looked none the worse for his ordeal; he was clean-shaven and neatly dressed.

'The longest two days of my life. How much longer do you expect me to put up with this?'

David was determined not to let the Dean's ill humour get to him. 'As long as it takes, Dean,' was his mild reply. 'You're being treated well, I trust?'

The Dean laughed mirthlessly. 'They haven't started using the thumbscrews on me yet, if that's what you mean. But this isn't exactly the Savoy, is it? The food is absolutely appalling.'

'As you say, it's not the Savoy.'

'Well, what progress have you made towards getting me out of this place?' Stuart Latimer demanded, adding with a sneer, 'Isn't that what I'm paying you some vastly inflated fee to do?'

David frowned; his voice was quiet but firm. 'Dean, if you're not happy with my services, you're quite free to find someone more to your liking. But I won't be bullied by you. Insult me all you like – I'm still your best hope for getting out of here in due course, and I suggest that you remember that.'

Crossing his arms across his chest, the Dean subsided into sulky silence.

After a moment David went on in a normal tone of voice. 'I came to see you today to ask you about something. About the books for the music festival.'

'What about them?'

He decided to reveal as little as possible of what he had learned in an attempt to discover what the Dean might know. 'I understand from Canon Kingsley that you asked for the books to be handed over, and that subsequently Canon Brydges-ffrench gave them to you.'

'Yes, that's right. But what does that have to do with anything?'

David replied obliquely with another question. 'You examined the books, I suppose?'

'No, as a matter of fact I didn't. I had much more important things to do than to spend my time working through Brydges-ffrench's miserable crabbed handwriting. I put them in my study – I imagine they're still there, if you want them for some good reason.'

It would be necessary to be more direct, David realised. 'Canon Kingsley says that you were very insistent about having the books turned over to you. Did you ask for the books because you suspected that there might be some . . . irregularity . . . in them?'

'Good heavens, no.' The Dean waved a dismissive hand. 'I knew that Brydges-ffrench was stubborn and obstructive, but I never suspected him of dishonesty.'

'Then why were you so insistent?'

'That should be fairly obvious, even to you,' he said with snide emphasis. 'To show them who was boss, of course.' Seeing the expression on David's face, he leaned forward suddenly. 'You're not telling me that there *was* something fishy about the books, are you?'

'Well,' David admitted reluctantly, 'it's just possible that there might have been. The police seem to think that someone had their hand in the till. They're not sure yet who it was, or how . . .'

The Dean burst into peals of humourless laughter. 'Oh, that is rich!'

Puzzled, David said, 'I don't really see what is so funny . . .'

'Don't you?' Stuart Latimer pressed his fingertips together

and looked at them rather than at David. 'It's just that all that time I had the books right there in my study. They were all in on it together – you can mark my words about that. Brydges-ffrench, Thetford, and Greenwood – if one of them was guilty, they were all guilty. It all makes sense to me now, all that whispering in corners. They must have been terrified that I'd find out. That's the biggest joke of all – I had the means right in my own hands to get rid of the whole useless lot of them, and I didn't even realise it!'

Inspector Drewitt was as good as his word. He returned that evening, joining them at the kitchen table and producing a small notebook.

'You asked me about alibis,' he addressed David, consulting his notes. 'There's not really a great deal to say. Most everyone was home for the evening, pretty much from Evensong on. The married people can give each other alibis – Canon and Mrs Greenwood, and Bishop George and Mrs Willoughby.' He smiled sheepishly at the Willoughbys, apologetic that they even had to be mentioned. 'Claire Fairbrother worked late at the clinic that night, and wasn't home until just after nine, so her husband Canon Thetford was on his own at home till then. And the people who live on their own – well, none of them really have alibis. They all just said that they were home by themselves. That's you, Canon Kingsley,' and again he looked apologetic, 'Miss Marsden, Mr Bartlett, and Mrs Hunt. Todd Randall, who lodges with Miss Marsden, was away that night.' He snapped his notebook shut. 'I don't know if that's any help or not.'

'Thank you very much, Inspector,' said David. 'It remains to be seen if it's any help!'

'Tell me,' interjected Lucy with an innocent look, 'were the bell-ringers practising that night?'

'No, we always practise on a Tuesday,' the policeman explained.

'So you weren't in the Close that evening?'

He didn't hesitate, even fractionally. 'No, I was on duty that night. I was called out later, of course, to the scene of the crime, but as I said, I was subsequently taken off the case.'

Lucy and David exchanged brief quizzical glances. If Rowena Hunt hadn't been with Mike Drewitt, their eyes communicated to each other, what had she been doing that she was so anxious not to talk about?

'Have there been any further developments on what you were telling us last night – about the music festival books?' queried the Bishop.

'Only that our man has determined that the irregularities seem to have something to do with the fabric fund – apparently there were some rather large sums transferred.' Inspector Drewitt looked slightly uncomfortable. 'I shouldn't really have mentioned it at all, Bishop. It's all a bit awkward, you understand – until we're able to pin it down, and see what it has to do with this murder case.'

Dr Willoughby stroked his beard. 'Yes, I see.'

'So I'd appreciate it if none of you mentioned it to anyone just yet,' Drewitt went on, looking at David. 'At some point we'll have to question the cosignatories on the account, Canon Greenwood and Canon Thetford, and find out what they know.'

'And you don't want us getting in there first and buggering it all up for you,' David analysed wryly.

'That's it exactly.' Drewitt grinned. 'If you wouldn't mind . . .'

'It really does make it difficult,' David said to Lucy later in their room, 'not being able to ask Rupert Greenwood or Canon Thetford what the hell was going on with those books. I have a feeling it could be very important.' Absent-mindedly he went to the window and looked out at the black shape that was the cathedral.

'Rowena Hunt doesn't have an alibi,' Lucy stated flatly, kicking off her shoes. 'I think *that* could be important.'

He turned to watch her as she undressed. She was unselfconscious about being observed, her movements graceful without being deliberately seductive, yet the sight was always deeply arousing for David. He tried to keep his mind on the matter under discussion. 'What about Jeremy Bartlett?' he reminded her. 'He doesn't seem to have an alibi, either. And Drewitt said that the missing money has something to do with the fabric fund. Fabric, Lucy! That points the finger in the direction of your friend Jeremy, if you ask me. I'm sure he's the one who's had his hand in the till, and I wouldn't be surprised if he committed murder to cover it up, so that his cosy little arrangements with the Dean wouldn't be jeopardised.'

'I don't know why you're so determined that Jeremy should

be guilty, of murder or something else. I don't know why you dislike him so much.'

David was evasive. 'I just don't trust him, that's all. There's something sort of . . . shifty . . . about him.'

'You're being ridiculous,' she said, putting her arms around him.

But before David succumbed completely to her charms, he muttered, 'There's something I wish I could remember. Something that someone told me. I can't think what it is . . .'

Chapter 36

My voice shalt thou hear betimes, O Lord: early in the morning will I direct my prayer unto thee, and will look up.

Psalm 5.3

The following morning, David's unconscious mind registered what he had been struggling to remember, as he woke to the sound of the cathedral's eight bells ringing rounds.

'Lucy!' he said, suddenly wide awake. 'It was the bell-ringers!'

'The bell-ringers should be shot,' she moaned, burying her face in her pillow. 'Isn't it a bit early to be making that kind of racket?'

'Never mind that! It was the bell-ringers who said what I was trying to remember last night!'

'What time is it?' She turned over and peered sleepily at the clock. 'Half past eight on a Saturday morning – they must be mad!'

'Listen to me, Lucy,' David insisted. 'Todd told me at the breakfast here, after the service for Ivor Jones.'

'I thought you said it was the bell-ringers.'

'Todd told me something that the bell-ringers had said, something that he happened to overhear,' he explained patiently. 'At the Dean's garden party. When the Dean started giving them a hard time for drinking beer, and said that they were a scandal, one of them told the Dean that the real scandal was happening down in the cathedral!'

Lucy wasn't wide awake enough to follow. 'I don't understand. What does that have to do with . . . ?'

'Don't you see? The Dean thought that he was talking about the organist and the choirboys, which was why he said the things that drove Ivor Jones to suicide. But what if he really meant the scandal of the fiddled accounts? What if the bell-ringers know something about it? It makes sense, Lucy!' He reached to the floor for his dressing gown.

'You're not getting up, are you?'

'Yes, I've got to go and talk to the bell-ringers, and see what they know – no one has thought to ask them!'

'Don't go yet.' She put an entreating hand on his arm. 'There's plenty of time.'

It was tempting, but not tempting enough. 'Sorry, love. I won't be good for anything until I find out.'

Lucy sighed. 'Oh, be that way!' She pulled the covers over her head and stuffed her fingers in her ears to block out the sound of the bells.

Pat was up and in the kitchen when David came down, without Lucy. 'Saturday is our day for a cooked breakfast,' she announced. 'George should be back any minute from the eight o'clock service.'

'The bells have started awfully early this morning, haven't they?'

'They often start ringing a peal just after the eight o'clock service on a Saturday,' Pat explained. 'If the peal is successful, it takes something like three hours and twenty minutes, and Mike Drewitt often goes on duty at noon, so if they don't start early they won't have his services. And he usually rings the tenor, so they can't very well do without him. The people in the Close are used to it – most of us have to be up early anyway.'

'Lucy was a bit cross,' he admitted. 'I think she was hoping for a lie-in this morning.'

'Poor Lucy,' chuckled Pat.

David circled around the kitchen restlessly. 'I need to talk to the bell-ringers – I've just remembered something that could be important, and I think the bell-ringers might be able to help.'

'Well, you're not going to talk to them for the next few hours, unless they lose the peal,' she stated with unavoidable logic. 'So you may as well sit down and have some breakfast. How do you like your eggs, my dear boy?'

David waited for them at the bottom of the spiral staircase in the south transept; a few minutes after the bells stopped ringing they began issuing forth. Inspector Drewitt was the first down, in a hurry to report for duty at noon. 'I don't have time to stop,' he greeted David. 'I've got to go to work.'

'I'd quite like to have a chat with you some time, Inspector – just the two of us.'

Drewitt paused, thinking. 'All right. Tomorrow evening? We could meet at the Monk's Head for a drink, if you like.'

'Great. What time?'

'Eight o'clock?'

'Fine. I'll see you there.'

Drewitt was followed out of the stairwell by several young people, chattering noisily; their voices echoed in the vaulted transept. 'The ringing master?' David asked them tentatively.

'Barry's still up the tower – he'll be the last one down,' volunteered a sallow girl with spiky hair and a series of silver hoops in graduated sizes piercing the side of one ear. 'You can go up, if you want,' she added helpfully.

David gulped; he'd never been very comfortable with heights. 'No, thank you. I'll wait.'

It was only a few minutes later that the final group descended: a frail, wispy blonde girl, a sturdy young man with a prominent nose, and at last the tall, long-haired Barry Crabtree. David remembered having seen, though not met, the three of them at the Dean's garden party.

He stepped forward. 'Barry?'

The tall young man turned. 'Yes?'

David introduced himself, explaining that he was a friend of the Willoughbys; he had decided, while waiting, that that would get him farther with anyone in the Close than admitting that he was the Dean's solicitor.

'This is my wife Liz,' introduced Barry, 'and my mate Neil.'

'Are you in a hurry? I'd like to buy you a drink,' David offered.

Barry and Neil looked at each other. 'Why not?' Barry said.

'I never turn down a pint,' added Neil with a gap-toothed grin.

Liz Crabtree shook her head. 'I'm afraid not. I've left Caroline – she's our daughter—' she explained to David, 'with Mrs Greenwood this morning, so I must go and fetch her.'

'Oh, come on, Liz,' Barry urged. 'You know that Mrs Greenwood loves having Caroline. She wouldn't mind you leaving her a bit longer.'

'No, that's not fair. But you two go ahead,' she added. 'I'll see you at home later, Barry.'

'The Monk's Head?' David suggested, naming the only pub he knew of in Malbury.

'Fine,' Barry agreed. 'If you're paying. It's a bit dearer than our local, down at the other end of town.'

The two bell-ringers led the way into the town. David had spent very little time out of the Cathedral Close in the town of Malbury. Malbury, although technically a city by virtue of its cathedral, was in reality no more than a market town, albeit an ancient one, with picturesquely crooked black and white buildings elbowing each other closely along narrow streets in the town centre. Girdling the central area was a belt of substantial red brick Victorian dwellings constructed in the days of the railway boom, along with a number of more modestly proportioned terraced houses, built for brewery workers. The building boom between the wars had largely passed Malbury by, so there were few of the semi-detached villas of that period, but recent years had brought the inevitable additions, including a raw new housing estate at the edge of town, with identical boxy detached houses each on a tiny, treeless patch of lawn.

The Monk's Head, though, was situated near the cathedral, overlooking the open green space which separated the Close from the town. A rambling mock-Tudor building, it had pretensions of being more than a mere pub: it styled itself as an inn, by virtue of the accommodation it offered upstairs, several cramped, unimproved bedrooms. The pub downstairs, though, lived up to expectations, with oak beams and horse brasses and an open fire.

Despite their protestations, Barry and Neil were obviously well known in the establishment. They greeted the barman by name, placed their orders for pints of Ploughman's Bitter, and commandeered a table near the fire. David paid for and collected the drinks, then carried them, foaming and dripping, to the table.

'Careful, mate!' grinned Neil. 'I was hoping to drink most of that. Ta.' He raised the glass and drank deeply.

'Thanks,' Barry acknowledged.

David rarely drank beer, but on this occasion he thought it a good idea to partake of the local brew along with his guests. The Ploughman's went down surprisingly easily, he found, and they were on their second round before he got around to the real business at hand.

'I was talking to Todd Randall not long ago,' he began tentatively.

Barry nodded. 'The American bloke.'

'A nice bloke,' Neil put in. 'Bar tried to get him interested in bell-ringing.'

'Without success?'

'Oh, he came up in the tower once or twice,' Barry explained. 'Gave it a go. But he couldn't quite get the hang of the timing, so he gave up.'

'He said that he'd spent some time with you at the garden party after the Dean's installation.'

'That's right,' confirmed Barry. 'He joined us at our table, he and Kirsty Hunt.'

Neil grinned. 'It was the beer rather than our company that attracted him, I reckon.'

Taking a sip of his beer, David chose his words carefully. 'He told me that the Dean gave you a hard time about the beer.'

Barry snorted in derision. 'That self-important little clown.'

'But Bar gave it right back to him, didn't you, Bar?' There was relish in Neil's tone and he looked admiringly at his friend.

'Well, I wouldn't say that.' Barry swirled the beer in his glass, suitably modest.

'Cor, but you did!' Neil turned to David eagerly. 'He told him that we weren't the disgrace – that the scandal was really down in the cathedral!'

David held his breath, then said as lightly as he could manage, 'And what did you mean by that, Barry? Anything in particular, or were you just saying it to get at him?'

The young bell-ringer appraised him for a moment before replying. 'Oh, I meant it, all right. Something funny was going on down there.'

'Something funny?'

'It was the scaffolding, you see. It went up in the summer, after the Music Festival, in the south transept around the Becket window, and outside the window as well.' Barry took a deep drink, emptying his glass. 'And it stayed up until November, just before the Patronal Festival. But in all those months, in that whole bloomin' time, nothing ever happened. No workmen, nothing.'

'You're sure about that?'

'Oh, yes. We could see the exterior scaffolding quite clearly on the way up to the tower, and I'm up the tower a lot. Every day, near enough. No workmen,' he repeated. 'They put the scaffolding up, and they left it a few months, and then they took it down again. Nothing else happened. Don't you think that's bloomin' odd?'

Chapter 37

Deliver my soul, O Lord, from lying lips: and from a deceitful tongue.

Psalm 120.2

The more David thought about it, the more convinced he became that the Cathedral Architect was involved in the death of Arthur Brydges-ffrench. But to make Lucy happy, he agreed to pay a call on Rowena Hunt, to probe further into her lack of alibi.

He went on Sunday afternoon, after a subdued, even strained, morning service at which the Bishop presided, and a deliciously compensatory Sunday lunch.

Rowena raised her finely shaped brows at the sight of David on her doorstep; she invited him in politely enough, though she failed to offer him any refreshment. Her sitting room was tidy, with none of the Sunday paper clutter he'd left behind at the Bishop's House, and a fire burned cheerily in the grate. David wondered if she were expecting someone.

She sat down and gestured him to a chair. 'What can I do for you, Mr Middleton-Brown?' she said, emphasising that she did not consider them to be on first-name terms.

David remained standing and came straight to the point. 'I'm sorry to bother you like this, Mrs Hunt, but it really is most important that I get a complete picture of what happened in the Close on Monday night. So I'd like to ask you again to tell me where you were and what you were doing.'

Frowning in exasperation, Rowena stated, 'I told you once. I was here at home all evening. I didn't go out, and I didn't hear anything.'

'But what were you doing?' he repeated.

'That's none of your business,' she snapped immediately, then softened it by adding, with a strained smile, 'I don't really see what relevance it has.'

David decided to be forthright. 'It might be very important, if – say – you were not alone?'

Her smile faded; her mouth tightened. 'I'm not prepared to discuss that ... suggestion,' she stated coldly, through clenched teeth. Rowena rose. 'I repeat: it is none of your business. You have no right to ask me that. And now I really must ask you to leave, Mr Middleton-Brown.'

As David left Rowena's house, a woman came towards him from the other side of the Close, lurching unsteadily out of the shadow of the cathedral. He stepped aside politely to let her pass, but she stopped and accosted him. David had never seen the woman before, though as she opened her mouth he knew in a flash of intuition who she must be: Val Drewitt. At first glance she was not at all the type of woman one would expect to encounter in the genteel Cathedral Close, but Lucy had given him enough of a description of the policeman's wife for him to recognise her somewhat overblown charms. He was surprised to see, though, that she was not an unattractive woman, in a somewhat coarse but blatantly sexual way, her voluptuousness evident beneath the shiny hot-pink vinyl raincoat which she wore in deference to the autumnal chill.

'Have you got a light, luv?' She thrust a long, menthol-tipped cigarette towards him.

'No, I'm very sorry. I don't smoke.'

'Well, never mind.' She laughed philosophically, exuding a powerful whiff of gin.

David continued walking back towards the entrance to the Close; to his surprise she walked along beside him. 'So, you're another one, are you?' she remarked in a conversational tone.

'I beg your pardon?'

'Another one of that Hunt bitch's lays. She's not happy with just one, you know. You'd think that my husband would be enough for her – he's damned good in bed, even if she has to share the bastard with me. But she can't leave any man alone, can she? I watch her house sometimes, when I think Mike might come.' She chuckled to herself and chattered on, oblivious to David's stunned silence. 'He tells me he's on duty, but I know he sneaks off to her for a quick screw every chance he gets. It makes me laugh to see him rushing in there, not knowing that I'm watching. Sometimes I get a surprise, though. Like the other night, when it was that other one

270

instead. And today, it ended up being you. Funny. I would have sworn that Mike was going there this afternoon.' She dropped her voice confidentially. 'Tell me, mate. Just between the two of us. Is she really that good?'

'I'm ... afraid I wouldn't know,' David mumbled, acutely embarrassed. 'And now, if you'll excuse me—' Lengthening his strides, he soon left her behind.

That evening, David arrived at the Monk's Head before Inspector Drewitt. He bought himself a whisky and settled down near the fire, reflecting what a difficult and delicate task he had before him. He acknowledged to himself that Lucy was right: Rowena Hunt was definitely concealing something, and he had to find out if Drewitt knew what it was. To do that he would have to bring the policeman to admit that he was her lover, and then ...

'Hello, David.' Inspector Drewitt slid his powerful body into the seat across from him. 'Sorry I'm a bit late. I was ... delayed.'

With Rowena, thought David. 'What would you like? A pint of Ploughman's?'

Drewitt eyed David's drink. 'Actually, I'm more of a whisky man myself, if it's all the same to you.'

'Right. A double?'

'Great.'

He went up to the bar, returning with another whisky, and they drank in silence for a few minutes, Drewitt wondering what it was all about, and David steeling himself to ask the questions. Although the direct approach had not been met by any notable success with Rowena, he decided in the end that Drewitt was a blunt, straightforward man and more likely to be susceptible to it. 'I saw your wife this afternoon,' he began.

'Val?' Drewitt didn't seem unduly surprised or alarmed. 'I didn't know that you knew Val.'

'I didn't. Not until this afternoon, that is. I ran into her in the Close.' David looked down into the remains of his drink, avoiding Drewitt's eyes. 'She said some things about ... you and Rowena Hunt.' He raised his head in time to see the policeman's face redden; for an instant his visage hardened like stone, then he consciously relaxed.

'Oh, did she now?' Drewitt forced a laugh. 'I don't suppose there's any point denying it to you, though I'd prefer that the whole Close didn't know. Not on my account – for Rowena's sake.'

'Of course.' Again David looked down.

'Can I get you another drink?' Drewitt offered.

'Thanks.'

When the policeman returned, he began talking; it was as though he'd been waiting for a long time for someone to confide in about the affair, and circumstances had provided David for that purpose. 'It all started last summer,' he said. 'About the time of the music festival. It's been going on ever since, at her place, whenever I can manage a bit of time off work, or after bell practice. I usually just tell Val that I'm on duty.' He smiled reminiscently. 'I don't mind telling you, David. She's one hell of a woman.'

'But your wife . . .' David tailed off, unsure what he'd meant to say.

Drewitt gave a short, cynical laugh. 'You needn't think that Val's as pure as the driven snow, my friend.'

David hadn't imagined that she was, but he hardly knew how to respond, so he rushed on to the heart of the matter that was on his mind. 'Were you with her on Monday evening?' he asked bluntly.

The policeman looked surprised at the question. 'No,' he said, equally blunt. 'I told you that I was on duty that night. And whatever else I may be guilty of, I *don't* mix duty with pleasure.'

'I don't quite know how to say this,' David said uncomfortably, moving his glass around to make damp rings on the table, 'but I'm not entirely satisfied about Mrs Hunt's alibi for Monday night. I thought that you might have been there, and she didn't want to say so.'

Drewitt stared into the fire for a moment. He raised his hand to stroke his trim moustache, so that when he spoke his voice was muffled. 'I'm not so happy about it myself,' he admitted quietly. 'She told the officer who interviewed her that she was home all evening, that she didn't go out at all. But I rang her around nine, to see if I might stop round when I went off duty at midnight.'

'And what did she say?' David was almost afraid to speak, lest he break the spell of whisky-induced intimacy that had developed between them.

'That's just it, my friend. She didn't say anything. She didn't answer the phone.' Drewitt looked at him, shaking his head in hurt bafflement. 'She bloody well didn't answer the phone,' he repeated. 'So where the hell was she?'

Chapter 38

*Let not the ungodly have his desire, O Lord: let not his
mischievous imagination prosper, lest they be too proud.*
Psalm 140.8

With so much on his mind, David didn't sleep very well that
night. He woke early, determined to make yet another trip to
Shrewsbury prison to see the Dean. As early as was feasible, he
was on the phone to the prison, making an appointment to visit
his client.

'I've arranged to see him this afternoon, just after lunch,' he
announced to Lucy and Pat, coming through into the kitchen as
they ate their breakfast.

'What else do you have to ask him?' Lucy wanted to know.

'I need to know if I'm barking up completely the wrong tree
with this alibi business – if I'm putting far too much
importance on the fact that Rowena doesn't have an alibi, and
neither, apparently, does Jeremy.'

Lucy shot him a look over the cornflakes. 'You haven't even
talked to Jeremy yet, and he's your number one suspect – as
you keep telling me.'

'All in good time, love. You must admit that he's got a good
motive, if he'd been doing funny things with the fabric fund and
Brydges-ffrench found out.'

'And don't forget that Rowena is hiding something,' Lucy
reminded him.

Pat frowned, baffled. 'But how can seeing the Dean help?'

Sitting down and helping himself to a piece of toast, David
explained. 'The alibi issue may be a complete red herring. Lucy
was right when she said last week that it's not enough for
someone else to have a motive and no alibi – there's still the
matter of opportunity. I still can't see how someone other than
the Dean could have poisoned and then swapped the Turkish
Delight, even if they could have got into the Deanery unseen by

Miss Marsden. How did they know it was there? And what sort of time period are we talking about? The whole question of alibis for the evening may be totally irrelevant, given the amount of time between when the Dean bought the Turkish Delight and Canon Brydges-ffrench ate it. That's the sort of thing I need to pin down – who knew he'd bought the Turkish Delight, where it was all afternoon, and so on.'

Pat poured him a cup of tea. 'And what about the cellophane wrapper?' she suggested.

'Exactly! When did he remove the wrapper? Before Canon Brydges-ffrench arrived? Before their meal?'

'And it's not even just a question of opportunity,' Lucy pointed out. 'Logistics come into it as well. Take Jeremy, for instance. I've been thinking about this – even though he lives next door to the Deanery, there's a high wall in between. I can't really imagine him shinning over the wall, can you? For him to get to the Deanery he has to go around the west end of the cathedral and all around the Close. Surely someone in the Close would have seen him, even if Miss Marsden happened to be away from her window.'

'Couldn't he have gone through the cathedral?' suggested David, unwilling to hear anything that cast further doubt on his favourite suspect.

Lucy shook her head. 'He doesn't have any keys – he told me so himself, a long time ago.'

'I must admit,' said David, 'that I'm compiling quite a list of questions for Mr Bartlett, when I finally talk to him.'

'And when will that be?' Pat asked.

'It depends on what the Dean says, of course. But possibly this evening.'

'I could talk to him,' Lucy offered.

David frowned. 'No.'

'But I know him better than you do. He might tell me . . .'

'Absolutely not,' he stated firmly. 'If he has done something criminal with the fabric fund – and the evidence of the bell-ringers certainly points in that direction – then he's a dangerous man, Lucy. Whether he's committed murder or not. I don't want you alone with him.'

Pat, suspecting that that was not the only reason he didn't want Lucy alone with Jeremy, tactfully changed the subject. 'I forgot to tell you, Lucy, that Judith Greenwood rang before you came downstairs. She wondered if you might be able to have lunch with her today.'

Lucy looked enquiringly at David. 'Go ahead, love,' he urged her. 'I'll grab a sandwich on my way to Shrewsbury.'

It was a cold, cloudless day of the sort one occasionally gets late in November, when the damp mists of autumn give way without warning to the crisp bite of winter. Lucy, pulling her coat close around her as she walked back from lunch with Judith, looked at the cathedral in the sunlight: the buttresses cast sharp-edged shadows against the transepts, and the carvings on the west front stood out in vivid relief. She paused at the entrance to the Bishop's House, looking towards the south transept; the Becket window was not visible from that viewpoint, obscured as it was by the surviving two-storeyed cloister. Lucy remembered then something that Jeremy had told her several months ago, that first evening when he'd shown her around the Close: the best view of the Becket window was from his bedroom window.

She didn't dare to stop and think about what she was going to do, against all good sense as well as David's express wishes. Taking a deep breath, Lucy squared her shoulders and propelled herself towards Jeremy's house.

His face lit up at the sight of her. 'Lucy! Come in!'

At the warmth of his greeting Lucy's heart misgave her, but she quelled the impulse to flee, forcing a smile. 'Are you busy?'

'Never too busy for you, my dear.' He quirked one eyebrow in a consciously ironic way. 'I was just doing a bit of work in my study, but it's nothing that won't keep. Come in and have a cup of tea.'

'Yes, all right.'

'If you don't mind my asking, to what do I owe this unexpected pleasure?' he queried, stepping aside to usher her into the entrance hall.

She'd scarcely had time to think up a coherent story, but somehow it came out sounding plausible. 'I wanted to see how you'd hung my painting. Remember the last time we talked – you said that you'd moved it from the sitting room. Just my artist's vanity, I suppose – I wanted to make sure that you'd hung it to its best advantage.' She smiled.

Jeremy paused at the bottom of the stairs and looked at her questioningly. 'Of course. But you do remember that I told you

I'd hung it in my bedroom? It's rather a cliché, isn't it? "Come upstairs and see my etchings"?'

Lucy laughed; she hoped it didn't sound as strained to Jeremy as it did to her own ears. 'I'm sure that your intentions are honourable.'

His eyebrow inched higher and he kept his voice light, teasing. 'I wouldn't be so sure about that, my dear. You know that I'm absolutely mad about you.'

'Then I suppose I'll have to take my chances.'

'So be it.' He led her up the stairs and into the spacious front bedroom.

Although it was an airy room, illuminated by large windows, it was to Lucy's eye undoubtedly a man's room, with no feminine touches at all: the furniture was massive and dark, and there was a total lack of decorative items of the sort favoured by women. Even the walls were bare, save for the painting on the wall facing the bed. Lucy wondered, not for the first time, what Jeremy's late wife had been like. Had this been her furniture, in their marital home, or had he got rid of anything that might remind him of their life together, and begun anew? Impossible to say.

Stifling her impulse to pity, Lucy thought quickly how she might get an uninterrupted look out of the windows. She studied the position of the painting with every evidence of grave consideration. 'No,' she said at last. 'I don't like it there. The light's not right at all. I think it would look much better over here, on this wall. Then it wouldn't be fighting with the shadow from your wardrobe.'

Jeremy followed her pointing finger. 'Yes, I suppose you're right. You're the artist, after all,' he added humbly.

'Do you have a hammer?'

'Downstairs. I won't be a minute.'

As soon as he was out of the door, Lucy went to the window. Jeremy had been right: the view of the Becket window was superb, especially in the sunlight. For a window that was nearly eight hundred years old it was in remarkable condition. The stonework surrounding it, though, did not look as though it had been disturbed recently; there were no tell-tale differences in the colour of the stone, or marks indicating mending. Lucy remembered what the bell-ringers had told David about the scaffolding. She remembered a few other things as well, and suddenly all the pieces slotted together in her mind: the discrepancies in the fabric funds, Bishop George explaining that Jeremy had discovered the need for urgent repairs to the window, Jeremy telling the American tourist all those months ago that the window had been re-leaded and the stonework renewed some ten years ago, Todd mentioning at the Patronal Festival Evensong that the window looked exactly the same as it had before the urgent repairs. Of course it looked the same, she told herself – nothing had been done. The window itself was mute testimony: not a tribute to the restorer's art, but rather immutable evidence of fraud. David had been right. And if Jeremy had cold-bloodedly concocted this elaborate scheme to line his own pockets with cathedral funds, what else was he capable of doing to conceal his duplicity? She caught her breath at the possibilities.

Jeremy paused in the doorway, hammer in hand, struck dumb at the sight of Lucy at the window, her hair a flaming halo against the sun. All of his resolution to play it cool evaporated as his chest constricted with desire for her; scarcely aware of what he was doing, he crossed the room in a few strides, put his arms around her, and buried his face in her hair. 'Oh, Lucy,' he groaned, 'how beautiful you are.'

Gasping, she tried to pull away from him, but his arms were unexpectedly strong. 'Don't be afraid,' he murmured. 'I want you, Lucy. I could please you more than David ever could. Why don't you give me a chance to show you? Isn't it about time you stopped keeping me at arm's length?' With one hand he groped for her breast, and his mouth sought hers roughly.

In the few seconds that it all took, Lucy's emotions went from speculative apprehension to stark terror: terror at the look in his eyes, his face bending close to hers, and terror at the implications of the situation she had walked into. Was this man a murderer? At that moment she could well believe it. And the hand that was against her back, pressing her tightly to his chest, held a hammer.

Chapter 39

Deliver me, O Lord, from the evil man: and preserve me from the wicked man.

Psalm 140.1

Fighting the urge to scream, an action which she instinctively knew could be disastrous, with an enormous effort Lucy remained calm. She wrenched her face away from his, scraping her cheek cruelly against his beard. 'Let go of me, Jeremy,' she said firmly, amazed and grateful that her voice didn't quaver to betray her fear. 'Don't be so silly.'

Astonished, he complied; his arms dropped to his sides and he took a step backwards.

She decided to strike while he was as off balance as she was, realising as she spoke that she was taking an enormous risk. 'The window,' she said. 'The Becket window. There weren't any urgent repairs, were there? Nothing's been done to it.'

Jeremy stared at her. 'What do you mean?'

'I have eyes, Jeremy. I'm not stupid. Nothing's been done to that window in the last ten years. I heard you tell that American tourist last summer that it had been re-leaded ten years ago, and the stonework renewed. You can't expect me to believe that it had got in such a bad state since then.'

She spoke forcefully, almost aggressively, but Jeremy's reaction surprised her almost as much as anything else he'd done: he shrugged and raised his eyebrows in a characteristic way. 'You win the prize,' he said with a short laugh, tossing the hammer on the bed.

'But why, Jeremy? Surely you weren't so hard up for money that you had to come up with such an elaborate scheme to defraud the cathedral?'

His laugh this time was more prolonged, and he seemed almost genuinely amused. 'Is that what you think? Is that what you really think it was all about?'

'Well, wasn't it?' she demanded. 'What else am I supposed to think?'

Jeremy crossed to the window and looked out at the Becket window as he explained. 'I did it to help Arthur Brydges-ffrench out of a tight spot. The Malbury Music Festival was a financial disaster, as you should have realised at the time – all those expensive glossy programmes, and all the other expenses, and no one came. Brydges-ffrench was in a real panic about it, especially with the new Dean on the way. So we worked out a little scheme to transfer money from the fabric fund to cover the shortfall. I thought it was rather clever, myself.' He turned to her with a self-congratulatory smile. 'It was my idea – to use the excuse of the window for the outgoing funds. I didn't think that anyone would question it, when the scaffolding went up and there was every appearance of work being done. After all, as people are fond of saying, the Becket window is the cathedral's greatest treasure, and no expense is too great to preserve it. I even got Rowena Hunt to kick in ten thousand pounds from the Friends – and she'd already turned Brydges-ffrench down when he asked for her help in getting out of his predicament.'

Lucy was speechless. Before she could formulate a reply, the doorbell rang, breaking the spell. David, she thought irrationally, knowing full well that David was in Shrewsbury. Whoever it might be, though, she was very glad of the interruption; she followed Jeremy down the stairs with relief.

The caller at the door was Todd. He didn't see Lucy at first, behind Jeremy in the entrance hall. 'Hello, Jeremy,' he said in his usual open, friendly way. 'I just wondered if you by any chance still had Canon Brydges-ffrench's keys – I was supposed to get them back from you last week, but I forgot.'

'Yes, they must be here somewhere. Come in while I find them.' Jeremy moved to the hall table and began shifting papers around.

'Todd! I didn't know you were back in Malbury!'

He was nearly as surprised to see Lucy there as she was to see him. 'Lucy! I just got back a few minutes ago. I couldn't stand being so far away from what was happening here, so I had to come back.'

Jeremy located the keys and tossed them carelessly to Todd: a great fat bunch of keys on a massive ring. 'I would have returned them sooner, but you weren't around.'

'Thanks.' Todd turned to go.

'I'll come with you, Todd,' Lucy said quickly, following him out the door. 'Goodbye, Jeremy. I'll be seeing you.'

'Lucy . . .' Jeremy called after her. 'I think we need to talk some more.'

'Not now.'

Jeremy stood at the door watching them as they walked away, so they spoke quietly. 'What's going on?' asked Todd.

'It's a long story. Where are you going now?'

'I thought I'd stay at Canon Brydges-ffrench's house for the moment, but then I remembered that I didn't have the keys.'

'Come with me to the Bishop's House,' Lucy urged. 'I'm desperate for a cup of tea, and there's so much to tell you.'

'All right.'

'By the way,' Lucy asked, with a frown that was only partially for effect, 'what have you done with Sophie? Have you abandoned my poor cat?'

Todd had the grace to look shamefaced. 'I left her with your cleaning woman. She said she'd look after her – I hope you don't mind. But I just couldn't stay away any longer.'

'I don't mind at all. In fact,' Lucy confessed, 'I can't tell you how glad I am that you showed up when you did!'

Back in Pat's kitchen, Lucy suffered a delayed reaction to the shock she'd undergone and collapsed trembling into a chair, her head in her hands and tears running down her cheeks. She might even have become hysterical at that point, but for Pat's calm efficiency. The Bishop's wife made her a strong cup of tea and put it in her suddenly nerveless hands. 'Now, my dear. Tell me what's the matter.'

Lucy took a deep, shuddering breath and touched her abraded cheek. 'Promise me that you won't tell David.'

'Very well, if that's what you want.'

Bit by bit, with many painful stops and starts, the story came out of her spur-of-the-moment visit to Jeremy and its unforeseen consequences. Todd was aghast; Pat was sympathetic but practical. 'Don't you see, my dear – you must tell David. He'll have to know what you found out about the window.'

'Yes, I realise that. But I couldn't bear for him to know . . . the rest of it. He'd never forgive me for going there and putting myself in such a position, and he'd . . . well, I can't even imagine what he'd want to do to Jeremy.'

'Then you must tell him as much as you think he needs to know for the moment. Eventually, I think, you'll have to tell him the whole story.'

'I shouldn't have gone. I was foolish to go,' Lucy reproached herself. 'Oh, Pat! Why on earth did I do it?' Even to herself, she was unable to articulate the horror of what might have happened.

The other woman gave her a brisk hug. 'What's done is done. Unpleasant as it may have been, there was no lasting harm done. And at least we know about the window now.'

By the time David arrived back later in the afternoon, everything had been arranged: Todd was to stay at the Bishop's House. Pat wouldn't hear of him going to the vacant Subdean's house, and he admitted that he was not yet ready to return to his room at Miss Marsden's, so it was settled. Cain and Abel were ecstatic, thrusting their large wet noses under his hand as they vied for his attention and caresses.

But David scarcely paused to register Todd's presence, much less to inquire into the particular circumstances that had brought him back to Malbury, or the subsequent arrangements.

'It could have happened!' he announced with great excitement. 'Someone else *might* have poisoned the Turkish Delight!'

'But how?' asked Lucy, who had by now recovered her equilibrium.

He sat down and accepted a cup of tea from Pat. 'I asked the Dean about it. He wasn't particularly inclined to be cooperative, but I explained to him that it might be our only chance of getting him off. So he thought about it, and remembered that he'd talked to Jeremy after Evensong, and mentioned to him about the Turkish Delight.'

'That he'd bought it?' Todd queried; Lucy and Pat had filled him in on the state of the investigations, so he was able to keep up with the discussion.

'Yes, and that he'd invited Canon Brydges-ffrench to supper, after which he was planning to serve the Turkish Delight.'

'So Jeremy knew,' Pat said thoughtfully, looking at Lucy.

'But what about Rowena?' Lucy asked, unwilling to relinquish her prime suspect. 'Did the Dean tell her as well? Did you ask him?'

'I asked him – and he didn't tell her. But he thought it was possible that she might have overheard when he told Jeremy,' admitted David. 'She was standing nearby. So she can't be discounted yet.'

Todd's questions showed that he understood the nuances of the situation. 'When was the box opened? And where did he put it afterwards?'

David smiled appreciatively. 'After Canon Brydges-ffrench arrived. The Dean had planned to keep it until after supper, but to get over the awkwardness of the Canon's arrival he decided to offer him a piece straightaway, to get things off on a friendly footing. So he took the cellophane wrapper off and offered it to him. But the Canon said he'd wait till later, so the Dean put the box down in the entrance hall, where it remained until they'd finished eating, going on for ten o'clock. Lucy's father rang at ten,' he added, 'and the Dean said that it was only a few minutes earlier that he'd brought the box through to the dining room.'

'So,' Pat summarised, 'we can narrow down the period of time during which anyone could have tampered with the Turkish Delight. If Arthur arrived at the Deanery at eight o'clock, and John rang at ten, that leaves a period of less than two hours when something might have happened to it.'

'And Jeremy knew enough to have been able to do it. The bit I can't work out, though,' David admitted, 'is how he might have got *into* the Deanery, as well as getting *to* the Deanery unseen. As Lucy said, he would have had to go all around the Close.'

'The keys!' Todd's eyes shone with excitement. 'Jeremy had Canon Brydges-ffrench's keys!' He took the large ring out of the pocket of his jeans and deposited it on the table with a satisfying clunk. 'I just got them back from him this afternoon! The Canon had given them to him on Sunday so that he could take down his display in the library. I was supposed to get them back on Monday, but of course with everything that happened I forgot about it entirely until this afternoon.' He picked them back up and jingled them with a triumphant flourish. 'It's a complete set,' he explained. 'Here is the key to the Deanery – the Subdean had it because he was the Acting Dean in the interregnum. And this is the key to the Dean's door, and here's the one to the south transept door. So Jeremy could have gone into the cathedral through the south transept – the entrance is through the cloister right by his house – and come out through the Dean's door, right across from the Deanery.'

'Lucy's found out something that sheds a bit more light on

Jeremy's motivation,' said Pat; Lucy shot her a warning look but Pat went on calmly. 'She happened to see Jeremy today, and he admitted something quite astonishing about the Becket window.'

Twisting a curl around her finger and averting her face from David, Lucy told him about Jeremy's scheme to cover the Music Festival's deficit.

'And Jeremy actually *told* you this?' The incredulity in David's voice mirrored that on his face.

Lucy raised her eyes to his at last. 'Yes, he told me. But I'd guessed most of it already. I remembered what you'd said about the bell-ringers and the scaffolding, and then I remembered a few other things as well, and I realised that nothing had been done to the window. So I asked him about it, and he admitted it, then told me why – that it wasn't for his own personal gain, but to help out Arthur Brydges-ffrench.'

David couldn't suppress a momentary feeling of triumph that his assessment of Jeremy's character had been borne out. 'I *told* you that Jeremy wasn't a trustworthy person,' he stated smugly. But Lucy's reaction surprised him; she merely nodded and looked away.

'You were right,' she said in a quiet voice.

Thoughtfully, David chewed on his thumbnail. 'But what does this mean in terms of his motive for murder? If he wasn't actually lining his own pockets with cathedral funds, and if Brydges-ffrench knew about it all along . . .'

'But don't you see,' Lucy interrupted him. 'That doesn't really make any difference. It was still fraud, after all. The important thing isn't that Arthur Brydges-ffrench knew about it, but that the Dean *didn't*. Jeremy had a great deal to lose if the Dean found out.'

'Yeah, what if Canon Brydges-ffrench was threatening to tell the Dean?' Todd hypothesised. 'He'd had to give him the books, so maybe he thought that the Dean was bound to figure out that something was fishy, and that he'd get off more lightly if he told him it was all Jeremy's idea?'

'The Dean would *not* have been amused, and Jeremy would have lost his position as blue-eyed boy,' Pat stated. 'And probably the commission to design the Cathedral Centre as well.'

'Not to mention the matter of public scandal,' added Lucy.

'As motives go,' said David, 'that's not a bad one.' He smiled around the table at the others. 'I think, my friends, that we may be on to something.'

But as Lucy drifted off to sleep that night she found that, despite the revulsion she now felt at the thought of Jeremy, she still couldn't quite believe him to be a murderer: something still didn't entirely fit, though she couldn't decide what it was. And there was still the question of Rowena, who, as far as Lucy was concerned, had a motive at least as good as Jeremy's, with the added factor of a lack of alibi, and an unwillingness to discuss it. She remembered, suddenly, something that Jeremy had said: that Rowena had kicked in ten thousand pounds from the Friends' funds for the phoney window repair. Had she been a willing partner in the fraud and the cover-up? Lucy decided that she would have to confront Rowena about it all, the next day. David might not see the necessity, and probably wouldn't approve, but David wouldn't need to know until she'd done it. After all, if she didn't tell him what she intended to do, he wouldn't be able to stop her.

Chapter 40

*They reel to and fro, and stagger like a drunken man: and
are at their wit's end.*

Psalm 107.27

The next morning, while David was in the kitchen chatting
with Pat and Todd, Lucy quietly let herself out of the house and
slipped into the cathedral, going straight to the Friends' stall
in the south aisle. She felt guilty that she was taking such a
step without consulting David, but had told herself that,
convinced as he was of Jeremy's guilt, he would dismiss her
concerns about Rowena.

To Lucy's surprise, Rowena wasn't at the Friends' stall; it
was inhabited instead by an elderly volunteer who regarded
her with suspicion when she asked for Mrs Hunt. 'She's not
here,' said the woman.

'Yes, I can see that. Is she at home, do you know? I'm Canon
Kingsley's daughter,' she added with what she hoped was a
winning smile, counting on her father's popularity with
everyone at the cathedral to enhance her standing by
association.

The ploy was successful; the woman unbent at once. 'Oh, the
Canon! He's a lovely man.' She went on beneficently, 'I believe
that Mrs Hunt is at home. She rang me earlier this morning
and said that she wasn't feeling well, and would I mind keeping
an eye on the stall until lunch time?'

'Oh, dear. Well, thank you very much for your help.'

Lucy left the cathedral and continued around the Close
towards Rowena's house; now that she'd made up her mind to
tackle her, not even her reluctance to disturb a sick woman
would stop her. As she passed the Cathedral Shop, though, she
decided to see if they had some little thing that she could take
to Rowena as a get-well offering.

Victor and Bert both professed themselves delighted to see

her. 'My dear!' effused Victor. 'We haven't seen you for days!'

'Though of course it seems more like weeks,' Bert added with an attempt at gallantry.

'What can we do for you, Lucy darling? Or have you just called in to see us?'

'I heard that Mrs Hunt was under the weather, and thought I'd take her a little something.'

Victor threw up his hands melodramatically. 'Oh, you *are* an angel of mercy! The next time I'm feeling poorly, will you come and stroke *my* fevered brow?'

'I'm sure that Bert can take care of you very well. But Mrs Hunt lives alone,' she reminded him.

Bert rewarded her with a grateful grin as Victor produced an extended version of his gurgling laugh. 'That one may live alone, my dear,' he said archly when he'd calmed down, 'but I don't think she's very often lonely, if you understand me.'

They brought forth a few items for her inspection; at last she settled on a bunch of dried flowers as being potentially less offensive to Rowena's taste than anything else.

'Don't be a stranger, Lucy dear,' Victor called after her as she left the shop.

She rang Rowena's bell, expecting a lengthy pause for the other woman to come downstairs from her sickbed. But Rowena appeared almost immediately, the hopeful look with which she opened the door replaced instantly with an expression of guarded dislike. Lucy wasn't surprised that Rowena's greeting was less enthusiastic than Victor's and Bert's had been; she'd never had the feeling that Rowena liked her very much. Perhaps, she thought, her errand would be a waste of time – would Rowena tell her anything? If she hadn't been forthcoming with David, what made Lucy think that Rowena would be honest with *her*?

Lucy smiled, extending the dried flowers. 'The woman at the Friends' stall said that you weren't feeling well, so I brought you these.'

Rowena took them from her hand, and hesitated a moment. 'Come in, won't you?'

As she entered, Lucy had the opportunity for a closer look at Rowena. She didn't look at all well: her eyes were red and puffy, with mascara smudges under them, and her nose was likewise scarlet. But there was an unmistakable whiff of gin about her, and the first thing she said was, 'Would you care to join me in a drink?'

The table in the sitting room on which Rowena carelessly dropped the dried flowers contained a half-empty gin bottle. Unwilling to antagonise her hostess by refusing and thus implying that she was censorious of her morning drinking habits, Lucy nodded. 'Plenty of tonic for me, please.' She settled down in the chair indicated and took a very tiny sip of the drink which Rowena had poured out with an unsteady hand. At that point she was uncertain how to proceed; Rowena's manner as well as her appearance were far removed from Lucy's previous experiences with her.

After a few minutes of uneasy silence, Lucy decided to carry on with her plans. 'If you don't mind, Mrs Hunt, I have one or two questions I'd like to ask you,' she said with a smile.

'Whether I mind or not may depend on the questions, Miss Kingsley.' Rowena's voice was testy; she didn't bother to return the smile. 'And if it's about last Monday night, you may as well save your breath. I've said everything I intend to say on the subject to your friend Mr Middleton-Brown.'

'No, it wasn't about that. It's about the repairs to the Becket window – I understand that the Friends contributed a substantial sum towards the project.'

Rowena relaxed slightly. 'Yes, that's right. Given the importance of the window, we felt that it was something we ought to support. And we did do rather well financially out of the flower festival in August, so we were in a position to be generous.'

'When you say "we", Mrs Hunt, does that really translate to "I"?' Lucy asked without malice, seeking clarification.

Frowning, Rowena snapped, 'If you insist on being pedantic, I was the one who made the decision, though of course I consulted my committee. As you said, it was a substantial sum of money.'

'Ten thousand pounds, I believe?'

Rowena took a large gulp of gin before replying. 'I don't know who told you, or in fact what business it is of yours, but that is correct.' She emptied her glass, and to Lucy it seemed that the belligerence drained out of Rowena as rapidly and as completely as the gin from her glass. With a sigh, she leaned over to refill her glass with neat gin.

Lucy realised then that it would be impossible to ask Rowena about her knowledge of Jeremy's fraud without compromising David's, or indeed the police's, investigations. Rowena was in no fit state to answer questions, in any case. She had verified one fact, anyway; perhaps, Lucy thought, she ought to depart at that point and leave Rowena to her gin.

She set her still-full glass down and rose. 'Thank you very much for your cooperation, and for the drink. I'll go now.'

'No!' Rowena's involuntary exclamation caught them both by surprise. 'I mean,' she added almost pleadingly, 'I'd like you to stay. I'd be glad of the company.'

Lucy hardly knew what to say; she resumed her seat. 'Are you sure you're feeling all right?' she asked with a tentative smile.

Rowena didn't reply, but after a moment a tear rolled down her cheek, to be followed by others in increasingly rapid succession. She raised an ineffectual hand to wipe them away; the gesture seemed uncharacteristic and somehow pathetic.

As she had done with Evelyn Marsden a few days earlier, Lucy rose impulsively and went to her, putting an arm around her drooping shoulders. 'Is there something you'd like to talk about?'

Rowena shook her head, and her voice came out on a sob. 'No. I couldn't.' She fumbled in her pocket for a handkerchief. Lucy reached for a box of tissues and offered them to her. Soon the trickle became a flood. 'I'm sorry,' she wept. 'I didn't mean to . . . I can't help it.'

'Would you like me to help you upstairs? Perhaps a little rest would do you good.' Lucy had expected a refusal, but unexpectedly Rowena nodded in assent. Getting her upstairs was harder than Lucy had anticipated; Rowena's limbs seemed to have lost the will or the ability to move, so Lucy more or less propelled her up the stairs and into what she judged must be her bedroom.

It was a room quite unlike the one she'd been in the day before: this one was as feminine as Jeremy's had been masculine, with delicate furniture, a lacy spread on the bed, and floral watercolours adorning the walls. The pervasive scent of tea rose was even stronger than the smell of gin; there were photos in small wrought silver frames on the chest of drawers, and various pots of cosmetics, ointments and esoteric beauty preparations covered the dressing table. But as Lucy guided Rowena towards a chair, her attention was caught by something hanging from the dressing table mirror: unmistakably a pair of police epaulets, identical to the ones worn by Inspector Michael Drewitt when Lucy had last seen him. In a flash of intuition she knew what was wrong.

It would do Rowena good to talk about it, Lucy told herself. Less admirable, perhaps, was the unacknowledged thought at the back of her mind that in her current state of inebriation and emotional distress, Rowena might inadvertently give away some vital clue. 'Why don't you tell me what's upsetting you?' she suggested soothingly. 'It's something to do with Inspector Drewitt, isn't it?'

Rowena recoiled. 'You know . . . about me and Mike?'

Not sure whether that made things worse or better, Lucy nodded. 'You mean that everyone in the Close is talking about me?' Rowena gave a bitter laugh. 'That's all I need.'

'No, of course not,' Lucy hastened to assure her. 'I just sort of . . . guessed, that's all. But why don't you tell me about it? It will make you feel better to talk.'

Even in her current state, Rowena recognised the truth in that. With a shuddering sigh, she began. 'He came to see me this morning. To tell me that it was all over.' Saying the words aloud was a great release; she wept gustily for a few minutes. Lucy, wise enough not to probe, merely squeezed her hand in a comforting way, knowing that it would all come out eventually. After a number of snuffling sobs, Rowena continued. 'It was Mike's wife. She found out. And she told him that if he went on seeing me, she'd make trouble – tell his superior officers. She'd tell them that he visited me when he was on duty – it's a lie, the common bitch! But they'd believe it, and he'd be reprimanded, might even lose his job. He couldn't risk it, he said. So it's all over. When the doorbell rang, I thought perhaps he'd changed his mind, had come back . . . But it was only you, and he won't be coming back. I've lost him for good.' Restlessly she shook off Lucy's hand, got up and went to her dressing table, peering at her swollen face in the mirror. 'Look at me. I'm not young any more. What am I supposed to do now?'

Lucy spoke at last, in what she hoped was a convincingly reassuring voice. 'There are plenty of other men. You're a beautiful woman, Rowena, and he's not the only fish in the sea.'

'That's bloody easy for you to say,' Rowena lashed out bitterly. 'You're younger than I am, and you've got your man!

But who is there for me, here in this bloody town, in this bloody cathedral? No one but a load of dried-up old clerics!'

'There's Jeremy,' said Lucy. It seemed a reasonable thing to say, and she was completely unprepared for Rowena's reaction: Rowena laughed, on the verge of hysteria, for a very long time.

'Jeremy!' she spat out with scorn, meeting Lucy's eyes in the mirror. 'He may as well be a dried-up old cleric, for all the good he is to me!'

'What do you mean? He's . . .'

Rowena turned to face her, looking defiant. 'There's no reason why you shouldn't know, not now. Now that I've lost Mike.' Taking a deep breath, she went on in disjointed sentences. 'Last week. He came here for supper. We had things to discuss . . . things about . . . things. Cathedral business. He had Arthur's keys. He came through the cathedral – no one saw him. No one knew he was here. We ate. We talked. We got on better than we ever had before. He told me how lonely he was, since his wife died. I felt sorry for him. And I rather fancied him. So we . . . well, we ended up here. In bed. But he . . . well, he couldn't manage it. Nothing. We tried for hours, but he couldn't do a bloody thing. God, it was humiliating!' With a dramatic gesture she covered her face with her hands. 'Nothing like that has ever happened to me before!'

Lucy stared at her as the realisation trickled through to her brain. 'It was last Monday, wasn't it?' she whispered.

'Of course it was bloody Monday! Why do you think I wouldn't tell the police, or your friend David, what I was doing? Mike would have found out, and I would have lost him. But now . . . none of it matters any more. I've lost him anyway.' She caught her breath on a sob.

The questions had to be asked nonetheless. 'What time was he here? When did he come? When did he leave?'

Incurious, Rowena supplied the answers that would give an ironclad alibi not only to herself, but also to Jeremy. 'He came about half past seven. We must have been in bed when the sirens went – we didn't hear them. And he left after that, just gone midnight. We were together the whole evening.'

Chapter 41

*For he hath delivered me out of all my trouble: and mine eye
hath seen his desire upon mine enemies.*

Psalm 54.7

David was at the kitchen table with Todd and Pat, all with
mugs of coffee, when Lucy returned. 'Where on earth have you
been, Lucy love?' he demanded, his tone expressing concern
rather than irritation. 'I've looked all over the house for you –
you didn't say that you were going out.'

'I'm sorry – I didn't realise when I left that I'd be gone so long.
I've been to see Rowena.'

'Rowena?' David frowned. 'But Rowena had nothing to do
with it. Listen, love,' he went on enthusiastically. 'We were just
talking. If Jeremy had . . .'

'No.' Lucy felt numb with her new knowledge, and her voice
was flat, but it cut across his; they all turned to look at her.
'You're not going to like what I have to tell you, but Jeremy
didn't do it. Rowena didn't do it. Neither of them could have
done it: they were together when it happened.' She went on to
tell them what she had learned, omitting, out of consideration
for Rowena, the factors that had led the other woman to confess
to her.

'Good Lord,' said David into the stunned silence that
followed. 'Rowena . . . and Jeremy? But why would she have
told you, when she wouldn't tell *me*? And wouldn't tell the
police?'

'Never mind that. She *did* tell me – that's all that's
important. Neither she nor Jeremy could have been involved.'

'Unless they were in it together,' offered Todd. 'What about
that?'

Pat shook her head. 'No, I don't think so. It really wasn't that
kind of crime, was it?'

'But that means there aren't any suspects left,' stated the

young man in bewilderment. 'Just the Dean.'

'We *did* think about Victoria and Albert,' David remembered. 'They might have kept a box of Turkish Delight, and not mentioned it.'

Lucy protested. 'I can't picture it. Not Victoria and Albert – they're completely harmless.'

'Then how,' asked David, expecting no answer, 'could it have happened?'

At that point they rehashed all that they knew about the case, for Todd's benefit and in the hope that some hitherto overlooked fact would take on sudden illuminating significance. The discussion took them through lunch and well into the afternoon; they explained to Todd about Inspector Drewitt's role of unofficial informant, and told him what they knew of the police investigations from that most helpful source.

'So they've searched Canon Brydges-ffrench's house as well as the Deanery?' Todd asked.

'Yes,' said Pat. 'Mike said that they didn't find anything, apart from a half-eaten box of Turkish Delight, and a sheet of sermon notes that he seems to have been working on just before he died.'

'Sermon notes?' Todd frowned. 'But Canon Brydges-ffrench never made notes for his sermons – he always wrote them straight out, in ink, and never changed a word. I've seen him at it plenty of times, sitting at his desk or in his chair with a pad of paper and that gold pen of his, scribbling away. He never made notes,' he repeated with emphasis.

Pat raised her eyebrows. 'Then what . . .' said David.

'Did the police take it away?' asked Lucy.

'I don't think so,' Pat replied. 'They didn't seem to find it significant.'

'Let's go over there and see,' Todd suggested excitedly. 'I've still got the keys. We can go right now.'

Pat hesitated. 'I'm not sure that the police would be very happy about that.'

'They needn't know,' David countered. 'Come on, Todd. Let's go.' The young man didn't wait to be asked twice; he jumped up and went off in search of the ring of keys.

'I'm coming too,' stated Lucy.

'I'll stay here,' said Pat. 'So come back as soon as you can.'

* * *

The house had a closed-up feeling, an air of extended neglect, although it had been scarcely more than a week since the Subdean had left it for the last time. Neither David nor Lucy had been in the house before, so Todd led the way to the study, off the dim entrance hall.

Curtains drawn, the study was as dark as the hall. Todd was conscious of the potential hazards which lay in wait for the unwary explorer – the endless stacks of books which littered the floor – so he switched on the overhead light and picked his way through the books to the desk while David and Lucy remained by the door. 'But it's not quite right,' he whispered, puzzled and frowning. 'I don't think the books are where he left them. The piles are too neat. He always knew where everything was, but it was a mess.'

David found himself whispering as well, a natural response to being without permission in the hushed and dusty house of a dead man. 'What about the desk?'

Todd surveyed it carefully. The Turkish Delight box was clearly visible on one side, and on the other, to his surprise, he found a brown envelope addressed to him in Arthur Brydges-ffrench's crabbed hand. In the centre, tucked into an old leather-bound Bible, was the sheet of purported sermon notes. 'There's an envelope here with my name on it,' he announced. 'I wonder what it could be?'

'Bring it with you,' Lucy suggested softly. 'I don't think we should stay here.' She shivered.

David put a protective arm around her. 'Yes, come on, Todd. Let's go. Bring the box of Turkish Delight, and the notes as well.'

'They're inside his Bible,' Todd reported.

'Well, bring that too.'

Todd retraced his steps, carrying the various things. They left the house quickly, locking up behind them, and hurried back through the Close to the welcoming warmth of Pat's kitchen.

'Well, what did you find?' she asked immediately.

Todd put his burden down on the table. 'Here's his Bible, with the notes inside. And we brought the Turkish Delight as well.'

'And he's left something for Todd,' added Lucy.

'What is it?' Pat queried.

'I'm not sure.' They all expected him to rip into the envelope to find out, but he seemed curiously reluctant to do so. 'Let's have some tea,' he suggested. 'Then I'll open it.'

While the kettle boiled, they sat in silence and looked at the array of items on the table. The doorbell rang; Pat went to answer it and the rest of them jumped guiltily as Pat ushered Inspector Drewitt into the kitchen.

'The Inspector has come to join us for a cup of tea,' she announced.

Todd, following the Inspector's curious gaze to the table, felt compelled to explain. 'We . . . um, we went to Canon Brydges-ffrench's house and brought a few things back.'

Drewitt looked amused at their sheepish expressions. 'It's quite all right. We've finished there, as I explained last week. There wasn't anything of particular interest to us.'

Pat opened the box of Turkish Delight and looked inside. 'It's about half empty,' she observed. 'And it seems to be missing its wax lining paper.'

'I suppose he threw it away,' Drewitt said easily. 'Or perhaps it was a manufacturing fault at the factory. The one at the Deanery had two, so I suppose it just shows that those machines make mistakes all the time.'

The tea having brewed sufficiently, Pat poured it out; while the others drank, Todd picked up the envelope and examined it, tracing his name on the front with a tentative finger. 'It's kind of like a last message to me,' he explained softly. 'I'm almost afraid to open it. I don't understand what it means.'

'Get on with it,' David urged. Todd slit the top of the envelope with a knife provided by Pat, and peered into it apprehensively, then shook it out on to the table. There was no letter, no note: only a tiny, flat book.

Lucy stated the obvious. 'A book?'

It was bound in leather, with no title on the cover; Todd opened it and read out the title. '*Sir Walter Raleigh's Instructions to his Sonne, and to Posterity.*' He looked around the table, puzzled. 'I don't understand.'

'It's a present, obviously,' Pat said. 'Something he wanted you to have, because he was fond of you.'

'But why *then*? It's almost as if he knew . . .'

'Perhaps, as he'd planned to resign, he thought he'd be gone before you returned to Malbury, and he wanted to leave it for you to find later,' Lucy suggested.

David spotted a slip of paper as Todd turned the book over in his hands. 'Is that a marker in it?'

The young man opened the book and read aloud from the last page. '"Serve GOD, let him bee the Author of all your actions, commend all your endeavors to him that must eyther wither or prosper them, please him with prayer, least if hee frown, he confound all your fortunes & labours like drops of Rayne on the Sandy ground: let my experienced advice and fatherly instructions sink deep into your heart; So GOD direct you in all his wayes and fill your heart with his grace." But what does it mean? He hasn't left a letter or anything with it.'

'He's left this.' David picked up the Bible and took out the sheet of paper. 'Samson,' he read. '"Out of the strong came forth sweetness. Judges 14.14. Judges 16.29–30." Does that mean anything to you, Todd?'

'Let me see that.' Todd scrutinised the paper for a moment. 'It's not sermon notes,' he stated. 'As I said, he never made them. No, I think it's a kind of a riddle. Or a puzzle.'

'A riddle?' echoed David, with rising excitement. 'A puzzle?'

Pat demonstrated knowledge gained from years of teaching Sunday School. 'Isn't that Samson's riddle? "Out of the eater came forth meat, and out of the strong came forth sweetness"?'

'Yes, of course!' David confirmed, looking up the first reference in the Bible.

Todd looked at the list again. 'It's like clues to a croossword puzzle, or something like that. You know how fond Canon Brydges-ffrench was of his crosswords and his riddles. He used to play around with things like this sometimes, to amuse himself.'

'Read them out,' commanded David. 'I'm sure they must all mean something. Perhaps it has something to do with the decision he was trying to make, whether to resign or not.'

'Well, it looks like they're in two sections,' Todd analysed. 'Underneath Samson, and the two references from Judges, it says Abraham and Isaac, Genesis 22.7–8. Then there's a space, and it says Matthew 7.6, Amos 6.12, Psalm 109.20–30, and finally Psalm 109.7.'

'A mixture of Old Testament and New Testament passages,' observed Pat. 'What do they have in common?'

'Two sections,' David said. 'Pro and con? To resign, or not to resign?'

The Bishop chose that moment to poke his nose around the kitchen door. 'Is there any chance of a cup of tea, my dear?' he inquired mildly.

Pat turned to him, stricken. 'George! I'm sorry – I forgot that you were in your study! Would you like to join us?'

His brain still engaged with an obscure facet of the Albigensian Heresy, Dr Willoughby only then registered the fact that his kitchen was full of people. 'Oh! All right. I suppose I ought to be sociable.'

'Bishop George,' David put in before he could sit down, 'do you by any chance have a few spare Bibles lying about that we could use?'

To the Bishop, having a Bible Study at the kitchen table over cups of tea was a natural activity and not to be questioned. 'Yes, of course. They're in the study – shall I get them for you? How many would you like?'

He did a quick count. 'Five, please.'

When the Bishop had returned, with an armload of Bibles, David explained his strategy. 'If we each take one, and look up one passage to read out, it won't take as long.' They all agreed, and the passages were shared out around the table, one for each. David read his out first, from Arthur Brydges-ffrench's Bible. 'It's another passage about Samson,' he explained. 'This one is about the end of his life, when he pulls down the house to kill the Philistines, realising that he will also die himself. Judges 16.29–30: "And Samson took hold of the two middle pillars upon which the house stood, and on which it was borne up, of the one with his right hand, and of the other with his left And Samson said, Let me die with the Philistines. And he bowed himself with all his might; and the house fell upon the lords, and upon all the people that were therein. So the dead which he slew at his death were more than they which he slew in his life."'

Pat came next. 'Mine is about Abraham and the sacrifice of Isaac,' she said. 'You all know the story, I'm sure – how God asks Abraham to sacrifice his son, and Abraham is willing to do it because he trusts in God's promises. "And Isaac spake unto Abraham his father, and said, My father: and he said, Here am I, my son. And he said, Behold the fire and the wood: but where is the lamb for a burnt offering? And Abraham said, My son, God will provide himself a lamb for a burnt offering: so they went both of them together." It looks to me,' she added, 'that both of those passages are about sacrifice. David may be on to something with his theory – perhaps these were the ones prompting him to self-sacrifice, in resigning. What have you got, Lucy?'

'It's the one about casting pearls before swine. Matthew 7.6: "Give not that which is holy unto the dogs, neither cast ye your pearls before swine, lest they trample them under their feet, and turn again and rend you." Do you think that's a reference to the Dean?'

David and Pat both nodded. 'It could be,' Pat encouraged her. 'I've heard him called much worse than a swine, and not a million miles away from this room, either.'

'Mine is a bit more obscure,' volunteered Mike Drewitt. 'Amos 6.12: "Shall horses run upon the rock? will one plow there with oxen? for ye have turned judgement into gall, and the fruit of righteousness into hemlock."'

At the word 'hemlock' there was a general intake of breath around the table, and they turned to Todd to see what was next.

'It's a fairly long passage,' he said. 'Psalm 109, verses 20 through 30. I'll read you a few of the verses to give you the idea. "Let this be the reward of mine adversaries from the Lord, and of them that speak evil against my soul. . . . For I am poor and needy, and my heart is wounded within me. I am gone like the shadow when it declineth . . . I became also as a reproach unto them: when they looked upon me they shaked their heads. . . . Let mine adversaries be clothed with shame, and let them cover themselves with their own confusion, as with a mantle."'

David frowned. 'I'm afraid it doesn't make a great deal of sense. Bishop George, you have the last one.'

Dr Willoughby grinned cheerfully. 'I've got a short one, though it's none too sweet. Psalm 109.7: "Let his days be few, and let another take his office."'

This time they all looked at each other, and no one had to articulate the thought that hung unspoken in the room: Arthur Brydges-ffrench may have wished that fate upon the Dean, but it had been his own fate instead.

'It's beginning to make sense,' David said slowly, after a moment of thought. 'I think I finally know what happened, but I'll be damned if I can see how. And I don't see how I can possibly prove it, without even a shred of evidence.' He picked up Canon Brydges-ffrench's Bible and shook it gently over the table. 'I just wondered if he might have left a note, stuck in between the pages or something,' he explained. 'But it doesn't look like it.'

'That's the sort of thing he'd do,' Todd affirmed. 'To have one puzzle lead to another. Maybe we should go back to his study and look through all the books.'

Mike Drewitt laughed. 'Don't you think the police have thought of that? I assure you that it was done – all part of the routine.'

'So that's why the books had been moved,' Todd realised, disappointed. Pat turned to David, intrigued by his claim that he knew what had happened. 'Aren't you going to tell us what you think?'

But David shook his head. 'Not yet. As I said, it's just a feeling – I don't have any proof. Why don't you all tell me what you think – perhaps it will get the wheels turning, and we'll end up with something.'

Before they'd had a chance to discuss the implications of the passages, John Kingsley arrived in search of his daughter. He was mildly surprised to see so many people around the table, earnestly studying their Bibles. As the Bishop went to find an extra chair, and Pat rose to refill the kettle, the Canon saw the box of Turkish Delight on the table. 'Where on earth did that come from?' he asked.

'It was the one that Canon Brydges-ffrench had on his desk when he . . . died,' Todd explained. 'We brought it over here to see if there was anything significant about it, but it's just an ordinary, half-empty box of Turkish Delight.'

Canon Kingsley stood very still for a moment. 'I've just remembered something,' he said. 'Something I hadn't thought about since last Monday night.' That captured their attention; they all turned to look at him. 'When Arthur came by to see me, just before he went to the Deanery, he gave me a box of Turkish Delight. It seemed an odd gesture at the time – he said it was something he wanted me to have, I remember.'

'But what did you do with it?' David asked eagerly. 'Where is it now?'

The Canon's brow wrinkled with the effort of remembering; so much had happened since that night. 'I didn't open it. I think I put it on the hall table,' he said at last. 'Would you like me to go and look? Do you think it might be important?'

David nodded in vigorous affirmation. 'It may just be the piece of evidence we need.'

'I'll go, Daddy,' Lucy offered.

'Very well, my dear. Whatever you like.'

She was gone only a few minutes, but to those waiting around the kitchen table it seemed an age. 'If we're going to open Joanna Southcott's box,' quipped Dr Willoughby, with a nervous attempt at humour, 'don't you think I need to ring round and get a few more Bishops here?'

Lucy was out of breath, peering at the top of the box as she entered. 'There's something written on the box,' she observed, pointing to a tiny mark on the lid. They all gathered around to squint at it.

'It looks to me like another Scripture reference, in Arthur's writing,' added Pat. 'What does it say? Todd, you have young eyes – you ought to be able to read it, even though it's written very small.'

Todd examined it closely. 'I think it says Hebrews 11.4,' he deciphered.

David riffled through the Bible to the New Testament. 'It says, "By faith Abel offered unto God a more excellent sacrifice than Cain, by which he obtained witness that he was righteous, God testifying of his gifts: and by it he being dead yet speaketh."' He looked up to meet six sets of eyes in various stages of comprehension. 'He being dead yet speaketh,' he repeated. 'Good Lord. This is it. I think that Arthur Brydges-ffrench is about to give us our evidence.'

It was John Kingsley, as recipient of the box, who opened the lid at last. Inside was not Turkish Delight, but a tiny old-fashioned chalice of the type used for home communions. Gingerly, he lifted it out to show them all; a minute slip of paper fell out of its bowl and fluttered to the floor.

Todd stooped to pick it up. 'I think this must be the last clue,' he said.

'Another verse?' guessed Pat.

'Yes. Matthew 26.42.'

David felt himself to be unendurably clumsy and slow as he turned the pages; all eyes on him, it seemed as if he would never find the reference. '"He went away again the second time, and prayed, saying, O my Father, if this cup may not pass away from me, except I drink it, thy will be done." Good Lord.'

'"This cup",' said John Kingsley. 'Does that mean . . .'

'Just a minute,' breathed David. 'That's not all. There's something written here in the margin of the Bible, on the same page as the verse.'

'Is it Arthur's writing?' Pat asked.

'Yes.' David turned the book around and looked at it closely, then read the words of the tiny crabbed script aloud. '"Thomas à Becket suffered martyrdom to preserve his principles and save the Church from the power of an evil king. Brother Thomas gave up his life out of love for this place, also against an evil man. I follow after them: God is calling on me to offer my life to save this cathedral, which I have loved for many years, from a man who would destroy it. Eventually my clues should lead you to this, and you will know that I found it necessary to take my own life. But it was also necessary for him to be discredited, and to suffer. I pray that my sacrifice may not have been in vain, and that Malbury Cathedral might yet be saved."'

There was a prolonged, stunned silence.

'Good Lord,' said David at last. 'Good Lord.'

Drewitt rose, addressing David with respect. 'Do you have any idea how it happened?'

David looked thoughtful. 'I think so, yes.'

'Then perhaps you can explain it to me on our way back to the station.'

'We're going now? You and I? What's the rush?'

'There's the tiny matter of the Dean to be cleared up.' Drewitt shook his head and sighed, a sigh of bafflement mingled with regret. 'You're his solicitor, and I'm sure you'd be the first one to tell me that if we don't get the little sod out of prison immediately, you'll have us for wrongful arrest.'

Laughing, David sat back down. 'Just between you and me, my friend, the Dean can wait a few minutes longer. I think we all need another cup of tea!'

Epilogue

Recompense them after the work of their hands: pay them that they have deserved.

Psalm 28.5

Christmas Day in Malbury: throughout the town trees twinkled, children squealed with greedy delight, and great quantities of food were consumed. In the Close the low-slung sun bathed the cathedral in a sharp-edged glow against the clear blue frosty sky.

At the Deanery, the Latimers observed their first Christmas in Malbury. Christopher and Stephen, the two young Latimers, were of course home from school, so the Deanery was more than usually lively; Jeremy Bartlett was with them for lunch as well, deep in discussion with the Dean about their ongoing plans for the Cathedral Centre. The unfortunate incident of the Dean's arrest and imprisonment was not even mentioned, although it was implicit in every controlled move and disapproving glance of the largely silent Anne Latimer.

Next door, Todd had not returned to Evelyn Marsden's house, but she was not alone; her house was the scene of unaccustomed hilarity as she entertained Victor and Bert to a delicious and carefully prepared meal.

The trio of red brick houses at the east end of the cathedral were now all empty: the Subdean's house, the organist's house, and now the Precentor's house as well, for Rupert and Judith Greenwood had left Malbury for London just before Christmas. Further along the Close, though, there was evidence of activity – not at the Canon Missioner's, where the Thetfords dined alone, quietly, on their festive nut roast, but at Rowena Hunt's house. Rowena had invited the bell-ringers to join her for a drink after the morning service, in the confident hope that Mike Drewitt, newly reconciled, would be staying on after the others went home to their respective lunches.

Christmas lunch at the Willoughbys was a traditional and convivial affair, complete with crackers and turkey and a flaming Christmas pudding. As an added note of festivity there was even champagne, provided by David.

In addition to the two dogs, who waited patiently and hopefully beneath the table for their anticipated turkey scraps, there were seven of them present at the meal: the Willoughbys, David and Lucy, John Kingsley, Todd Randall, and the Bishop's secretary, Olivia Ashleigh. As they pulled their crackers, read out their jokes, and donned their paper crowns, conversation was lively, moved along by Pat, who had made a conscious decision that on that day they should not dwell on the unhappy events of the past few months. But the toast to 'absent friends' brought those events all too poignantly to mind, and it was perhaps inevitable that they should be mentioned.

Olivia was the only one of the seven who had not been in Pat's kitchen on the day, four weeks earlier, when the riddle of Arthur Brydges-ffrench's death had been unravelled. She was, naturally enough, curious to hear the details from the others, particularly from David. So when she raised the subject, Pat decided to let it ride.

'Poor old Canon Brydges-ffrench,' said Olivia, shaking her head. 'It's dreadful to think of him being so unhappy that suicide seemed the only way out.'

David turned to her. 'Oh, but there was much more to it than that. His suicide was more than an escape from an untenable situation – it was his way of trying to rectify that situation. In dying, he was attempting to preserve a way of life that he had loved, in the only way he thought possible. He had reached the point where he had convinced himself that nothing less than the sacrifice of his own life would be enough to save Malbury Cathedral.'

'But how did he really think that his death could accomplish that?'

'By casting suspicion on the Dean, the man whom he held responsible for all that was threatening the cathedral,' David explained. 'He had arranged things so that suspicion would inevitably fall on the Dean, and he knew that even when the Dean was cleared, as he would be eventually, some of the mud would stick.'

'You know how people are,' Pat added. 'No smoke without

fire, they all say. People are always ready to believe the worst, especially of someone as unpopular as Stuart Latimer.'

'At the very least he would suffer humiliation,' David went on. 'And as Pat says, he was bound to be discredited to some degree just by being arrested, no matter how unjust or unjustified it was.'

'How on earth, though, did he actually accomplish it? He fooled the police, and he fooled everyone else. Why didn't they suspect suicide?'

David smiled wryly. 'Why didn't any of us suspect it? A gesture like that was very much in keeping with his character, and after Ivor Jones's suicide, Canon Kingsley preached a sermon in which he implied that suicide might be justified under certain circumstances.'

'That's not exactly what I said,' John Kingsley put in, defensively. 'I just said that we're in no position to judge. I still feel that way, but I can't help feeling guilty – perhaps that sermon *did* influence Arthur in some way.'

Lucy reached for her father's hand. 'Daddy, that's enough,' she stated firmly.

'As to why we didn't suspect it,' continued David, 'the police told us that it wasn't possible. They said that he couldn't have ingested the poison before he arrived at the Deanery – the timing wasn't right, and there was definitely poison in the box of Turkish Delight at the Deanery. And they'd found nothing – no traces in his clothing or anything in which he could have brought it – to indicate that he'd carried the poison in with him. Besides, the police reasoned that if he'd wanted to commit suicide, he could have done it in a much simpler and more straightforward way. They couldn't know that the whole point of it was to implicate the Dean, so that it had to look like murder.'

'I may be dim,' Olivia laughed, 'but please explain to me how he *did* do it. How did he poison the Turkish Delight?'

'This is where David was so clever,' Lucy said with pride.

He shook his head self-deprecatingly. 'Not at all. I just overheard something that gave me a little idea. It was Canon Brydges-ffrench who was clever to think of such a thing. I just put two and two together and came up with four.'

'Or rather,' added Lucy, 'you put two and naught together, and came up with two.'

'It was the wax lining papers,' David amplified. 'I heard Pat say that the box of Turkish Delight on Canon Brydges-ffrench's desk was missing its lining paper, and then Inspector Drewitt remarked that the box at the Deanery had two. It was after that I realised how it was done: he carried the poison to the Deanery folded in the lining paper from his own box of Turkish Delight. He'd arranged for Canon Kingsley to ring the Deanery at ten o'clock, so while the Dean was out of the room taking the call he just emptied the poison on to the Turkish Delight in the box, and slipped the extra lining paper into the lid.'

'Very neatly done,' Pat declared. 'But David was the one who twigged about the significance of the extra lining paper. No one else, including the police, thought anything of it. And now,' she went on with determination, 'I think we ought to change the subject to something a little more in keeping with the spirit of the season.'

'Can't I ask one more question?' Todd, who had been quite silent up to that point, requested.

Pat nodded. 'Go ahead.'

'What *is* going to happen to the Dean? I mean, I know he's been cleared, and is back at the Deanery, but surely he can't just go on here at Malbury as if nothing has happened.'

A rumbling chuckle issued forth from the Bishop. 'Good question, young man.' He looked sideways at Pat. 'It is my wife's opinion – and I must tell you that she's usually right about these matters – that before long he will do the decent thing and find himself another preferment.'

'With any luck,' she added, smiling, 'it will be a nice remote bishopric somewhere in the Colonies – that's the way these things used to happen, at any rate.'

'It all rather depends on what happens with his plans for the Cathedral Centre, I should have thought,' ventured John Kingsley. 'The Chapter is going to be changing quite significantly over the next few months, with Arthur and Rupert gone, and if he can get his own people appointed as Precentor and Subdean, then perhaps he'll want to stay on and push that through.' He paused. 'I was actually thinking of retiring soon, myself,' he revealed with an apologetic look at the Bishop. 'The last few months have been rather too much for a man of my advanced years.'

'Nonsense!' George Willoughby roared robustly. 'You're younger than I am, John Kingsley, and I'm not about to retire!

No, you must stay on! Whatever happens, the Chapter will need a man of your experience and wisdom. *I* need you, John. I'm telling you: there will be no more talk of retirement from you for a good many years yet.'

Canon Kingsley bowed his head in silent acknowledgement of defeat.

'But about the Cathedral Centre,' said Olivia. 'Do you think it's still on?'

The Bishop nodded. 'In my last conversation with the Dean, he was determined to go ahead with it.'

David cleared his throat. 'I'm afraid,' he said in a quiet but authoritative voice, 'that won't be possible.'

They all turned to look at him. 'In the last few weeks I've done a bit of investigation,' he revealed. 'Pat said something to me when I ran into her at the Patronal Festival, and it got me thinking. She said that part of the Abbey church had belonged to the monks, and part to the town. At the Dissolution, she told me, the townspeople tore down their bit, hence the green space at the west end.' He looked to Pat for confirmation.

She nodded. 'Yes . . . But I don't see . . .'

'I've done some legal research. And I've discovered that if that part of the church belonged to the town, so did the land that it stood on – and it still does, up to the present day. The cathedral can't build on that land,' he concluded triumphantly, 'because it doesn't own it. That space belongs to the city of Malbury, and I can't imagine them handing it over to the Dean to satisfy his edifice complex.'

'Well, that does it,' Pat declared at once. 'He'll definitely go if he can't have his new building.'

'And what about Jeremy Bartlett?' asked the Bishop. 'He won't be any too pleased about this.'

David smiled complacently. 'I know.'

'I suppose I'll have to tell him,' Dr Willoughby mused, stroking his beard.

'No,' said David. 'I'd like to tell him myself.' Glancing at Lucy, he thought back to the various humiliations he had suffered at Jeremy's hands, and realised, with some shame, how much he was going to enjoy it.

After lunch it was time to open presents. Lucy sat quietly on the sofa as the many gifts were distributed, opened, and enthused over, attending with only part of her mind to the proceedings. The moment was drawing near, she realised, when she would be called upon to declare a decision.

The night before, after they'd returned from Midnight Mass at the cathedral, David had detained her under the mistletoe and kissed her thoroughly, then had produced a small jewellery-sized box. 'Your Christmas present,' he'd said. 'Do you want to open it now, or will you wait until tomorrow?' She'd decided to wait, to give herself time to decide. For she knew it must be a ring, and he would want an answer.

Through the night she'd been wakeful, wrestling with the issue of marriage as she had so many times before. This time, however, she had reached a different conclusion than all those other times; in the past few weeks she had learned a few painful truths about herself, as she tried to analyse why she seemed to be attracted to the most unsuitable men. For, she admitted to herself at last, in a certain sense she *had* been drawn to Jeremy, a man who had turned out to be not unlike her ex-husband in many ways: both facilely charming older men with well-concealed darker sides. Even as she had protested to David that she wasn't interested in Jeremy, she had found him unaccountably fascinating, until circumstances had proved how wrong she'd been. But through it all, it was David whom she loved, and his solid, unassuming strength had never seemed more attractive to her than it did now. David was gentle, and kind; he was decent, and good. David loved her to distraction, and she loved him; she couldn't imagine any circumstances that would change that. If he asked her to marry him tomorrow, in front of so many people whom they both cared about, she would say yes.

So now she waited for the moment with a mixture of excitement and trepidation. The little box was practically the last thing left under the tree when David brought it to her. 'With all my love,' he said, putting it into her hands.

Todd craned his neck in benign curiosity. 'I'll bet it's a ring,' he predicted as her fingers fumbled with the wrapping paper. 'An engagement ring. Is it a ring?'

She had the box open at last. It was an exquisite gold and amethyst brooch, intricately wrought. 'No,' she said involuntarily. 'It's not a ring.'

Fatally, David failed to hear the disappointment in her voice. 'Not a chance,' he laughed. He explained to the others, 'I've lost count of the number of times I've asked this woman to

310